THE KEY OF ASTREA

NICHOLAS MARSON

MAPIE
&PINE

Published by Maple and Pine

Visit our Web Site: www.mapleandpine.com

Library of Congress Cataloging-in-Publication Data is available.

First Edition

ISBN-13: 978-1-7334642-1-5

Printed in the United States of America

To my wife Natalie Perrin for being my partner in everything, and my daughter River for keeping the child inside me alive.

1

UNITY

In the depths of outer space, there was a flash of light as hundreds of ships appeared out of nowhere. The newly arrived spaceships exited the Terminal, and new ones quickly took their place, huddling together in a ball like a school of fish. Day by day, hour by hour, thousands of people and goods traveled by Terminal across the galaxy.

One of the newly arrived vessels bristled with antennas, like some enormous hedgehog. It immediately began broadcasting the daily news. Data transmission was limited to light speed, and with the galaxy being over 100,000 light-years across, travel by Terminal was by far the fastest method to exchange information to other stellar systems.

First to receive the news was a space station composed of concentric rings plus 240 pods. Inside one of these pods, a thin man glanced nervously through the skylight at the Terminal. His name was Hocco, and he sat on a couch in a large common room, surrounded by two dozen armed members of the rebel group Unity.

Some of these rebels wore old fatigues and sat cleaning their rifles and counting their ammunition. Others sat nearby eating breakfast. A pile of pans and dishes sat unwashed on the kitchen counter. At the far end of the common room, more Unity members whooped and cheered as they made bets on spaceship races. They were all here for a common purpose, to protect Hocco—or, more accurately, the secret he carried.

"You look nervous, Hocco," said a man with a thick black beard and long gray hair that hung in front of his creased face. "You're starting to make me nervous, and when I'm nervous, I lose my appetite," he said before taking another bite of synthetic meat covered in gravy.

"Sorry, Boros," Hocco said as he tore his gaze away from the Terminal and wrung his hands. "I've got a bad feeling today."

"Have something to eat." Boros pushed a plate across the table toward him. "You'll feel better, and you need it."

Hocco was whip-thin. A result of genetics and a constant state of nervousness due to living in fear over the last few months. His guts clenched at the sight of the synthetic meat. *Stop it*, Hocco thought. *We've been here for weeks. If Tyr knew where we were, then they'd have attacked by now.* He pulled the plate closer.

"You know," Boros said as he sipped from a yellow mug, "you do make a damn fine cup of coffee."

When you lived on a space station millions of kilometers from the nearest plantation, your coffee-brewing technique was invaluable. Hocco was the best brewer on Lan station, and had often been called an artisan of the craft.

"I know how good my coffee is." Hocco didn't mean to sound flippant, but his nerves didn't allow for a sweeter tone. He brushed his long black hair behind one ear and took a sip from his own mug. The warmth settled his stomach but failed to calm him down.

Boros laughed. "I suppose you do." He nudged the plate closer. "Eat." Hocco didn't move.

A boy who was no more than twenty spoke up. "Is it true what they say about him? About the admiral?"

"Vae Victus?" Boros chewed the simulated meat. "Depends. What did you hear?"

"That he has an eye as black as space. That he can take over your body with just a look—"

Boros interrupted. "That he's assassinated world leaders by possessing their bodyguards, closest friends, and even their lovers." He waved his fork at the boy. "I don't think any of it is true. It's all a bunch of propaganda meant to keep us in line. All I know for sure is that we're safe here, and my breakfast is getting cold."

At the thought of Admiral Victus, Hocco's stomach twisted, and he pushed his food away.

~

The warship *Tamarack* arrived at Lan Station in a flash of light. It was a huge ship that stretched across the entire two-kilometer diameter of the Terminal. Accompanying it was a strike group—mostly corvettes and cruisers—that immediately joined in the organized chaos around the station's docks.

With so much traffic, nobody noticed a single transport launching from one of the *Tamarack*'s many hangars as it drifted silently, in the shadow of a cruiser. Admiral Vae Victus sat in the copilot's seat of the transport.

A direct message arrived from the *Tamarack*: "Sir, we've located the rebel's vessel. It is docked outside pod L-145."

At once, the transport peeled off from its host and approached the ring-shaped Lan Station. After matching the space station's orbit, it docked at a maintenance airlock near pod L-145.

Victus rose from the copilot's seat. The confined space forced him to bend his two-meter frame in half. He patted the pilot on the back. "Good flying."

"Thank you, sir."

Victus brushed his white-blond hair back and pulled on his helmet, trading the recycled air of the ship for the stale air of his suit. He drifted back toward the crew compartment. The ship bucked as docking clamps fastened to the transport, and Victus bumped against the hull. Inside his armored black suit, he barely noticed, and his magnetic boots held him to the ship's floor in the absence of gravity.

Four armored marines occupied the crew compartment. They stood nearly three meters tall in their hypersuits. Red skulls adorned their black face masks and grinned evilly down at Victus.

One of the marines stepped forward. "Admiral Victus," a woman's voice broadcasted into his helmet. "Sergeant Alberta of Fireteam Draco."

"Sergeant." Victus stood before the fireteam. "We have located the terrorist group. They call themselves Unity," he said, growling the word. "It is Tyr who put an end to the First Galactic War. We secured peace, and now the galaxy puts its faith in us to keep it."

The marines raised their right fists.

"These terrorists want to undermine that trust and unseat us from our rightful place as Terminal defenders. Will we let them?"

"No, sir!" The four marines spoke in unison.

"What are your orders?" Alberta asked.

"Set your guns to stun. You must capture the rebels alive for me to interrogate. We must discover the location of the escaped Selkans."

Alberta turned to her marines. "Draco!"

"Oorah!" they responded as one and slammed their heavy fists against their broad, armored chests.

"Lead the way, Sergeant," Victus said.

"Yes, sir." Alberta turned and led them into the airlock.

Victus shut the airlock door and stood face-to-face with the marines. After the airlock's red light switched to green, Alberta pressed a button, and the hatch opened with a hiss. The marines rushed out and took up defensive positions in the hallway. Red lights in the ceiling illuminated the metallic alloy of the walls. The system's star, Lan, was visible as a large, bright dot through a bank of windows. The corridor, which ran the circumference of the station, provided access to the 120 pods on this side. An identical passage on the opposite side of the station connected another 120 pods.

"Remain on alert," Alberta said. "With the arrival of the *Tamarack*, the rebels will be prepared for us." She pointed to the door on her right. Stenciled numbers indicated pods 140 through 149. "This way."

The marines followed the sergeant.

"Wait." Victus closed his eyes and held his hand up to his face mask. "We go this way." He pointed left to pods 130 through 139.

"Sir, the rebels docked their ship at L-145," Alberta said.

"That is a diversion."

"How do you know?"

"I can feel it," Victus said.

"Based on your Æon senses?"

"Yes, sergeant." Victus turned and walked down the left corridor toward pods 130 through 139.

Alberta paused for a beat before turning to the left. "You heard the admiral. This way," she commanded.

The marines followed her without question. Inside their enormous suit, they were forced to duck through the hatch leading to the interior corridor.

Victus stopped outside pod L-137. "Here."

Alberta raised a fist and the team halted. "Sir, if you're wrong..." she started.

"I am not wrong."

Alberta pointed at one of the marines and gave a hand signal. The marine withdrew a canister from a satchel and traced the seams of the heavy pod door with gel. Within moments, the gel spread into the seams, eating away the hinges and locks that kept it secure. Victus was thankful for his helmet as a heavy cloud of caustic smoke billowed into the hallway.

Next, Alberta approached the door and dug her fingers into the seams. With a whir of her suit's motors, she ripped the door off the pod. All at once, the squad activated their shields and formed a wall in front of Victus. One of the marines made a throwing motion, and a flash grenade exploded inside the pod. Then, the marines moved like a serpent through the door, with Alberta as the head.

Victus watched the chaos from the doorway. The infrared sensors in his face mask marked cool objects in blue, and warm objects—like people—in red. Guns flashed and shields pulsed, all highlighted by the smoke of the grenade. Men and women screamed as suppression rounds shocked their nervous systems. Victus tilted his head to the side, and a ceramic bullet screamed past his helmet and shattered against the wall.

A thin man with an angular face and long black hair fled from the pod. Victus grabbed him by the neck and held him off the ground with one hand. A handgun clattered to the floor. The man tried to insert something into his mouth. *A pill.* Victus grabbed his arm and shook the pill loose. He carried the man over the broken door and into the pod.

The station's air scrubbers were already dissipating the smoke, revealing a communal living area with two tipped-over couches and a table covered in half-eaten meals. The marines confiscated all the weapons and then lined the men and women against a wall. A score of bodies lay immobile throughout the room.

Victus ground his teeth. "What happened? Why are there only five left?" Victus stared up at the nearest marine. "I said stun only."

"We did, sir, but they took suicide pills before we could stop them."

Victus thought about the pill he'd shaken from the man's hand, then shoved the rebel against the wall with the others. The man dropped to the ground, gasping for air. Victus stepped backward until all the prisoners were visible. Three wore the uniforms of the Balt System; the others were in civilian clothing. Their faces showed fear and panic. Some sobbed, while others bared their teeth.

Victus needed answers. One by one, he approached each prisoner and asked for the location of the escaped Selkans. Of course, they would all deny knowing the Selkans' location, but Victus could tell when people were lying.

As Victus interrogated the prisoners he thought, *What if I'm wrong? What if nobody here knows where the Selkans are?* He leaned in close to the thin man. Like the others, he'd denied knowing where the escaped aliens were, but when he asked the question, the man's aura flickered.

A lie.

Victus fought against smiling while a thrill shivered through his gut. He pulled the man away from the wall.

"You are all enemies of Tyr," he said to the rest of them. "Your cause is not just." He looked at Alberta. "For the sake of the galaxy, we must protect the secret. Kill them."

"No," the man gasped.

With a nod, Alberta and the other marines aimed their arm cannons at the prisoners. The pod exploded with gunfire.

The man shuddered as his comrades were torn to shreds. Tears traced paths down his dusty face. "We will never surrender." He spat, and a streak of saliva slithered across Victus's face mask.

Alberta stepped forward and pressed her arm against the man's head. A thin line of smoke still trailed from the cannon.

Trembling, the man dropped to his knees, and wetness spread down his leg. "I will not talk."

Victus chuckled, a sound void of amusement. "There is no need." He nodded to Alberta, who lowered her arm. Victus crouched in front of the prisoner. "You won't need to tell me anything...Hocco."

"How?" Hocco recoiled. "How do you know my name?" He tried to stand up, but Alberta held him in place, like a cat with a mouse under its paw.

Victus removed his helmet. The acrid smoke of the flash grenade joined with the smell of blood and human waste, and stung his nostrils.

"It's true," Hocco looked up and shuddered. "What they say about you is true."

"Excellent, then you know that it is useless to resist me. Tell me where the Selkans are."

"Kill me, please." He grabbed Alberta's arm and aimed the barrel of her cannon at his head.

Victus pinched the bridge of his nose. "You helped the Selkans escape, and now I'm going to find out where they are." He sat down cross-legged in front of the rebel.

With a deep breath, Victus closed his eyes, and his consciousness manifested into an ethereal form. Strange creatures of shadow teased the edge of his supernal vision. His spirit was as beautiful as the archetypal angel, but invisible to the ordinary human. His power radiated in waves of rainbow light as he walked through the pool of blood that crept across the floor.

Then, Victus was staring at his own face from Hocco's eyes. He saw his own high cheekbones and aquiline nose that emphasized his angular features. Thick, dark eyebrows framed his strange eyes—one crystalline blue on white. The other black on black.

Victus almost laughed aloud as Hocco's consciousness attempted to fight back. The other man's struggling quickly grew tiresome. Victus squashed him like a piece of ripe fruit forcing his spirit out of his body. The ghost appeared in the common room as a dim specter, barely holding human form. Confusion and fear warped the spirit's face. Without a body, there was nothing to protect him from the dark shapes. They pounced, pulling him into their horde.

One day, Victus thought, *I, too, will sink into that darkness. Then my payment will come due. For now, I have a galaxy to protect. Right after I get a clean pair of pants.* Victus tugged at the urine damped cloth.

"What's going on?" Alberta whispered as she looked down at Victus's unresponsive body.

In Hocco's body, Victus felt the Sergeant's restraining arm, like a docking clamp holding him in place. "You can let go now, Alberta."

"How—how do you know my name?"

Victus felt a slight tremble as the sergeant released her grip and stepped back.

"It's true," she said. "You really can possess people."

Victus ignored the Sergeant and browsed through Hocco's memories as if he were reading the morning news. After a minute, he stood up and tugged at his wet pants away from his leg. "The Selkans have fled to Sol."

"The closed system?"

"The same." Victus followed trails of thoughts until he found what he wanted. "They plan to unlock the Terminal," he whispered. A thrill of excitement ran through his mind. *A closed system. A locked Terminal.* He smiled. *They must have a Riftkey.*

As he tore open mental doors and gleaned the contents within, a name surfaced from Hocco's memories. Jack Spriggan. Ex-military pilot and former smuggler. *He'd be willing to help, for the right price.*

Victus/Hocco turned to face the sergeant and her marines. Though he looked like the thin man, he still carried the authority of an admiral. "Return to the *Tamarack* and inform Captain Hoff that he is to remain near Lan Terminal."

"Yes, sir," Alberta replied.

She motioned to Victus's body, which still sat motionless on the floor of the pod. "Sir?"

Victus looked at his unconscious self. "Take my body to the sickbay. I plan on keeping this one for a while."

2

CURSED

It was Saturday, June 15, 2024, and it was a clear winter day in New Zealand. Jenny Tripper parked her aunt's sedan at the Wellington Regional Hospital and turned the car off. She rubbed at her temples and tried not to think about why she was there. She didn't want to remember that three months ago, her mom, Ruby, had been diagnosed with a rare form of leukemia. She was only thirty-nine, and the doctors had been helpless against the rapidly spreading disease.

Worried that her tears had ruined her makeup, Jenny flipped the visor down and opened the mirror. She wanted to look happy and healthy for her mom, and part of that was to hide her sadness.

Jenny's eyes were dichromatic, one brown like chestnuts and the other green as an emerald. It was a favorite feature, unlike her black hair, and her brown skin.

Jenny's hair crunched against the headrest as she leaned back in the seat and opened the door. She oozed out of the driver's side door. Her breath was visible in the chill air. She wrapped her black coat tightly over her long lace-and-tulle black dress and pulled the collar up to her cheeks.

From the passenger-side of the sedan, her aunt, Beatrice Tripper, stepped out of the car. "I'd love it if you put on a happy face, Jenny." She pursed her artificially bright-red lips. "People are actually dying in there."

Jenny ignored her aunt as she walked to the car's back door to help the third member of their group out. She pulled at the door handle, but the door had frozen shut on the way over. Jenny gave it a hard tug, and it flung open in a shower of sheet ice.

"I still don't understand why a ghost needs you to open doors," Bea said as she flipped her curly brown hair behind her shoulders and straightened her colorful dress around her thin frame.

Jenny rolled her eyes. "So she can get out of the car." She didn't know why the ghost couldn't pass through solid objects, but this was Jenny's first and only specter. The ghost had been with Jenny since she was eleven. Jenny had even given her a name, Sally, after the dead heroine in *The Nightmare Before Christmas*. Being dead was where their similarities ended. Jenny's ghost wasn't a solid, stop-motion animated doll. She was ethereal, like a reflection in a car window. Though she was bound by hard objects like doors, and the ground, she could pass through living matter, like plants and animals. It didn't make sense to Jenny, so she tried not to think too hard about it.

As they reached the doors to the Blood and Cancer Centre, Jenny's heart started pounding in her chest, and Sally's form, which was normally steady, now flickered, like the flame of a candle.

"It's okay." Bea reached out to touch Jenny's shoulder.

"I'm fine." Jenny pulled away and stepped through the automatic doors.

The smells of laundered sheets, industrial-strength cleaners, and rubber gloves inside the hospital building irritated Jenny's already queasy stomach. She, Sally, and Bea took a lift to the third floor and checked in at the nurse's station. From there, they continued down the brightly lit linoleum walkway to Room 317.

Jenny paused at her mother's door and peeked through the small window. Green text broadcasted life signs on a dark-gray monitor. A large plastic mug of water with a thick bendy straw stood next to an empty pill cup on the bedside table. Ruby rested on an inclined hospital bed; her pale scalp was all that remained of once luxurious black hair; her thin blue hospital gown rose up and down over deflated breasts.

Ruby wore a virtual reality headset, and her thumb and fingers twitched over a controller.

Jenny took a breath and turned the doorknob. Her aunt and Sally followed Jenny inside. Bea took her place at the end of the bed. Sally sat down in a chair in the corner of the room. Jenny brushed Ruby's hand and attempted to imbue her voice with a cheerfulness she did not feel. "What are you watching?"

Ruby smiled at the sound of Jenny's voice and removed the headset with shaky hands. Her tired eyes were framed by dark rings and sunken cheeks. "It's Billo," her voice croaked. She pushed herself upright and winced in pain. "She's on a trek through the rainforest to base jump into a giant cave."

It was called vexing, for "virtual exploring," and Billo Misra was her mom's favorite guide. The young Indian woman had risen to worldwide stardom. Her charisma made people feel like they were an essential part of every adventure. Ruby had talked about her first experience, diving in the Bahamas, for weeks. After that, it was hiking to the top of the Giza pyramids, then visiting the Grand Canyon National Park.

At least she got to travel the world in her final days on this Earth, Jenny thought.

"Are you ready to come home?" Bea asked.

"More than ready." Ruby nodded and gazed warmly at her daughter. She patted the bed with her gaunt hand, "Sit by me, Djangini."

Jenny cozied up next to Ruby. Only her mother still called Jenny by her Romani birth name. Jenny had wanted to fit in at school, but it was difficult. She had been teased and bullied for being a Gypsy her entire life. She knew that the word "Gypsy" was originally given to her people in ancient Europe because they were foreign and exotic, and anything foreign and exotic was known to be from Egypt. "Egyptian" was shortened to "Gipcyan," and then "Gypsy." Jenny didn't mind the word, as some Roma did, but she didn't like being teased about it. So, after moving to Wellington, she changed her name from Djangini to Jenny, cut her hair short, and started wearing black clothes to hide her origin.

"How are you feeling?" Bea asked from the foot of the bed.

"It hurts." Ruby smiled at her sister. "But we knew this would happen."

"I'd love it if it had been different this one time." Bea shook her head.

Jenny's lips became a thin line, and her nostrils flared. Ruby and Bea believed that their family had been cursed. Male infants never survived birth, and all females in their bloodline died before the age of forty. "How can you be so laissez-faire about this?"

"Are you okay, Djangini?"

Jenny's temper flared. "No, Mom, I'm not okay. I hate this. I hate school. And you're dying. So, no, I'm not okay."

Ruby pulled a bronze amulet from her hospital gown and said a silent prayer. Like Aunt Bea and many Roma, Ruby put her faith into talismans and religious symbols. She kissed the amulet and tucked it back into her gown.

"Why do you believe in this stuff?" Jenny asked. "It hasn't kept the curse away."

"Because there is more in this world than what we can see."

"No, there's not."

Ruby sighed and shook her head. "I wish you would believe."

"Why?"

"That way, when I tell you that I'll always be with you, even after I'm gone, you'll believe me."

Jenny's eyes watered and a lump formed in her throat. She weaved her arms through the tubes and wires and hugged her mom's shrunken body. "I believe in you."

"I'll always love you, Djangini, no matter what."

"I love you too." As Jenny gave herself over to the tidal wave of emotions, a vibration ripped through her skull. She winced in pain as the pressure grew behind her eyes. Sally, who stood at the foot of the bed next to Bea, looked more solid than ever. Jenny pulled away and massaged her temples.

"Are you okay?" Ruby asked.

"It's just a headache." In fact, these migraines were such a persistent problem that Jenny invented a form of meditation to fight them. She turned her focus inward and imagined the pain as angry blue flames. Jenny gathered the tendrils into a ball and pushed it out of her. A warm buzzing sensation filled her head and spread through her body. After a minute, the tremors abated, and Sally returned to a fuzzy outline. Jenny looked at her mom and laughed.

"What's so funny?"

"You're the one dying of cancer, and you look so worried about me."

"You're not crazy, Djangini," Bea said.

"The rest of the world would say otherwise."

"Your mom and I don't have your gift, but we can feel her presence."

Jenny saw and heard things that other people couldn't, like auras and shadowy objects. Bea and Ruby accepted their own extrasensory perceptions, not that they compared to hers. Jenny just wanted to be normal.

Ruby gasped. "I think I see her. There's a faint outline next to your aunt. If I just concentrate..." She pointed at the foot of the bed. "She has long, dark hair, and she's wearing medieval clothing."

Jenny's mouth went slack. No one had ever seen Sally before. She looked at her ghost, then her mom. "How?"

Suddenly, Ruby's eyes rolled back in her head. Her arms went rigid against her chest, and the tendons in her hands looked like spiderwebs. She arched her back, then hunched forward as if her abs and back muscles were playing tug-of-war with her torso.

Jenny stood frozen. A piece of her soul seemed to die as the machine monitoring her mother's vitals beeped violently. The nurse ran into the room and checked Ruby's airway, breathing, and circulation. He moved on to make sure the lines from the saline were clear. "She's okay, it's just a seizure."

"What do we do?" Bea asked.

"There's nothing to do, except to keep her comfortable and safe. It will stop on its own."

The bed rattled in an unsettling manner as Ruby continued to seize for two more agonizing minutes. After it was done, she fell asleep.

"Your mom will need some rest before she can leave," the nurse said as he pulled them out of the room. "And we have some paperwork for you to fill out."

Jenny half-listened as Bea discussed palliative care with the doctor. She looked back at her mom's room. *This is finally going to end,* Jenny thought. *No more waiting. I'm finally going to have my life back.* She instantly regretted the selfish thought.

~

Bea's house was a straight drive south from the hospital along Adelaide Road. The narrow street sloped gently down toward the ocean, giving Jenny a view of the charming, well-kept houses of South Wellington.

"Do you have any plans for your birthday next week?" Ruby asked.

"No." There was no one she wanted to celebrate with, except for her mom. "It's enough that I get to spend it with you."

They drove past two large parks and turned onto The Parade. Residential blocks transitioned into downtown, where two-story, mixed-use buildings lined the street. Jenny pulled the car into a narrow alley and parked behind a green building at 137 The Parade, Island Bay. Jenny helped her mom out of the sedan and in through the back entrance. Painted on the front window of the building was a sign that read:

The Fortuna Niche, Madame Tripper, Clairvoyant
Predict the Future, Find Lost Treasures, Conjure True Love

It was lunchtime, so Jenny prepared cucumber sandwiches while Bea readied some tea. Ruby and Bea recounted stories as they ate. Afterward, Jenny helped her mom upstairs. In Romani tradition, Ruby's bed was surrounded by candles to light her way to the afterlife. As Ruby settled into bed, Onyx, Bea's black cat, jumped into her lap. Ruby scratched between its ears and it purred.

Bea came into the room holding a large quilt. "Jenny and I made this for you." Jenny and Bea had spent three weeks crafting each square of the quilt with meaningful shapes and pictures.

"Thank you, it's beautiful." Ruby took the quilt and admired each square as tears welled in her eyes.

"Well, I've got some work to do," Bea said, "so I'll let you two have some alone time."

"Thank you, Bea," Ruby said as her sister left the room.

Jenny retrieved an old photo album from the bookcase. This was one of her favorite activities with her mom, and it was the only way she learned of her family. She loved asking her mom to describe the people in the pictures. Jenny liked to imagine that she knew them. She sat next to her mom and put the album in her lap.

"Before I forget." Ruby reached up to her neck and pulled a chain over her bald scalp. "I want you to have this."

"Your amulet?" Jenny traced the triangle inside the circle. A long leather cord had been tied through the opening so that it could be worn as a necklace. The rough craftsmanship made the amulet seem ancient.

"It belongs to our family. Passed down for generations. It's part of who we are and represents our culture better than anything else I have. I have a feeling that it will help you one day."

Jenny hugged her mom. "Thank you."

They sat in silence for a while as Jenny leafed through the photo album. It made a ripping sound as each of the cellophane pages came unstuck. "So, how are you doing with your aunt?"

"She wants me to become a fortune-teller, like her."

"I'm not surprised," Ruby said. "She took us in when we needed her. Please do whatever you can to help."

"Fine." Jenny shrugged. "Only for you." *But after you're gone,* Jenny thought, *I'm out of here.*

Ruby sighed and collapsed onto the pillows. "You remind me so much of your father."

Jenny perked up. Ruby never talked about her dad. "How so?"

Ruby brushed her cheek. "How are things at school?"

Jenny's shoulders slumped. "Okay, I guess."

"There must be something you like."

"I like to fence."

"Of all the things you could have picked up." Ruby shook her head. "Your father loved to fence too."

Jenny snapped the album shut. "What else did he love? Do you have a picture of him?"

"Jenny, I'm sorry. You know I can't talk about him. I really want to, but I promised him. You wouldn't understand, but it really is for the better."

Jenny pouted.

"If you knew, what would you do? Would you track him down and tell him you're his daughter and hope that he adopts you into his family?"

"No." Jenny's eyes dropped to the album. Part of her understood why she couldn't know who he was, but she also resented her mother for making her miss out on having a father. "I don't know." They were silent for a long time. Jenny felt numb; even blinking seemed too loud as she stared down at the photo album. What would she do if she knew who her father was? She always imagined that he'd be happy to meet her. But what if he wasn't? She couldn't handle that, not right now.

～

Jenny hit the snooze button on her smartphone's alarm with practiced ease. *Was that the second or third time?* Jenny thought as she snuggled back into the covers. *And why is my bed the most comfortable at the moment between asleep and awake?* Before Jenny drifted off to sleep again, her bedroom door swung open.

Bea stood in the doorway. "Jenny, why are you still in bed?" She crossed the room and flung the curtains open.

Jenny shaded her eyes against the sudden brightness. "I don't have school today." She pulled a pillow over her head.

"You still have to work. Get up. Now."

"Ugh, fine." Jenny threw her covers off and stretched her arms with much exaggeration. She rubbed her eyes, relishing the squishy sensation. She picked up her smartphone. It was 8:15 a.m., June 19, 2024, Wednesday. Four days had passed since she had picked her mom up from the hospital, and Jenny had been given the week off from school to be with her.

"How'd you sleep?"

"Miserable, as usual." Jenny knew she was being melodramatic, but it was true. Several pill bottles sat on her desk. As her doctor had said, "They fix chemical imbalances." When she had migraines, exposure to lights and sounds made her feel like her eyes were going to pop out of her head. Glancing down, she saw the scars on her arms and pulled the long sleeves of her black shirt down to cover them up.

"Play music," Jenny said to her computer. A program examined her mood from the tone of her voice and played an appropriate playlist based on her listening history. Bauhaus's "Bela Lugosi's Dead" played from a pair of speakers on her desk.

"I know this song." Bea smiled. "I used to have all of Bauhaus's albums on vinyl."

Jenny raised her eyebrows in surprise.

"In fact, I think I still have them in a crate in my closet."

"So?" Jenny asked.

"So," Bea said, "I could pull out my record player sometime and we could listen to them."

Jenny looked down and remained silent. *I can't let myself get close to her,* Jenny thought. *It will just make it harder on her after Mom dies, and I run away.*

"I'd love it if you'd get ready for work and joined me downstairs." Bea turned and left the room.

Jenny dragged herself out of bed a minute later. Even though she had the day off from school, Jenny still planned on attending fencing practice at ten-thirty a.m. She wasn't about to miss out on the one activity that made her happy. After getting dressed, Jenny pulled out her duffel bag and added her fencing jacket, trousers, gloves, and breast shield. The plastic chest cover was molded and sized like a bra. It was bulky and awkward, but it was better than getting jabbed in her tender areas. Sally watched her approvingly. The ghost always seemed more vivid, and maybe even enthusiastic, when Jenny prepared for practice.

Jenny dropped her duffel bag by the front door and entered the kitchen. She had prepared two types of cookie dough last night, one for Anzac biscuits and the other for Afghans, delicious cookies popular in New Zealand. Jenny preheated the oven and pulled the two bowls from the refrigerator. She dropped spoonfuls of dough, evenly spaced, onto two cookie sheets.

Back in the 1980s, this building had been a restaurant, and the appliances were never upgraded. Early on, there had been some tragic cookie failures until they bought an oven thermometer to sit on the rack. Jenny slid the baking sheets into the oven and set a timer for ten minutes. She started cleaning up.

There was a knock at the door. Jenny glanced at the timer. *Three minutes left.* "Can someone get that?" Jenny shouted. Nobody answered, but she didn't want to abandon her cookies. *Where's Bea?* The knock came again, more insistent this time. Jenny sighed and hurried to the front door. She unlocked the deadbolt, pulled the chain, and swung it open.

Michael Creme stood in the doorway. He was a college-aged man with a short, hipster-style black beard. Michael worked at the Black Rabbit Cafe down the street, a place Jenny considered her second home. He held a large dark-gray package in his tattooed arms. A stylized image of a cabin and the letters *VRGo* were embossed onto the wrapping paper.

"Michael?"

"Happy Birthday, Jenny!" Michael held the package out. "Do you like puzzles?"

"Um, yeah." Jenny took the pizza-sized box from Michael and almost lost her balance. It was heavier than it looked.

"You got it?"

"Yeah." Jenny adjusted the package in her arms. "Thanks." *Why would Michael give me a puzzle?*

"You need to open that right away."

"Why? My birthday isn't until Friday."

"I know, but it's sort of time-sensitive. And because it's your birthday, I'll give you a free milkshake at the cafe."

"Okay." Jenny smiled.

"Is your mom home from the hospital?" Michael leaned against the entryway.

"Yeah."

"How is she?"

Jenny's smile faded. "She's on lots of painkillers, so she's as good as someone can be who's about to die."

"I'm sorry."

"It's okay. It's hard, you know? But I'm dealing." Jenny heard the timer for her cookies and sighed. *Saved by the bell.* "Well, I've gotta go save my cookies from the oven. Thanks for the present."

"Oh yeah. I'll see you later for that free milkshake."

"Yeah, bye." Jenny closed the door with her foot and set the package down before rushing to the kitchen.

"Who was that?" Aunt Bea called.

"Michael, from the cafe. He brought me a birthday present."

"Oh? That's odd."

"Yeah, a bit."

Bea walked into the kitchen. "Those smell wonderful."

Jenny smiled. They were a bit on the brown side, but they weren't ruined. "I hope they taste better than they look. I'm about to take some up to Mom."

"I'm sure she'll love them."

Jenny poured tea into a porcelain cup and placed six cookies on a plate, three of each type. Carefully, she climbed the stairs and peeked into Ruby's room. Seeing that her mom was awake, Jenny set the tray on the bed and sat down.

"Yum." Ruby sat up and hugged Jenny.

"I made these for you."

"They look delicious."

They ate in silence for a time, enjoying the shortbread cookies and tea in each other's presence. Ruby turned to Jenny and said, "Tell me more about school."

"Okay, what do you want to know?"

"Have you made any friends?"

Jenny hadn't, but she had only been at her new school for a couple of months. Not that any more time would have mattered. She wasn't the best at making friends, and she didn't really want to. Yet, with the way her mom was looking at her, she had to tell her something. "There is this one boy."

"A boy?"

"He's on the fencing team with me."

"Hmm." Ruby raised an eyebrow. "What about Adriana Thatcher?"

Jenny frowned. "Miss goody-goody, popular, and pretty? What about her?"

"Have you tried to be friends with her?"

"She looks at me like I'm a freak."

Ruby looked Jenny up and down. To be fair, Jenny was not trying to conform with the popular crowd—or any crowd, for that matter. All she wanted was to be left alone with her music and her books.

"Why would I be friends with her?" Jenny asked.

"Because she's Roma."

"What?" Jenny squinted. "She doesn't look Roma."

"Yeah, she inherited her mother's looks."

"Still, that's no reason for us to be friends. We have nothing in common."

"How do you know that?"

"I just do."

Ruby looked away from Jenny and wiped at her eyes with the back of her hand. "Still, I'd like you to try."

Jenny held her mom's bony hand. "If it means that much to you..."

"It does, thank you." Ruby set down her cup and yawned. "I'm tired all of a sudden, Djangini. Will you help me get ready for bed?"

"Sure."

Lately, it seemed that her mom spent more time asleep than awake, but that was better than always being in pain. Jenny helped her mom use the bathroom and get back into bed. She lifted the homemade quilt to Ruby's chin, kissed her forehead, and turned out the light. Then, she took the empty tray down to the kitchen and cleaned up.

The phone rang in the other room, and Jenny heard Bea pick it up.

Jenny checked the clock. It was just after nine. She still had an hour before she had to leave for practice, which gave her time to open the package that Michael delivered.

"That was Rebecca," Bea called down the stairs. "She'll be here in an hour."

"What?" Jenny answered. *Rebecca? Oh crap, I forgot.* Rebecca was her regular tarot-reading client. Jenny looked down at the duffel bag holding her fencing gear. *Before we came, Bea used to do all the readings by herself.* "Can you do the reading this time? I have fencing practice today."

"No, she's your client, and you can play with your friends another day."

"Fine." Jenny huffed. *I guess I won't be fencing today.* Jenny looked down at the box in her hands. *At least I have time to see what this is.*

The old wood stairs creaked and popped as Jenny carried the package up to her room. She set it on her desk, waking up her computer as it nudged the mouse. A Web page about a foreign exchange program displayed on the monitor. One of Ruby's biggest regrets was that she had never traveled outside of New Zealand. *I'm not going to let that happen. I'm going to see the world. I'm going to discover my true potential.*

Jenny retrieved a wood-handled pocket knife from her desk drawer and carefully cut the gray wrapping paper away. Inside was a shiny block of silver metal that was strangely warm. As Jenny touched it, a tone filled her head, not unlike the ringing in your ears after a loud concert. On top of the block was a card with her name on it. She picked it up, revealing a quarter-size depression in the otherwise perfect silver surface. Jenny opened the card and read it.

Jenny Tripper,

We seek gifted individuals to take part in a secret mission. If you are interested, use every one of your senses to solve the enclosed puzzle.

I look forward to meeting you on the other side,

Lance LaGrange,
Founder and Chief Executive Officer
Cabin, Inc.

Secret mission? Is this part of the puzzle? She examined the box. There didn't appear to be a single seam or mark anywhere on the metal block, nothing to open or rotate. Nothing but that quarter-size depression. *Maybe it's a button.* Jenny pushed her finger into it, and something jabbed her fingertip.

"Ouch!" Jenny screamed and jerked her hand back. She squeezed her finger, and a drop of blood bloomed from the tip. She looked closely at the depression. Something black oozed from the tip of a hypodermic needle. *What the hell?*

A strange humming filled her mind, and the edges of the room became fuzzy. The silver block glimmered with fugitive lights deep within. The air shattered into thousands of crystal fragments that coalesced into a woman who smiled and said, "Hello, Jenny Tripper. My name is Lin Yuan Song." The woman stood on the floor facing Jenny, looking as real as herself. A large white collar stretched across her black suit like the wings of an albatross. "You have been selected to take part in a test that will determine your candidacy for a special mission." Lin's dark brown, almond eyes looked through Jenny as she spoke, as if not seeing her

"Hello?" Jenny waved her hand in front of Lin, but the woman didn't even blink in response. "Can you hear me?" Jenny looked over at Sally, who shrugged in response.

"We've been looking for people with an exceptional genetic background."

Jenny sat down on her bed. The holographic display of Lin remained between her and the silver block. *It must be some sort of augmented reality projector,* she thought.

"Unique markers in your mother's genome brought you to our attention, and our agent, Michael Creme, has verified that your mental disorders are indicative of a latent ability."

Michael? Jenny's mouth dropped open. She felt violated and intrigued all at once. *What do they mean by "latent ability"?*

The woman disappeared and was replaced by the same stylized logo of a cabin that was on the package. The logo faded, and a tall, handsome, dark-haired man, probably in his thirties, phased into view. Like Lin, he stared straight ahead as he spoke.

"Hello Jenny, I am Lance LaGrange, owner and CEO of Cabin. I wish you luck on the test, and I look forward to welcoming you as a member of our team."

A thrill ran through Jenny. Somebody thought she was more than a fortune-teller. Somebody believed in her. Not like her aunt. Not like her mom.

Sally waved her arms excitedly and pointed at Lance LaGrange.

"I know," Jenny said to Sally. "This whole thing seems crazy. It must be some elaborate hoax."

The ghost sighed heavily and crossed her arms in response.

Lance faded away and Lin reappeared. "We are assembling a team of unique young people with potential abilities. Abilities that are needed to save a group of people called Selkans. In exchange for your help, Cabin promises to develop your natural talents and cure your ailments."

Could they really cure me? And what about my mom?

"You have seventy-two hours to solve the VRGo puzzle. After completing the test, you should pack supplies for at least two days before you enter—"

Aunt Bea shook Jenny's shoulders. "Jenny, wake up."

Jenny blinked and looked around. Lin was gone. The message had ended. *Was it all just a hallucination?* Jenny wondered.

"Jenny?"

"What?" Jenny glared at her aunt. "Why'd you barge in here?"

"You were in some sort of trance. I knocked and called your name, but you didn't answer." Bea looked at the strange box on Jenny's desk. "What is that thing?"

"That's what Michael delivered." The cube had ceased glowing.

"Why'd you scream?" Bea asked.

"I poked my finger." Jenny held the finger with the drop of blood out for Bea to see.

"Well, wash it off and get yourself presentable. Rebecca will be here any minute."

Jenny took a long, slow breath. "Fine. I'll be downstairs in ten minutes."

"Make it five."

"Fine, now get out," Jenny said as she pushed her aunt out of the room and closed the door.

3

JOB OFFER

People flocked to Lan Station with visions of striking it rich mining the asteroids. Others dreamed of touring the galaxy. The station's residents made their living providing food, drink, and pleasure to these entrepreneurs and tourists. Jack Spriggan knew all these people had one thing in common: they flew spaceships, and ships needed maintenance. So he'd done the logical thing and opened a repair shop.

Jack turned on a hot-water kettle and arranged a reusable filter over a glass urn. As a member of Lan Station's Coffee Enthusiast's Club, he had recently learned how to make a pour-over. While he waited for the pot to heat, Jack looked out through the skylight of his loft.

When you lived on a rotating space station, up was the same thing as the center. And at the center of the space station was the Terminal, where hundreds of spaceships swarmed like insects. Small black fighters escorted green cargo ships. White cruise ships carried tourists to faraway destinations. The control station configured them into a sphere to maximize the efficiency of each activation.

As Jack watched, the blue glow of the Terminal intensified. For a moment, everything in the workshop took on a blue hue. Then the Terminal climaxed in a flash of brilliant white. The ball of ships disappeared, and in its place, a massive pill-shaped warship appeared along with its strike group.

Jack recognized it as one of the Terminal Defenders. At a length of 1,914 meters and with a beam of 610 meters, it reached from one side of the station to the other. With crews of over ninety-six thousand each, the Defenders were cities unto themselves. These warships were impressive, but what truly made them formidable was their ability to teleport short distances through space on their own. They were the only ships capable of this feat, and it allowed them to jump behind their enemies, or away from projectiles, making them undefeated in battle. Terminals, however, were still required for traveling the thousands of light-years between systems.

Jack turned from the skylight, lifted the kettle, and poured hot water over his ground coffee, careful to avoid the light spots where the coffee was blooming. He leaned over and inhaled the rich aroma as the brew dripped into a stained ceramic mug. *Too bad the beans are flavorless crap,* Jack thought. *If I ever get planetside, the first thing I'm going to do is buy my weight in gourmet coffee.*

Taking his steaming mug, Jack climbed down the stairs from his living quarters to his workshop. Lan Station's pods measured forty meters wide, twenty meters tall, and eighty meters long. They were attached by spokes strung to the outside of the station. With the Terminal being tidally locked, one side always faced the star, leaving the other in shadow. Dark side pods were considered unsuitable for living, so they were primarily used for storage, and they were cheap. It was all Jack could afford.

A narrow window to his left provided a glimpse of his ship. It was a Harbinger. Back in his home system of Balt, harbingers were large birds of prey. Even before he'd enlisted as a pilot in the First Galactic War, Jack was in love with the mighty warcraft. Like the birds, the ships were known for their stealth. Their armor and shield technology absorbed and reflected radar and lidar signals. Active cooling systems concealed their heat signatures. Cloaking devices hid their electromagnetic radiation. Their hulls were capable of shifting color from white to black. With its thrusters off, his Harbinger was invisible to all forms of detection.

Jack had trained hard to become one of Balt's best pilots and had created a name for himself. He was proud to serve under fleet admiral Brigham Newton, who had led them to victory after victory. Piloting his ship into battle, confident of Admiral Newton's plans, Jack had felt alive in those days. But not even the invincible Newton could win against Tyr. After the war, Jack's home system, Balt, had been forced to retire its entire fleet. He'd pulled some strings, bought a Harbinger before it was scrapped, and named her the *Celestial Strider*.

One positive thing came from Tyr winning the war, for the first time in Jack's memory, there were peace and prosperity in the galaxy. Jack was even getting used to the idea of being ruled by Tyr.

Jack pulled his eyes away from the *Celestial Strider* and checked the day's schedule on a data tablet. *I'm scheduled more than a month out,* he noted. Just then, the pod door chimed. *And there's the first client of the day.* Jack climbed down the stairs.

The heavy pod door slid into the wall. A birdlike alien, called an Avian, stood in the corridor. He held a box in his feathery hands and looked more frantic than was typical for his species. "Are you Jack Spriggan?"

"I am."

"I—I heard you could fix anything."

There wasn't much Jack couldn't fix, given the right tools and parts. And what he didn't have, he could mostly manufacture in his own shop. "That's true." Jack sipped his coffee.

"I need your help." The Avian lifted the box up to Jack. His beak clicked in anticipation, and a crest of feathers rose from his neck. "The last shop told me that a replacement will take weeks to arrive, and no one else will even touch it."

"Let me see." Jack set his mug down and took the Avian's part out of the box. He turned it over, pulled on a lever, and looked inside. *To get at the coil,* Jack thought, *I'll have to disassemble the ignitor.* He removed the access panel and pulled the actuation lever back. A spring shot into the air. Jack caught it. "I can have it fixed by this afternoon—"

"Thank you, thank you, Jack. It's true, you are the best."

"As long as you have the money," Jack finished.

"How much?"

Jack looked the part over. It was an ignitor from the engine of an ice hauler. *I bet they're losing money every minute.* "Three fifty."

The Avian's eyes went wide, but he nodded. "Okay, okay. Please hurry. My job is on the line."

Jack retrieved his tablet and handed it to the alien. "Fill this out."

As the Avian filled out the form, Jack set the part on his worktable. "You need a new coil. Lucky for you, I can mill one."

"Here." The Avian set the tablet on the table.

Jack looked it over and nodded. "Looks good. I'll contact you when it's ready."

"Thank you, thank you," the Avian said as he backed out the door.

Before the door slid shut, another man stepped in. The patches on his blue-and-gray uniform read *TCS*—the Terminal Courier Service, the premier delivery service of the Terminal Space Station. Behind the courier, a giant blue-gray alien called a Snibb held a large plastic crate in its massive arms.

"You Jack Spriggan?" the courier asked as he thrust a tablet out to Jack.

"Yeah, that's me."

"Sign here."

"Who's it from?" Jack asked as he set the Avian's ignitor on the worktable.

"Anonymous."

Jack was no stranger to receiving ship parts from clients, but usually there was some notice. "What is it?"

"Look, you gonna sign it or what? I got more deliveries to make."

"I didn't order..."

The courier stared at him.

Jack took the tablet and scribbled his name in the signature field. "Put it inside, I guess." He moved out of the way and returned the tablet to the courier.

The Snibb shuffled forward on four stout legs. He breathed hard through the slits of his nose. Massive muscles rippled under his thick, wrinkly skin.

"Not there, you idiot," the courier yelled and smacked the Snibb with the back of his hand. "You'll block the doorway."

"There's no need for that," Jack growled at the courier. He believed in equal rights for all species. Which wasn't a common, or popular, point of view in the galaxy. "Right there is fine."

The Snibb set the large black crate near the door. The station courier held his hand out for a tip. Jack dug around in his pockets and shrugged.

"C'mon, let's go," the delivery man grunted to the alien and muttered to himself as he walked into the corridor. "Maybe there's still time to watch the *Elemental* qualifiers."

The *Elemental* was a galactic racing event inspired by the evolution of human technology and represented by each of the four elements. The first race was carried out on boats and symbolized water. Next was a car race that represented earth. The third race was in planes and symbolized air. Last was a spaceship race that represented fire. Every four years, each of the nine stellar systems sent their best teams to compete. The prize money was astronomical and often tilted the winning system's political power in their favor. Yet, with great reward there was often great risk, and the *Elemental* was no exception. Many racers died while competing, which of course made it more entertaining to the spectators.

Jack tapped the Snibb's shoulder and offered his hand. The Snibb reached out with one of his smaller arms and grabbed it. The alien's eyes widened as Jack slid a handful of credits into his palm. Jack winked, then walked back to his tool rack as the alien disappeared down the hallway.

Jack grabbed a crowbar from the rack and approached the crate. *Time to see what's inside,* he thought. He hefted the thick steel bar in one hand and wedged it under a strap on the crate. He cracked his large, calloused knuckles and pulled up on the end of the bar. The band gave way with a snap. As he slid the bar under the next strap, he noticed a whip-thin man standing in the doorway.

"Hocco." Jack straightened his back with a crack. Jack and Hocco had served together in the military. Now they only saw each other at the Coffee Enthusiast meetings. Most recently, Jack had heard that Hocco was running errands for his ex-wife, Pepper. "What are you doing here? Don't just stand out there, come on in."

Hocco stepped inside the workshop, and the doors slid shut behind him.

Jack was intrigued by this surprise visit from an old friend. "It's been months. Can I offer you something to drink, some coffee maybe?"

"Another time."

"This must be serious. It's not like you to turn down a cup of coffee."

Hocco only grunted in response.

"What are you here for?" Jack rubbed his nose with the palm of his hand and walked over to the worktable.

"I came by to offer you a job."

"I already have more work than I can handle." Jack picked up the Avian's part and waved it at Hocco.

"I'm talking about a real job." Hocco looked over at the *Celestial Strider*. "Wouldn't you rather be out there?" He pointed up to the skylight where the curve of the Terminal cut a path across the stars.

Jack looked up, then over at the hangar. Restoring the *Strider* had been difficult. With the war over, military parts were hard to come by. That had led him to the black market and a young woman who called herself Pepper. She was a dynamo who dreamed of running the black market on Lan Station. Using the *Celestial Strider*, they ran one successful smuggling campaign after another. It was the biggest thrill he'd had since the First Galactic War, and it fanned the flames of their romance. They were married in a casino at the end of the month.

Their marriage began to suffer after Lan System began using its military forces to police illegal activities. Smugglers were being fined, sentenced to jail, and even killed. Fearing he would lose his ship, his shop, or his life, Jack quit smuggling. Pepper didn't quit. She still dreamed of being the queen of the black market, so she doubled her efforts. She found a new ship and a new pilot.

During that time, Jack and Pepper fought constantly, and after a couple of years, they divorced. Sometimes Jack missed that old life of excitement, but he was a different person now and had responsibilities to his clients. Not to mention a massive debt to Pepper to pay off.

"You're wasting your time here," Hocco said. "Don't you want some excitement in your life?"

"I've got plenty of excitement," Jack said defensively.

"Look." Hocco leaned on the large crate. "I know we haven't been the best of friends lately, but we always helped each other in the past, right?"

Hocco plucked the ignitor from Jack's hand and fidgeted with it. "I know you miss the thrill, the uncertainty of battle. The—"

"I've changed."

"Listen, just this once, and I'll never bother you again." Hocco tossed the ignitor to Jack.

Jack caught the part and set it on the worktable. Then he walked to the back of the workshop, picked a thin rod of carbon from a rack and said, "Not interested."

"Just hear me out," Hocco pleaded.

Jack inserted the rod into one end of his milling tool and turned it on.

Hocco raised his voice over the hum of the machinery. "This isn't about smuggling. This is about uniting the galaxy."

"Are you with Unity now?" It was more an accusation than a question.

Hocco shrugged. "C'mon, Jack, you believe in alien equality as much as anyone."

Jack took the tooled rod and set it next to the ignitor. He flipped the activation lever, held the spring down, and inserted the tooled part. As he released the lever, the spring held.

Hocco looked over at the *Strider*. "I know you haven't flown her in months."

"Exactly. You don't want a rusty pilot for your job."

"You're still a great pilot. Give yourself some credit."

Jack looked up from the worktable and smiled. "I always give myself credit, but it's suicide to oppose Tyr."

"We know where to find Tyr's secret to the defender's teleportation."

"*What?*" With a twang, the lever and coupling blasted off in opposite directions. Jack gathered the parts from the floor and put them back on the table. *If Unity figures out how to disable the defender's teleportation, then they might have a chance against Tyr.*

"It's true. This is the chance you've been waiting for. It's a chance for all of us to win." Hocco grabbed the crowbar from the crate. He slid it under the strap and pulled with a grunt. There was a twang, and the strap popped loose.

Jack watched Hocco guide the crowbar under the last strap. It broke with a snap, and the crate panel fell open. Jack grabbed a large envelope from inside and read the package label aloud. "One military-grade negative-energy buffer." Jack's mind reeled. Negative-energy buffers (NEBs) were only used for traveling through a Terminal, and due to capacity limits, a limited number of buffers were available. Corporations bought most of the public registration numbers, making the waitlist almost infinite. The military, however, had its own registration numbers and didn't use half of them. Jack looked at Hocco. "How did you get this?"

"Trade secret."

"Why me?"

"You're the best pilot."

"You mean I'm the only pilot with a Harbinger." Jack set the label on his work table and pulled the molded foam away from the package. He whistled. Underneath was a masterpiece of premium military hardware, black and red, polished and perfect. "So, what's the mission?"

Hocco pulled a sphere from his pocket and twisted it. A three-dimensional image of a pentagon-shaped vessel appeared in the air. "We need you to locate the *Endeavor*, a Tyran stellar lab."

"Why?"

"When we find this ship, we'll uncover the secret to teleportation."

Jack studied the holographic image and asked, "How do you know?"

"Because we were the ones who stole it from Tyr in the first place. But, before we could get our engineers to study it, a group of nonhumans, called Selkans, hijacked it from us and fled through a Terminal."

"Selkans? Never heard of them."

"Neither had I, before this." Hocco twisted the sphere, and a sturdy, brown-gray creature replaced the hologram of the *Endeavor*. Short, dense fur covered its broad, humanoid body. Sharp tusks jutting down from its upper jaw gave it a fierce appearance.

Jack studied the hologram. "Selkans, huh? What system are they from?"

Hocco shook his head. "I don't know."

Jack grabbed a shop towel to clean his hands. "So, if I take this job, Pepper will surrender her half of the shop?"

"Don't worry about Pepper," Hocco said. "If you find that ship, you'll earn enough credits to pay her off and more."

"And what's my guarantee?"

"I'm coming with you."

Jack's mouth dropped open. Hocco wasn't the type to put himself in harm's way. He narrowed his eyes. "If you're lying, you're gonna have to get used to eating without teeth."

Hocco grinned. "You have my word," he said, extending his hand.

Jack gripped Hocco's soft hand with his calloused one.

"I'll be back at 09:00 with more details." Hocco pulled away and walked toward the door.

"What system did the Selkans flee to?" Jack called after him, but there was no answer. Hocco was already gone. Jack suspected that Hocco wouldn't have told him anyway.

4

THE WEDDING

Jenny had five minutes to get ready to meet her fortune-telling client, Rebecca. *No fencing practice*, Jenny thought, *no fun, just work, work, work. I guess that's my life, so I better get used to it.*

No time for this now, either. Jenny moved the silver VRGo puzzle to the floor. Its shiny surface was impossibly smooth, almost slippery. And warm. Her head buzzed, and twelve strange blue symbols lit up around the needle-equipped depression. Using her foot, Jenny pushed the puzzle all the way under the desk.

"Computer," Jenny said out loud. "Play music." Radiohead's "Paranoid Android" played from a pair of speakers on her desk.

The buzzing in her head persisted. She opened a drawer and took out her prescription bottles. She twisted each cap off, shook out the proper dosage, and chased the pills with a swig of water. This buzzing in her head was familiar. It reminded her of a night six years ago. Jenny looked at Sally. *It was the same night you came to me.*

Jenny walked to her bookshelf, where books of paranormal fiction, H. P. Lovecraft, Dante's *Inferno*, Edgar Allan Poe, and Tolkien lined the shelves. The Rubik's Cube she solved when she was nine years old sat next to an assortment of iron puzzles. She'd been obsessed with puzzles

for most of her life. On top of her bookshelf was her most prized possession—a handmade, mechanical diorama of the Mad Hatter's tea party.

Jenny turned the toy over and wound it with a metal key. She flicked
a tiny switch and set it down on her shelf. Teapot lids bobbed up and
down to the tune of "The Unbirthday Song" while Alice, the Mad Hatter,
and the March Hare hopped from one eccentric chair to another. *It was
the same night I received this diorama, and the last time I went by the name
"Djangini."*

~

Eleven-year-old Djangini Tripper played spaceplane out the window of
her mom's hatchback by moving her hand up and down in the wind. "It's
so beautiful out here!" she shouted at her mom over the road noise.
"Where are we going?"

"All I know is that it's a wedding." Ruby Tripper was a pleasantly
plump woman with a perpetual smile in her eyes. Her long black hair
had a hint of red in the sun that Djangini always found so beautiful. It
framed her round face and prominent rosy cheeks. "We're supposed to
follow the caravan."

The caravan had led them north, out of the Gypsy Fair in Inver-
cargill. Djangini smoothed her skirt, with fractal patterns in blue, yellow,
and green, across her legs. She played the fiddler's music in her mind
and pictured the men wearing silk shirts twirling women in skirts of
every color.

The sun dropped behind the snow-capped mountains that zigzagged
across the horizon. The caravan skirted Te Anau, taking a road that ran
south and bordered Lake Te Anau. The lake's glassy surface glittered
from countless stars and the sliver of a moon.

The hatchback skidded on the dirt road. Headlights and taillights
jumped and swayed, leaving tracers in Djangini's vision. The road
became little more than a rutted trail, and Ruby's knuckles turned white
from gripping the wheel. Their front tire hit a deep pothole, making
Djangini's teeth chomp.

The caravan turned off the bumpy road and onto a grassy meadow
bordered by evergreens. People bustled around an enormous tent held

aloft by tension rods and thick poles. Ruby gave Djangini's hand a squeeze. The vibration of the road still echoed through Djangini's nerves, and she let out a bubbling laugh.

They were finally here, wherever here was. Djangini flung the car door open and jumped out. She rubbed her arms for warmth against the chilly April night and looked around. A waxing moon backlit the tree-tops, and stars appeared like tiny holes in a black satin sheet.

Around the meadow were house trucks, houses built atop trucks of all shapes and sizes. Some were merely pickups, while others were converted school buses and lorries. Whimsical designs and bright colors adorned their sides.

The driver's side door of a vintage black lorry opened. A man wearing a bright floral shirt and a dark-blue vest stepped down. He looked like a lumberjack, with a thick black beard that hid all but his gentle eyes. His gaze locked on to Ruby's. She smiled and waved him over.

"Hey there." His voice was deep and rich.

"Hi." Ruby twisted her dress with both hands.

"And who's this?" He looked down at Djangini.

"Thatch"—Ruby sounded breathless—"this is your—this is Djangini."

Thatch smiled and held out a hand with grease packed under the fingernails. "Hello there, Miss Djangini."

"Hi." Djangini's hand wrapped around two of his calloused fingers.

"So, uh..." Thatch rubbed at his beard like he might find something interesting to say buried deep within. "You in school?"

"Yeah, sixth grade." Djangini kicked at the back of one foot with the other.

"You like it?"

"I guess so." Her gaze shifted to the tent and the colorful people bustling around it.

"I have a daughter about your age, Ana. She goes to school in Wellington."

"Cool."

"I uh, would have brought her, but she's with her mother this weekend."

Ruby lifted an eyebrow at Djangini and nodded toward Thatch.

Djangini rolled her eyes, looked around for something to talk about, and settled on his vehicle. The circular headlights and curved fenders gave it a lively, cartoonish appearance. The emerald-green dwelling trimmed with gold was beautifully crafted. "I like your truck."

The vehicle's chrome accents seemed to sparkle at the compliment, and an infectious smile spread across Thatch's face. "Alice is a real beauty." He put a hand on her side. "She's a converted 1962 Mack truck that I found abandoned at a farm. The owner sold her to me for five hundred dollars. Of course, she didn't look this good back then." He raised an eyebrow at Djangini. "You want to see inside?"

"Yeah." Djangini grasped her hands together.

"Thank you, Thatch," Ruby said. "We'd love to."

"Great." Thatch opened the back door. A sign above the door read, "Nonsense." Stepping onto the back fender, he hopped inside and lowered a ladder.

The dwelling was roomier than Djangini had imagined, and it smelt pleasantly of pipe smoke. A loft with a bed sat over a kitchenette and dining area that doubled as an office space.

Thatch looked at Ruby. "You remember how it all works?"

Ruby ran her hand along the wall, and something clicked.

Djangini gasped in wonder as hundreds of lights glowed from dozens of shelves that lined the walls. They were dioramas. To her right were scenes from a storybook. She saw the Three Bears, Humpty Dumpty, Little Red Riding Hood, and a dozen others. The mechanical creations hummed as their moving parts came to life. Goldilocks ate each of the bears' porridges. Humpty Dumpty fell off the wall. Red Riding Hood talked to the wolf dressed in her grandma's clothes.

Dioramas from *Alice in Wonderland* filled the opposite wall. Djangini watched Alice, with her bright yellow hair and a sky-blue dress, leap from scene to scene. At first, she crawled into the White Rabbit's hole. In the end, Alice fled from the Queen of Hearts and a pack of cards.

Thatch smiled from ear to ear as he watched Djangini. "I want you to have one."

"What? Why?"

"As a gift. To remember me. Think of it as a late birthday present."

"Really?" Djangini looked at the priceless toys. Each one was a work of art. "No, I couldn't."

"They aren't meant to live here, on the walls of my truck. They are meant to be loved and admired. Please, take one."

"Any of them?"

Thatch nodded.

Djangini was overjoyed, but how could she pick? She knew it had to be an *Alice in Wonderland* scene. The first time Djangini had seen *Alice in Wonderland*, she'd fallen in love with the idea of exploring a world of nonsense. Thatch seemed to have captured that idea perfectly in his dioramas. There was Alice, shrunken and crawling through a tiny door, a bottle with the words "Drink Me" on a table. She ran around the dodo in the caucus race. A caterpillar smoked a hookah on a mushroom. The Cheshire Cat grinned in a tree. Alice ate from a box with the words "Eat Me" and filled the White Rabbit's house. The Queen played croquet. But the Mad Hatter embodied nonsense more than any other character.

She lifted the Mad Hatter's Tea Party from the shelf. "This one?" Djangini asked in a small voice.

"Good choice, one of my favorites." Thatch fished a small metal key out of a wooden box. He took the diorama and showed her how to wind it up.

Djangini followed Thatch's instructions and flicked the switch to activate it. A music box played "The Unbirthday Song" while the characters moved from chair to chair and the teapot lids danced. Djangini giggled with pure joy.

Ruby squeezed Thatch's hand. He smiled at her.

"I ought to be getting ready." Thatch picked up a large green duffel bag and tossed it down to the ground. Then, he pulled a long, thin sword from a closet and dropped it into the bag.

"Where are you going?" Djangini asked.

"To get ready for the performance." Thatch nodded toward the tent. "See you inside?"

"Absolutely." Ruby nudged Djangini.

"Thank you for the present!" Djangini shouted.

"You're very welcome." Thatch pulled Djangini in for a hug before hopping out of the truck. Hoisting the duffel bag over his shoulder, he waved and jogged toward the tent.

"What'd you think of him?" Ruby asked.

Djangini shrugged. "He seemed cool."

Ruby turned off the lights, and the Lilliputian creations stopped their merry movements.

"Did Thatch really make all those?"

"He did. I have no idea how he does it, but he's always been good with machines." Ruby shook her head. "It's people he has trouble with."

Djangini stored the diorama in the hatchback before crossing the meadow to the tent. The white canvas glowed with yellow light, and a delirious mix of music and conversation spilled into the air. Inside, flags in every color hung from a long rope that wrapped around the ceiling of the tent.

A five-piece band composed of an accordion, two clarinets, a double bass, and a guitar played live Gypsy folk music in the back. They provided accompaniment for a beautiful dark-haired woman.

Off to one side, a group of women in white aprons set platters of aromatic food onto long tables. Romani food was the little-known soul food of Europe, and here in New Zealand it was downright exotic. Djangini's mouth watered at the sight of janij, a tomato-based beef and vegetable stew. There were sarma rolls stuffed with meat and tomatoes, and a pile of fresh-baked rolls and flatbreads.

Before Djangini could pick up a plate, an elderly couple approached.

"Ruby, it's good to see you." The little old woman set her plate down on a nearby table and hugged Djangini's mom.

"Djangini"—Ruby took Djangini's hand—"I'd like you to meet some old friends of our family. This is Abigail and Seth Sanford; they're the parents of the bride, Nadya."

Djangini smiled and nodded at the short couple. Seth had a scarce amount of hair on his head, and his green velvet suit was straight out of the 1960s. Abigail's dark-brown hair hung in tight ringlets around her face, and she wore a gorgeous white dress with emerald embroidery. Her eyes crinkled behind her Coke-bottle glasses as she smiled.

"Welcome." Abigail opened her arms and embraced Djangini. Though Djangini was only eleven, the two of them were the same height.

"It's good to see you again." Abigail stepped back and looked Djangini over. "My, you've gotten so big. I remember when you were this tall." She held her hand near her knee. "Do you remember?"

Djangini smiled and shook her head. "No, sorry."

"Ah, I wouldn't expect you to. You were a toddler, after all." Abigail winked and turned to face Ruby. "I'm so glad you made it. Where have you been all these years?"

"Trying to find out where I fit in and being a mother. Now, I'm trying to introduce Djangini to our culture. I just hope it's not too late." Ruby shrugged. "But it's a different world from when I was a kid." She smiled. "Gypsies are cool now."

Djangini crossed her arms. No, not cool. Whenever the bullies found out, they called her names. Though, to be fair, they called everybody names.

"Well, we have a beautiful celebration planned tonight," Seth spoke in a deep and musical voice.

"Thank you so much for having us. Is there anything we can do to help?" Ruby asked.

"No," Abigail said in a firm tone. "Everything's taken care of. You two enjoy yourselves. Grab some food and drink, then find us." She motioned toward the stage at the rear of the tent.

"We'll do that." Ruby moved toward the food table.

Djangini filled her plate and poured some punch while her hips swayed to the music. At the center of the tent, two teenage boys unfolded and positioned wooden chairs onto stadium steps of an indoor amphitheater. The steps led down to a hole in the wooden floor where something dark glinted from the torches that lit the tent.

"Mom, what's that down there?" Djangini asked.

"Hmm, I don't know. Let's take a closer look."

Careful not to spill their plates and cups, Djangini and Ruby climbed down the steps and peered into the hole. A large obsidian-like bowl rested on the ground underneath the floor. It felt significant, like a henge or a fairy ring, timeworn and formidable.

A sudden chill made Djangini shiver. "What is it?" Djangini felt the urge to rub her arms, but her hands were full.

"I don't know. I've never seen it before." Ruby gave herself a small shake, chuckled, and nudged Djangini with her elbow. "C'mon, let's find a seat."

They found Seth and Abigail sitting on a plush rug near the dance floor. On the stage, soft lantern light illuminated the colorful clothing and bright jewelry of the performers. The female lead looked at the guitarist and bobbed her head three times before starting her next song.

I'm a Romano Rai, just an old didikai,
I build all my temples beneath the blue sky,
I live in a tent, and I don't pay no rent,
and that's why they call me the Romano Rai.

The wood floor creaked and bounced as people danced. Djangini watched women in colorful dresses whirl about. Men stomped their boots in time to the beat. As the music picked up, hips swayed, and the men leaped about. By the time the song ended, Djangini was scraping the last remnants of her stew from her bowl with a piece of flatbread.

The next song started, and Djangini watched Ruby moving her feet in rhythm with the music. "Mom, do you know this dance?"

"I used to. Let's see." Ruby stood up and tried a few steps. She found the rhythm and pulled Djangini up. The music infected Djangini like a fever, and she picked up the steps in no time.

As the singer called out commands, groups of people danced together as one. Everything was a haze of clapping and stomping. Faces glowed orange and red from the lantern light, and everyone laughed in merriment.

When the song came to an end, Djangini clapped her hands and jumped with joy. She gazed up at her mom. "That was so much fun!"

As Djangini made her way back to her seat, she felt dizzy. She swayed backward, feeling as if a bottomless pit opened up behind her. "Mom, did you feel that?"

"What?" Ruby asked.

Djangini stared back at the amphitheater and the obsidian bowl. "Nothing, I just got a bit dizzy." The sweat from dancing had grown cold on her skin.

"Have some water," Ruby replied, grabbing Djangini a glass as they worked their way back to their seats.

Two young men in purple satin pants and white silk blouses took the stage next. They bowed to the audience, then gathered a set of three clubs. Their shirts billowed as they juggled in arcs above their heads and to each other. Their movements and skill were hypnotizing. Next, they dipped their clubs into a bucket and swung them through the flame of a torch. The clubs caught fire, and the crowd whooped in appreciation as a flaming infinity symbol formed in the air. The jugglers twisted, cartwheeled, and flipped before dousing the clubs and bowing to the audience.

Djangini let out a deep breath, wiped her hands on her dress, and applauded. As the jugglers left, a man in medieval period garb approached the stage. He wore an olive-colored vest over a drab tunic and a pair of dark leather pants.

Djangini gasped. "It's Thatch."

Thatch looked across the stage where a woman with long blond hair bent over a basket of baguettes. He turned to the audience and mimed an hourglass with his hands. While staring at her ankles, Thatch approached the lady with his hands held out.

The woman turned in feigned surprise, and a melon fell out of her voluminous white blouse. Her most surprising feature, however, was that she had a full red beard. Thatch stuck out his tongue in disgust. The audience erupted in laughter as the lady stuffed the melon back into her blouse.

Thatch looked back and forth between the woman and the audience. Then, he picked up a giant beer stein and made a show of drinking it all. He stumbled and squinted at the lady and shrugged. Thatch sauntered forward and took the lady's hand. He leaned in and whispered into the lady's ear. She turned her head and giggled.

A third actor jumped onto the stage. It was a woman dressed as a man, wearing a black beard and shoulder pads under a black shirt. The man in black pulled off a leather glove, pantomimed that Thatch had besmirched his honor, and slapped him.

The red-bearded lady pulled an enormous paper fan from her blouse and fanned herself. Thatch grabbed a French baguette from the basket and stood *en garde*. The man in black also grabbed a length of bread and stood ready. Thatch thrust the bread forward, and the other man stepped aside. They swung and dodged as the crowd shouted encouragement.

In no time, the bread turned to crumbs, and the fighters returned to the basket. This time, they pulled out rapiers and faced each other. This was too much for the red-bearded lady, who swooned. Thatch rushed to her side as she collapsed to the stage, but the man in black shoved him off. Their duel renewed.

Djangini's hands were sweating as the two fighters lunged, dodged, and shuffled their feet in an elegant dance. In the end, the man in black disarmed Thatch. Thatch knelt down, prepared to receive the finishing blow. The man in black knocked him out with a pommel strike to the head. The red-bearded lady jumped up and embraced her hero, then rewarded him with a kiss.

"They're married," Ruby whispered to Djangini, indicating the two cross-dressed actors who had portrayed the man in black and the bearded lady.

"Oh." Djangini nodded, curious how her mom knew all of these people.

The audience cheered and applauded. Thatch stood up and bowed along with the other actors, then hopped off the stage and joined in ushering everyone to the amphitheater.

Djangini approached the center of the tent with a feeling of trepidation. She took nervous glances at the glittering bowl on the ground as she took her seat. Only after she settled down and nestled up to her mom did she notice the musicians at the top of the steps, but her eyes kept returning to the bowl.

A ripple of excitement spread across the room, and the audience looked toward the entrance. "That's the groom," Ruby said. "Marco."

Djangini tore her eyes away from the bowl and looked. A handsome man with dark hair and warm olive skin had entered the tent. He wore a navy jacket and pants and a white shirt, and a tie that glowed emerald in the lantern light.

Marco welcomed guests as he walked down the amphitheater steps.

After squeezing shoulders and shaking hands, he stopped at the edge of the opening to the obsidian-like bowl.

The music changed, and everyone stood up and turned toward the entrance. The night sky framed the bride, Nadya, who wore a long white dress with lace sleeves. More lacework bordered her neckline, and an emerald silk scarf draped over her shoulders and down to her waist. An elaborate silver headpiece adorned her head like a crown, and delicate silver chains veiled her eyes and crisscrossed her face.

Ruby sighed. "Oh, she's beautiful."

Djangini nodded in agreement.

Seth stepped up to his daughter and smiled. Nadya offered him her arm. Seth took it and escorted her to the groom.

Marco hopped down through the opening and slid on the smooth obsidian-like surface. Once he had his feet, he helped the bride into the bowl. When they stood in the center, the floor of the amphitheater was level to their waists.

The officiant approached the opening. She had dark hair pulled into a complicated bun and wore a gold-embroidered emerald dress. She cradled a plain wooden box in her arms.

"Good evening." The officiant looked around the amphitheater. "We have been invited here today to share with Nadya Rose Sanford and Marco Donovan Barrett a crucial moment in their lives." She looked down at the obsidian bowl. "This location has a feeling of grandeur appropriate for the public affirmation of their love."

With hands clasped tight, the bride and groom gazed up at their officiant and nodded.

The officiant looked down at the wedding couple. "Do you choose to be married today?"

"We have so chosen," the couple responded as one.

The officiant continued. She spoke about love and the meaning of marriage and quoted verses in a strange language. She opened the wooden box. "You will need to nurture each other." She withdrew a silver knife and handed it to the bride.

Nadya took the knife with trembling hands.

Next, the officiant took a small loaf of bread out of the wooden box and gave it to the groom. Marco took the bread and broke it in half.

"You are each other's support system now; do not take that task lightly."

With a flash of the blade, Nadya pricked the tip of her ring finger.

"What are they doing?" Djangini asked in a shaky voice.

"It's a traditional bonding ceremony," Ruby said.

Bonding. Something about that word seemed significant to Djangini. Especially near this strange bowl.

Djangini watched as the bride squeezed a drop of her blood onto one half of the bread. The groom ate the blood-stained part while looking into her eyes. Nadya exchanged the knife for the bread, and the ritual was repeated.

After the bride and groom exchanged vows, the officiant invited them to wear their rings and complete the ceremony with a kiss.

The audience applauded and cheered, and the musicians started playing. A few seconds into the song, a low-frequency sound hummed from the bowl. Djangini's heart pounded with an overwhelming feeling that something was wrong. She looked at the opposite side of the tent, behind the last row of the amphitheater. A peculiar non-substance, like fog, was forming out of thin air. As Djangini watched, the mist solidified into a dark shape. It was a ghost, she realized. From here, she could see that it was an older woman, maybe in her late thirties, with dark hair and strange clothes. "Mom." Djangini tugged at Ruby's dress. "What is that?"

"Where?" Ruby looked.

"It's right there, can't you see it?" Djangini said as she pointed at the ghost across the tent

"Djangini, what are you pointing at?" Ruby sounded irritated.

"A ghost."

Nearby, a gray-haired man looked at Djangini, and her face heated up as more people glanced in her direction. She dropped her arm, worried that she was drawing even more attention to herself. Candles and torches flickered along the tentpoles, and the silvery shape had vanished. "Nothing, a funny shadow, I guess."

Djangini placed her hands in her lap and focused on the wedding couple. The audience grew silent in anticipation as an old Roma woman, bent over with age, approached the officiant. A strange noise buzzed from the old woman's throat, and she simultaneously sang in a commanding voice. It was the most incredible thing Djangini had ever seen or heard.

The gray-haired man leaned over to Ruby and whispered, "Music activates the senses—"

"Mmm," Ruby replied.

"Mom, how is she doing that?" Djangini leaned forward, enthralled that a human could create such a sound. The words were arcane, like a magical spell.

"It's called throat singing."

The old man nodded, closed his eyes, and listened to the strange song. Three of the musicians circled around the wedding couple and played their fiddles. The sound reverberated off the tent walls and willed Djangini's heart to match.

She still felt that something was wrong. A danger lurked somewhere in the tent, but she wasn't sure if it was the obsidian bowl or the shadowy figure. Djangini squirmed in her seat as the wedding couple danced slowly inside the bowl. The audience clapped in time to the musicians and the old woman.

Across the tent, Djangini caught sight of the ghost again. It had moved about halfway around the amphitheater. This time, she wasn't going to take her eyes off of it. She watched as the ghost drew nearer. It climbed down the stadium steps, passing through a woman's leg in the process. As it drew nearer, Djangini could see that the ghost's dark hair was braided, and her clothing looked like something out of a Renaissance fair. To her surprise, the expression on the ghost's face was one of hope.

Suddenly, Djangini's senses heightened and colors, smells, sounds, and tastes flooded into her brain. She felt the vibrating fiddle strings and smelled the rain outside. She heard the rustle of clothing and tasted the coppery tang of blood-soaked bread. But there was a new sensation as well, one which her mind struggled to define because it was completely inside her mind. Djangini could tell that something was off about this new sense. It didn't taste quite right, and she needed to fix it. Like adding spice, she tried a few brain exercises until something worked. It seemed that by humming inside her mind, the sensation changed. So, she experimented with the pitch and timbre until something clicked.

That's when the colors inside the tent became more vivid, and the obsidian bowl thrummed in response. A globe of shimmering mist enveloped the wedding couple. It looked like they were trapped inside a snow globe. Djangini's heart skipped a beat and she stopped humming, but the obsidian bowl continued to thrum. She looked around in horror at all the smiling faces. *Why is everyone still clapping?* The bowl's thrumming peaked, and with a bright flash, Nadya Rose Sanford and Marco Donovan Barret vanished.

5

THE FORTUNA NICHE

Jenny wasn't a naive eleven-year-old any longer, but the guilt of making the wedding couple disappear had been eating at her for years. From that point on, she wanted nothing to do with Gypsy culture. That eleven-year-old still existed, somewhere, locked in the deep recesses of her mind, a defense mechanism that kept her from reliving that night. As well as the part of her that enjoyed dancing, bright colors, and folk music. She'd grown to accept that Sally's presence was her punishment.

Now, coming from the strange puzzle under her desk, were the same sounds and vibrations from that night. *I don't know what this VRGo puzzle is,* Jenny thought, *but if it has anything to do with that obsidian bowl, I don't want it.* She slid the silver block into her closet and shut the door.

Jenny traded her black shirt and pants for a black dress and pulled on a pair of black boots. Then, she went to the bathroom and stared at her bloodshot eyes in the mirror. *I have work to do,* she thought. After splashing cold water on her face, she set out her makeup. She outlined her eyes and darkened her eyebrows with black eyeliner. Next, she added some putty to her flat, dull hair and pulled it into chunky spikes. It was about as rebellious as she was willing to go. She'd thought about piercings or tattoos but always chickened out before going through with it.

Jenny grabbed her smartphone and stomped down the stairs in her heavy boots. The bottom floor of Bea's shop catered to the guests of her trade. Jenny enjoyed the crystals and bright colors of the shop, though she would never admit it to her aunt. A yellow-fabric sofa with dark wood legs sat near the front door. Bea bought and sold sofas as if it were her mission in life. Last week it had been a high-backed pink loveseat.

"What's all that noise for?" Bea stood in front of Jenny with her arms crossed over a billowy white blouse. A bright-red silk scarf was tied around her black hair. Bronze bangles clanged on her wrists and silver hoops dangled from her ears. A black skirt with moons, owls, bats, and snakes embroidered onto it hung off her bony hips.

"You're such a stereotype," Jenny groaned.

"Look who's talking," Bea retorted. "Do you have to wear so much black?"

"It's a reflection of the darkness in my soul."

Bea rolled her eyes. "Fine, but I'd love it if you'd keep the darkness away from our client."

Bea led Jenny into the workroom, where figurines of cats sat alongside handmade talismans. Rose petals floated in bowls of rainwater. The skulls of various animals sat next to dusty tomes.

"Don't forget that Rebecca needs another talisman."

"Yeah, sure," Jenny replied.

In the fortune-telling business, first visits were the realm of tourists. The spiritually curious. For Bea to make a living, she needed long-term, highly superstitious clients. Jenny didn't hate working for her aunt. Some parts of it were fun. She liked running the website and maintaining her aunt's social media presence. She even enjoyed the tarot card readings. But, she didn't like taking advantage of gullible people.

People don't want to hear the truth; they want pretty fortunes. Bea's clients *wanted* to believe that Bea could see into the beyond, so they did. Her aunt then manipulated them into buying more talismans. Jenny was different. Call it auras or vibrations or whatever, but she could sense what people were feeling. It made it both easy and hard to take advantage of them.

In the workroom, incense smoke curled up to the ceiling. Relaxing music played on a speaker hidden inside an antique cabinet. Bea lit twelve candles to optimize the ambiance, then set out a pot of tea along-side Jenny's homemade cookies. "I brewed Darjeeling," she said.

"Rebecca's favorite," Jenny answered. She had wrapped a red scarf similar to her aunt's around her neck and shoulders before sitting at a plain wood table polished from years of use. Onyx, Bea's black cat, jumped in Jenny's lap and purred. Sally took her usual seat in the corner on a red settee with gold embroidery.

Jenny opened the table drawer and drew a single card from a worn tarot deck. It was the Eight of Swords. The card represented imprison-ment and powerlessness, caused by self-victimization. *Not the most uplifting card*, Jenny thought.

While she waited for Rebecca to arrive, Jenny pulled her smartphone from her pocket and searched for "Selkans." Nothing significant appeared in the search results. She tried "VRGo" next, but there was no mention of a test or a puzzle by that name.

The bell hanging above the front door jingled. A lovely woman of about twenty-five entered the waiting room. Her long black hair framed birdlike features, large, round eyes, and a hooked nose, which made her more interesting rather than unattractive.

"Good morning, Miss Shepherd," Bea said. "Would you like some tea and cookies?"

"Yes, please." She smiled as she took two cookies and placed them on a small plate.

Bea made small talk as she led Rebecca into the workroom.

"Oh! That's weird," Rebecca said. "I could have sworn I saw Jenny outside. I even said 'hi' to her."

"I assure you, she's been here the whole time. Perhaps you saw her psychic twin."

Rebecca's eyes went wide. "Really?"

Bea smiled as if she knew a great many secrets. "Did you bring the offerings?"

"Yes, of course." Rebecca took a sip from her cup before placing it onto a narrow table. She knelt down at the altar in the corner and made the sign of the cross. A statue of the Madonna, the skull of a humming-bird, a raven's feather, and an empty ceramic bowl rested inside the altar.

Rebecca removed a small jar of honey from her purse, followed by a candle and a warm, fresh bread roll. Rebecca placed the offerings into the wooden bowl, along with a wad of dollar bills.

"I'll need one of your hairs for your talisman," Bea said. Rebecca plucked one of her long black hairs and handed it to Bea. Bea blew out the flame of a large candle and fed the hair into the melted wax. "The hair represents the path you've taken in your life." Bea held the candle over a large abalone shell filled with blessed water. "Now think of a question you want to be answered."

After a moment, Bea poured the melted wax into the water and observed the abstract shapes that formed. She spoke in a stream of consciousness. "Significant forces are working against you. One who has been away will return and bring trouble. Now is the time to take chances." Bea plucked the wax from the water and turned it over. "You lack focus and spirituality in your life. You will go on a distant trip, experience new activities, and rediscover yourself."

As Rebecca stared at the lump of wax, Jenny rolled her eyes and typed "Cabin Inc" into her phone. If this VRGo Cabin company was as big as they claimed, then they should be near the top of the search results. Yet again, there was nothing relevant.

Bea added the lump of wax to Rebecca's offerings. Then she took the bowl to a worktable where a plethora of crafting materials awaited. "I will have your talisman ready by the time Jenny finishes your reading."

"Thank you," Rebecca said, and approached the table where Jenny sat.

Jenny slid her phone under her leg and leaned forward. She smelled lavender on Rebecca's skin. "It's lovely to see you again." Jenny took Rebecca's ring-laden hands and studied her face. Jenny knew that her dichromatic eyes helped convince clients of her mystical nature. "You said that you saw me outside?"

"Yes. At least I thought so."

"It was probably my doppelgänger." Jenny laughed. "Shall we begin?"

Reading tarot was more of a performance than a scientific process. It involved listening to a client's tone of voice and watching for subtle tells in facial expressions and gestures. She had to give Rebecca what she came for but leave her wanting more.

"I'm ready." Rebecca bit her lip and sucked air through her teeth.

Jenny opened the table drawer and withdrew a silk-wrapped bundle tied with a blue string. A series of four tiny bells jingled as she unraveled the cord and wound it around her hand. Jenny set the parcel of black silk on the table in front of her, unfolded the cloth, and withdrew a well-worn deck of tarot cards. She placed the cards on her right, folded the silk, and set it next to the circle of blue string on her left.

Together they shuffled the deck, then Jenny formed a cross of five cards, with four more lined up on the right. A faint pressure bloomed in Jenny's skull as she went through the cards in order. She provided Rebecca with an explanation of each. "Ace of Pentacles, inverted," Jenny began. "You have power and strength, but it is unclear to you now. You are being blocked, and the weight of it causes you to diminish."

As she explained the cards, Jenny watched for Rebecca's reactions. What she did wasn't magic. She had a knack for knowing what people needed before they knew they needed it, and the forethought to commit a person's secrets to memory until such time as they might be of use. Yet, even as she tried to focus on Rebecca, her mind kept wandering back to the puzzle in her room.

"The card in the west position illustrates your past. Inverted pentacles again, this time the three. You lacked a clear male role model in your childhood, like a father figure. But from this absence, you acquired an essential gift."

Jenny's skin tingled. *This reading isn't for Rebecca anymore, it's for me.*

Her face flushed at this betrayal of their session, but it was too late to back out now. All she could do was hope that Rebecca would find the reading applicable to her life as well.

"The north position holds the card of strength, indicating that you are more than capable of overcoming any obstacles before you. The Ace of Wands"—Jenny pointed at the southern card—"means a new opportunity, one that will help you grow and mature. Your future path begins here in the east. The Page of Pentacles. Your horizon line. These three cards"—she waved her hand over the middle of the cross—"are all pentacles. The Page represents new beginnings. Its upright orientation indicates that you will have the strength to cast off the negative influences that are blocking you."

What's blocking me? Jenny's blood grew cold. There was a wish that she had buried deep down in her subconscious. It was painful to watch her mom wither away. But it was worse to watch her own life and dreams die.

"Are you alright?" Rebecca asked. "You look pale. Well, paler than usual."

"I'm okay. I was just meditating on these cards." Jenny indicated the line of cards on her right. "Your future path holds challenges. You may experience the darkest shadow you can imagine. The Moon, as it manifests, often appears to us when we are unsure of our destination. It will help you on your path, though you may not see it immediately.

"Your next card, the Hanged Man, implies that you will experience a period where you feel unable to conquer life's obstacles. When this happens, you must push past it. Do not act selfishly or refuse the help of others during this time, for you will only succeed through cooperation.

"The Nine of Cups. Once you accept and face your challenges, you will find the satisfaction you seek. But beware of complacency. The people who help you on your way should not be forgotten.

"The Nine of Wands. Do not allow yourself to revert to old habits or behaviors. This path is a growth process. Be mindful and allow yourself to be unburdened from any pressure you are feeling. If you do not, you may be consumed by fear from within."

Jenny reached again for the deck, laying out three more cards. Her thoughts traveled upstairs and into her closet. *I need to figure out what that puzzle is.* Jenny thought about Michael Creme. *He delivered the VRGo puzzle; he must know something.*

"The High Priestess, inverted. You're intuitive, but you're intentionally disconnecting yourself. You must heed your internal voice." She pointed at the next card. "The Five of Swords is an unusual card. I can read it two ways. The first is that you must be sure to be aggressive in your pursuits. Passivity will not win the day. The other warns you against engaging in conflict or unnecessary disagreements with others. Alienating friends and family will only hurt you in the long run. Lastly, the Four of Wands has only positive meanings associated with it." Jenny leaned back. "Home, community, celebration, it's all good news and a lovely way to end your reading."

"Excellent," Rebecca exclaimed. "This has been so helpful. I don't know how you do it."

"It's not me," Jenny said in a deadpan voice, "I'm merely a vessel of a higher power."

"Wow." Rebecca's eyes widened. "Thank you."

"Do you have any other questions?"

"Oh no, I'm just giddy with excitement." Rebecca rose from the table and picked up her purse. "I'll be taking what you said about growth and family and friendships to heart. I wouldn't want to alienate anyone on my rise to the top."

Oh no, I forgot Bea's talisman, Jenny thought. Rebecca wasn't supposed to be in such a positive mood. Ideally, she should feel cursed. But relationship issues or problems in her career would also have worked. *What do I care anyway? If I interpreted this reading correctly, then something life-changing is about to happen.*

Suddenly, Jenny's head throbbed in pain. Her neurons created a tumultuous racket that almost drowned out her inner voice. She massaged her aching head with both hands as she watched Bea and Rebecca.

"Oh, I won't be needing a talisman this time." Rebecca held up her hand. "I feel empowered after Jenny's reading."

Bea looked past Rebecca and glared at Jenny. Then she picked up the talisman and handed it to Rebecca. "You are a good customer. Take it, free of charge."

"Thank you." Rebecca accepted the token. "Both of you." She took another cookie on her way out the door.

Jenny prepared for the worst as Bea approached.

"What was all that about home, community, celebration? Do I have to remind you that you're earning your keep around here?"

"I know, I'm sorry." She rubbed her head and pressed the heels of her hands against her eyes. *The prospect of joining Cabin is sounding better every minute,* Jenny thought.

"We could do so much with your talent to see ghosts. Imagine what people would pay to speak with their loved ones."

"I told you, I don't see *ghosts*, plural. I just see the one." Jenny looked at the red settee. Sally was more defined than usual. Jenny could see the ghost's full lips, almond eyes, and long dark hair.

Bea shook her head. "What's wrong with you?"

"I'm sorry. I'm distracted, okay? I couldn't stop thinking about Mom."

"Oh, Jenny, I'm sorry." Bea stepped forward and pulled Jenny into her chest. "I'm hurting too. It's just that you're so good at this." Bea held Jenny by the shoulders and looked into her eyes. "I'd love it if one day you had your own shop."

"That's the last thing I want." Jenny jerked away and covered her face with her hand. "I don't want to be a Gypsy fortune-teller." She tore the scarf off and tossed it back at the reading table. "I'm going to check on Mom."

6

LOCKED TERMINALS

The Avian clutched the repaired ignitor in his feathered hands. He backed out of the door as he showered Jack with praise. Once it was clear, Jack locked the door. *It's time to prepare for my mission with Hocco,* he thought. *How long will this mission take?* Jack picked up his data tablet. *Just to be safe, I should cancel all my appointments. If Hocco is true to his word, I won't need the money anyway.* Jack set the tablet down and walked up to a panel by the door. *It's been a while since I used this.* Jack touched a few buttons on the panel and the pod jolted into movement.

Lan Station generated artificial gravity by rotating around the Terminal once every two minutes. The pods could move independently along spokes extending from the Terminal to the primary and secondary rings of Lan station. By moving the pod closer to the Terminal, he could decrease the artificial gravity to half a G. At half the standard gravity, Jack would be able to lift the crate as easily as the Snibb.

The pod came to a stop after a few minutes, and Jack carried the crate through an umbilical that connected his workshop to the airlock on the *Strider*. The entire hangar was kept in vacuum. This made it easier to launch, and he didn't have to waste money maintaining an atmosphere or heating a large space.

Once he was inside, Jack set the crate down on the metal floor of the cargo bay and breathed in the stale recycled air. *It's been too long,* he thought as he sighed with pleasure. The interior of the ship was not at all homey. Harbingers were designed for battle. Latticework frames optimized the *Strider's* strength and weight distribution. Her structure, wiring, and pipes were on full display. Jack preferred this practicality to the smooth interior of luxury vessel as it made repairs easier.

Jack pulled out his old leather military jacket from a locker and put it on. Now he was ready to direct his focus onto the crate. He started by removing the buffer and separating its parts onto the cargo deck. He found a silver envelope. Inside was a chipset that would be needed to integrate the NEB with the ship's computer. Without it, the buffer would be just an expensive hunk of precious metal. Jack folded the envelope and slid it into a pocket inside his jacket.

I have less than twenty hours to install something that should take a week, he thought as he rifled through the NEB's installation instructions. Any ships caught inside a Terminal without a NEB got vaporized when it activated. It was a side effect of opening a wormhole. A good chunk of his work came from servicing NEBs, and every month, Jack heard of some fool who got vaporized due to a malfunctioning buffer. Even though he knew better, Jack would have to forego testing to meet his deadline. The buffer had to work perfectly on the first try, or he and this mission would be dust.

After twenty hours of non-stop work, Jack now stood in the kitchenette of his loft and watched coffee drip into his mug. He pulled back the jacket's sleeve to read his wristwatch. It was already 08:17 by the Standard Galactic Spacetime Interval. It had taken him all night to install the buffer. He picked up his sixth cup of coffee and activated the program that would return the pod to the main level of the station.

At 08:30, the door buzzed. The supplies Jack had ordered for the journey had arrived. Jack transferred the vegetables, grains, proteins, and fats to a large cooler.

Hocco arrived at 09:00, and they talked about the mission over a cup of coffee. While he divulged some details, Hocco still refused to tell Jack where they were going.

After finishing their coffee, Jack and Hocco made their way to the *Strider*. Jack stored the food in the galley, then showed Hocco to his quarters.

When they were ready to launch, Jack and Hocco went down to the locker room to trade their civilian clothes for spacesuits. First, Jack took off his leather jacket and hung it up in the locker, followed shortly by the rest of his clothes. He pulled on a thin, flexible bodysuit, then slid into the rigid spacesuit that would protect him during high-G maneuvers

Jack and Hocco reached the Strider's cockpit at 09:46. Jack fastened his restraints and inhaled the warm electrical air from the ship's vents. He hit a series of switches and buttons using pure muscle memory. The engines hummed and the lights sparked to life. "Start preflight check."

The computer read the status of various systems out loud, and when they were ready, Jack initiated the program to exit the pod. The entire roof of the hangar opened to the vacant Terminal and billions of stars. The ship groaned and lifted off the floor. Free of the station's rotation, it became weightless and drifted through the open doors.

The Harbinger's distinguishing feature was its two arms. They extended the length of the craft and connected to the hull by a joint midship. While in storage, the arms were kept parallel to the fuselage, but once they were clear of the pod, Jack set their orientation to be perpendicular. This was better for fighting and maneuvering, as it gave the thrusters maximum torque. It also provided the gun pods—at either end of each arm—a greater firing solution.

As they drifted toward the center of the Terminal, the control tower contacted them. From here, it was standard protocol to surrender control of the *Strider*. Jack hated to do it, but he understood that it was necessary to avoid collisions. The station's computers would then arrange each ship's position within the Terminal and fit them together like a big puzzle.

Jack leaned back as the *Strider's* main engines powered down. Maneuvering thrusters fired in rapid bursts that only a computer could manage. After a few minutes, they stopped in the dead center of the ring. The Terminal, which had been part of Jack's view for years, now loomed around him in 360 degrees. His ship may have been a large fighter, but it felt tiny and insignificant compared to the ring-shaped artifact.

Jack checked his watch. "It's five after ten." He faced Hocco. "You've got fifty-five minutes to take care of any personal business."

Hocco ran a flight simulation on his panel.

Jack cocked his head. "I didn't know that you could fly?"

"I've had some experience." Hocco hit a series of buttons and jerked the stick left. "And I'm using intention controls."

With intention controls, the computer would correct decisions that would jeopardize the ship. Like when someone knew what you meant to say, even if you said the wrong thing. Jack never activated intention correction. Time always seemed to slow down for him when it mattered, allowing him to make the right choice in the heat of battle.

"That's odd."

"What's odd?"

"We're the only ship in the entire Terminal. I've never seen that before." Jack checked the holographic lidar. Hundreds of ships were queued up outside, but no one crossed the invisible boundary of the Terminal's activation sphere. "Oh wait, there's one. Not just us after all." A single spaceship had edged closer to the boundary, but had yet to cross it.

Hocco looked up from his simulation. "There shouldn't be any other ships joining us."

Suddenly, red lights flashed on the control panel, and a loudspeaker blared. "Alert. Alert," the voice repeated throughout the *Strider*. "Negative-energy buffer not detected."

"I thought you installed it."

"I did," Jack said as he simultaneously ran through every step of the process in his head. Then he remembered the thin chipset he slid into the pocket of his jacket. "Damn it!" Without the chipset, the station couldn't sync the buffer, and they'd be disintegrated when the Terminal activated. Jack released his restraints and pushed off toward the cargo bay. He flung open his locker and pulled out his jacket. He reached inside and groped with gloved fingers.

"We should cancel the transfer," Hocco said over the comm. "We can try again tomorrow."

"No, I can fix it," Jack answered, still fumbling in his jacket. The constant blaring of the ship's alarm had turned Jack's brain to mush. "Can you shut that alarm off?"

"Got it," Hocco said, and a moment later the alarm went silent.

Jack sighed in relief as he pulled a small static bag out of his jacket. He carried the chipset back up to the cockpit. Then, he ran his gloved finger between two panels on the corridor wall. A hidden lever flipped open. He used the lever to remove the panel door. He let it float inside the hallway. Warm air and the scent of silicon hit his face. Holding the static bag in his teeth, he paged through the circuit boards and slid one out. A hologram displayed the name and function of each component. He took a deep breath and let the hum of fans and the deep rumble of the ship's engine soothe him.

"We're running out of time," Hocco reminded him.

Jack ignored Hocco and scanned the circuit board. "There." He ripped the static bag open and pull the chipset free. Holding the wafer between his gloved fingers, he inserted it into an empty socket. Then, he slid the board inside and flipped it. The hologram displayed a progress meter of the installation. The loading bar sped forward and paused at 95 percent.

Outside the ship, the Terminal glowed an ominous blue as it activated, filling the cockpit with blue light. Jack became acutely aware of the sweat under his arms. Finally, the loading bar reached 100 percent, and the negative-energy buffer appeared on the list of active modules. Everything was green.

"Negative-energy buffer detected," the computer announced. "You may now safely travel through the Terminal."

Jack sighed and headed back to the cockpit. He noted that Hocco was gripping the chair arms.

"I thought you said, 'No problem.'"

"Yeah, well, I fixed it, so no problem." Jack settled into his seat. The blue glow of the Terminal increased in intensity and a one-minute warning played over the ship's speakers. "See, we even had time to spare."

"We're not completely out of danger," Hocco said. "That ship is still out there."

Jack shrugged with his hands. "She's probably trying to boost. Sometimes ships cross the threshold right before the Terminal activates." Jack scanned the mystery vessel, and a hologram appeared. It was a Tiburon ship with blue-and-white detailing. This one had illegal missile banks, laser turrets, energy capacitors, and armor. Then, the ship did something odd: It moved inside the launch perimeter. If they were hitching a ride, they should have waited until the last second.

"I don't like it," Hocco said as he unfastened his restraints.

"Where are you going?" Jack demanded.

"To a gun pod." Hocco pulled his helmet down.

"Why? The Terminal has everything locked down."

"I can override computer control and switch it over to manual."

Good idea, Jack thought as Hocco dropped out of sight

Suddenly, the *Strider's* shield flashed blue. "They shot at us!" Jack said. He turned and shouted at the retreating Hocco, "Hurry up and get secured."

The shields continued to flash as the enemy ship fired on them. Jack slammed his hand on the unresponsive controls. "Sorry, baby," he mumbled to the *Strider*. "Why are they shooting at us?" Jack asked Hocco over the communicator.

"It has to be the Selkans," Hocco said. "They must have followed me. Now, we've got to destroy that ship before they kill us."

"I'd like to, but the station still has us in lockdown," Jack said. "Why aren't they shooting it down?" *They're probably trying to communicate with them*, Jack thought. *Waste of time.* Finally, the Lan Station's ion towers opened fire. The Tiburon ship's shields glowed green as blasts of charged ions hit it. *That should at least confuse their sensors*, Jack thought. The console flashed. Jack checked the notification. Pod three was online. Hocco had done it. With only manual control, aiming would be difficult. Jack checked the timer. "Just a bit longer," he whispered to the *Strider*.

"Final sequence initiated," the computer said.

The blue glow of the Terminal intensified. A thick black mist surrounded the two ships. Outside, a mote of perfect black exploded from the center of the ring, swallowing them in an instant. Inside the ship, white light stretched out until it encompassed the entire visible spectrum. It looked for a moment as if a rainbow had wrapped itself around them. Then it was gone, and a foreign starfield surrounded the *Strider*. They were no longer in the Lan System, which meant that the station no longer controlled Jack's ship.

"Hey baby," Jack said to the *Strider*. "Let's show 'em what you can do." Jack fired the primary drive and the ship lurched forward.

"We have to destroy that ship," Hocco said over the communicator.

I know, Jack thought to himself as the Tiburon opened fire. He twisted the sticks and the Strider twirled away from the projectiles. Jack increased thrust and they surged past the enemy ship. He flipped the *Strider* around and set all weapons on automatic fire. Purple plasma erupted from the rail guns, and hypersonic slugs slammed into the Tiburon.

"Whoo, that got 'em!" Hocco shouted. "Nice flying."

Jack grinned in spite of himself. The enemy ship wasn't done however. It flipped around to face them. Jack heard the familiar beeping of a target lock. *They're firing missiles.* At this range, they couldn't miss.

The *Strider* lacked missiles, but she had several countermeasures. She could scramble the enemy's sensors in a flood of ions, or fire flak to confuse the missiles. The point-defense cannons could shoot the missiles down, but Jack chose the one countermeasure that outshone them all. He disabled the primary drive and activated the ship's cloaking device. To all forms of detection, he was now invisible. The beeping of the target lock ceased, and the missiles drifted out into space.

The Tiburon had only one course of action left: They ran.

"Chase after them," Hocco urged. "They're going to warn the Selkans."

Jack would have preferred to sit here and let them go, but Hocco was right. He'd never locate the stellar lab if they managed to warn the Selkans that they were coming. Jack cursed and jammed their communication. Then, he fired up the primary drive and gave chase.

Now that they were cloaked, all the Tiburon could do was fire backward blindly with their point-defense cannons. A few lucky shots hit the *Strider*'s shields, causing it to light up in flashes of green, but it wasn't enough to make him back down.

Jack set all four rail guns on auto, and a volley of hypersonic slugs slammed into the rear of the enemy ship. The Tiburon's shields overloaded in a shower of blue particles, and its main drive went dark.

"Finish them off," Hocco said.

"Wait," Jack said as his console beeped. They had received a message from the Tiburon. "They sent a message. Maybe we can get some answers."

Jack hit play and a man said in a panicked voice, "This is the *Redeemer*. We surrender."

Jack sent them a message. "Who are you?" he demanded. "Why did you attack us?" Then, he matched the *Redeemer's* velocity and pulled close to the derelict ship.

Before the *Redeemer* could answer, the rail gun in pod three fired, and the enemy ship's reactor exploded in a flash of blinding light. The *Strider* rattled as debris struck them, and a wave of energy spun them around.

"*Hocco?*" Jack shouted over the ship's intercom, and his hands shook with adrenaline. "What were you thinking? You could have killed us."

"They attacked us, remember? I wasn't about to take the chance that they were bluffing."

Jack narrowed his eyes. He didn't agree with Hocco, but he wasn't wrong. The *Redeemer* had no reason to tell them the truth. With the enemy ship gone, Jack turned the *Strider* around to face the pitch-black Terminal behind them. *That's odd,* he thought, *where's the space station?* He checked the star charts. Nothing looked familiar. *Where are we?*

7

BLACK RABBIT

Jenny's head thundered as she stormed away from Bea. She looked at Sally and said, "Can you believe she actually thinks I'd want to be a fortune-teller for the rest of my life?" Then, she thought to herself, *She probably wants me to find a husband and be a good little wife too. Ugh, I'd rather die.*

A dizzy spell hit Jenny as she took the first step up the stairs. White spots swam before her eyes. She swayed and used the rail to pull herself up to the landing. Onyx ran up the stairs and into Ruby's room. Jenny followed Onyx inside. Her mom was snoring softly under the patchwork quilt. Jenny tried to recall a time before her mom was sick, a time when the sounds of laughter echoed throughout the house, but they were distant memories.

Jenny stumbled into her bedroom and collapsed onto the bed. Jenny focused on the pain, visualizing it as a blue flame. Then she gathered it into a ball and pushed it away. A warm feeling spread through her, and after a minute the tremors in her head quieted. She opened her eyes and smiled. The pain was gone.

"Now"—she looked at Sally—"let's find out what this VRGo puzzle is all about."

Jenny slid her closet door open. The silver cube rested under a rack full of dark dresses. Jenny slid the block to the middle of the room. As her fingertips lifted from the warm surface of the puzzle, twelve glowing symbols lit up around the divet on the surface. Jenny noted that one of the symbols was a triangle inside a circle, like her mother's amulet. *Probably just a coincidence,* Jenny thought as she felt the necklace under her shirt.

One of the symbols flashed blue, and a tone played. Yet, she didn't hear this tone with her ears. Somehow it played inside her mind. Jenny shivered. *It is just like that strange obsidian bowl at the wedding.* Jenny looked at her *Alice in Wonderland* toy. *It's not time to be afraid,* she thought, *it's time to be curious. After all, they did say I'd have to use all my senses. I guess that includes this bizarre extra sense I have.*

Jenny took a deep breath and tapped the symbol. It flashed back at her. A different symbol lit up, accompanied by a new tone. *If this is anything like* Simon Says, *then I need to copy the pattern.* She touched the two symbols in order. Then three and four. Each time Jenny solved a previous sequence, the VRGo puzzle added another symbol, another note to the series, and the tempo increased.

After completing a pattern that involved all twelve of the symbols, the block made a strange clicking noise. The four, thin rectangular sides of the *Simon Says* block dropped to the floor with a clack. Jenny gathered the four narrow strips together. They were as thin as poster board but inflexible and strong, like titanium. She set them down on her left. Then, she removed the top piece of the puzzle. Underneath was another silver block, identical to the *Simon Says* block, but slightly smaller.

Do I have to do this again? Jenny groaned as she placed the top piece on the floor to her right. It suddenly felt too quiet in her room. "Computer, play music." Radiohead's "Paranoid Android" continued to play from where she had paused it earlier. She pulled the slightly smaller silver block toward her, and to her surprise, it slid apart. It wasn't solid. It was a stack of cards. Eighteen, altogether, plus four squares on the bottom that were slightly larger. These were the same size as the top piece she noted, so she put them on her right, with the top piece. She now had three piles. One with eighteen square metal cards, five slightly larger from the *Simon Says* box, and the four narrow rectangular strips.

The squares were much too large to lay out on her floor, so she inspected each piece in turn. After five minutes of careful investigation, she didn't find any useful details. *I bet Michael knows what to do,* Jenny thought. *Maybe I should go ask him.* But her stubborn side wouldn't allow her to give up just yet. *What if I try different combinations?*

With the music playing, Jenny found it easier to perform the monotonous task of testing each square to each of the other squares. On her twelfth try, she heard a humming sound inside her head, like during the *Simon Says* portion of the puzzle.

"Volume down," she said aloud, and the music coming from the computer quieted. Jenny needed to use all of her brain as she focused on the pieces that produced sounds. After several more minutes, Jenny had sorted the eighteen cards into three stacks of six. Now she had five piles. *Hmm,* she thought, *I haven't exactly simplified things.* Then, an idea came to her. *A cube has six sides.* Jenny took two squares and placed their edges together at a ninety-degree angle. Nothing happened, but Jenny didn't give up. She rotated one of the squares until suddenly, the two pieces snapped together with a clack. Blue lines raced across their shiny surfaces in a weave of geometric patterns then vanished. The connection was so precise that she couldn't find a gap where they had joined.

Jenny gave a little cheer, then she continued by snapping the other pieces together until she had formed a simple cube. After that, she quickly formed two more cubes. Next, she tried the five remaining cards from the *Simon Says* block. After some trial and error, they also joined together and formed an open box.

Jenny rolled back on her heels. *So, I have three cubes and a box. Now what?* She looked at the pile of four narrow rectangular strips. She flipped and rotated them until they snapped together as well. However, these pieces didn't form a cube, or a box, they, they formed a peak. It looked to her like a roof, so she set it onto the open box. The finished product looked like a little silver house. The roof even opened and closed on an invisible hinge.

Now I have three cubes and a house, Jenny thought. *Is that it? Did I complete the puzzle? If so, I don't get it.* Jenny's stomach growled. She checked the time. *Wow, it's already time for lunch.* She pushed the puzzle into her closet and closed the door. *It's time to get some answers from Michael...and my birthday milkshake.*

After checking on her mom, Jenny said goodbye to her aunt and left the house. She crossed the street to the Black Rabbit Cafe and opened the battered door. Inside, she heard "How Soon Is Now?" by the Smiths playing from four black speakers mounted to the ceiling. Dark wood and brass adorned the interior. A few solitarily patrons sat at small tables and worked on their laptops.

Michael Creme pushed the drawer shut on the antique cash register and walked over to Jenny. He wore a stylish vintage button-up shirt and tight indigo jeans. Michael leaned over the bar and said, "Welcome back."

"What?" Jenny looked into his dark eyes. "This is the first time I've been here today."

"No. You came in earlier, then you just disappeared."

Jenny shook her head. "My doppelgänger again."

Trudy, Michael's coworker, steamed a latte at a big silver espresso machine. She was around Michael's age and had pink hair and several facial piercings. Trudy poured steamed milk into a travel mug and handed the drink to a couple in matching tracksuits.

Jenny set her smartphone on the bar and sat down on the barstool. "I heard the message—I know you work for Cabin, whatever that is."

"Where I'm from, it's a household name, like Apple or Microsoft, only Cabin is like a hundred times bigger."

"Okay..." Jenny didn't entirely believe Michael's claim, but living with Sally made her accept the strange and unusual more easily than most. Even that a corporation one hundred times bigger than Apple could exist. "I need some answers."

"And a milkshake?" Michael raised an eyebrow.

"Well, yeah, that too." Jenny smiled.

"How about a strawberry Milkquake?"

"A Milkquake? That's not on the menu."

"No, but it's popular where I'm from." Michael scooped ice cream into a steel mixer. "This dessert is so grand that it was honorarily renamed 'the Milkquake.' It isn't soft-serve ice cream defecated from a machine with some red flavor mixed in. This ice cream"—he gestured with the ice cream scoop—"is made fresh every day, from cows milked this very morning. This miracle of dessert is a closely guarded secret."

He leaned over the counter and whispered, "History tells us that the creator spent weeks experimenting with different temperatures, mixing devices, proportions, timing, and exotic ingredients." Michael flipped open a bin and added scoops of red strawberries to the mixer. "Sadly, the creator of the Milkquake passed away from a heart attack."

"Probably because he drank so many milkshakes," Jenny said.

Michael nodded slowly. "Yes, but lucky for us, he thoroughly documented his entire process. This secret formula has been passed down through generations." He picked up a squeeze bottle and added a healthy amount of caramel. "Who knows what he could have created if he had lived."

Michael thrust the tumbler under the mixer and flipped a switch. A loud whir whipped the contents and ground against the metal cup as Michael worked the tumbler. He poured half of the pink Milkquake into a fountain glass, then topped it with a dollop of whipped cream and a cherry. "Critically acclaimed across the world, and even farther. On the house."

"Thank you." Jenny pulled the milkshake toward her and ate the cherry, then took a big bite of the shake. "Mmm." The flavor ignited her taste buds: creamy, sweet, and fresh. She looked up and smiled.

"Good, huh?"

"As good as you claimed." She sucked hard through the straw, then focused her gaze on Michael. "So, what can you tell me about Selkans?"

"I don't know, I haven't heard of them before."

"What about the VRGo puzzle?"

Michael shrugged. "There's not much I can help with." Then he leaned against the bar and whispered, "It's supposed to test for some ability. Something that only you can do."

"Well, I got it open," Jenny said, "and I put the cubes together—"

"That's great!"

"Yeah, but now what?"

"Hmm." Michael stroked his sculpted beard in thought. "Let me think. There may be some clue I can give you..."

Jenny waved her smartphone at Michael. "I couldn't find anything about VRGo."

"I'm not surprised."

"So, what am I supposed to do with a bunch of cubes?" She set her phone down and spun it on the bar.

"I just remembered." Michael slapped the counter. "Do you know what a tesseract is?"

"No. Not really."

The bell on the door jingled. A little girl, maybe four years old, rushed inside and peered into the ice cream case. Her parents followed closely behind.

"Look it up." Michael pointed at Jenny's phone. "I've got to take this."

Jenny saw that Trudy was busy bussing tables.

Michael approached the new customers. "Would you like a sample of anything?" he said to the little girl as she peered through the glass case. Her dad picked her up and nuzzled his bearded face into her neck. Her mom smiled at her giggling daughter before ordering a coffee.

Jenny's heart ached. She had often dreamed of a life with a mother and father. A life full of people who cared about her and supported her choices. A family that wasn't cursed. She turned and looked at Sally. *At least I have you.*

Jenny unlocked her smartphone and typed "tesseract" into the search bar. She selected a Wikipedia article from the results: "A tesseract is a four-dimensional analog of the cube, consisting of eight cubical cells. It's also called a hypercube." The picture in the article resembled an M.C. Escher drawing. Jenny remembered that the stylized Cabin logo looked like this. *So, I'm supposed to make one of these?*

Jenny sipped at her shake as she scanned the other search results. Next, she selected a short video about "Understanding 4D—the tesseract." A hypercube made sense from a mathematical perspective, but it was hard to imagine in reality.

Basically, four lines made a square, and six squares made a cube. That meant eight cubes formed a tesseract. *Even if I could push all the cubes into the fourth spatial dimension, I only have four cubes.*

"Did my hint help?" Michael peered at Jenny's smartphone.

"I think so, maybe. It's a hard concept to wrap my head around."

"Yeah, but you're an exceptional young woman, Jenny. Otherwise, Cabin never would have contacted you. I'm sure you'll figure it out."

"Thanks." *If they're testing me for an ability—something that only I can do*—*then it must be the humming inside my mind. But how would they know about that?*

Together, Jenny and Michael watched an animated video with Carl Sagan demonstrating the concepts from Edwin A. Abbott's *Flatland*. It described an encounter between an apple and a square in a two-dimensional universe. From the square's perspective, the apple was an object that changed shapes as it passed through the plane of Flatland. The square refused to believe that the apple was what it said it was, so the apple pushed the square above Flatland. From there, it was able to see all of Flatland.

Just as the square had no concept of up, Jenny had no perception of four-dimensional space. *I have to think outside the box.* "I'm ready to give the puzzle another shot."

"Good luck."

Jenny finished her shake and placed her empty glass in the bus bin. The family with the little girl was leaving at the same time.

The little girl approached Jenny. "Why are you wearing a costume?"

Jenny knew that her makeup, clothes, and hair were unusual. She knelt down and looked at the little girl eye to eye. "It's not a costume, this is how I dress. Do you wanna feel my hair?"

The little girl reached up to touch Jenny's hair. "It's all spiky."

"Yup." Jenny smiled. "That's how I like it."

"Me too."

As Jenny crossed the street from the Black Rabbit, a murder of crows flocked around her aunt's shop. She shooed them away and stepped inside and found Bea waiting by the door.

"Jenny, I'd love it if we could talk."

Before Jenny could shut the door, a crow flew into the room. It squawked and flapped against the walls. Jenny and Bea screamed. A black-and-white picture of an old Roma woman, her great grandmother, hit the ground with a bang. Glass scattered across the floor. Jenny flung the door open and waved her hands at the crow. The crazy bird knocked magazines off the table and tipped the trash can over before making its exit. Jenny and Bea looked at each other in horror. This was a bad omen. In her culture, these were signs that someone was about to die.

"Go check on your mom. I'll take care of this." Bea tossed the broken bits of glass into the waste bin.

Jenny's stomach felt sick from dread as she climbed the stairs to her mom's room.

Ruby was sitting up in bed as if waiting for Jenny. "Come here." She patted a spot next to her. "Sit down."

Tears streamed down Jenny's cheeks as she noticed her mom's yellow, bloodshot eyes. Some of the tender capillaries had even ruptured, and blood had dried in the corners of her eyes. Jenny sat next to her mom and laid her head on her mother's bony sternum. She listened to the rattle in her mom's lungs.

Ruby embraced her daughter with skeletal arms and looked toward the door. "Bea, I'm glad you're here."

Bea's cheeks were wet as she embraced her sister and niece. As they held each other, Jenny wished that this moment would last forever. But, when Ruby's nose started to bleed, Jenny was first out of bed to retrieve a warm washcloth. From there, Jenny and Bea knew what they had to do.

Sally stood in the doorway and watched as Jenny and Bea prepared Ruby for her last night. After washing her, they dressed Ruby in a rose-patterned dress and silk stockings. Then, Jenny and Bea lit the candles around the room.

Jenny retrieved a photo album from her mother's bookshelf. "Mom."

"Jenny," Ruby's voice was a rasp, but she still managed to smile. "You've heard every story I know."

"It just makes me happy." Jenny squeezed the amulet that hung around her neck. The family heirloom, the last thing her mom would ever give her.

"Well"—Ruby smiled and took the album—"if it makes you happy."

After a time, Ruby could no longer keep her eyes open. She fell asleep with her hand on a picture of Jenny's grandma. Jenny flipped a tear-soaked pillow over to the dry side. She lifted the quilt and nestled up to her mom. Bea and Jenny spent the rest of the day close to Ruby. That night, Jenny watched the flickering light of the candles and tried not to think of tomorrow. Her eyes were puffy and swollen, and a hard lump filled her throat. As Jenny's eyes blurred with sleep, she fixed her gaze on a sliver of moonlight. A small shape, like a mote of dust, rose from the floor to the ceiling with a hiss.

In the morning, Jenny felt a sense of peace as she woke. She took her mom's wrist and checked her pulse. There was none. Ruby Tripper had finally escaped the pain of cancer on Thursday morning, June 20, 2024. After straightening her mom's limbs, she kissed her forehead and left the room to inform Bea.

Jenny and Bea sat at the kitchen table and finalized the funeral arrangements. They spent the rest of the day notifying friends and relatives that the funeral would be Saturday morning at ten. Focusing on these tasks helped to distract her, but Jenny found that there were still plenty of tears to shed as she delivered the news.

That Friday, Jenny and Bea sat at the kitchen table eating cucumber sandwiches. The tick of the clock was the loudest thing in the room. Jenny didn't want to talk about her, and yet Ruby was all she could think about. Her heart was on fire, and her body felt numb. Her mind was a fog, and the line between dreams and reality had become blurred. She needed to get away. Go somewhere that didn't remind her of Ruby. Jenny forcefully swallowed her bite and looked up at Bea. "Now that Mom is gone—"

"The other day," Bea interrupted, "when I said I needed to talk to you..."

A feeling of dread enveloped Jenny like a lead blanket.

"I was going to tell you that I'm close to losing my house and my business. Selling your mother's things will cover some of the funeral expenses, but I'd love it if you could help out more with the business."

Jenny shook her head and laughed. "I'm never going to be anything but a fortune-teller. Up until the day I die from the family curse."

"Jenny, this is who we are. We're carrying on a centuries-old family tradition." Bea took a bite, and her eyes went wide. "Oh, Jenny, I forgot that it's your birthday today."

"To be honest, I forgot too." Jenny looked down at her plate. "It's okay."

"No, it's not. We should do something." Bea reached out to take Jenny's hand.

Jenny pulled away. "Don't worry about it." The food had gone tasteless in her mouth.

"It's not every year you turn seventeen. Maybe we can have a party next week."

"I said forget it!" Jenny dropped her sandwich and stood up.

"Where are you going?"

"Looks like I'm going nowhere." Jenny ran to her room, slamming doors along the way, and wishing that her connection to the Romani had died with her mom.

～

It was Saturday, and it had rained the entire day of Ruby Tripper's funeral. As tradition demanded, Jenny and Bea did not bathe, brush their hair, or eat during mourning. Jenny wore a lacy black dress and a wide-brimmed black hat. Bea wore a red dress in a simple cut.

Almost two hundred people came to see Ruby off to the afterlife. Jenny recognized many of the same people from the wedding. Funny how tragedy and celebration bring everyone together. She even saw Thatch, the man who owned the curious collection of Lilliputian wonders. Ruby would be happy to know that so many of her friends and family members came to celebrate her life.

As they marched to the funeral home, mourners cried and wailed. Some tossed coins into Ruby's casket for goodwill. Most of the attendees wore white, to represent purity, or red, to represent vitality. Storm clouds roiled above while people delivered their eulogies. Jenny had helped her aunt plan everything from food to music. She had been surprised at the number of funeral-song playlists. Traditional, modern, uplifting, religious.

Jenny hugged her long black coat around her. It was cold enough to see her breath. The grass—wet from the rain—leached heat out of her tall black boots. A breeze rattled the bare tree branches. Crows cawed and took flight. Self-pitying thoughts stormed in her mind as the priest spoke. Then, a ray of sunlight pierced the gray blanket of clouds and bathed the funeral-goers in its warmth.

Jenny smiled. *Mom could always brighten my day.* Others viewed the coincidental act of nature as a meaningful blessing. They took comfort in the knowledge that her mother's spirit was pleased.

At the reception, the mourners imbibed liquor and coffee and waited in line to offer their condolences to Jenny and Bea. Death was familiar to Jenny. She had been prepared for this day. Everyone born into her family knew that life ended before forty. She mourned properly and cried at the remembrance of Ruby's life, but she wasn't broken.

Jenny stood alone in front of her bedroom mirror. She had been compulsively straightening her long black dress and tracing the amulet through the fabric. Gathering her courage, Jenny turned and left for her mother's room.

It smelled of linen on a summer day and fresh-cut grass. Clear tape screeched as Bea built boxes and added items to them. "One is for things to sell," she explained in a strained voice, "and the other is for stuff, that, well, we have to get rid of." Her red lips relaxed, and her eyes softened as she looked at Jenny. "I know this is hard, but it's our tradition."

Jenny peered into a box filled with knickknacks: sculptures of silver, brass, and wood, plus found objects like precious rocks and crystals. These were memories in physical form. All the clothes and personal effects that made up Ruby's life had to be sold or burned to keep evil spirits away.

Bea picked up the quilt they had made together and added it to a box. Jenny choked back a sob. Hypothesizing about a future without her mom was like wondering what life would be like without the color blue. It wasn't something her mind was capable of understanding, let alone knew how to deal with. "I can't do this. Not right now."

"Jenny."

Jenny's breathing was short and fast as she looked around the room. "I have to get out of here."

"Can you sort through the books, at least?"

Jenny took a deep breath to calm herself. "Okay."

"What about the photo albums?" Jenny asked Bea.

"They can stay."

Internally, Jenny sighed in relief. Still, every item of her mom's that was packed up was a reminder that she was never coming back. Ruby was gone forever. She wanted to be done, so she didn't have to deal with any more painful reminders.

As she read through the titles, she found a book titled *Flatland: A Romance of Many Dimensions*, by Edwin A. Abbott. A thrill ran down her spine as she remembered the video about Flatland she had watched just three days ago. It seemed like more time had passed. She thought about the half-completed VRGo puzzle in her closet, and the strange message from Cabin. *Lin said I had seventy-two hours*, Jenny thought. *Maybe it's not too late.* Jenny finished sorting the books and turned to her aunt. "I'm all done with the books. Can I go to my room now?"

Bea sighed. "I'd love it if you took the full boxes downstairs first."

"Okay." Jenny picked up a box. "Thanks, Aunt Bea."

After Jenny had completed her tasks, she went to her room and flung the closet doors open. The silver cubes of the VRGo puzzle peeked out from under her black dresses. *This is how I escape a life as a Gypsy fortune-teller.*

"Play music." The Cure's "A Forest" played from her desk speakers. She dragged the VRGo puzzle from her closet. The three cubes came out as one. Somehow they had gotten stuck together, like magnets. She pried them apart and arranged them next to the little silver house.

Jenny looked at Sally. "So, how do I make a hypercube?"

The ghost shrugged.

"Lot of help you are."

As Jenny picked up one of the cubes her head buzzed with energy. *Michael said that Cabin's testing me for some ability. It's got to be related to this strange buzzing.* She focused on it and closed her eyes. An image, like a waveform with peaks and valleys, formed in her mind. It was tumultuous, stormy, so Jenny worked to put it in order. She hummed until she found its harmony. The effect was immediate. The mountains smoothed into hills. Meandering rivers became straight. She opened her eyes. The cube looked just the same as before. *A hypercube is an object made of cubes*, Jenny thought, *so maybe I need to put them all together.*

As Jenny stacked two of the cubes on top of each other, the buzzing energy in her mind changed, and she saw two waveforms instead of one. When she hummed, the peaks and valleys reacted in different ways. Jenny experimented with her tone and pitch, like tuning a guitar until it sounded right. The waveforms matched. She had found their harmonic rhythm, and the two cubes merged together into one supercube that occupied the same space.

Jenny wouldn't have thought it possible if she hadn't just seen it with her own eyes. Her body shivered with excitement as she picked up the third cube and set it on top of the supercube. As soon as she found their harmony, it slid into the supercube, and they became one, and electric-blue lights swam across the surface of the combined cubes. *Is this a hypercube?* Jenny wondered to herself.

Sally knelt down to inspect the cube's swirling patterns. She turned and nodded at Jenny in approval, or maybe she was just impressed with what Jenny had done.

"Now, let's see if it fits inside." Jenny flipped the lid of the house open and picked up the hypercube. It was much heavier now, as if it contained the weight of all three cubes. She lifted it over the open box and let go. Slowly, the hypercube slid down to the bottom of the box and disappeared. Then, a reflective bubble formed inside the empty house followed by a flash of light and the top of a simple wooden ladder emerged out of a thick black mist.

A ladder? Jenny stared in disbelief. Last week, this would have blown her mind, but after seeing Lin in her room, and assembling a tesseract, it was merely odd. Jenny reached inside the completed VRGo puzzle and touched the mundane object. It felt real, like the kind of ladder you'd find attached to a tall bookshelf. It was immovable, as if mounted to a wall. Jenny placed her hands on the top rung and lowered her head into the box. A tingling sensation enveloped her as she passed through the black mist. It was neither cold nor warm, but she did feel a bit dizzy. Jenny withdrew her head.

Lin had said to pack for two days. Maybe there was some type of orientation or retreat. Jenny set her duffel bag on the bed and removed her fencing gear. Then, she packed her bag with extra clothes and her psych meds. She tossed a toiletry kit inside that contained her makeup and hair products. She pulled a rectangular food container from under her bed. It was filled with Lamingtons, her favorite snack. The thought of coconut and moist sponge cake was already making her mouth water. She stuffed it into her duffel.

With her bag packed, Jenny exchanged her long black dress for a more practical pair of black jeans, and a black concert T-shirt. She took a wide-brimmed hat, that was hanging by the door, and ran the woven material through her fingers before putting it on.

"What am I doing?" Jenny asked Sally. "Is this crazy?"

Sally shook her head.

"Good." Jenny zipped up her bag and slung it over her shoulder. "I'm not going to be a fortune-teller like Aunt Bea wants." *After all,* Jenny thought, *Bea did just fine before we showed up. She's better off without me. On second thought, I should at least leave her a note.* Jenny pulled open her desk drawer and found a piece of paper and a pen. She wrote that she was going away for a while and told her Aunt not to worry.

"Jenny!" Bea shouted.

Oh no, I have to go before Aunt Bea sees me. Jenny dropped her duffel into the box and watched the black mist consume it. Then, Sally jumped in. *Right, well, nothing's going to seem weird after this.*

"Jenny," Bea called out again.

"I'll be right there," Jenny shouted back. *I probably shouldn't leave this in the middle of the room,* Jenny thought. *What if Bea found it and tried to follow me?* She flung her closet open and pushed the VRGo puzzle inside. Jenny parted her clothes and pulled the closet doors shut behind her.

It was claustrophobic and dark inside her closet, and it smelled of linen and lavender. To her surprise, light shone from inside the VRGo box. *A ladder...* Jenny shook her head. *So weird.* Placing both hands on the sturdy walls of the box, she thought, *I'm finally going to be free of the family curse.* She reached down with her foot until she found the top of the mounted ladder, then she slowly put her weight on it. It held. She let out a breath and pulled in her other foot. As she lowered herself into the dark mist, it looked as if her body were disappearing one piece at a time. She held on to her hat as her eyes slipped below the lid.

Suddenly, the box lid started to close, and Jenny felt a tug somewhere behind her navel. Jenny couldn't tell if she was moving cosmically fast or if she was standing still. It was as if space and time were being stretched to their breaking point. It made her dizzy and nauseous, so she closed her eyes and gripped the ladder until her knuckles turned white.

8

RUINS

Jenny opened her eyes. She was no longer in her room. The ceiling was crisscrossed with roughly hewn beams, and the walls were made of stacked logs. *Is this a cabin?* Jenny thought. *A bit on the nose for a company named Cabin.* There were no rooms, no toilet, not even a sink. One end of the ladder rested on the cabin's wooden floor, but the other end terminated inside another fully assembled VRGo puzzle that was attached, upside down, to the ceiling of the cabin. *Is this how they invite all their visitors?* Jenny thought. *Seems a bit convoluted.*

Outside, a brisk wind rattled the single door. *I wonder if someone is going to meet me here or if I should have a look around.* The smell of mildew permeated the room, and something else. *Wet dog?*

Aloud, she said, "I'm here, now what?"

Jenny climbed down and bent over to retrieve her duffel bag. As she did, her black hat fell off and passed through Sally's ethereal form. It landed near a pile of glowing rags. *Glowing rags?* The pile stirred, and a furry white ear peeked out. The pile rolled over, and Jenny saw that the ear was attached to a creature with a round Pomeranian face and enormous eyes. The glow was coming from the fur that covered his entire body.

"Oh!" Jenny jumped back.

"Heather leaving," the strange creature said as he stood up.

"What?" Jenny cocked her head. "Did you just say something?" *No, that's silly. Dogs don't talk...and they don't walk on their hind legs.*

"Yes, Heather leaving." He backed toward the door.

Is it a talking dog, or a human with a furry condition? She noticed that a chunk of one of his large fox-like ears was missing. "No, stop, please."

He stopped.

"Your name is Heather?"

"Yes." His long ears bobbed as he nodded. "Heather Bibtwit."

Jenny shook her head. "I'm sorry. I've never met anything like you before. What are you?"

"Heather is Alfur."

"What is an Alfur?"

"Alfur is Heather."

"Clear as mud," Jenny mumbled. "Well, Heather, it's nice to meet you. My name is Jenny Tripper."

"A pleasure." The little creature clapped his hands to his sides and gave a small bow of greeting. At his full height, he reached Jenny's belly button.

"Heather leaving." Heather turned and walked toward the door.

"Wait, where are you going?"

"Home," the little glowing man continued.

Maybe this is some sort of test from Cabin. "Wait, don't go." Jenny rushed forward and grabbed Heather's small, wiry arm. As she did so, her mother's amulet swung loose from her shirt.

Heather stood transfixed by the brass amulet. His long fox-like ears lay flat against his back. "Jenny have food?" He looked up at Jenny expectantly.

"Oh yeah. Sure." Jenny blinked at the abrupt change of subject, but she was willing to play along if this was part of her Cabin initiation. She opened her bag and presented the package of raspberry Lamingtons.

Heather grabbed for them.

Jenny jerked the box out of his reach. "First, I need you to answer some questions."

"Yes, yes." Heather licked his lips.

"Can you take me to Lin?"

"Yes, yes. Jenny lucky Heather here. Forest dangerous place. Give Heather food. Heather take Jenny to Lin."

"You can have one now"—Jenny pulled the lid off and held out one of the coconut-covered morsels—"and one more after we find Lin."

"Yes, deal, deal. Give, please."

Jenny dropped the Lamington into his outstretched hands.

Heather gobbled the snack with his fox-like jaws and licked his hands clean. "Mmm, good." Bits of coconut and raspberry clung to the glowing fur around his mouth, which he cleaned with a long pink tongue. "Come, come." He walked to the cabin door and swung it open.

Jenny followed him outside. The smell of moss, wood, and decomposed leaves filled her nose. Ancient, colossal trees swayed and groaned. The base of a single tree was as large as the cabin. Ferns and bushes were the size of cars. A spiral of branches formed a dense canopy that created a permanent night. No clear paths led through the thick underbrush, and besides the cabin, there was no sign of civilization.

"Wow, this place is prehistoric."

Movement caught Jenny's eye. A butterfly the size of her hand fluttered through the air. Then a dragonfly the size of a bird. *What a strange place for a megacorporation to send me. I expected an office building, maybe a park in a city, but not this. Thank goodness Heather was here to guide me.*

"This way." Heather took a path that Jenny had not seen at first glance. If it hadn't been for Heather's glowing fur, she would have lost him in these dark woods. The Alfur hopped through the dense underbrush, somehow managing to avoid the thorns that snagged Jenny's duffel bag and jeans. While Jenny had to climb over shrubs and under branches, Sally walked through them.

It was dark. The light of the day failed to penetrate the dense canopy. After several minutes of hiking, Jenny stopped to catch her breath. "Hold on." The moss that covered the trees and earth absorbed her voice like a sponge, making her feel small and claustrophobic. "Can we take a break?"

"Yes, Jenny."

Jenny sat on a large root and inhaled the forest's earthy aromas while she rested. She wished that she had thought to bring a water bottle. "Heather, what makes you glow?"

"Alfur glow." Heather shrugged. "Alfur eat glowing food."

"Where do you find glowing food?"

"In cave."

"Why were you sleeping in the cabin?"

"Cabin safe." His eyes followed a moth the size of a dinner plate fluttering nearby. "Forest dangerous."

"If it's so dangerous, why would you come here?"

"Big, juicy bugs." Heather leaped into the air and caught the moth in his mouth. He snapped his jaws shut, crunching the large insect in meaty bites until he swallowed it. He mistook Jenny's horrified face for jealousy and said, "Jenny have next one."

"No. Thanks." Jenny's stomach roiled. "I hate bugs, especially the flying kind."

Heather shrugged.

"Ok, I'm ready." Jenny got to her feet. To her frustration, Heather led them deeper into the forest as he rushed after every insect he saw, which was quite a few. She wasn't accustomed to long hikes through the woods, and the muscles in her legs began to burn. "Are you sure you know where you're going?"

"Yes, yes, Heather take Jenny to Lin."

A stream had been growing louder as they walked. Soon, it appeared through a break in the undergrowth. The water babbling over stone, the smell of damp earth, and the rustle of the wind through leaves reminded Jenny of happier times with her mom. On the edge of the muddy bank, a giant frog watched then with its big wet eyes. Warty growths covered the mottled brown skin on its back. It let out a loud croak, then it stood up on stubby hind legs, revealing a soft white potbelly and flabby chins.

"Did you see that?" Jenny pointed. "That huge frog stood up on its hind legs—" She turned and caught a glimpse of Heather in the dark woods as he chased after a large, furry moth. "Wait!" Jenny ran after him and stumbled into a spiderweb. Spitting the sticky silk from her mouth, she called out Heather's name, but he didn't hear her. She charged recklessly into the undergrowth, and a slender, thorn-covered vine grabbed her black jeans. By the time she freed her herself from the thorns— earning several blood-oozing scratches—the Alfur's glow was nowhere to be seen. She ran to where she had last seen him, calling his name, but the dense moss absorbed all sound.

The forest seemed bigger and darker than before. She called Heather's name and scanned the dark woods for anything that glowed. Jenny kept walking until she found a narrow path free of undergrowth. *Why didn't we use this?*

Jenny stumbled over something soft. The wind seemed to hold its breath as she looked down. A lump formed in her throat. It was a man in a gray uniform with half his head crushed. She gagged at the smell and the sight of his misshapen purple face. Yet she didn't run. Instead, a morbid fascination drew her closer. Blood had congealed in his black hair and pooled onto his collarbone. *I wonder what happened to him.* The blood looked wet and fresh, but a few green flies were already buzzing around the wounds. *It looks recent.* Seeing another human, even a dead one, gave her some relief. *But what if whatever killed this man comes back?* She looked around, aware of how vulnerable and alone she was. Didn't Heather say this forest was dangerous? Gnarled branches seemed to reach down for her, and the air grew stale.

Jenny looked to Sally, who seemed brighter and more detailed than ever in this forest. Sally motioned for Jenny to follow. "Do you know where to go?" Jenny asked with relief. Sally nodded. Jenny shrugged and followed her ghost into the dark woods. The thick undergrowth made passage difficult for her, but not for her ethereal companion.

After an hour, the trees transitioned from giant evergreens to groves of fruit and nut trees. Jenny's throat had grown sore and dry from breathing through her mouth, and her stomach was cramped with hunger. She had the Lamingtons, but she'd gladly trade the sweet cakes for a drink of cold water.

Soon, Jenny had her wish as Sally led her down to a stream. A thick fog concealed the opposite bank, and a distant tree line formed a jagged outline against the fog-cloaked hills. Jenny picked her way down smooth gray stones to the stream's edge. There, she drank from the clear water to relieve her dry mouth and throat. After wiping at her chin with the back of her hand, Jenny dug through her bag for her Lamingtons. As she devoured the treat, she watched the fog crawl across the water. She washed the Lamington down with more water as Sally crossed the stream and entered the fog.

"Wait for me!"

Jenny put her food away and followed her ghost. Her duffel bag bounced against her hip as she hopped across the stones. Thunder cracked overhead, and cold raindrops found their way to Jenny's warm skin. That's when Jenny realized that she had lost her hat. As they climbed the hill, she mentally retraced her steps. *That's right, I dropped it back at the cabin.*

Sally beckoned Jenny forward toward dark, square shapes that emerged from the fog. They crossed a field of wild grasses to a floor of cobblestones. Jenny grew more miserable as water ran in rivulets down her back and into her jeans. She picked her way over a crumbled wall to a scattering of ruined buildings crawling with vines and moss. Remnants of rooms lined the inner walls. At one end of the courtyard, a rusted lattice portcullis hung within a gatehouse; at the other end was a grand cathedral. Its large doors promised a treasure of secrets to explore.

Jenny could feel the history of this place. She looked around in wonder at the enormous stones and imagined what life had been like here. Water gathered into streams on the ground and rushed to a large square hole in the middle of the courtyard. Sally sat on her heels and watched the water spill into the dark depths of the drain. Jenny walked over and crouched next to her ghost companion. Every detail of the ghost's face was distinct.

Suddenly, a feeling of helplessness and intense loneliness crashed into Jenny like a tidal wave. She felt lost, both physically and mentally, and she struggled to maintain her hold on reality. "What am I doing here?" She looked at Sally. "Why am I here with you?" Jenny's eyes filled with tears. "Why can't I see my mom instead?"

Sally reached out her hand. Jenny took it and gasped. It felt solid. Sally grabbed her and pulled her into an embrace. Jenny collapsed into Sally's arms as the dam on her emotions exploded. Hot tears flowed down her cheeks, and a strange numbness spread through her body. The air grew dense, more like water. Circular waves moved languidly out from the depths of the drain. A wave hit her, and the world spun.

9

ASTREA

Jenny walked down a dark, arched stone corridor lined with tapestries. Half the art depicted men in plate armor attacking giants with bladed polearms. The other half illustrated the path of Christ from birth to death. Jenny tried to turn and study the tapestries in more detail, but her body would not respond. She walked differently too, from toe to heal rather than heel to toe. For a few frightening seconds, she fought to control her body. Failing that, she surrendered to the strange vision. She heard the sound of footfalls. *I'm not alone.*

A man wearing full plate armor and carrying a tallow candle walked next to her. A long sword hung from a leather scabbard at his waist. "We must abandon Fort Esperanza," the man said.

She faced the man. "I agree, Father." Her voice and words were not her own. "But where could we go that the Risi would not follow?"

His brown forehead wrinkled. "Home."

A sense of panic washed over her. "I will not take our people back to Spain. We lived on the edge of society, begging and stealing to survive. The people feared and loathed us. They treated us worse than animals." She gripped an object hanging around her neck. It was warm and slippery to the touch. "I would rather die."

"There is another way, Astrea."

"The Riftkey?" Astrea looked down past her leather cuirass to her leather boots. "But Ramus warned us that it was dangerous."

"But he also encouraged you to practice with it, and he said that one day it would save our people."

"He didn't know what I could do with it."

The man—Jenny somehow knew his name to be Walther—placed a gauntleted hand on her shoulder. "We are the last tribe of Simeon. This may be our only hope of survival."

Astrea took a deep breath. "You are right." She looked into her father's eyes. "I will use the Riftkey."

Walther held the candle out and led them down a narrow stone staircase. The air chilled as they descended. They reached an underground vault through a long hallway. Wooden stands for holding weapons and armor littered the columned room, but the light of the candle failed to reach the distant walls.

Walther picked up an empty grain sack and walked over to a barrel filled with arrows. Astrea continued walking toward the back wall of the vault. She stopped in front of a wooden table where a long, thin mirror seemed to float a few centimeters above its top.

Astrea reached under the mirror and lifted it free of its resting place. The object was more substantial than Jenny had expected. It had a handle, and the proportions were that of a longsword. But where the blade would have been, there was a rectangular prism. The sides of the prism were impossibly black, as if there was a chasm instead of a solid edge. The top and bottom were mirrors that felt slippery and warm to the touch.

This is one strange sword, Jenny thought. *No, this is the Riftkey,* Jenny heard inside her mind. She shivered. Jenny wasn't sure if the thought was Astrea's or hers.

Astrea transferred her grip to the handle. A moment later, there was a loud crack, and the black edges of the Riftkey sparked with blue light. Astrea swung the Riftkey. It resisted movement as if passing through water and trailed blue sparks. The air filled with the clean, chlorine-like smell of ozone.

Suddenly, a surge of energy exploded inside Jenny's mind. She felt herself drift away from Astrea's body and gained control of her movements. She looked down at herself and gasped. Her body was insubstantial and had a silvery mist quality to it. She looked like her ghost, Sally, or more accurately, Astrea. Jenny turned around and faced her host.

Astrea's open-faced helmet revealed almond eyes of green and brown, a sharp nose, wavy black hair, and brown skin. "Sally?" Jenny asked.

"Nimue?" Astrea cocked her head as if she could see Jenny. She looked closely at Jenny's short hair and dichromatic eyes. "No, you are not her."

"What did you say?" Astrea's father asked as he filled up another grain sack with arrows.

"Nothing, Father." Astrea returned her attention to Jenny and lowered her voice. "Who are you?"

"My name is Jenny. I'm, uh, Jenny Tripper."

Astrea shook her head and whispered, "I do not know why you are here, but I pray you do not interfere."

The Riftkey's light faded and the room plunged into darkness. Astrea turned and joined her father. They left the basement, and hurried down the passageway. Though Jenny finally had control over her own movements, she soon found that there was a limit to how far she could be away from Astrea. When Jenny strayed, she was dragged along behind Astrea like a fish on a hook.

Up ahead, Jenny heard the shouts of men echoing down the tapestry-lined hallway. They reached the end of the hall, and exited into a grand space. Clerestory windows lit rows of pews. The scent of wood and perfumed oil mixed with polished stone. Astrea and Walther ran down the side aisle and out through a set of massive wooden doors. Jenny was pulled along behind them.

The shouting was louder out here. A dozen men wielding spears and halberds lined up behind the gatehouse. Some were armored in chain mail, but most wore boiled leather. More men wearing padded armor and armed with bows lined the battlements. Fat drops of rain fell from a dark-gray sky and passed through Jenny's ethereal form.

I know this place, Jenny thought. *These are the ruins that Sally led me to.*

"Tristan." Astrea turned to a lanky, black-haired boy. "Gather everyone in the courtyard."

Tristan hefted an iron-tipped spear and ran off in the direction of a large building.

A soldier wearing chain mail and a pot helm approached them. "Walther, we need you at the wall."

Astrea's father handed the sack of arrows to the soldier. "I will return," he said to Astrea as he pulled a helmet over his head. As he marched to the wall, Walther called out orders and pointed to areas with weak defenses.

Outside the fort, huge drums boomed, deep voices chanted, and metal clanged. The lanky boy, Tristan, returned with a group of thirty women, children, and elderly men. They huddled together in the muddy courtyard, clutching at each other and sobbing. As a group, they flinched at every beat of the drum.

Astrea was the same height as Jenny, but at that moment she appeared a head taller than any of the men. "You have a choice." Her voice rose above the din. "Come with me now and hope to live, or take your chances here. I warn you, this is not without risks, but it is our only chance to save the last tribe of Simeon." She wiped the rain from her face.

The crowd murmured to itself, and within a minute, they'd all agreed to join her. Walther returned with four young men in gambeson armor. He instructed them to guard the villagers while Astrea used the Riftkey to open a portal.

Astrea took a stance in the center of the courtyard. Even from a distance, Jenny felt the explosive power as the Riftkey activated. Steam billowed out of its glowing blue edges. Starting with the tip pointing at the ground, Astrea swung the Riftkey in a circle. A ring of blue sparks hung in the air, then fizzled out. Astrea cursed.

Meanwhile, arrows twanged from atop the battlement. Men shouted directions and pointed outside. "The Risi are scaling the wall!"

At that moment, a huge head emerged between the crenellations, followed by a hand the size of a dinner plate. An enormous body rose from the wall. Arrows stuck out from the Risi's thick, padded armor, giving him the appearance of a monstrous porcupine.

"To arms!" a halberd-wielding soldier shouted as he charged along the wall. He sank the spiked tip deep into the Risi's shoulder, but the giant didn't flinch. The monster hauled himself onto the wall and grabbed the shaft of the polearm in one hand. The soldier looked like a child as he struggled to free his weapon from the giant's grip. The Risi took a club from his waist and swung it with the force of a falling tree. It struck the soldier's neck and sent him flying outside the fort. A nearby archer jumped from the wall. His leg snapped with an audible crack on the cobbled stone of the courtyard.

Two more soldiers approached the giant from behind. One ran forward and sank the long point of a halberd deep into the Risi's back. The giant turned and swung his club, knocking the man from the wall. The other soldier thrust his polearm at the giant's face. The Risi slapped the halberd away with his open hand and slammed his club against the man's head. His helmet crumpled like an aluminum can, and his halberd clattered to the deck.

The Risi reached back to remove the polearm stuck in its back. Gobs of thick blood pumped from the wound. Within seconds, he tipped and fell off the wall, landing on top of the archer with the broken leg.

A Risi wearing padded armor and brandishing a falchion gained the wall. He shouted in a voice like thunder, "This is our land!"

"To me!" Walther yelled as he charged up the stairs to the wall. The shield on his back clattered against his armor as he climbed the steps. Astrea's father leaned down and grabbed the fallen halberd. Four young soldiers in chain mail and wielding halberds followed him onto the battlements.

The falchion-wielding Risi charged at Walther. Astrea's father propped the butt against the stone grout and waited. The Risi swung his sword at Walther's head. He ducked. The giant stumbled forward. Walther raised the polearm, and the halberd's long spike embedded itself into the Risi's chest.

The giant wasn't dead yet. He swung his falchion. Walther dodged to the side, and the sword sparked against gray stone. The shaft of the halberd snapped into splinters, and the Risi tumbled to the courtyard where a soldier finished the job with his sword.

Two more club-wielding Risi gained the wall. Nearby archers fled from the monster. Walther slid his shield onto his arm and pulled his sword from its scabbard. "To me!" He took the lead in a formation with the four soldiers who followed him onto the wall.

"Simeon!" Walther yelled the name of their clan as he charged. The giant swung his club at his head. Walther deflected the attack with his shield and spun to the giant's side. He thrust the tip of his sword into the Risi's exposed armpit until it sank to the crossguard. The monster stumbled for a moment, then fell off the wall.

The other giant moved to attack. Two soldiers thrust their polearms over the top of Walther's head. The Risi twisted away, but one of the spikes managed to pierce his neck. Enraged, he swung his club in a wide arc that knocked Walther off the wall. He landed in the courtyard with a crunch. His helmet and shield skidded in opposite directions across the wet stones.

Astrea looked frustrated but determined as she swung the Riftkey in a circle for the sixth time. Another curse passed her lips as the blue sparks faded away. She looked up and watched as three more Risi gained the wall. They fought past the inexperienced soldiers. From there, they descended the stairs and ran toward the gatehouse. A horde of giants waited outside the gate. More than enough to eradicate every man, woman, and child in the fort. "We are all doomed if they open the gate."

Jenny moved closer to the three intimidating giants. Even in the rain, their body odor was overpowering. They had thick, hairy arms and thicker legs. One held a cruel, curved falchion, while the other two wielded large clubs. Though their bodies were massive, their heads were only large and very human-looking. She'd seen eyes, noses, and hair like theirs on other men.

Astrea ran to join the two swordsmen guarding the gate controls. Water sparked and misted on the edge of the Riftkey as she stared down the three giants. Nearby, Walther rose to his feet; blood matted his dark hair and corrupted his white beard. He stumbled to his daughter and raised his long sword and shield against the Risi. The eight remaining soldiers, each armed with a halberd, moved behind the giants.

Astrea charged with her Riftkey. The foremost Risi swung his club with enough force to knock down a tree. She ducked under the blow and slid on her knees along the wet stones. As she came within striking distance, she swung the sparking Riftkey up between the giant's legs.

The Risi let out a blood-curdling cry as a gray aerosol mist filled the air. The giant split open from crotch to chest. His guts spilled out, striking the courtyard with a wet smack. With his pelvis destroyed, the Risi's legs wobbled, then collapsed.

The destructive power of the Riftkey made Jenny stagger backward, and the sight of the bisected body made her sick. She wanted out of this terrible nightmare.

The falchion-wielding giant swung down at Walther's unprotected head. He dodged to the side and stabbed at the giant's gut. The Risi swung sideways, hitting Walther in the shoulder and knocking him to his knees. Walther slashed at the giant's thigh, scoring a shallow gash. The giant swung again, aiming for Walther's exposed neck.

Before steel met flesh, the giant's sword arm fell to the ground. A cloud of gray mist exploded into the air and mixed with the rain. Astrea aimed her next attack at the giant's chest. After she pulled the glowing Riftkey free, the dead Risi fell to the ground.

Two polearms protruding from the chest of the third giant. One of the soldiers lay on the ground with a smashed face. It reminded Jenny of the man in the gray uniform she'd discovered in the woods earlier. The giant batted the halberds away, but other spikes found their mark. The Risi collapsed, and the soldiers cheered.

Walther recovered his shield and helmet. "Astrea, you must open that portal."

"But you need my help."

"No. Even with your help, we will lose the fort to the Risi. Our only hope is to escape."

"Tch." Astrea gritted her teeth. "You are right, Father."

Walther nodded and led the remaining seven soldiers toward the wall. Together, they held back two more Risi making their way down the stairs. These giants soon fell under a barrage of spear thrusts. Yet the last tribe of Simeon wasn't without their own casualties. Another man fell, leaving their total count of able-bodied soldiers at six.

Astrea ran back to the villagers and skidded to a stop in the center of the courtyard. Streams of water poured into a drain beneath her. She took a deep, shaky breath and focused. "Take us to an Earth where I never found the Waypoints."

As she spun the Riftkey, the blue sparks remained, and a window opened to a world of yellow grasses, sunflowers, and cypress trees. A thin blue line separated this world from the rift in space and time. When viewed on edge, Jenny realized that the portal was all but invisible in the rain.

A cacophony of deep shouts erupted from outside the fort. A wild-looking Risi with a red Mohawk jumped onto the wall. His dark skin was bare, tattooed, and pierced. Four more naked giants joined him a moment later. The berserkers ran along the wall, slashing through the remaining archers with knives the length of long swords.

These giants were a stark contrast to the first attackers. Their speed and agility belied their vast size. Their whoops and screams paralyzed the defenders. The red-Mohawked giant jumped from the wall with ease and ran toward the gatehouse.

Seeing the berserkers, one of the guards struck the gate latch with a hammer. The inner portcullis dropped, but it was too late. The Mohawked Risi slid under the falling gate. He swung his large knives and cut the legs out from under the guard. When he stood, the Risi's red Mohawk brushed the ceiling of the gatehouse.

Outside the wall, over twenty heavily armored giants roared and pounded their shields. Three of these grabbed the outer portcullis and heaved. Inside, the Mohawked giant hauled at the winch. Soldiers stabbed through the inner portcullis with the butts of their halberds in an attempt to distract the giant. Behind them, the four other berserkers leaped from the wall.

In the center of the muddy courtyard, villagers screamed and clutched at one another. The sun-drenched land beyond the portal stood out in stark contrast to the bleak setting of the fort. Astrea pointed to Tristan. "Get everyone through the portal." Astrea turned and rushed toward the berserker giants.

Tristan touched the butt of his spear to the portal's edge. A slice of the handle fell to the ground. People gasped in fear and awe at the power of this magic. Gathering his wits, Tristan directed the children and their mothers through the portal first. He kept them away from the edges of the portal. Mothers clutched their children to their breasts as they passed into the golden lands beyond. Next through the gateway were the men and women unable to fight.

With the portal open, Astrea joined Walther in the fight against the berserkers. Even with the soldiers' skills and advanced weaponry, the Risi drove the humans into a defensive posture. In spite of their best efforts, one of the berserkers broke free of the defenders and ran toward the portal. Jenny watched in slow motion as the giant's footfalls blasted water over the courtyard. His blood-curdling cry sent shivers down her spine. Jenny stood close enough to see his red-rimmed yellow eyes.

Tristan directed the line of people behind the gateway and stood so that he was between the charging berserker and the portal. He raised his spear. The Risi grinned and brandished his knives. Spittle flew from the giant's mouth as he lunged for Tristan. Instead of cutting Tristan in two, the giant's forearm disappeared through the portal.

The Risi stared at the stump of his arm in confusion. Tristan took that moment to stab the giant in the neck. The berserker gurgled and fell forward into the side of the portal. A red line bisected the giant from shoulder to groin.

The villagers backed away from the eviscerated giant, and a few vomited. Jenny struggled to banish the horrible sight from her mind. Tristan continued the evacuation, and the villagers gave the edges of the portal a wide berth. Lastly, an old man with a beard down to his knees crossed over to his new home.

"Everybody is through," Tristan yelled over the din of the battle.

Jenny turned back to the wall. A new fighter had joined Astrea's side. He was a very tall man, wearing black armor that looked too futuristic for this period. He wielded a tall black bow which he was using to fire arrows at the giants.

Astrea turned toward the remaining defenders. "Retreat, retreat, retreat!"

Hearing the order, the soldiers turned from their fights and ran for the portal. Walther rushed to the stairs and guarded the defenders as they made their escape. Astrea swung the Riftkey at an arrow-riddled giant. Flesh parted and filled the air with gray dust. The Risi fell, but the red-Mohawked Risi still held the gatehouse. The outer portcullis stood open, and armored giants filed into the gatehouse. The tall, mysterious man approached Astrea and Walther as the inner portcullis lifted.

"Rygelus, I fear you are too late. We have lost the fort, but you are welcome to join us."

"I cannot." Rygelus shouldered his massive bow and pushed up the faceplate of his helmet. Dark-brown hair framed a sharp face with thick eyebrows perched above angled brown eyes. A significant bump stood out from his forehead.

"I understand." Astrea clapped him on the shoulder. "I will miss you, friend."

Rygelus gave her a short nod. The rain fell in a torrent and funneled through a slotted drain cover. As the soldiers retreated through the portal, Walther joined Astrea at the gatehouse. Sweat and blood plastered his black hair to his head.

As the inner portcullis lifted higher, a Risi clawed its way through the gap. Astrea swung the Riftkey into its exposed head, killing it and blocking the way for the others. She faced Rygelus and pulled the tuning-fork object free from around her neck. "Here." She lifted the chain over her head and placed it in Rygelus's hand. "Someone else may need this one day."

Pain showed on Rygelus's face. "I had high hopes for you." He closed his hand around hers and looked into her eyes. "I wish you luck on your journey, and I hope you return one day."

"I will, I promise."

"Be safe." Walther gripped Rygelus's shoulder.

"I will take the hidden passage."

As Astrea and Walther made their way to the portal, Rygelus disappeared through the grand double doors of the church.

"This is my path. These are my people," Astrea chanted as she followed her father through the portal. "They are my responsibility now." Astrea stepped through the opening to the golden world beyond. She stopped short. The Riftkey would not pass through the portal. She pulled with all her might. She gave Jenny a look of desperation and confusion. The gateway shrunk. Astrea had to make a decision. Either let go or lose her hand. She let go, but the Riftkey remained stuck to the surface, like a pin to a magnet. When the portal finally closed, the

Riftkey fell and hit the stone drain cover, shattering it. For a moment, it balanced on the edge of the hole, then it tumbled into the darkness. A splash echoed up from below.

The rain passed through Jenny's hands as she stared into the drain. The inner portcullis opened, and a horde of Risi ran for the courtyard. They searched the buildings and alleyways and inspected their dead comrades. Sounds grew muffled, and Jenny's vision faded to blackness.

Images played across her mind like a deranged slideshow. A triangle inside a circle, the same as the talisman her mom had given her. The triangle became a pyramid, carved out of the inside of a massive cave. Small, furry, glowing humanoids, like Heather, worshiped in front of an immense serpent-like statue. It cradled a silver human in its coils.

10

A DISGUISE IN A FRIEND

Jack sat in the cockpit of the *Strider* and watched the remains of the *Redeemer* scatter into space. Victus sat in the third gun pod. The dark Terminal loomed behind them. *There may not be a station,* Jack thought, *but maybe there are some transmissions.* "Scan all frequencies," Jack said to the computer.

The console beeped a moment later. Jack looked down and saw that there was a message waiting for playback. The source of the communication was a nearby satellite. Jack pressed play, and a cheerful male voice spoke over the ship's speakers.

"Welcome to the Sol System. We have registered and logged your spacecraft. Please proceed to one of the four spaceports at Sol-3, or, as we call it, Earth."

Jack's temper rose with each word of the automated message.

"There are 365.25 days in an Earth year," the message continued. "Days are divided into twenty-four hours. Years are divided into twelve months. It is currently the year 2024, the sixth month of the year, and the eighteenth day of the month. The primary species is human. Seventy-one percent of the planet is water, and the land is mountainous. We have included the coordinates in this broadcast. Proceed to the nearest

Department of Transportation to begin your application for citizenship. Your well-being is our goal. Have a wonderful day."

"What the hell is Sol?" Jack asked.

"Sol is the star of this system," the computer answered.

"I wasn't talking to you." Jack disconnected from the broadcast. "Hocco." Jack scratched his scalp with both hands.

There was no answer.

"Hocco, where the hell are you?"

A moment later, Hocco floated into the cockpit. He calmly took a seat in the copilot's chair.

Jack's hands shook with adrenaline. He stared at Hocco and said, "You owe me some answers."

"Jack," Hocco answered, "do you know how many systems are part of the Terminal network?"

"There are nine," Jack said. "Everyone in the galaxy knows that." He clenched his fist. "What are you playing at?"

"Wrong." Hocco spun the chair around to face Jack. "There are twelve."

"No." Jack thought back to his lessons. "That's not possible."

"Why not?"

"Somebody would know," Jack said. "I would have heard something."

"If there's no reason to suspect another system, then why would anyone seek them out? Besides, only a Terminal master could confirm such an allegation, and why would they lie?"

"What was your reason?" Jack asked.

"Have you heard of a locked Terminal?"

"Locked, like a door?"

"Sort of. You can travel to a locked Terminal, but you cannot return through it."

"And Terminal masters allow people to travel there?"

"They do."

"Why?"

"Use your imagination."

Jack thought. There were times in his life when he'd wanted to escape. Even now, he spent most of his time alone, locked in his shop, married to his work. Hocco watched him think it over and remained quiet. *Why would Hocco tell me this?* Jack thought. *Unless...* "We're in one of these locked systems, aren't we?"

After a short silence, Hocco answered. "Yes."

"You trapped us here. You tricked me. *I would punch him right now if he wasn't wearing a helmet.* Why?"

"To find the Selkans."

"And the Defenders' secret weapon," Jack whispered. "Teleportation." Hocco wouldn't trap himself here unless he knew of a way out. But the key to getting home was finding Selkans. Jack entered the coordinates sent by satellite and fired up the primary drive. The seat pressed against Jack as the *Strider* sped away from the locked Terminal toward the planet called Earth.

Jack dreamed that he was being hunted by a monster aboard the *Strider*. Panting heavily, he removed a panel in the engineering section and crawled inside. The sound of footsteps echoed in the hallway. The panel was torn open, and a wave of heat blasted into his face.

Jack jerked awake to a buzzing sound in the next room. Consciousness returned like a planet completing a rotation. His eyes wouldn't open. Like him, they refused to acknowledge reality. The sound, Jack realized, was the buzz of electric clippers. *That's right, I'm searching for Selkans with Hocco.* Jack hadn't even bothered to remove his pants and shirt before jumping into his bunk. He checked his watch. *And I've only been asleep for three hours.*

The *Strider*'s floors were arranged like a four-story building, with the thrusters at the bottom. It accelerated at ten meters per second, producing the standard, galactic artificial gravity. So he shuffled over to the mirror rather than float. The skin around his reddened eyes sagged, and his shoulders slumped. Staying up all night to install the buffer had taken its toll. *And why do my knuckles hurt?* He ran his aching hand under running water and combed his hair with his wet fingers.

Jack plopped down on the edge of the bed and grabbed his boots. They were timeworn and rugged, and more than leather and gold. They were a symbol of a Harbinger pilot. Years of drills in the corps, hundreds of hours of flight school, and merciless combat missions had earned him these boots.

Jack left his small cabin and inhaled the rich fragrance of fresh-brewed coffee filling the *Strider's* galley. Caffeine wouldn't make this catastrophe go away, but it would drastically improve his mood. Jack was a skilled brewer, but he was nothing compared to Hocco. And even though the man never gave any presentations, Jack was sure he could get some tips out of him.

Jack smiled when he saw Hocco. His shipmate sat at the table reading from a tablet and drinking from one of Jack's favorite mugs. The mug was from a Lan station vendor who had misspelled it as an alien curse word that sounded the same. It always made Jack smile when he saw it. This time, Jack smiled because of a large purple bruise decorating Hocco's right cheek. *That's right*—Jack grinned—*I did* get *to* punch *him right before I went to sleep.* Jack also noticed that Hocco had trimmed his long black hair into a short military crop. *The man loved his hair,* Jack thought. *Why would he cut it now?*

Hocco pinched the bridge of his nose as he studied the tablet. "I found some coffee in the food stores. There's more in the pot."

Jack rubbed his big knuckles and said, "I'm not going to apologize for hitting you, and I still want to know your plans for getting us out of here." Jack took a mug from the cabinet and poured himself a cup of Hocco's brew. He inhaled the steam and sighed at the aroma.

"And I plan on telling you."

"What's with the new look?" Jack asked.

"Oh, this." Hocco ran his hand over his shorn head. "I could not live another day with that hair."

Jack looked down at the tablet. The screen displayed a map of what he assumed was Earth. "What are you doing?"

"Searching for my contact on Earth." Hocco scrolled through data on the tablet.

"You know someone down there?"

Hocco nodded.

Jack took a sip and winced at the heat. Why did Hocco use such high heat? He should know that the water-soluble compounds would never be absorbed. He may have burned off the volatile oils. *That's an amateur move.* Jack scrunched his face at the taste. *Are the beans that bad? No, they're the same ones I used in my pour-over back at the station.* Jack forced the unpleasant black liquid down his throat.

"I hope Earth has some good coffee," Jack said to Hocco, "because this tastes like piss."

"Be thankful I made it at all," Hocco said.

Jack cocked his head. *What is he playing at? He's been acting unusual since he showed up at my workshop. I was willing to ignore the odd manner-isms and the haircut, but not this coffee.* Jack decided to test him. "I loved your presentation on pour-over coffee in variable gravities the other day. You said that four gees were the ideal for maximum flavor extraction, right?"

"Hmm?" Hocco set the tablet down and looked up at Jack in confusion. "Uh yeah, that sounds right." He shrugged and looked down at his tablet.

"You're not Hocco." Jack jumped across the table and knocked the other man off his seat. They fell to the hard deck in a tangle. Hocco banged his head against the wall and started laughing. Jack lifted him up by his collar and smashed his fist into his chin. "You never gave any presentations, you were always too self-conscious in front of crowds."

Hocco collapsed to the floor and wiped the blood from the corner of his mouth. "That is one hell of a punch." He snickered as he pushed himself up to a sitting position and leaned against the wall. "You should know, this is not my face."

"Who are you?" Jack grabbed him by the collar and shook him. "Tell me before I beat it out of you."

Hocco worked his jaw. "Unless you want to stay in this system forever, you will not strike me again."

"Who the hell are you?" Jack let him fall back to the floor. "Tell me."

Hocco stood up, straightened his shirt, and thrust his chest out. "I am Admiral Vae Victus of the Defenders."

Jack stepped back in shock. "You're an Æon." He'd heard stories of the supernatural humans who could control people's minds. Covert assassins who could make wives kill their husbands or bodyguards kill their clients. He'd always believed they were myths. Jack clenched his fist. He wanted to beat this man to a pulp, but he'd have to control his emotions if he was going to get home. He slammed the table instead, causing the coffee mugs to bounce. "What happened to Hocco?"

Victus shrugged. "He's dead."

Jack tried to feel something for the loss of his colleague, but he couldn't. He was in too much shock. Jack picked up Victus's tablet and examined the map of Earth. "How do we get out of this system?"

"The same way we got in." Victus grabbed his chin and moved his jaw around.

"But you said that the Terminal is locked."

"When a door is locked, you find a key."

"This isn't a normal door we're talking about."

"You are correct. We're not looking for a normal key. If you want to get back to your home, then we need to find the Riftkey before the Selkans do.

11

TREEHOUSE

Heavy rain chilled Jenny to the bone where she lay on the wet cobblestones. She opened her eyes and saw Sally—no, Astrea—standing above her. It seemed like the battle had raged only minutes ago. Jenny could still smell blood and sweat, but she saw only moss-covered ruins around her.

Jenny rolled onto her knees and stood up. "This is where you created the portal."

Astrea nodded and pointed at the timeworn storm drain.

Jenny looked down. "After the portal closed, the Riftkey fell down there."

Astrea nodded and then jumped into the hole.

Jenny gasped and dropped to her knees to peer into the dark drain for her ghost companion. Years of water erosion had widened and smoothed the opening, and she had to choose her hand position carefully to avoid falling in. "Do you expect me to follow you down there?" Jenny called out.

There was no answer, of course, except for the rain that pelted the back of her head and dripped off of her face. Jenny straightened up and tightened the strap on her duffel bag. "I can do this."

Jenny sat on the edge and swung her feet into the hole. After wedging her fingers into the cobblestones, she found a foothold and lowered herself into the drain. As she shimmied down the slick rock, the muscles in her arms and legs started to burn. After a minute, she couldn't take it anymore. Jenny shoved her foot into a gap and allowed herself to rest.

Suddenly, the chunk of the wall her foot rested on gave way. Her stomach shifted into her throat. She scratched at the wall for a hand-hold, but only succeeded in splintering her black-painted fingernails on the rough stone. Gravity yanked her down, and she slammed into the drain channel.

Jenny screamed as pain shot up her back. Her scream turned into a gurgle as the iron taste of blood filled her mouth. She had bitten her tongue before and knew it took weeks to heal completely; she couldn't imagine how long this gouge would take. Still, this fear was nothing compared to a realization that gripped her chest in a cold, iron fist. She couldn't move. *I'm paralyzed, and no one will ever find me. I'm going to die here, alone. I never should have run away.*

Soon, the murky water rose past her ears and tickled her nose. It was colder than she thought possible, and her breathing came short and fast as water found its way into her sinuses and lungs. All she could do was lie there and stare at the opening six meters above her. Astrea stood over her with a look of concern, sunlit rain passing through her ethereal body.

Then, a warm buzzing sensation traveled up and down Jenny's spine. After a minute, tingling pain, like pins and needles, spread throughout her body. Her fingers twitched, and a minute later she rolled onto her side and coughed up the wetness that had settled into her lungs. She stood up, and a dizzy spell made her stumble. She leaned against the stone wall for support, and rivulets of water slithered over her hands. She touched her burning back and winced. Her fingers came back spotted with blood. She turned around and inspected her surroundings. She stood in a channel about the size of a twin bed with one end that tapered toward a dark tunnel and was clogged by a darker shape.

"My bag!"

Inside, she found that her spare clothes were thoroughly soaked. Her hair and makeup supplies were fine, but her smartphone was ruined. A hollow pit formed in her chest. For two years, she had meticulously customized her phone's apps and settings until it was perfect. *It knows me better than I know myself, and I just got this new case with pink skulls too. I might as well have lost an arm.*

Next, she pulled out the box of Lamingtons and saw murky water sloshing around the confections. She dropped the box of treats into the channel and watched it disappear into the pitch-black tunnel.

This couldn't get any worse. Jenny sighed. *I guess I should get to work.*

She sank to her knees and thrust her hands into a thick mat of humus. As she shoveled the ancient sludge, a dank, musty odor assaulted her nose and made her gag. Jenny persevered, tossing pound after pound of slick mud into the tunnel. Thankfully, the task helped her forget about her aching back and her bleeding tongue.

After several minutes of digging, she felt a hard, straight edge—about a meter long—in the muck. A buzzing sensation shivered down her body. Jenny pushed her fingers under the object and lifted it free from the humus. She looked over at Astrea with a feeling of pride and accomplishment.

Astrea gazed back at her with an expression of relief and sadness. *Thank you, Jenny.*

The voice echoed in her mind. Jenny gasped. "Astrea?"

The ghost nodded. *You have freed me from my bond.*

"How can you speak now?"

The Riftkey has connected us.

There were a million questions Jenny wanted to ask, but only one that mattered. It was a question that had haunted her life even more than Astrea's ghost. "That night, at the wedding, when I first saw you—" Jenny squeezed the Riftkey with both hands. "I mean, there was a strange sound in my head that night, and I hummed along with it. Whatever it was, I fixed it. There was a flash, and they...disappeared. Was it my fault?"

Astrea shook her head. *That was not your fault. The Riftkey sought a new master and found you. It activated the Waypoint.*

Jenny let out a loud sob and moved toward Astrea.

The ghost looked up at something unseen. *I must go now.*

"No, no, no. You can't leave me here." Jenny looked frantically around the narrow space.

Astrea squeezed Jenny's shoulder once before fading into a silvery mist and vanishing. Jenny stared at the spot where Astrea had been. The ghost had been her last connection to home. She stared up into the gray clouds. Rain mixed with the tears that flowed down her cheeks. Jenny looked down at the Riftkey. *It's so dirty.*

With nothing else to do, she knelt down and rinsed the sword in the dank water. Soon, she exposed the mirrored flat of the blade that sandwiched the blunt black edges. Now that it was clean, she examined herself in the Riftkey's mirror finish.

Jenny flinched at the sight of her own face. Black streaks of makeup ran down her eyes, and blood coated her chin from the bite on her tongue. It already hurt to swallow, and it would be worse tomorrow. She examined the Riftkey from tip to base. She found a triangle inside a circle on the pommel. *Like my amulet.* She touched the heirloom under her wet black T-shirt and thought of her mom. *What does it mean? Is my family related to Astrea's clan in some way?*

Suddenly, Jenny's entire body hummed like she had drunk twelve cups of coffee, and a buzzing chaos exploded in her mind. The muscles in her arms seized. She moved to pry her frozen fingers loose of the hilt, but she couldn't.

Please do not drop me, said a pleasant, singsong male voice. *I have spent enough time buried under organic matter, unable to activate without my master.*

What was that voice? What did it mean by master? Jenny spun around, looking for a person and finding no one. *There's nobody here. So, the voice is definitely in my head. Am I having a schizophrenic hallucination?* A ball of ice formed in her stomach. *When did I last take my pills?*

This isn't a hallucination, the voice said.

Jenny looked down at the Riftkey and asked, "Did you speak to me?"

Is there anyone else here?

"N-n-no," Jenny stammered, shaking, "but you're a sword."

Who said I was a sword?

Jenny thought back to Astrea's vision and remembered how Astrea had sliced a Risi in half. "That's how Astrea used you. So, if you're not a sword, then what are you?"

I am a Terminal key, or Riftkey.

Jenny shook her head. "Keys don't talk."

And swords do?

"Good point. So, what is a Riftkey?"

A life form for Terminal management. I was assigned to the Tricaster in support of the Sol expedition to unlock the Terminal. But my mission failed, and my master perished. But, that was so long ago, you know.

"I do not know, and I can't just call you 'Life Form for Terminal Management.' Don't you have a name?"

Cobol.

"Okay. Well, Cobol, it's nice to meet you."

How should I refer to you?

"Oh, my name's Jenny Tripper." *This is so weird,* Jenny thought. *I'm talking to a sword. I wonder if Astrea talked to it too?*

She did.

"Oh, you really can hear my thoughts."

Yes.

"You know, I saw you earlier, in a dream, or a vision, or something."

Yes, I remember. You released Astrea from her bond after touching me.

"Her bond? What does that mean? What did I do?" She looked down at the Riftkey and saw that a red welt had formed on the inside of her forearm. It was in the shape of a triangle inside a circle. "What is that?"

A mark that represents our new bond.

Jenny loosened her grip.

Wait. We both want to get out of here. We can help each other.

Jenny stopped struggling against her grip. "I'm listening."

Follow the water out.

"You mean crawl in there?" Jenny shivered as she stared into the tunnel's impenetrable darkness. A squeak echoed off the stone walls.

Unless you can climb out of here...

"No." Jenny sighed in defeat as she looked up. "I couldn't even climb down."

Then the only way out is through the tunnel. I can provide you with light.

"You can?" Jenny looked for a switch. "How?"

Blue fire formed inside her mind. It reminded her of her method for curing migraines. A sound, like hitting a baseball, resounded in the tiny space, and the sharp tangy odor of ozone filled the air. Jenny squinted as the air around the Riftkey sparked with a fierce blue light.

Careful of my edges. They will disintegrate anything they touch.

"Anything?" Jenny asked. *That explains the sparks,* Jenny thought, *and the ionization of the air.*

Well, almost. The Riftkey cannot cut through the same material it is made of.

"That makes sense," Jenny said as her body shivered from the cold.

We should hurry before you suffer hypothermia.

"Agreed." Jenny's teeth chattered. She held Cobol up to the tunnel's opening. A meter gap separated the water from the roof. With a sigh, she got down on her hands and knees and crawled. Her duffel bag scraped the green-and-yellow-slime-covered arch of the tunnel. The Riftkey caused the water to fizz like soda as she slid it along the floor. Up ahead, she heard something skitter and shivered.

I need to take my mind off the creepy-crawlies, Jenny thought. "So," she said out loud, "Astrea's bond to you made her a ghost?"

Yes, and we are bound until another Æon takes your place.

"What does it mean to be bound?"

It means that only you can use me. We share memories, senses, so you don't have to speak out loud. I can hear your thoughts, as long as you direct them at me.

Jenny crawled through a spiderweb and picked the sticky silk off of her face and hair. *It would be nice,* she thought, *if I didn't have to open my mouth in this tunnel.*

Yes, that is one good reason, but more importantly, we can talk in secret, and be heard where your voice should not.

Cool, well, now that I found you, what should we do?

Find my body and break Nimue's bond.

Who's Nimue?

She was my original master.

Something squeaked and skittered up ahead and made her scalp itch. *What happened to her?* Jenny asked.

She died in a crash.

And where is your body?

I do not know.

Can't you detect it or something?

Could you locate an amputated limb? Cobol asked.

Fair enough.

There are ways to detect the material my body is made of, but the technology was likely lost in the crash.

Jenny's teeth chattered as she crawled. The stones under her hands transitioned from mildewed to muddy. The roots dangling in her path pulled at her hair and tickled her back. *Wait. At the end of Astrea's vision, I saw a silver statue. Was that your body?*

Yes, but I have no memory of the location.

Light at the end of the tunnel beckoned her onward. Soon, Jenny stumbled out of the drain and into the brightness of the day. Shielding her eyes, she studied her surroundings. Thick grasses and shrubs bordered a stream. Bent trees leaned over the bubbling water. Behind her, a small, stacked-stone structure housed the drain's exit. Farther up the hill, the walls of the ruined fort were visible through a cluster of trees.

Jenny followed the outflow of the drain to the stream. Carved gray rock and smooth, colorful stones were visible through the clear water. Holding the Riftkey out for balance, Jenny stepped onto the nearest rock. Her black boots provided good traction as she walked from stone to stone. When she was halfway across the stream, a booming voice echoed out of the woods ahead of her. The silhouettes of two large men appeared through the mist on the opposite bank. Her mind conjured up memories of the Risi. She turned, and her foot slipped off the stone and splashed into the cold water.

As Jenny struggled to regain her balance, the Riftkey slipped out of her hand. The moment she lost contact with it, its glowing blue edges turned black as the Riftkey deactivated. It plunked into the water and settled into a deep section of the stream.

"Wait!" a man's voice cried out.

The voice sounded familiar, so Jenny stopped.

"Are you Jenny Tripper?" he asked.

"Lin sent us to find you," said the other man.

Each man stood at least two meters tall and wore full body armor painted in greens and browns that blended in with the surrounding woodlands.

I know him, Cobol said in her mind. *His name is Rygelus.*

Rygelus resembled a Greek god, like Adonis. Pointed ears extended from wavy brown hair. A bump protruded from his forehead, just above his thick brown eyebrows, which accentuated his deeply angled brown eyes.

"Oh, thank g-g-goodness," Jenny chattered. "Ry-Ry-Rygelus?" *That's right, I saw him in Astrea's vision, but how could he still be alive? He'd have to be hundreds of years old.*

Thousands, Cobol amended.

A fully formed ghost, like Astrea, stood next to him. She wore a black bodysuit and had the same angled eyes, pointed ears, and a bump that protruded from her forehead.

Don't tell me this is Nimue, Jenny asked Cobol inside her mind.

Cobol remained silent.

Cobol?

You told me not to tell you.

Is she Nimue?

Yes, this is Nimue. She is Rygelus's daughter.

Isn't it strange that she's right here, right now?

No, she would want to remain close to the Riftkey, and her father. What is strange is that Rygelus is here.

Rygelus studied Jenny like he was reading her soul. "How do you know my name?"

"I—I—" Jenny debated whether or not she should tell Rygelus about her vision. Ultimately, she decided to wait until she knew more about what was going on. "How did you find me?"

"Tracking you was easy enough." The other man held out the soggy box of Lamingtons in a hand the size of a baseball mitt. He looked like a comic-book version of Thor. Broad-shouldered, with a smooth, rugged face and a cascade of golden hair that danced in the breeze. His trimmed, reddish-blond beard framed a powerful jawline. He waded out into the stream and bent down to retrieve the fallen Riftkey.

Rygelus's eyes went wide. "No, Brock." He splashed into the stream. "Don't touch it!"

"What's the big deal?" Brock lifted the Riftkey from the water. Suddenly, his body went stiff and shook like he had grabbed a downed power line.

Jenny felt odd, as if something was touching her mind.

The next moment, Rygelus tackled Brock. The Riftkey flew from his grip, and together, they splashed into the stream. Rygelus sprang to his feet and pulled Brock upright. The blond man gasped for air. Rygelus stared at the Riftkey and laughed. "It was here the whole time." He withdrew a wool blanket from his backpack and wrapped it around the Riftkey.

The cold stream had numbed Jenny's extremities, and she hugged herself as her teeth chattered. Her injured tongue felt huge in her mouth, and she was growing light-headed.

You are about to lose consciousness, Cobol said in her mind.

Okay. Jenny nodded. *That sounds nice.* She giggled because her head felt like it was stuffed full of cotton. Her vision narrowed to a single point of light, and she collapsed face-first into the frigid water.

Jenny dreamed of giants with faces twisted in rage, and Alfur worshipping in front of a faceless silver statue. A blur of light- and dark-brown hues filled Jenny's vision. Someone lifted a damp cloth from her forehead and stroked her skin with a rough hand. As she woke, Jenny rolled over and found herself lying on a bed. A chest of drawers sat in the corner of the rustic bedroom. A single window revealed a thick canopy of tree branches.

"How are ya?" Brock sat on a stool next to the bed.

"Better," Jenny croaked. "Thanks."

"I never got a chance to properly introduce myself." He held a giant hand out to her. "My name is Brock Holger."

"Jenny Tripper." She took his hand, and he shook her entire arm.

In another corner of the room, Rygelus screwed the cap onto a copper flask and thrust it into a coat pocket. The ghost of Nimue stood next to him with a look of sadness on her face.

I should be able to trigger a vision if I touch her, she thought to Cobol.

Perhaps, he answered.

Jenny's hand passed through the ghost.

That is what I thought; it will only work if you are near the object she is bound to. Which means—

That your body is not nearby.

Well, how do we find it?

I do not know.

Rygelus cocked his head toward Jenny as if confused. He picked up a glass of water from a small table and approached her. "Thirsty?"

"Yes, thank you." She took the cup and drank greedily.

"I'll be right back," Brock said, then left the room.

"I'll be here," Jenny called out.

Rygelus took the empty glass and exchanged it for a granola bar. "Have an energy bar. I make them myself."

Jenny thanked him and took the bar. She winced from the pain in her tongue, but she forced herself to chew. The bar tasted of nuts, fruit, and some sort of thick, rich syrup. "I know it sounds weird," Jenny said between bites, "but I watched you fight alongside Astrea at the fort."

He glanced at the Riftkey and nodded. "That was a long time ago, in the year 1405."

Jenny's mouth opened wide. Even though she'd seen it in her vision, hearing him admit it, and so nonchalantly, was entirely too real.

Soon, Brock returned and handed Jenny a steaming mug of something like cocoa. She wrapped both hands around it and took a sip. The warm liquid slid down her throat and heated her from the inside out. She shivered as if the heat reminded her of how cold she had been.

"Where am I?"

"You're in our treehouse."

"Treehouse?" Jenny lifted an eyebrow and took another sip. Visions of boys with signs that read "No Girls Allowed" flashed into her mind. There was a sound of a door opening in the other room. A woman wearing a red trench coat over a patterned yellow button-up shirt entered the room.

Jenny sat up straight, feeling the stiffness in her soiled shirt and jeans. "Hi, are you Lin Yuan Song?"

"Please, call me Lin." She sat at the edge of the bed. "Sorry, I'm late."

Red ringed Lin's dark-brown irises, and dark circles framed her bloodshot eyes. Compared to the holographic message, Lin's skin appeared dull, and her once shiny, straight black hair was frizzy.

"No, it's my fault for getting lost." Jenny smiled and shook her head. "I shouldn't have followed Heather."

"That should never have happened, and I take full responsibility."

"I'm just happy to see you."

"So, what happened?" Lin asked.

"I fell down a hole and scraped my back." Jenny turned and lifted the back of her shirt to show the bloody scrapes. "Then I passed out."

Lin sucked air through her teeth. "That looks bad. Does it hurt?"

"Not as much as this." Jenny stuck out her tongue, showing the red bite marks in the tender flesh.

Lin frowned.

"We found her in the stream outside the fort."

"I—" A shiver racked Jenny's body and her teeth chattered uncontrollably.

"We tracked her from the cabin," Rygelus said.

"It seems Heather found her first," Brock said.

"How can that little Alfur cause so much trouble? Wait, what is that?" Lin looked at where the tip of the Riftkey jutted out from the wool blanket in Rygelus's arms.

"The Riftkey." Rygelus set the blanket between Lin and Jenny.

"I thought it was gone," Lin said. "To the Astrea realm."

"Apparently not," Rygelus said. "Jenny found it in the ruins."

"Amazing." Lin looked at Jenny.

Brock stepped backward as Jenny reached inside and slid the Riftkey out from Rygelus's blanket. "Lin, why did the Riftkey shock Brock and not me?"

"Because you're an Æon," Lin said.

"What's an Æon?"

"Someone who can sense the patterns that make up our universe," Rygelus said as he rolled up his empty blanket.

Is that why I can see ghosts? Jenny thought as she looked at Nimue.

"How did you find the Riftkey?" Rygelus asked.

Jenny told them about her vision at the edge of the storm drain, and how she had seen Rygelus help Astrea fend off the giants long enough for her people to escape.

"And why did you go to the fort?" Lin asked.

"After losing Heather, I got lost. Then—" Jenny gasped.

"What is it?"

"After seeing so many people die in the vision, I almost forgot that I found a dead body in the woods," Jenny said.

"Where?" Lin asked.

"On the path between the fort and the cabin," Brock said. "I'd estimate that he was killed about four hours ago."

"Killed?" Lin asked. "Did you recognize him?"

Rygelus shook his head. "No, but he was wearing a gray Cabin uniform."

Lin put a hand to her mouth. "It must have been Mister Torres. I'll send someone through the Waypoint to recover the body." She shook her head. "Sadi will not take this well."

"Who's Sadi?" Jenny asked.

"The dead man's girlfriend," Lin said. "It's probably best to not say anything to her until we've verified his identity."

"Okay."

"Jenny." Lin looked serious. "I want you to keep the Riftkey hidden."

"What, why?"

"The Selkans brought one with them, and there should only be one Riftkey per system, but now we have two."

Where did they take it from? Cobol asked Jenny.

Jenny echoed Cobol's question. "Where did they get the Riftkey? Did they take it from another system?"

"No," Lin said. "One of the Selkans, Kett'l, crafted it in his forge."

That is impossible, Cobol said to Jenny. *They should not be capable of creating a Riftkey.*

How do you know it's not possible? Jenny asked Cobol. *You're a talking sword—*

Key, Cobol reminded her.

Key, sorry, but you shouldn't be able to speak into my head, and there shouldn't be ladders inside boxes leading to cabins.

What's that about ladders? Cobol asked.

I'm just saying, we have no idea what's possible. So what if there are two Riftkeys? Jenny looked at Lin and asked, "I still don't understand. If you have a new Riftkey, why do I have to keep this one hidden?"

"We invited you here to compete against other Æons for the right to possess the Riftkey. If the other contestants knew you already had one, they'd be jealous. Some may even try to steal it, or worse..."

To use a Riftkey, Cobol said, *the previous bond must be broken—by death.*

Jenny gulped. "Why would anyone want to...steal it?"

"Any Æon who owns a Riftkey is granted power and prestige in this galaxy. It is a prize worth killing for."

A chill traveled up Jenny's spine, and her hands felt clammy. "Okay, I get it. Where should I hide it?"

Lin unstrapped her backpack and handed it to Jenny. "In here."

Jenny looked at the simple bag, which was even smaller than her duffel bag. She narrowed her eyes. "It's too small."

"Just take it and look inside. You might be surprised."

Jenny took the bag and opened it. The dark, smooth fabric of the lining shimmered. She reached inside and felt a large, hard box instead of the lining. Her hand brushed against a stack of books, knocking them into a pile of clothes. Somehow, there was more than enough room for the Riftkey inside the bag.

"Kett'l calls it a burstepi. You can fit a trunk's worth of supplies inside, and it will never weigh more than it does now."

"It's amazing. Thank you." Jenny placed the Riftkey inside. As Lin said, the bag weighed the same. *These four-dimensional whoosy-whatsits sure are handy*, Jenny thought.

"But I'll want it back after the mission. Deal?"

"Deal." Jenny transferred her personal items from her bag to the burstepi, followed by the empty duffel. When she tried to put it on, she became confused by the straps. There was one long, wide belt; two short, thin straps; and a set of straps for adjustments. She figured the belt should come over her left shoulder, and the two smaller straps should wrap around her waist and clip to an attachment point at her chest. That way it wouldn't shift as she moved.

Rygelus pulled the flask from his jacket and took a sip. He tucked the flask back into his jacket and turned to Jenny. "How are you feeling?"

"A bit better," Jenny said as Lin helped her adjust the straps. "Still a bit cold, though."

When they were done with the burstepi, Rygelus wrapped the woolen blanket around Jenny's shoulders. "That should help."

"Thanks."

"You should at least stay until you've finished your drink," Brock said.

"Yes," Lin said. "That's a good idea."

"Moving around should help too," Brock offered.

Jenny nodded and stood up. Holding the blanket around her with one hand, and the warm mug in the other, she explored the treehouse. Everything, including the furniture, was constructed of the most beautiful handcrafted wood. Not a nail or screw was in sight. Jenny had no doubt that these men had built everything by hand. She noticed a set of hand-carved wooden animals lining some shelves. Each one had a brass plaque. Whittling tools sat on the nearby chest of drawers. An unfinished Barney Beaver sat next to them.

"Brock carved these forest creatures himself." Lin picked up a wooden badger.

"It passes the time." Brock shrugged.

"Where's Shelly Squirrel?" Jenny pointed at the plaque marking an empty slot on the shelf.

"Brock doesn't like squirrels," Rygelus said.

"It's their bushy tails." Brock shuddered. "They give me the willies. But I'm not the only one with a hobby." Brock huffed. "Rye has shelves full of steamy romance novels."

"Epic poetry," Rygelus corrected. "Not romance novels."

Jenny pictured Rygelus reading his poetry while Brock whittled his wood figures and sniggered.

Lin looked over at Jenny and asked. "How are you feeling now?"

"Warmer," Jenny said. "I think I'm ready."

Brock opened a trapdoor in the floor of the treehouse and dropped through. He caught himself on the floor and lowered his massive frame through the opening and onto a rope ladder.

Jenny looked through the trapdoor. Brock had already covered half the length to the forest floor, fifteen meters below. *How did they get me up here?* She sat at the edge of the opening and stretched out with her foot until it touched the first rung of the rope ladder. Putting a hand on the floor, she lowered herself, rung by rung, down the ladder. From here, she could see the roof of the cabin through the trees to her left and the ruins of the fort on top of a hill straight ahead.

"You should consider installing an elevator," Lin said as she lowered herself out of the treehouse.

"Why did the VRGo puzzle bring me to a cabin in the woods?"

"The cabin contains one half of a tesseract, and the VRGo puzzle is the other half. When you activated the puzzle, the tesseract became whole and formed a pocket universe—similar to the interior of the burstepi—with one end opening into your room, and the other into the cabin," Lin said. "But why it's here in this forest is a rather unusual story. You see, five years ago, a bride and groom were found wandering through the woods, as if they had come straight from their wedding."

No, it couldn't be the same couple. Jenny's hands and feet went numb.

"Rygelus found them in the exact location of the cabin. They had no idea as to how they came to be here."

Jenny's foot slipped off the ladder, and she stumbled backward. With one flailing arm, she managed to hook her elbow around the rung.

"Jenny, what's wrong?"

Jenny found her footing and took a deep, shaky breath. Though her body trembled with adrenaline, she stepped off the ladder onto the roof of a shed. She swallowed past a lump in her throat.

Lin stepped off the ladder and rubbed Jenny's shoulders.

"I was at that wedding." Her voice shook with emotion. "Their names were Nadya Rose Sanford and Marco Donovan Barrett. For a long time, I thought—no, I knew—it was my fault that they disappeared."

"Well—" Lin lifted a trapdoor on the roof of the shed. A wooden ladder waited inside. "It's a good thing they did."

"What?" Jenny looked at Lin. "Why?"

"If they never came here"—Lin stepped onto the ladder—"then we wouldn't have known about your realm."

Jenny stood frozen. "My realm, like a different universe?"

"Exactly."

That would explain the strange journey through the VRGo puzzle, Jenny thought. *Not to mention Heather, the visions of giants, and a talking sword.*

"The appearance of Nadya and Marco was proof of an alternate universe," Lin continued. "Cabin established a research program and hired me to lead it."

Jenny followed Lin down the ladder and out of the shed. She jumped as Brock's colossal hand gripped her shoulder. Jenny turned and looked up at the modern-day Viking.

"I've never seen Rye look so alive," Brock said. "You've got to come back."

Are you kidding? Jenny thought about the distraught man taking sips from his copper flask. "I don't know."

"I'm a great cook." Brock winked. "I'll make you dinner."

Jenny looked over at Lin.

"He is a great cook."

Jenny shrugged and looked up at the treehouse. It was an elaborate series of structures connected via spiral staircases and ladders. Five catwalks stretched out to neighboring trees. Rygelus stood on the roof of a wooden shed that wrapped halfway around the base of a titanic tree. He took another pull from his flask before climbing down the ladder. Jenny felt pity for the man. After all, she knew what it was like to lose a loved one. Losing a child must be even worse than losing a mom. Jenny looked back at Brock. "Okay, I'll think about it."

"Think about what?" Rygelus asked as he stepped out of the shed.

"I invited Jenny back for dinner."

Rygelus looked down at Jenny, and with no emotion in his voice, he said, "I would like that."

Jenny felt as if Rygelus could read her soul by looking into her dichromatic eyes. After a moment, it unnerved her enough to look away.

"This way." Brock turned and led them into the woods.

"Where is this place?" Jenny asked Lin as they followed Brock. "Is this even Earth?"

"Yes, this is Earth." Lin held a branch back for Jenny. "But it does get confusing to refer to each world as Earth. So, we call your universe the Astrea Realm, after the woman who created it."

"You mean"—Jenny gasped—"she created a universe using the Riftkey?"

"Maybe not created, but she did form a connection to it." Lin looked around the forest. "And we call this one the Nimue Realm."

Nimue. Jenny looked at the ghost following Rygelus. "Wait." Jenny cocked her head. "*This* Earth? Are there more?"

"At least one more, and as far as I know; it's the original one. We call it the Prime Realm."

They passed through a ring of deciduous trees and into a clearing. Sunlight kissed Jenny's face, and warmth seeped into her damp clothing. A natural gazebo stood at the center of the green grass. Jenny walked up to the gazebo and caressed the thin trees that had been bent and woven into one another to form a domed shape.

"This is where we leave you." Rygelus stopped. "Goodbye, Jenny Tripper."

"Let's do this again," Brock said. "I don't mean finding you in the woods or carrying you to our house. I mean, you should visit sometime—"

Jenny touched Brock's arm. "Thank you for finding and saving me." Though she usually shied away from physical contact, Jenny hugged each of the big men in thanks.

"Be safe." Rygelus turned and walked into the forest.

"It's been a pleasure," Brock said before he turned and followed Rygelus.

Lin led Jenny inside the tree-woven gazebo. Jenny's chest tightened, and a chill ran down her back as she recognized the object that lay within. It looked like the obsidian bowl that Nadya and Marco had stood on before they disappeared.

Lin studied Jenny's dirty face, which had grown pale. "You've seen this before, at the wedding."

Jenny hugged herself and nodded.

"These are Waypoints." Lin stepped onto the edge and slid into the bowl. "They were first discovered by Astrea Baillie in the early fifteenth century."

Jenny's eyes widened. "The same Astrea from my vision?"

"The same." Lin held her hand up to Jenny.

Jenny took a deep breath. *If Lin can do it, so can I.* She took Lin's hand in a death grip and walked herself down the bowl.

"Ow." Lin shook her hand. "That's quite a grip."

"Sorry."

Eerie red and blue light swam in the obsidian depths of the Waypoint.

Lin smiled at Jenny. "Are you ready to discover your destiny?"

"Yes." She rubbed at the goose pimples forming on her arms. The scratches on her back and the pain of her tongue seemed secondary to getting warm. "Especially if it involves getting clean and dry."

"I know just the place." Lin reached into her yellow button-up shirt and withdrew a silver tuning fork. It was identical to the object that Astrea had given to Rygelus. "This is a Waypoint key." She knelt down at the center of the Waypoint and inserted the forked end into a hole.

The entire Waypoint thrummed with power. One of the sixteen blue symbols around the perimeter lit up. Jenny noted that one of the symbols matched the pattern on her amulet. The same symbols were on the VRGo puzzle too. *Are they numbers?* Jenny thought.

Lin twisted the key, and a different symbol lit up. "Stay close to me." Lin waved her forward. "I don't want you getting hurt when I activate the Waypoint." Jenny jumped and moved closer to the center of the bowl. Then, Lin pushed down on the key.

Jenny waited, but nothing happened. She was about to say something when her stomach lurched. Forest sounds faded away, and the air around them crystallized. A thousand faceted surfaces twisted the trees and grass into shifting fractal patterns. The crystal walls formed a mist that became a light that flowed like liquid. This gave Jenny the sensation of flying backward at incredible speed. Her ears pounded. She tried to yell, but she couldn't hear her own voice. The process played out in reverse. Liquid light became a mist, and then a crystal wall. This time, the fractal patterns gave the impression of architectural elements.

Solid ground materialized under Jenny's feet, and she stumbled forward. Her stomach was doing backflips, so she sat down in the bowl to catch her breath. The natural gazebo was gone. As was the forest. Six stone columns, carved to appear like tree trunks, surrounded them. The upper branches formed a lattice roof above their heads. A park, with paths through landscaped trees and shrubs, bordered the gazebo. Beyond that was a city. Buildings of red, yellow, and blue built of old-world architecture. Tourists shopped at street vendors and sat at outdoor tables. Jenny sighed at the sound of so many voices, and her mouth watered from the smell of cooking meat.

Lin smiled. "Welcome to Acacia City."

12

MARCHING ORDERS

"Deceleration will begin in T minus five minutes," said the *Strider*'s computer in an authoritative female voice. It had been twenty-two hours since Jack and Victus had set off for Earth from the Sol Terminal, and it was time to begin deceleration. The *Strider* shut off its engines. Without continuous acceleration, artificial gravity disappeared. Jack jerked awake as he floated up from his bunk. He checked the ship's status. *Huh, we're halfway there.* Jack had spent most of these last twenty-two hours in his cabin. Now, he made his way into the cockpit and strapped into his seat. Victus entered a moment later.

Jack had to keep reminding himself that even though Hocco's body was alive and well, his soul was dead. Jack clenched his fists. *Vae Victus tricked me, and now I'm trapped in the Sol System with the fleet admiral of the Terminal Defenders. Even worse, he's my only ticket back to Lan Station.*

Jack ignored Victus as he reviewed the flight plan with the computer. Their current velocity was over four million kilometers per hour. To avoid slamming into Earth, they would have to turn completely around and reactivate the engines. Jack confirmed the flight plan, and the maneuvering thrusters fired until they were pointed backward from their destination. The female voice of the computer counted down from ten. As it reached zero, the *Strider*'s engines activated. Jack's seat slammed into his back, and his stomach lurched.

Under constant acceleration, artificial gravity was restored. Jack unfastened his restraints and climbed down to the galley. He opened the cooler and set an airtight package of rehydrated meat and vegetables on the counter.

Victus climbed down after him and said, "I can find no sign of the *Endeavor*." He took a fatty, protein-rich white sauce and a package of tortillas from the cooler.

Jack grabbed the items from Victus's hands. "You mean the stolen ship isn't here?"

"A lack of evidence is not a lack of existence."

"Oh, that makes me feel much better."

"It is likely hidden." Victus leaned on the counter.

Jack spread the protein-based condiment onto his tortilla. Then he added the rehydrated white meat and crunchy green vegetables.

"Which means I will need you to go planetside—"

"And do what?" Jack interrupted. "Look under every rock?"

"You need to meet my contact, Randolph Torres, in person." Victus took the ingredients after Jack had finished making his wrap.

Jack pointed at Victus. "What will you be doing while I'm completing your mission?"

"After you deliver proof—"

"Why doesn't your contact send you proof?"

"I will not commit the *Tamarack* until after you deliver proof that Selkans are on Earth."

"You don't trust this contact of yours?" Jack took a bite of his wrap.

Victus ignored Jack and grabbed a data tablet. "Here is your destination."

Jack leaned in to look at the screen. It displayed a map of a city, Acacia City, on a large island called New Spain.

"You will fly in here." Victus zoomed in on the map until street details were visible. "A festival is being held on the day we arrive in Earth's orbit. Odd traffic in and out of the city will be expected. Your airport of entry is the Acacia City Airfield."

Jack took the tablet from Victus and studied the map.

"You have been precleared for entry," Victus continued. "Randolph Torres will meet you at the Waypoint Plaza at nineteen hundred. He will provide you with a job as a pilot. I volunteered your spaceplane."

Jack narrowed his eyes at Victus.

"Once you have visual confirmation of the Selkans, send a sensor scan to the *Celestial Strider*."

Jack studied the itinerary Victus had prepared. He tapped on a thumbnail image of Randolph. The picture of a young man filled the screen. He had sad eyes, long dark hair, and a close-cropped beard. Jack handed the tablet back to Victus. "Got it."

"He has a picture of you as well," Victus said.

"Hope it's a good one." Jack walked toward his cabin. He intended to eat in solitude.

"Do not fail."

Jack answered with an offensive finger gesture as he shut the door behind him.

13

MOONLIGHTER AND TINMAN

Acacia City's distant skyscrapers formed a jagged skyline against red-tinged clouds. The evening sun cast abstract shadows through the stone canopy of the Waypoint gazebo. Two men in ornamental armor stood between the treelike columns of the gazebo with their backs to Jenny and Lin. Feather-like scales ran from their shoulders to the tips of their fingers. They each held long halberds, like the ones in Jenny's vision with Astrea. Their helmets were styled in the likeness of a bird's head. Shaded glass visors hid most of their faces. Plates of carbon fiber and a flexible Kevlar-like material covered the rest of their bodies.

One of the guards turned and saw Jenny and Lin in the obsidian bowl. He stumbled backward in surprise. His foot missed a step and he fell hard on his backside. The guard's polearm clattered down the steps.

"Oh, Pat." Lin rushed forward to assist the fallen guard. "Not again."

Jenny and Lin pulled Pat to his feet.

The other guard stood statue-still and bit his lip to keep from laughing.

"Jenny"—Lin straightened the man's shoulder piece—"this is Pat O'Brien."

"Nice to meet you." Jenny brushed at her dirt-caked clothing before offering her hand. His grip felt like carved wood. "I'm Jenny Tripper."

"It's a pleasure to meet a friend of Lin's." Pat removed his helmet and wiped at his brow. Wispy silver hair blew in the wind. He retrieved his halberd with a heavy sigh that wobbled his jowls and rosy cheeks.

"Pat's worked here as a Songbird for..." Lin started.

"Forty-five years." Pat smacked the butt of his polearm onto the steps as he climbed. "And this Waypoint has seen more use in the last week than in all those years combined."

"Did you see anyone else go through today?"

"Besides you?" Pat stroked his stubbly chin in thought. "Yeah, one of yours. He wore a gray uniform."

"Was he alone?"

"Yes." Pat rubbed his chin and nodded to the other guard. "But Johnny might remember more."

"It's John," the guard corrected. "I remember he had long black hair and a short black beard."

"Sounds like Trey." Lin sucked air through her teeth.

The temperature was dropping fast. Jenny shivered and hugged her arms around her chest. Lin put an arm around her and rubbed her shoulders.

"Johnny's been working here for, what?"

"It's been about—"

"Almost a year," Pat interrupted. "He used to be a soldier, but he moved here to be close to his wife and little girl. Isn't that right?"

"Yeah, and it's John." He sighed in frustration.

"Back in my day, things were different," Pat continued. "People looked up to us. We meant something."

"Thank you, Pat, but we have to get Jenny some new clothes." Without another word, Lin led Jenny down the eastern walkway.

"Pat's a sweet man," Lin whispered, "but once he gets started, he'll never stop."

Jenny looked back at the gazebo. "Why are they wearing bird armor?"

"Oh." Lin grew animated as they walked down a path that took them next to a tree with pink flowers. "It's ceremonial. But, back in the fifteenth century, it used to be dangerous to travel. People hired armed guards to protect themselves and their goods. It was common for Waypoint cities, like this one, to provide guards to protect their patrons.

The four Waypoint cities styled their gazebos after different trees. And the guards began calling themselves Songbirds.

"Their armor is for more than just looks. It's designed to fight the Risi."

The giants from my vision, Jenny thought. She shivered as a sunbeam snaked its way through the tall buildings and warmed Jenny's skin and she realized how cold she was. "Can we sit in the sun for a minute?"

"Sure." Lin walked over to a black cast-iron bench. "How about here?"

They sat down on the bench. Jenny looked around at the people and the landscaped plaza.

"Now, where was I?" Lin asked.

"You said that the Songbirds fought the Risi."

"Oh yes." Lin smiled. "The Risi made travel to the Nimue Realm, where you arrived in the cabin, quite a risk."

"Did they know it was another universe back then?"

"Oh no." Lin shook her head. "It took almost a hundred years before the first theory of an alternate universe surfaced. Then another hundred before it could be proved. Before that, the Catholic Church considered it a crime against God to acknowledge another Earth and burned heretics at the stake."

"Oh!" Jenny gasped. "That's awful. So, what did the Church have to say about the Risi?"

"Actually, the Bible mentions giants. They're called Nephilim, and I'm sure you've heard of David and Goliath."

Jenny nodded. "Oh yeah, that's right."

"The existence of giants helped to strengthen the faithful's convictions. Others even converted to Catholicism. Still, the Risi were a liability to Waypoint travelers, so the cities offered a considerable bounty for every Risi's head. Even an ear or a scalp would fetch a price. In those days, a skilled warrior could become wealthy. Even today, people refer to any large sum of money as a 'killingsworth.' These days, the Songbird's role is mostly ceremonial, as are the Waypoints themselves."

"But...the Waypoints work? We just traveled across universes."

Lin nodded. "Yes, in the fifteenth century, the Waypoints were an amazing method of travel. They were safer and faster than ships, and invaluable for the transfer of goods and information. They connected the world in a time before ships circumnavigated the planet. But they're not needed anymore, now that we have airplanes to deliver goods and satellites to send information."

"But a jet can't beat instant travel."

"It's a matter of convenience." Lin held out her tuning-fork-shaped Waypoint key. "You need one of these to use a Waypoint. As one of the few key holders, I'm not willing to spend my day ferrying people back and forth through a Waypoint."

"Then why not give it to someone who will?"

"This key is thousands of years old and has been in my family for generations. I'm not about to loan it out."

Jenny traced her mother's amulet through her shirt. She understood how sentimental a family heirloom could be. "Okay, then make more."

Lin shook her head. "It's not that easy. They're not made of any material you can mine from the Earth. The only person who knows how to make one is the Selkan, Kett'l. According to him, it's terribly expensive and time-consuming. One day, we may lend these keys to Waypoint operators, but not until we have a surplus."

The scents from restaurants and bakeries were making Jenny's mouth water. Outdoor lights blinked to life, and the sun dropped below a building. A sudden chill made Jenny shiver.

"Shall we?" Lin asked.

Jenny nodded and stood up from the bench. She felt worse than ever. *Maybe taking a rest was a bad idea*, she thought. Even her skin seemed to drag her down, and her stomach rumbled its dissatisfaction at not being fed.

"Sounds like you're ready for some food." Lin chuckled as she looked Jenny up and down. "But first, we've got to get you clean and dry."

Lin led Jenny down the sidewalk to a cobblestone road that circled the plaza. Five streets radiated outward like the spokes of a wheel, and brightly painted buildings bordered each spoke.

"Where is Acacia City? I mean, where would it be on my Earth, the Astrea realm?" It still felt weird to think that there were parallel universes. It was even stranger to think that her universe was named after her ghost, Sally.

Lin chewed her lip in thought. "In your world, this would be Sydney, Australia."

Jenny's eyes went wide. She looked around to find some similarities between this city and Sydney. It looked like an old European city, but the trees, shrubs, and flowers were thoroughly Australian. A panoply of tourists browsed merchant booths around the circular pedestrian street of the plaza and ate delicious-smelling food while listening to live folk music.

"Lin!" a man called out. He was bald and wore a gray uniform. A young woman and a young man were with him. They all sat at a white-painted outdoor table with a yellow-and-black umbrella blooming out of the center. A big yellow sign spelled out "The Buzz" in black letters.

As Jenny followed Lin across the street, she brushed at her hair and, to her horror, pulled out a clump of mud and a spiderweb. She side-stepped a waiter wearing a yellow polo shirt and black pants and hid behind Lin.

"These are Lance's aides," Lin said, pulling Jenny forward. "Cassadi Stevens and Aindriu Ward. Everyone, this is Jenny Tripper." A young, dark-skinned man also sat at the table, but he kept his eyes down, so Lin didn't introduce him.

"Some call me Moonlighter," Cassadi said in a very British accent, "but you can call me Sadi." The corners of her lips turned up. Cassadi tilted her head to the side, and a bush of light-brown hair tumbled past her shoulders. She adjusted a pair of thick black glasses and stared straight through Jenny, as if looking at something behind her. The look gave Jenny the chills.

"Hi, Sadi."

"Hey, Jenny," said Aindriu Ward in a thick Irish accent. He cocked his head, and the sunlight glinted on an enormous scar that wrapped around his neck. Ropelike muscles rippled along Aindriu's forearm as he flipped a coin across the back of his fingers. "I'm also known as Tinman."

"Hey, Tinman."

"Nicknames?" said the third member of their group, a young man wearing a pair of tortoiseshell sunglasses. His bright white uniform contrasted against his dark skin. "Can I get one too?"

Aindriu raised a blond eyebrow. "You have to earn your nickname, newbie."

The newbie pulled the bill of a purple Lakers hat over his eyes and slumped back in his chair.

"It's nice to meet you all." Jenny nodded toward the table.

"Sadi and Aindriu are taking part in the testing," Lin said, "but right now they're helping me onboard our other new recruit, Kensei Drake. He arrived a couple of hours before you did, that's why I was a bit late in meeting you."

"Hi," Jenny said.

"Hey," Kensei answered.

"Did you say, Drake?" Jenny looked at Kensei. "Like the hip-hop star?"

"Yeah." Kensei pulled the bill of his hat lower.

"What's hip-hop?" Aindriu asked.

"Who's Drake?" Sadi asked.

"We really are in another universe," Jenny said.

"No kidding." Kensei grabbed a slice of bread from a plate at the center of the table and added whipped butter and a dollop of honey. Jenny's mouth watered.

"Are any more of them coming over here?" Sadi made a face like she smelled something foul.

"No," Lin said. "Jenny is our last one and she arrived just under the deadline."

"Good, can we head back to the *Endeavor* now?"

"As soon as we get their keys."

Sadi sighed and leaned back in her chair.

Kensei pulled out a strange gray tablet device and tapped at its screen.

Aindriu studied Jenny. "What happened to you?"

"I fell through a hole and crawled out through a dr—" Jenny sneezed.

"Bless you," Aindriu said.

"You know why people say 'bless you'?" Kensei asked without looking up from his tablet.

"No, why?" Jenny rubbed her itchy nose.

"People used to believe that sneezing expelled your soul from your body." Kensei set the tablet down. "They would say 'bless you' like some magical charm until your soul could return." He picked up his glass of milk and swallowed several gulps.

Sadi turned to Jenny. "Do you believe your soul can escape?"

"Uh, no." Jenny laughed awkwardly. "It's just a silly superstition."

"It's an involuntary reflex to bronchial irritation," Aindriu said.

"Actually"—Jenny rubbed her nose—"I think I caught a cold."

"That explains it." Lin rubbed her hands together.

Sadi reached for the platter of bread.

Jenny licked her lips unconsciously.

"Are you hungry?" Aindriu picked up the plate and offered it to Jenny.

"Yeah." Jenny grabbed a thick slice of crusty bread. "Thank you."

She slathered it with layers of butter and gobs of honey. As she tore a chunk off with her teeth, she winced and held her face as the crust scraped her injured tongue. Jenny pushed the bite to the less painful side of her mouth and sighed. *I'm going to be miserable until this heals.* Jenny caught Sadi looking at her with a sly smile on her thin lips and turned away.

"Are you joining us?" Aindriu reached back to pull an empty chair from a neighboring table.

"Not yet, Tinman," Lin said. "I need to get our recruit cleaned up and in uniform. Will you still be here in about half an hour?" Lin looked up at the tall clock tower, which read 4:41.

"Yeah, we'll be here." Aindriu sipped at something that looked like beer. "When you get back, can you take Kensei to get his key? I've got to run an errand for Trey."

"Of course." Lin turned her smile to Kensei. "The more, the merrier."

Lin led Jenny clockwise around the plaza and took a street that angled to the southwest. Tinges of pink and yellow painted the sky. Live music echoed off the colorful buildings. A small parade passed by them, on its way to the plaza. Jenny backed against a wall as characters in papier-mâché heads walked by on stilts. Musicians followed close behind, playing trumpets, drums, and other parade instruments. More people in Songbird costumes brought up the rear.

"What's the big celebration?"

"It's like your..."

"Queenstown Winter Festival?" Jenny offered.

"Sure. In truth, I can't keep track of all the holidays. It seems like there's a parade almost every week. There's a lot of history and culture to celebrate."

"That sounds incredible."

Lin nodded. "This city relies on tourism, and the history behind the Waypoints is a big part of it."

The buildings here were all two or three stories tall, with storefronts on the bottom and apartments up top. Hand-painted signs—advertising makeup and perfumes, sweets, records, and books—extended down the street.

They stopped in front of a brick building with three mannequins modeling beautiful dresses in a large picture window. The sign on the forest-green door read "Mary Ann's Fine Custom Tailoring."

"A tailor?"

Lin looked Jenny up and down. "Well, we need to do something about this."

"You just indicated all of me."

"Well..." Lin smiled at her.

A brass bell dinged as Lin opened the door. Dresses, suits, and uniforms were on display around the shop. The sweet scent of cloth and well-oiled sewing machines filled Jenny's nostrils. It reminded her of the vintage natural fabrics of thrift shops and her sewing machine back home. She made most of her clothing, and always sought out black linen, cotton, and silk from thrift shops.

A stunning emerald-green dress caught her eye. Jenny wanted to run her hands over the beautiful fabric, but she resisted and instead carefully lifted it by its hanger and admired its shape.

A plethora of antique mirrors hung along one wall. Jenny caught sight of herself, and her face grew pale, then red with embarrassment. She looked like a zombie. Black makeup had run down her cheeks. Her hair was full of dirt and debris from the storm drain. Her black clothes had become brown with dirt.

The people at The Buzz must have thought I was a vagrant.

From the back of the shop, the sound of a sewing machine stopped, and a middle-aged woman with curly blond hair joined them. "Lin," the woman said with a smile.

"Hello, Mary Ann." Lin smiled back. "Do you have time for us?"

Mary Ann looked like her bones were too large for her skin. Her cheeks, collar, and wrists protruded, and her arms and legs seemed out of proportion to her body.

I bet she became a tailor because she couldn't find clothes that fit, Jenny thought.

"For you? Always." Mary Ann looked Jenny up and down, then shook her head at Lin. "Looks like she'll need the works." She turned to Jenny. "Do you want to keep the clothes you're wearing?"

Jenny gave her once-black clothes a glance and probed the rip in the back of her shirt. "Um, I guess not."

"Good." Mary Ann perched her hands on top of her bony hips. "What's your name?"

"Jenny Tripper."

"Stand up straight," she barked. "Hold up your chin."

Jenny clapped her arms to her sides, straightened her spine, and lifted her head.

"Now step up here." Mary Ann pointed at a platform surrounded by three floor-to-ceiling mirrors.

Jenny stepped onto the platform. The mirrors reflected her horrendous appearance from every angle.

Mary Ann held measuring tape up to Jenny's arm. "By the time you're clean, your new clothes will be ready."

"Clean?"

"Yes, we have bathing facilities here." Mary Ann tutted as she examined Jenny from head to toe. "How did you get so filthy anyway?"

"It's a long story," Lin said, "and I'm afraid we need to rush."

Jenny turned to Lin. "How much is this going to cost?"

"Don't worry about that." Lin waved. "Cabin is paying for everything."

After the measurements, Mary Ann led Jenny past the sewing room and into the bathroom. Large black-and-white tiles covered the floor, and a white marble countertop stretched from wall to wall. Mary Ann approached a large white porcelain bathtub and turned a pair of brass dials. Jenny sighed as steamy water gushed out. She studied her reflection in an enormous mirror. An array of bright lights highlighted every horrific feature of her tangled hair and mud-caked face.

"I'll be in the next room," Mary Ann said. "Adjusting your new clothes."

Lin picked up the burstepi. "And I'll see that your things get clean and dry."

"I believe you owe me a story," Mary Ann said to Lin as they walked out the door.

"Thank you," Jenny shouted as the door closed behind them. As the latch clicked shut, Jenny pulled her t-shirt off. Her filthy clothes were so caked with dirt that they held their shape on the floor. She lowered herself into the half-filled tub. Warm water caressed her tender skin. A wave of pleasure caused her to shiver with delight. A row of essential oils lined a nearby shelf. Jenny added a few drops of lavender to the running water for its calming scent, and a few drops of peppermint to clear her stuffy nose.

The scratches on her back stung as the water rose, but the pain faded after a minute. Jenny shut off the water, closed her eyes, and floated. From the other room, Jenny heard the pocka-pocka-pocka of a sewing machine. She replayed the day in her mind, beginning with solving the VRGo puzzle. Jenny thought about this incredible opportunity. She could start over fresh and reinvent herself. No longer would she be labeled as a Gypsy. Jenny focused on that part of her identity. That eleven-year-old girl who had loved Romani culture. She pushed it deep inside, hiding it where it would never surface again. Jenny pulled the stopper and dried herself. Then, she took a robe and left the bathroom.

Mary Ann pursed her lips, looked Jenny over, and nodded. "Based on the state you arrived in, I wasn't sure a bath would be enough." She waved toward two mannequins. "Here are your Cabin uniforms. This one has a nano-weave, carbon-fiber fabric, which means it is highly resistant to heat, punctures, and most stains. This other one is for formal events, and is made of cotton."

Jenny pulled her white bathrobe tight and studied the uniforms. Each included a pair of pants and a long, asymmetric white shirt with a mandarin collar and a large pocket on one side. She thought about how much time and effort she'd spent crafting her goth appearance. A pang of sadness flashed across her face.

"Don't worry," Lin assured her. "You don't have to wear a uniform all the time."

At least no one will mistake me for a Gypsy in this outfit. "Do I have to wear it now?"

"Yes." Lin pulled the formal uniform off the mannequin. "After all, you'll be meeting our entire team, along with the CEO of Cabin, this evening."

Jenny straightened up and thrust her shoulders back. "Lance LaGrange?" She felt a bit queasy and anxious as she took the uniform from Lin. He was the person who would determine her future here, on this Earth. If she didn't make a good impression, would he send her home?

"That's right. Now, get dressed." Mary Ann pointed to a door. "You can use that changing room."

Jenny entered the changing room. She removed her robe and put on the formal uniform. It fit like a dream, and the fabric felt soft on her skin. Next, she pulled on a pair of black socks followed by a pair of black leather boots. Jenny stood in front of a mirror and studied herself. She had to admit, she did look good in a uniform. Finally, she tried to massage her dark hair into spikes, but it was futile without any product. Jenny left the changing room.

"Are you the same girl I found in the woods?" Lin asked.

Jenny smiled.

"You look fantastic." Mary Ann adjusted the uniform near Jenny's hip. "A complete transformation. Still..." Mary Ann lifted a bundle from behind her sewing machine. "I think this would look better on you."

Jenny took the bundle and opened it up. It was the green dress Jenny had admired in the waiting room.

"I saw you looking at it," Lin said.

"It's beautiful." Jenny held the dress up to her body. The light, silky fabric felt amazing against her skin. "Is this for me?"

"If not"—Mary Ann put her hands on her hips—"then I wasted my time adjusting it."

Lin handed the burstepi to Jenny. "I did my best to clean and dry your clothing. We have people who can fix your communication device."

"Thank you." Jenny slung the burstepi over her shoulder. She looked at Mary Ann. "And thank you so much for your work. It's more than I could have dreamed of."

"You are very welcome, my dear."

"Okay, we've got to run." Lin pulled Jenny toward the door. "Thank you, Mary Ann."

Mary Ann waved. "I'll send Cabin my bill."

The open door to Mary Ann's shop cast a wedge of light on the darkened street. A warm breeze carried the smell of the sea from the east. Overhead, the sun had ignited the sky like fire. Fireworks lit the lowermost clouds in flashes of white, red, and blue.

"What do you do for Cabin?" Jenny asked as they walked toward the plaza.

"I'm an archaeoastronomer," Lin said.

"What's that?"

"I study alien artifacts. The Waypoints are my specialty, and I've spent my life researching their effect on our history."

"Then you know a lot about the Waypoints?"

"Yes, it's my life's focus. After inheriting a key, I became obsessed with their history. I traveled to Nimue and studied with Rygelus."

In the plaza, a man with a long pole lit gas streetlights that circled the interior of the cobbled walkway. Diners sat at small tables sipping wine from crystal glasses. Lin and Jenny returned to the table where Aindriu, Sadi, and Kensei waited for them. Empty plates sat in front of them. Jenny's stomach growled.

"Hello, who's this?" Aindriu looked Jenny from head to toe in confusion.

"It's me, Jenny."

"No," Aindriu said, "this can't be the same girl from before."

Sadi narrowed her eyes and glared at him.

"Sorry to make you wait," Lin said.

"No worries." Aindriu pulled up two more chairs to their table. "Have a seat."

Jenny and Lin sat down.

"Hi again." Kensei pushed up the brim of his hat and studied Jenny over the top of his glasses. "You look a lot better." He tore a small chunk of bread and fed it to a little fuzzy animal on his lap. The creature took the food with tiny, almost human hands and bit into it.

"I told you," Aindriu said, "do not let it eat at the table."

Kensei's shoulders slumped as he opened his backpack and placed the little critter back into his bag. He fidgeted in his chair, looking two sizes too small, then settled for slumping backward.

The waiter came by to clear plates and promised to take Jenny's and Lin's drink orders when he returned.

Jenny snacked on the bread appetizer while she studied the menu. Prices were surprisingly inexpensive. Items that would be over ten dollars back home weren't even two dollars here. She also noticed a theme for this restaurant. Everything used honey as an ingredient.

The waiter returned and took their drink orders.

Aindriu ordered another beer, Lin chose mead, and Jenny decided on an Italian raspberry soda. While they waited, Jenny watched an old man putting a chessboard away. He counted each piece out loud as he dropped them into a drawstring bag. In the plaza, costumed characters had joined a group of street musicians. They were performing a mock battle between the Songbirds and the Risi. Two soldiers used a blunt halberd to take down a giant. The giant wore a large papier-mâché head. It was styled after a human, but with more grotesque features. The man stood on short stilts, and his body was wrapped in a long robe. When the halberd struck, he tumbled to the ground. The entire act reminded Jenny of Walther's men attacking the Risi that first scaled the fort's walls.

The waiter returned with their drinks and asked Jenny and Lin for their food order. Jenny ordered the honey-ham sandwich, and Lin got the honey-glazed salmon. When Aindriu took a sip, Kensei fed a piece of bread to the furry face poking out of his backpack. While they waited for their food, Aindriu asked Jenny about her trip. Jenny provided an abbreviated version of her journey, from finding Heather in the cabin to getting lost in the woods. She decided to leave out the part where she followed Astrea's ghost and had a vision, and told them about Rygelus and Brock finding her.

"Did you see Trey while you were over there?" Sadi asked.

"Trey?" A horrified look crossed Jenny's face as she remembered trip-ping over the dead body in the woods. With her memories of Astrea's people defending the fort, she had forgotten about the corpse she had tripped over. She stared down at her hands and avoided answering the question.

"I haven't heard from him all day." Sadi looked at Lin. "Last I heard was that he went through the Waypoint." She looked over at the gazebo.

"No"—Lin looked at Jenny—"we don't know."

"What's going on?" Sadi stared at Jenny. "You know something." She narrowed her eyes. "Tell me."

A tingling sensation spread over Jenny's body, and her tongue itched where she had bitten it. Jenny squirmed.

The corners of Sadi's lips curled up. "What did you see?"

Trey's blood-soaked, bruised head flashed into Jenny's mind. She winced and rubbed at her cheek as her tongue blazed in pain.

"Sadi, stop it," Aindriu said. "She doesn't know anything."

"I..." Jenny stared at Sadi. *Is she doing this to me?* Jenny trembled. Her mouth felt like fire, and her tongue was the fuel. "I..." Jenny forced the words out through the pain. "I found..." She shook her head. "I mean, I tripped over...a body, a dead body."

"Sadi, that's enough!" Lin shouted.

Sadi glared at Lin, then turned her focus back on Jenny. "What did he look like?" Her eyes widened until the whites encircled her brown irises.

"A week of kitchen duty," Lin said.

Jenny squirmed in her chair like a mouse caught in a cat's claws. "I don't know!" she screamed. Several diners turned to see what was happening.

Aindriu stood behind Sadi and lifted her out of the chair as if she were a doll.

Tears welled up in Jenny's eyes. "He was wearing a uniform," Jenny said. "Like yours. He had blood on his face, and in his hair."

"You thought that taking a bath and getting new clothes were more important than telling me?"

"It's my fault, Sadi," Lin said. "I told Jenny not to say anything. We don't know for sure that it's Trey."

Sadi twisted out of Aindriu's grip. She leaned on the table and looked at Jenny with pleading eyes. "What color was his uniform?"

The pain in Jenny's tongue faded away. She rubbed at her face with the heel of her hand and sucked on her tongue. "Gray. It was gray."

Sadi clenched her jaw and glared at Lin. Without saying a word, she stood up and stormed off toward the Waypoint.

"Sadi, there's nothing to be done," Lin called out.

Sadi pushed through the performers and their mock battle, toppling a man off of his stilts.

Aindriu started to follow her, but Lin held him back. "Let her go."

"Are you okay?" Kensei asked Jenny.

"I think so." Jenny took a deep, racking breath and wiped at her eyes. She turned to face Lin. "What was that?"

Lin shook her head. "Sadi can use any memory of pain and enhance it."

"How is that possible?"

"She's an Æon. In time, you may discover similar gifts."

"Some gift," Jenny said.

Andriu said, "She can also reduce pain."

"She should stick to that," Jenny replied.

"But, Sadi had no right to do that to Jenny," Kensei said.

"No, she didn't," Lin assured him, "and we will punish her."

"She's usually not like this," Aindriu assured Jenny.

Lin nodded. "She's just distraught about Trey."

"You should have said something earlier," Aindriu said to Lin.

"You're right," Lin said. "I'm sorry, Jenny."

"It's okay." Jenny forced herself to smile.

"You want to know why we call her Moonlighter?" Aindriu asked.

Jenny shrugged. "Does she have a night job or something?"

"There's a tree that grows in the rainforests of Australia. It has these stinging hairs that deliver a neurotoxin that can last for days, weeks, or even months. The pain is so excruciating that it has driven its victims to suicide. One of this tree's names is Moonlighter."

Just then, the waiter arrived with Jenny's sandwich and Lin's salmon. At the sight of food, Jenny drove all thoughts of Sadi's impropriety from her mind. She lifted the massive honey-ham sandwich from the plate and took a bite. She felt every layer. Soft bread, crisp lettuce, and thick honey ham. Flavors flooded her mouth. The pain in her tongue even seemed more tolerable now. As her stomach filled, her anger toward Sadi lessened.

All too soon, Jenny looked down at an empty plate and still felt hungry. She sipped the last of her soda and wondered if she could order some flan. The waiter dashed her hopes when he returned with a check and a loaf of bread in a blue-and-yellow bag.

Lin took the bread and handed it to Jenny. "I know you're probably still hungry, and you never know when a loaf of bread will come in handy."

Jenny took the bread and inhaled the yeasty aroma. After thanking Lin, she slipped it into the burstepi.

"Tell me, what are you doing here in Acacia?" Lin asked Aindriu.

"I am supposed to meet someone named Jack Spriggan. Trey told me that he is a new member of the team."

Lin cocked her head. "I was not notified of a new hire. Does Lance know about this?"

Aindriu pulled a dark-gray tablet from the front pocket of his uniform. After pressing his palm against the surface, he tapped the screen and handed it to Lin. "Have a look at his resume."

"Looks like he has a military background." Lin nodded. "Oh, he served in two operations, Pakistan and Syria. Hmm, and then he went on to freelance. Oh, this is good."

"What?" Aindriu asked.

"It says here that he already has the appropriate security clearance, and he's a pilot."

"With his own plane too."

Lin raised an eyebrow. "When can I meet him?" She handed the tablet back to Aindriu.

Aindriu looked up at the clock tower. "He's supposed to meet me at the Waypoint in an hour."

Aindriu looked at Jenny. "Sorry again about Sadi."

"It's okay."

Aindriu turned and walked toward the center of the plaza. Finding a bench near the Waypoint, he sat down to wait for Jack Spriggan.

14

KEY CEREMONY

Rain fell on the streets of Acacia City and the scent of wet stone mixed with the sulfur of the fireworks. Lin led Jenny and Kensei toward the north end of the plaza where a large building with neoclassical architecture loomed above them. It was at least twelve stories tall. White granite framed tall windows, and a great brass clock told the time. A bas-relief sign near the entrance read "Cabin Department of Transportation."

A drop of rain landed on Jenny's forehead as they climbed the white marble steps. She looked up and noticed a little pink nose peeking out of Kensei's backpack. "Kensei, can I see your pet?"

"Sure." Kensei unzipped the bag, and a furry animal climbed up his arm and perched on his shoulder. Dark stripes ran from his short pointy ears to his long furry tail. "His name is Leon. He's a sugar glider."

"Hi, Leon." Jenny stroked his furry back. "He's so cute. Did you bring him from home?"

"Yeah, he goes everywhere with me." Kensei gave Leon a sideways glance. "Even when I don't know it."

"Did he sneak into your bag?"

Kensei nodded and scratched between the sugar glider's ears with his long brown fingers.

They passed through a revolving door. The sounds of fireworks and tourists vanished, replaced by the din of voices echoing inside a large chamber. In the foyer, the walls were lined with signs requesting donations for clothing, food, and money to help refugees. From there, they entered a cavernous lobby. It had the feeling of being outside. Large, leafy plants and small trees filled the vast space. To their left and right, brick walls rose five stories tall. In front of and behind them, huge windows revealed the night sky. An exact replica of the cabin in Esperanza Woods stood in the center of the floor.

"Aliens?" Jenny stared openmouthed.

Two large humanoids with thick, wrinkly, bluish skin walked out of the structure. They had four stout legs, two huge arms that swung at their sides, and two smaller arms near their heads. One of them held a huge baby.

A creature resembling a chewed-up pile of bubble gum slithered across the marble floor. Six short, thin legs and two tentacled arms propelled it forward. Its skin changed color and flashed complex patterns. Leon squeaked and ducked into Kensei's backpack.

"What is this place?" Kensei looked around the lobby.

"This is where extrasolar entities register to live and work here on Earth."

Jenny watched two extraterrestrials with wrinkly skin working a strange handheld device. Then, a group of compact aliens with scaly gray skin rushed by them as they entered the cabin. Inside, relics of the past adorned the shelves. Interactive signage detailed the rise of Cabin and the CEO's humble beginnings in a cabin like this one.

Through the cabin window, Jenny saw a pair of brass elevator doors open in the outer wall. Two thin and feathery birdlike humanoids stepped out, and a sizeable human woman with a lot of upper lip approached them. The aliens waved their long, delicate arms and their voices rose to a loud chirp. A thick bun of black hair bobbed in rhythm as the woman spoke.

"Why isn't everyone outside celebrating?" Jenny asked as they walked out of the cabin. "There's a festival with fireworks and everything."

"That's for the tourists," Lin answered. "These people just arrived in a new stellar system. They don't know it's Independence Day, and it wouldn't matter to them anyway. As for the rest of us, festivals and parades happen every week in Acacia City. After a while, it gets dull. I hardly notice them anymore myself." Lin looked up at the fireworks visible through tall windows high in the lobby.

"I guess the allure would wear off after a while." Jenny stared at the aliens. "But right now, I'm a fish out of water."

Lin led them into the same elevator that the birdlike aliens had recently used. It was utterly silent inside and smelled of oiled metal.

"You use the duodecimal system?" Kensei pointed at the elevator's keypad.

There were two extra call buttons between nine and ten. One looked like the letter *X* and the other was a backward *3*. Even odder was that a triangle had replaced the number three.

"What's that?" Jenny asked.

"It's one of the quirky differences between our universes," Lin said. "We use twelve digits in our numbering system."

Kensei sighed. "I wish we used base twelve. It makes for much cleaner fractions."

Lin nodded and pressed a metal card against a gray panel. It beeped. She then pushed the B button on the keypad.

Jenny's stomach jumped as the car descended. After a moment, her weight increased as the elevator slowed to a stop. The doors opened to a basement that was nothing like Jenny expected. The hallway was well lit by bright lights in its tall ceiling. White walls met white granite floors. Across from them were two large freight elevator doors.

"Is this where we're taking the test?" Jenny asked.

"Yes, but first I need to get you two inoculated." Lin turned right and led them down the hallway. Her footsteps echoed down the stark white corridor.

"Inoculated?" Jenny asked as she followed a step behind Lin.

"Have you ever traveled to a foreign country?" Lin asked.

"No."

"I have," Kensei replied. "I was just doing a foreign exchange program in China."

"Did you have to get travel vaccinations?"

"Typhoid, hepatitis, and influenza."

"Oh, I get it." Jenny nodded in understanding. "We didn't just travel to another country, we're in another universe."

"Plus, you're surrounded by aliens that share a lot of biological similarities. We need to get you vaccinated before you catch something more horrible than that cold." She looked at Jenny.

Jenny sniffed.

Lin placed her hand on a black panel on the wall next to a set of double doors. A red light scanned her palm, and something clicked. She shoved the door open. Inside was a vast room filled with tall shelves, and a myriad of electronic equipment that lined the walls. A male and a female lab worker stood at a worktable with their backs to them.

Jenny looked at the metal shelves. There was something strange there. Something that pressed against her mind, beckoning to her like the call of the siren.

"Welcome to our laboratory," Lin said. "This is where we store and study a vast collection of artifacts. I used to work here as a researcher."

A cylindrical aquarium rested on a nearby table. A strange creature that looked part worm and part jellyfish swam inside. "What is that?" Jenny pointed.

"That's our pet, Legion." The female tech pulled latex gloves off her hands and approached them. "It's a siphonophore."

"What's a siphonophore?" Kensei asked.

"It's a relative of corals and jellyfish. They're a group of individual organisms called zooids that operate as a single animal. Isn't it incredible?"

Jenny leaned in closer and saw hundreds of tiny, translucent organisms, each the size of a grain of rice. "Yes, it is."

"Legion reminds us that we're all just a collection of single-celled organisms working together as one," The male tech said.

"And it's pretty," The female tech added.

"Cora," Lin said, "I'd like you to meet our newest recruits, Jenny and Kensei."

"Welcome aboard. You must be so excited."

The male tech approached and stood beside Cora. "Hi, I'm Joseph. You're here for vaccinations, right?"

"That's right," Lin said.

"Oh." Cora hopped. "I'll get them." She took a hard-plastic case down from a shelf and set it on the table next to Legion. Inside were a set of vials containing dark fluid and a stainless-steel injector.

Jenny leaned back and narrowed her eyes. "Why is it black?"

"Normally, antigens are suspended in clear solutions," Cora said as she took a vial out of the case, "but you would need over a dozen standard shots to inoculate yourself from all the different viruses, bacteria, and parasites in our universe." She held the vial out. "But with this, you'll only need one dose."

Kensei lifted his sunglasses and peered closely at the dark vial in Cora's hand. "I don't know."

"Saying this is a vaccination is like saying the sun is just a bright light in the sky," Joseph said. "This serum allows for complete environmental adaptation, and it cures allergies, heart disease, and cancer. In addition, it grants rapid healing and heightened endurance."

"Best of all," Cora added, "the effect is permanent because it creates a new organelle within your cells, just as mitochondria did millions of years ago."

"It also optimizes your microbiome," Joseph added.

"Like my gut bacteria?" Jenny asked.

"And worms?" Kensei asked.

"A hookworm infestation can prevent autoimmune diseases and overactive allergic reactions. There's a fungus that controls an ant's body, and a bite from a tick produces an allergy to red meat. This cure makes all the organisms living in your body work together as one. Which is why we call this serum 'siphonophore,' like Legion over there." Joseph set the vial back into the plastic case.

Jenny looked at the cylindrical aquarium with Legion swimming inside, then she turned her gaze on Lin. "Could this have saved my mom?"

"It's possible." Lin nodded. "If we had found her in time."

Jenny inhaled sharply and looked up at the ceiling to keep her tears away.

"Her death was not in vain," Cora said as she placed the vial into the injector. "If it weren't for your mother's cancer, we would never have found you."

"How *did* you find us, exactly?" Kensei asked.

"When we searched your universe for potential Æon we looked for several common factors." Cora counted on her fingers. "A family history of early death, schizophrenia, migraines, hallucinations, and any unexplained phenomena."

Joseph looked at Jenny. "As direct descendants of Astrea Baillie, your family inherited a mutation that causes familial acute myeloid leukemia."

"So, this serum, siphonophore, will keep me from developing cancer?" Jenny asked.

"Yes," Lin said.

I could break the family curse, Jenny thought.

"I'm deathly allergic to peanuts," Kensei said. "Will I be able to eat them after this?"

"You bet," Joseph said.

"Then I'm in." Kensei rolled up his left sleeve. "I've always wanted to taste a Reese's Peanut Butter Cup."

Joseph gave him a puzzled look. "Something from your universe?"

"Yeah," Jenny said.

"First, we'll need to take a blood sample from each of you," Joseph said as he gathered up six blood bottles with colored caps.

"Okay." Kensei held out his arm.

"You'll feel a sharp pressure." Joseph said before filling three of the blood bottles with Kensei's blood. Using a pen from his shirt pocket, he wrote something on the labels and set them aside.

Next, Cora stepped forward with the siphonophore injector, and pressed the tip into Kensei's arm. As she depressed the plunger, the inky fluid vanished.

"Ow," Kensei said rubbing his shoulder.

"Yeah, that one burns for a bit," Cora said.

Joseph looked at Jenny and asked, "Are you ready?"

Jenny took a deep breath. *I can't turn back now.* "Okay."

"Which arm?" Joseph asked.

Cora removed the empty vial and the needle from the injector and inserted fresh ones.

Jenny shrugged. "Whichever."

"Ambidextrous?" Joseph said.

"Yeah." Jenny always felt like it was bragging to say it. It meant that she could do most tasks with either hand. She rolled up her left sleeve. First, Joseph collected the blood samples, which hurt, but it wasn't too bad. Then, Cora pressed the injector to Jenny's skin. She felt pressure, like the blast of a water gun, and fire spread up her arm and into her chest.

"It's going to be sore for a while"—Cora looked at both of them —"and you might feel a bit sick or dizzy, so take it easy and keep well hydrated."

Jenny rolled down her sleeve and rubbed her arm. A dull pain throbbed in time with her heartbeat.

"Can you give my pet a shot too?" Kensei asked as he lifted Leon from his backpack.

"Uh, sure." Joseph searched the table for something. "We keep test samples around, which should be about the right dose." He found a small syringe and injected the sugar glider in the thigh.

Leon squeaked and scurried back into Kensei's backpack.

"How soon until I can eat peanuts?"

"I'd give it a couple of days to be safe," Joseph said.

It may be too late to save my mom, Jenny thought, *but I wonder if I could still help Bea with this?* "Can we bring this home with us, to help our relatives?"

"Absolutely," Lin said. "Before you leave for home, we'll supply each of you with as many doses as you need." Lin rubbed her hands together. "Now, let's get you tested for your keys."

Jenny looked around the room. "I'm ready."

Lin smiled. "Not here. It's a special kind of test, one that requires a more meditative space."

"What do you mean?" Joseph looked offended. "I find it plenty relaxing here."

Lin grinned at Joseph and ushered Jenny and Kensei out of the laboratory. She led them down the hallway, past the elevator, and into a large, bare room at the end of the hall.

"I used to come here to relax on my work breaks," Lin said. "Now this area is solely for testing new recruits."

Jenny couldn't see why. The walls and floor were black and dark, and at its center was a tiny, windowless box with a single entrance.

"Run Chinese tea garden," Lin said.

A trill sounded from a console near the door, and the walls and floor of the room flashed white. Suddenly, they were standing on a stone path leading to a small bridge spanning a bubbling stream. Jenny spun on one foot to take it all in.

A soft breeze carried the smell of sunflowers and jasmine to Jenny's nose. A green bamboo forest waved in rhythm with the wind. Above them, a bright-blue sky peeked out from behind ponderous white clouds. Koi fish swam in a nearby pond and dragonflies kissed the water's surface. Even the plain box in the center of the room had transformed into a traditional Chinese teahouse.

"This is incredible." Kensei looked all around.

"Have either of you meditated before?"

"Oh yeah, lots." Jenny had been meditating with her mom since she was four. Over the years, they had practiced every form and method, from A to Zen. At one point, they believed it would help with her schizophrenia. Most recently, Jenny had been using the techniques she had developed to control her headaches.

Leon climbed out of Kensei's backpack and onto his shoulder. Then, the sugar glider leaped for a nearby tree and hit the wall of the room. Kensei hurried over to Leon and made sure he was unharmed.

"How about you, Kensei?"

"I did a relaxation session at school one time," Kensei said as he put the dazed sugar glider back into his bag. "It wasn't very informative, but I learned a little about breathing and muscle control."

"That's great, you'll both have a head start." The bridge creaked as they crossed the stream and entered the teahouse. It smelled of aromatic leaves mixed with oiled wood. Lin caressed a dark wood column. Intricate gold-leafed carvings adorned the woodwork. "This space is my oasis within the city."

"It's hard to believe that it's all a simulation." Jenny looked at the maple trees and water features through the square windows. "It's beautiful."

"Please, have a seat." Lin indicated a circular table with a jade carving of a tree, and four chairs that bore ornate carvings of cranes and dragons.

Jenny and Kensei sat down.

Lin set an iron kettle onto a stove before setting a beautiful porcelain teapot on the table. She walked over to a wall of wooden shelves that held glass jars filled with dried leaves, flowers, berries, and who knows what. She pulled a jar from a shelf and spooned its contents into the teapot.

"Jenny?" Kensei asked. "I feel weird, do you?"

"Yeah." Jenny's body and mind felt disconnected. "You think it's the vaccination?"

"It is," Lin said. "The tea should help with your focus."

"How will tea and meditation help us with the test?" Kensei asked.

"You know that buzzing sensation you feel sometimes?"

"Yeah."

"That is your brain struggling to perceive the patterns you're sensing, and unless properly developed, these sensations will manifest as hallucinations that will lead to mental illness, or worse." The kettle whistled and Lin filled the teapot. "This tea, combined with some focus and meditation, will allow me to determine the best way I can help you."

That made a lot of sense. Jenny thought. The doctors had told her that she was mentally ill because she could see a ghost, but that wasn't all. There were headaches, and buzzing, and maybe even a doppelgänger.

Lin poured the brewed tea into three matching porcelain cups. Jenny lifted her cup and took a sip. Her face scrunched up, and she shared a look with Kensei. The tea was highly bitter, but refusing to offend Lin, Jenny drank it all.

Kensei drank all his tea, closed his eyes, and shivered. "So, these patterns are all around us," He said, "like in nature?"

"Sort of," Lin said. "The patterns are the field vibrations that forge the matter and energy of our universe."

"Vibrations?" Jenny asked.

"I know it sounds like pseudoscience. But field vibrations are literally everywhere and in everything. It's the vibrations in energy fields that determine whether something has mass, feels solid, or carries an electric charge. Even in the most remote parts of outer space, there are fluctuations in the electromagnetic field. What we take for the complete absence of matter and radiation is an infinite field of possibility from which particles emerge. In fact, there is a field for every elemental particle, just waiting for sufficient energy to define each its own existence."

"How we can see these fields?" Kensei asked.

"Well," Lin cradled her cup in her hands and chuckled. "Your eyes read electromagnetic radiation, your ears detect pressure waves, and your skin measures thermal energy."

"And what organ sees field vibrations?" Jenny asked.

"Your brains have the innate ability to detect vectors of field transformation and process the amount of stretching or compressing that occurs." Lin set her cup down. "And like a hearing or eye examination, we have a method for testing your ability to sense these vibrations." She retrieved a beautiful wooden box from a shelf and set it on the table. Engraved onto the lid was an owl holding four rings in its mouth. She put two fingers into the owl's eyes on the box lid and rotated its head. The brass rings spun, and the box swung open. Inside, four tuning-fork-shaped keys rested on red velvet, each inset with gemstones of heliodor, ruby, sapphire, or emerald. They were the largest gemstones Jenny had ever seen. Like something British royalty or a movie star would wear. "These four keys represent different frequency ranges."

"Wow." Kensei lifted his sunglasses. His eyes glittered at the sight of the gems. "These must be worth a fortune."

"The gems are for identification only. Their worth is negligible compared to the key's material."

"What material is that?" Jenny asked.

"We call it nexum. The process used to create it is a mystery. Which is frustrating, because most of Cabin's revenue comes from reverse-engineering alien technology. It's what made Lance LaGrange the world's first and only trillionaire. And yet, he'd trade it all to know how to recreate nexum."

As Jenny gazed at the four brilliant keys, she remembered Astrea handing a very similar one to Rygelus. At that moment, she wanted nothing more than to feel the weight of one in her hand again. To feel the slippery warmth of the strange metal against her skin.

Lin took the teapot and their empty cups away. "Jenny, since you have more experience with meditation, would you mind going first?"

"Sure, what do I have to do?" She rubbed her left arm, which still ached from the shot.

"Start by clearing your mind, and when you're ready, place both hands on the brass plate."

Jenny sniffed at her runny nose and closed her eyes. She inhaled the herbal scents of the teahouse and regulated her breathing. Outside, the wind rustled bamboo stalks, and dragonflies flitted above the burbling stream. She focused inward. Her heart beat steadily in her chest. A sense of calm spread through her body, and her muscles relaxed. She slowly opened her eyes and looked down at the open wooden box. Then she placed both hands on the cold, brass plate.

Lin lifted the first key. It had a ruby set into the shaft. "Tell me if you feel anything."

"Like what?"

"A vibration, or a tone that resonates inside your mind. I'll go through each of the keys, and you tell me which one feels the strongest."

"Okay."

As Lin inserted the key into the slot in the bronze plate between Jenny's hands, chaos exploded in her mind. The world moved in slow motion. Sounds lowered in pitch. It seemed like it took minutes for Lin to remove the key, and then the world returned to normal.

"Wow, that was weird."

"No comments until we've tried every key, okay?"

Jenny nodded. "Okay." With the next key, she felt the same chaos, but the world didn't slow down. Instead, Jenny experienced temperature to an extreme degree. She could sense the heat emanating from everyone's skin and the teapot cooling on the shelf.

As Lin swapped the second key for the third key, Jenny's head buzzed and something strange happened to her vision. Lin's fair Chinese skin had transformed to deep violet, with splotches of turquoise. A second later, Lin looked more normal, but all the colors became impossibly vivid. Her yellow overcoat beamed like a sun. Finally, Lin's face turned red, with glowing orange blotches around her eyes and lips. Lin removed the key, and Jenny's vision returned to normal.

With the fourth key, Jenny felt a rushing sensation, as if she were being pulled down by a river's current. She crouched down in her chair and expected everyone else to do the same. Instead, Lin and Kensei continued sitting calmly.

Lin pulled the final key free of the brass plate. "Did any of them stand out?"

"They all made my head buzz, but I wouldn't say any of them stood out. The first one slowed everything down. With the second, I could sense the temperature of things. The third one made my vision go crazy, and the last one made me feel like I was caught in a river."

"But none of them felt any stronger than the others?"

Jenny shook her head. "Does that mean that none of the keys are for me?"

"No," Lin said as she shook her head. "This has never happened before. I guess it means you can take any of the keys."

Any of the keys? Jenny thought about each reaction and tried to decide which one would be best for her.

"But before you choose," Lin said, "Let's have Kensei take the test first."

"Okay," Kensei said and closed his eyes. He breathed deeply for a minute then opened them. He put his hands on the brass plate and nodded. Lin inserted the first key.

"It's buzzing," Kensei said.

"That's good, but remember, no comments until we've tried them all."

Kensei nodded, and Lin inserted the next key. As Jenny watched the test, she felt that siren call from the laboratory. It pressed against her mind with a persistent humming sensation. Lin inserted the last key.

Kensei jumped and jerked his hands back as if shocked. "Whoa."

Lin grinned. "That's how it's supposed to work."

Kensei massaged his hands. "What was that?"

"We just found your key." Lin lifted the key—inset with an emerald—from the box. "You're the first one to pick the emerald key." She attached it to a silver chain necklace and handed it to Kensei. "Wear it at all times. You can use it to activate the Waypoints, but more importantly, it'll help attune your senses."

Kensei nodded as he took off his purple Lakers hat, revealing short, curly black hair. He slipped the chain over his head and put the hat back on.

"Congratulations," Jenny said to Kensei, trying to sound earnest.

"Kensei, let's see you hold your key," Lin said. He wrapped his long fingers around the silvery haft. Lin corrected his grip to be more subtle and to free the fork end. "Focus on it. Feel the energy of it, and try to match its vibration."

Kensei stared at the fork until his eyes crossed.

Jenny giggled at the sight.

Lin grinned. "It will take some getting used to." She turned to Jenny and tilted the box toward her. "Have you decided which one you want?"

Jenny considered the remaining keys. What she wanted was the connection that Kensei had with his key. Again, she felt the pull toward the laboratory. "Is there another key? I keep feeling something from the laboratory."

Lin raised an eyebrow. "Show me." She closed the Key Ceremony box and placed it back on the shelf.

As they left the teahouse, Lin ended the program, and the garden disappeared. They made their way down the hall, and through the double doors to the laboratory. The lab techs, Cora and Joseph, gave them puzzled looks as they entered the laboratory. Jenny allowed the siren call to pull her into the heart of the steel shelving. Handwritten paper labels marked archaeological treasures. Objects covered in sheets lined the back wall, including one that had the silhouette of a Risi.

Jenny jumped back against the shelving.

"What is it?" Lin asked.

"I saw a giant."

"Oh." Lin chuckled. "That's just a suit of armor. We have many Risi artifacts in our collection, including complete skeletons, weapons, and camp supplies."

"You stole them?"

"No, we discovered them, mostly in and around Fort Esperanza."

Jenny bit her lip. *I bet the Risi wouldn't be too happy if they knew Cabin held this collection.*

"Is that a Waypoint?" Kensei pointed at a large obsidian disc held upright with carbon-fiber straps. Although it was a little smaller than the one they arrived in, the shape and material were identical.

"No." Lin covered the smaller Waypoint up with a canvas sheet. "Well, kind of, yes." She cleared her throat. "Anyway, it doesn't work the same. It only connects to one other Waypoint."

"Which one?"

Lin turned to Jenny. "Did you find what you were looking for?"

"Oh." Jenny turned away from the covered Waypoint and searched the shelves for the source of the emanations. "It's right around here somewhere." She closed her eyes and recalled the meditative state from the teahouse. She stretched out with her senses and followed the siren's call. When she opened her eyes, she was looking at a shelf with a black touch-combination safe. "It's coming from inside here."

"You're sure?"

Jenny nodded.

Lin tapped a six-digit sequence into the twelve-numbered keypad. She pulled the door open and removed an antique wooden box. The siren's call grew to a scream as Lin opened the lid. Inside, an unadorned Waypoint key rested on a bed of purple velvet.

"This key wasn't made by Kett'l."

"May I?" Jenny asked.

Lin nodded.

Jenny lifted the tuning-fork-shaped key free of the box. Her mind and body buzzed like she was on a quadruple-shot espresso high. A tone played in her mind, and like with the VRGo puzzle, Jenny hummed along. Something clicked inside her mind. She shivered as a tingling sensation raced down her spine.

"That's the effect we were looking for." Lin smiled. "And you just solved a century-long historical debate."

"How?"

"You see, by the time Astrea Baillie discovered the Waypoint, it had been hidden for thousands of years. She had to dig through layers of sediment and organic deposits to locate the obsidian bowl. Then, Astrea had to clear the bowl to find the key. Historians have debated how she had discovered the first Waypoint key, and now I know the answer. It must have called to her, the way it did with you."

"This was Astrea's key?" Jenny spun the heavy, silvery object between her fingers. She thought about the key's journey from Astrea to Rygelus, Lin, and finally to her.

Lin nodded. "And now it is yours." She pulled a silver chain from the pocket of her yellow coat and fit it to the key.

"Congratulations." Kensei put a hand on Jenny's shoulder and squeezed.

"Thank you." Jenny smiled and looked into Kensei's face as Lin hung the key around her neck. A eurythmic song played in her head. For the first time in longer than she could remember, Jenny felt complete.

15

PENWALES

The *Strider*'s main drive shut down as they entered Earth's orbit and the ship flipped around to face the blue-green sphere. The view filled the cockpit. In spite of being tricked into this mission, Jack couldn't help feeling a sense of awe. *This is a beautiful planet.* Even though he was trapped with Hocco's killer, he felt like celebrating his first visit to a planet in several years.

Jack unfastened his harness and floated up from his seat. Using handholds in the cockpit, he pulled himself to the galley. Jack rifled through the cabinets until he found a bottle of amber liquid. He squeezed a shot into a small cup. The grooved interior was designed to contain the fluid even in zero gravity.

The door to Victus's cabin opened, and the man masquerading as Hocco floated into the galley. Jack suppressed his anger. He wasn't going to let this man spoil his mood. So, Jack filled another grooved shot glass and handed it to Victus.

"To a smooth mission." Jack held up his glass for a toast. Without waiting for Victus, he sucked the amber liquid out of the grooves and savored its sweetness and warmth. It tasted smoky and slightly fruity. When he swallowed, it burned a trail of heat down his throat. He sucked air through his teeth and tossed the glass toward the sink net.

"I'm ready to go planetside, and while I'm down there, I'm going to pick up some supplies for the ship." *And maybe a little something for me*, Jack thought.

"Do not get sidetracked." Victus tossed his empty glass toward the sink. It clinked into Jack's before getting caught in the net.

"Don't worry." Jack pushed off a cabinet and floated toward his cabin. "Getting home is my number one priority."

After packing a duffel bag, Jack climbed down to the cargo bay. He grabbed his leather jacket from the locker and made his way through the airlock to his spaceplane. Jack had named the plane *Pepper*, after his ex-wife. As a wedding gift, he had commissioned an artist to paint her likeness—ice-blue skin and red hair—onto the side of the plane's tail. Even though they were now divorced, Jack couldn't bring himself to change the name or remove the painting.

Jack entered the plane and secured the door behind him. Out of habit, he kissed two fingers and touched the ceiling. He passed through the small cargo area—lined with eight vac suits—and strapped his duffel into an empty seat. Jack strapped himself into the pilot's seat and ran through the preflight routine.

Jack activated the communicator and said, "Ready for release."

"You are all clear," Victus said. "One thing, though..."

"What's that?"

"I cannot reach Mister Torres."

"Is that a deal-breaker?"

"No, he may not be free to talk, for security reasons."

"Or he learned that you're an evil body-snatching warlord."

"Amusing," Victus replied with no trace of amusement in his tone.

"Oh, sorry, I thought I had the comm turned off," Jack lied.

"In case he cannot meet you, he will send his colleague Aindriu Ward. They both know the situation and will lead you to the Selkans' location. This remains our best option."

"As much as I hate saying it, I agree with you."

The docking clamps retracted, and the spaceplane drifted away from the *Strider*. Jack turned the nose of the *Pepper* toward Earth's southern hemisphere. Then he hit the thrusters and dropped toward Acacia City Airfield. The airfield catered to clientele who owned private planes and spaceplanes like the *Pepper*, while the Acacia City Spaceport, or ACX, was primarily for commercial flights and arrival and departure of cargo.

As the *Pepper* drifted out of the exosphere, it started shaking from turbulence and roasting from air friction. Jack's knuckles turned white as he gripped the control sticks. *I hate this part.* It had been years since he'd been in atmosphere. He was afraid to blink as he passed through a cloud. By the time land came into view his armpits were a sweaty mess.

Jack notified the airfield's tower of his approach and received arrival instructions. The *Pepper* was capable of vertical takeoff and landing, so he was directed to a helipad. As he neared the city's limits, Jack reduced power and used the airfield's artificial lights to guide him toward the pad.

After landing, he taxied to the apron and searched for his parking spot. Airplanes and spacecraft of all shapes and sizes parked beneath massive, mushroom-shaped canopies. Jack found the seventeenth concrete mushroom and parked the *Pepper* at spot D. It was the farthest zone from the fixed-base operator, he noted. A yellow-and-white electric vehicle was parked near the supply station. With its three rows of seats, and a large covered cargo area, it had to be a transport vehicle.

After shutting off the *Pepper*'s engines, Jack set his watch for the local time and grabbed his bag. Victus had provided him a generous amount of local currency from an untraceable account. Even after the airport's hefty fees, he would have enough left over to buy some local goods. He opened a secret compartment in the floor and withdrew his A-159X handgun, a weapon that enthusiasts lovingly dubbed "the ax." Named for its ability to fell a tree with a single shot. It was a strange boast, but the only trees Jack knew of were the stunted kind that grew in Lan Station's small parks.

Jack shrugged off his jacket and slung the gun's holster over his shoulder. He connected the strap across his chest and adjusted the fit until the gun's handle rested under his left armpit. Jack drew the gun in a blur, a move he'd practiced at least a thousand times. Satisfied, Jack pulled his leather jacket on and walked down the ramp. Finding fuel and water supplies, he refreshed the *Pepper*'s reserves.

Jack checked his watch. There wasn't much time before his meeting. *I might still have time to shop.* By the time the *Pepper*'s tanks were full, the sun had set, and fireworks boomed over the nearby bay.

Jack walked over to the yellow-and-white electric vehicle and hopped into the driver's seat. He found the power switch and flipped it on. The car purred with electrical energy, and a single wiper cleared a path through a spattering of rain that peppered the windshield.

Jack checked the map on his data tablet and drove toward Acacia City's historic downtown district. He found that people assumed you knew what you were doing when you acted with confidence, and he was right, nobody tried to stop him as he exited the airfield.

As he neared downtown, a group of drunken tourists stepped out into the street. Jack beeped the little car's horn. A man made a finger gesture that Jack made a note of. Jack slowed his pace and searched the shop fronts. He saw art galleries, museums, jewelers, bakeries, patisseries, and ice cream shops, but not what he was looking for. The street ended at a row of yellow pylons that prevented vehicles from entering the Waypoint Plaza.

Jack backed the little yellow car between two other vehicles and parked. Nearby, a crowd gathered outside a window display. It was a women's clothing boutique, and two female models were displaying dresses in a soundless miming act.

Finally, Jack spotted a picture of a steaming coffee cup on a hanging sign above a door down the street. Painted onto the large picture window in perfect calligraphy was "Penwales Coffee Roasters." Jack entered the shop, and the heavenly aroma of roasted coffee almost knocked him over. Incredible coffee-making apparatuses lined the shelves. There were chemistry-like glass drip systems, and nitrous-oxide taps, and other brewing systems. Next to these were bags of beans in light, medium, and dark roasts from countries all over the Earth. Freshly roasted beans were like gold on a space station, so he grabbed an armful.

Jack felt a childlike excitement as he stood in line. Several people, mostly human, waited to order their beverages. In front of him, an Avian cradled a bag of decaf in his feathered arms. Jack took his time studying the vast menu.

"What will it be?" The cashier, a teenager with the sides of his head shaved, looked at him with glazed eyes.

Jack dropped the bags on the counter. He felt overwhelmed with options and grew more anxious at the sight of a dozen impatient faces behind him. He ordered the only thing he recognized on the menu, a pour-over.

As he waited for his order, Jack thought about the mission. So far, he had seen several aliens: Taalo, Avian, and even a hulking Snibb. Nothing that looked like a Selkan.

A female barista called his name and handed Jack his pour-over. He wrapped his hands around the tall white paper cup and sighed in ecstasy at the aroma. When Jack said thank you for his coffee, it was genuine. He was truly grateful for the barista's expert work in addition to this opportunity to indulge in a luxury few could experience where he was from.

Jack took a long, slow sip. He waited for the bitterness and acidity he usually experienced. Instead, he tasted fruit, nuts, vanilla, and a bit of smoke. "Now, that's coffee!" he shouted.

Everyone in the shop turned to stare at him, but Jack didn't care. He couldn't remember having had a better cup of coffee in his life. He walked out with a bag full of coffee beans, and breathed in the heady scent of Earth air. *What if I just stay here?* He thought, *I could hide here, drink good coffee, and never have to worry about my debts again.* Then, he thought about Victus. The Æon would never allow Jack that freedom. So, with a heavy sigh, Jack walked toward the Waypoint Plaza. He skirted a group of characters wearing papier-mâché heads and bird masks and made his way toward the center of the plaza. He passed landscaped trees and shrubs as he approached a stone gazebo. With minutes to spare, he sat on a park bench and sipped his coffee.

"Hey!" a muscular young man with a terrible neck scar shouted. "Are you Jack Spriggan?"

16

WAYPOINT INSTRUCTION

Outside the Department of Transportation, Jenny rubbed her hands together and hugged herself against the cold. Silky clouds formed a canopy that reflected the reds, blues, and greens of the fireworks. Yellow light spilled from storefronts and reflected off the rain-soaked cobblestone streets. The paraders had abandoned the plaza, but a few brave musicians remained to serenade the tourists.

Lin led Jenny and Kensei down the landscaped path to the Waypoint gazebo. She pointed up at a majestic stone cathedral lit from below by powerful lights. It was the second-tallest building in the plaza, next to the Department of Transportation. The cathedral's towers pointed up to heaven, and a huge dome stood eight stories tall. "Waypoint travel paid for that and most of this plaza." Lin looked at Jenny. "The same Church that condemned the Roma and drove—"

Jenny shook her head. She didn't want Lin to tell Kensei that she was Roma, because she didn't want to be teased for being a Gypsy.

"—Astrea and her people away," Lin finished.

Did he suspect? Jenny glanced at Kensei. *No, how could he?* Her black hair was short and spiked with a red streak on one side, and she kept out of the sun so that her brown skin was paler than other Roma.

Lin cleared her throat and continued. "After finding the first key,

Astrea soon discovered the other seven original keys. Her people rapidly grew wealthy from their magical transportation devices. This got the attention of the Catholic Church, which held authority in Europe at the time. They claimed that the Waypoints were a gift from God and the rightful property of the Church. Astrea's clan were Roma, and in Spain, they lacked even the most basic human rights. The Church mobilized a task force, and over the course of three days, those seven keys were stolen, and the bearers were found dead.

"The Catholic Church was now free to increase tolls to build more forts, missions, and cathedrals. Meanwhile, Astrea's clan went into hiding from the Church, until one day they heard of a fort that had been abandoned by the church. Astrea's clan saw this fort as their salvation. They fled from Spain and took refuge in the abandoned fort. Of course, that's all in the past. Today, Cabin owns the Waypoints."

"Why would Cabin want them?" Jenny asked.

"For use in off-world travel."

"Wow." Kensei looked up to the sky. "That would be incredible. Imagine, visiting the moon, or Mars, or even Titan in an instant."

Jenny wondered how he could see anything behind those sunglasses at night.

"That's the idea." Lin nodded. "With the Waypoints, we could support off-world colonies, or transport people and goods to and from a spaceship."

The two Songbirds, Pat and John, nodded to them as they neared the gazebo. Nearby, Aindriu stood alongside a solidly built man in his thirties. The man saw them approach first and turned to face them. The man had shaggy brown hair and a clean-shaven face. His leather jacket was well worn, as were the rest of his clothes. He clutched a shopping bag from Penwales Coffee Roasters in a big fist.

"Hello, Aindriu," Lin said. "Is this Jack Spriggan?"

"It is." Aindriu turned to face Lin. "Yeah, it is. Jack, this is Lin Yuan Song, Jenny Tripper, and..." Aindriu gulped as he looked at Kensei, causing his Adam's apple to warp the thick scar encircling his neck. "Umm."

"Kensei Drake," Jenny spoke up for Kensei.

"Nice to meet you," Jenny said as she held out her hand. Jack had stubby fingernails with dry and cracked cuticles, she noticed.

"Welcome to Cabin, Jack," Lin said. "It will be good to have another pilot around." She looked at Aindriu. "Any sign of Trey or Sadi?"

"No." Aindriu's blond eyebrows lifted over his gray eyes. "No one's come through since Sadi left."

"Well, I'm about to show Jenny and Kensei how to use their new keys..."

"By all means." Aindriu stepped aside to let them up the gazebo steps.

Lin climbed into the Waypoint and signaled for Jenny and Kensei to follow. Jenny and Kensei scrambled down the bowl. The tree-like gazebo canopy provided some shelter from the rain, but heavy drops still formed on the lower branches before falling onto their heads.

"When you first insert your key"—Lin freed her shiny key and knelt down in the base of the obsidian bowl—"it is set to this Waypoint." She pushed the fork end of her key into a hole at the base of the Waypoint, and one of the sixteen number-like symbols lit up with blue light. "As you turn your key clockwise, the other locations will light up." She rotated the key inside the hole, and the other symbols lit up. "There are sixteen total, including this one. Eight in this world, and eight in the Nimue Realm."

"Where do they all lead?" As Kensei dug a sketchbook and pencil out of his backpack, Leon ran up his arm to perch on his shoulder.

"Let's see...there's Spain, Argentina, China," Lin counted each Waypoint off on her fingers. "South Africa, California, Greenland, and Antarctica." She put her hands down. "Now if you're ready, please take out your keys."

Jenny gripped the silver chain and pulled her newly found Waypoint key out of her uniform shirt.

Kensei finished writing in his sketchbook, then pulled his own key out by the chain. The movement caused Leon to jump from his shoulder onto his purple Lakers hat. "Get back in there." Kensei grabbed Leon and put him and his sketchbook into his backpack. He zipped it up and focused on Lin.

"Now this is important, so listen up," Lin warned. "Before activating a

Waypoint, make sure that everyone who is traveling is completely inside the gazebo."

"Why's that?" Kensei asked.

"Because you don't want to transport half a person."

Jenny shuddered as she recalled seeing the Risi losing an arm to Astrea's portal, and then getting cut in half.

"When you're ready to activate the Waypoint, just push down. Your key will lock in place until the Waypoint cycles. Afterward, you can remove your key." Lin lifted her key free of the slot and jumped to her feet with surprising agility. "Now, who wants to give it a try?"

Kensei looked down at his feet.

"Me," Jenny said, raising her hand.

"Okay Jenny, just do what I did."

Jenny knelt down as Lin had done, but before she could insert her key, water bubbled up from the keyhole. She knitted her eyebrows together and looked up at Lin. "What's happening?"

"Someone's coming through. Quick, get out of there," Lin said as she pulled Jenny and Kensei out of the gazebo.

"What's the water for?" Kensei asked.

"It's a safeguard. Whenever someone activates a Waypoint, water bubbles up at the destination to warn people to get clear."

"It's probably Sadi." Aindriu pushed them aside to get a look.

The air above the Waypoint took on a shimmering, spherical shape, like a soap bubble. There was a bright flash of light, and four enormous figures filled the gazebo. Each stood around three meters tall and their heads almost reached the canopy. Their giant heads rotated inside steel helmets as they examined their surroundings. The Risi had changed little in six hundred years. Their armor looked more protective, their weapons were more deadly. They looked so out of place in this modern city that Jenny's brain struggled to accept this reality. She shook her head and pinched her arm. It wasn't a dream. Then, she noticed a human-sized figure in a black cloak crouched between their thick, elephantine legs. A large hood hid his face in shadow.

Jon and Pat, the two Songbirds, were the first to react. They ran up the gazebo steps with their halberds.

"Keep them in the bowl!" Pat shouted as he thrust his polearm at the nearest giant. The long spike found its way through the Risi's leather armor and sank into his gut. The enraged giant swung his massive club at Pat. The old man caught the attack on the shaft of his halberd. The polearm bent at the point of impact but didn't break. Instead, the spike ripped through the giant's gut in a spray of viscera. The Risi roared and clutched at his eviscerated abdomen. Dark blood pumped between his thick fingers and poured into the obsidian bowl.

Pat lost his grip on the halberd. Exploding fireworks echoed off the buildings as Jenny watched the polearm clatter down the steps until it rested at the base of the gazebo. She turned her attention back on the battle in time to see another giant shove his wounded comrade aside. He swung an ax the size of a stop sign at Pat, but the Songbird's armor deflected the weapon downward where it struck the stone gazebo in a spray of sparks. A studded club smashed into one of the gazebo's columns. Chunks of granite sprayed outward. Jenny turned away, and rocks struck the back of her head. Pat was knocked out of the gazebo.

Jack rushed to Jenny's side and pulled a futuristic-looking gun from his jacket. A thunderous boom rocked the plaza, and a fist-size hole opened up in a Risi's chest. His blasted armor peppered the other Risi with molten shrapnel. The giant dropped with a splash into the obsidian bowl.

Only a few seconds had passed since the Risi arrived, and already two of the four were dead. Feeling confident, Jenny looked down at Pat's halberd. *I should do something,* she thought. *I've seen how to fight these things in Astrea's vision. I could help.* Jenny ran down the steps and picked up the fallen polearm. The shaft was a composite material as light and flexible as wood but as strong as steel.

"What are you doing?" Kensei asked. "We should get out of here."

Jenny knew that it was foolish to stay, but she couldn't run. "Help me." Jenny held the halberd midshaft, keeping the tip low.

"I've never killed anything," Kensei said.

"Neither have I. Nothing bigger than a spider." The rumbling voices of the Risi prickled the back of her neck, and she turned around. The angry yellow eyes of a giant met hers. Jenny lifted the halberd's head, with its long spike, toward the Risi. The giant charged. His footfalls shook the cobblestone path, and the halberd trembled in Jenny's hands.

Suddenly, the massive polearm slipped from her rain-numbed fingers. She dropped to her knees and picked it up. "Hold it steady!" she shouted at Kensei.

Kensei grabbed the end of the halberd. "How?"

The Risi's metal armor clanged loudly in Jenny's ears.

"Brace it against the stone."

Kensei jammed the polearm into a joint in the cobbled path and put a foot on it. Jenny lifted the tip of the halberd toward the giant. Her heart thundered in her chest.

The Risi raised his enormous ax, which could easily cut Jenny and Kensei in half with one stroke. However, the giant slipped on the wet stone pathway. His eyes bulged with shock. The momentum carried him forward. The halberd's spike punched through the giant's neck and hit the roof of his skull. The Risi gurgled and gasped. Hot blood flowed down the polearm's shaft and warmed Jenny's cold hands. Then, the weight of the giant's body yanked the halberd from her grip.

Jenny looked down at her blood-soaked hands and was overcome with nausea. She scrambled away from the grisly scene and vomited into a trash can. Jenny felt a hand on her back. She spun around and saw Lin. She was talking, but Jenny couldn't understand what she was saying. Her mind was too numb. Slowly, it came into focus. She looked over at the gazebo just in time to see it flash a brilliant white. The man in the black hood had disappeared, along with the remains of the fallen giants.

"What was that?" Jack looked around for additional threats. With the hostiles dead or vanished, he opened his jacket to holster his gun.

"You should keep that out," Aindriu said.

"You think there will be more?" Kensei asked.

"Positive."

"Look." Jenny pointed at the gazebo. A giant soap bubble formed, and with a bright flash of light, four large, dark figures materialized around a smaller hooded and cloaked figure.

One of these new giants stood a head taller than the others. His mane of bright-orange hair brushed the roof the gazebo four meters above the base of the Waypoint. He wore a leather skirt over skin the color of asphalt. Two knives the size of long swords hung from a belt at his waist. Long, slender fingers with black fingernails gripped an enormous sword with a wavy blade.

"I got him." Jack leveled his gun at the gazebo. A thunderclap sounded, and the air ignited, leaving a trace of the hypersonic projectile. The orange-haired giant stumbled backward. But, instead of creating a hole in his chest, the bullet left only a minor smoking flesh wound. Jack fired twice more. Each shot hit, forming visible divots in the giant's bare chest, and the Risi stumbled out of the gazebo. "Finally." Jack sounded relieved.

The two Songbirds recovered their halberds and rushed at the remaining three giants. These Risi were lightly armored in leather. They dodged and performed counterattacks with long knives that put the Songbirds on the defensive. One giant jump-kicked Pat, knocking him down the gazebo steps. The other smashed John with a gauntleted hand, sending him headfirst into a stone column. With a loud whoop, two of the Risi fled from the gazebo toward the Department of Transportation.

To Jenny's surprise, Aindriu had engaged the third Risi barehanded. He even managed to disarm the giant. With a twist of his wrist and a quick kick, Aindriu dropped the Risi and broke his knee. The giant roared in pain. Aindriu calmly flipped the fallen knife to his hand with his foot and slit the Risi's throat. Aindriu jumped backward just as the Waypoint flashed a bright white, and the cloaked figure disappeared.

In the distance, people screamed as the other two giants reached the outer plaza. Then, a deep rumbling sound erupted from the opposite side of the gazebo. "I am Blunderbore!" The lithe, dark giant with the orange mane of hair rose to his feet. His yellow eyes shone like the moon. "No weapon can harm me." He snorted out of his wide, flat nostrils and walked around the gazebo.

Jack found a clear shot between the columns and fired at Blunderbore. The round exploded with a thunderclap. Blunderbore's shoulder jerked backward, but he continued his slow walk around the gazebo. "You are a nuisance." Then he charged, knocking Jack to the ground with a grunt. Instead of finishing him off, Blunderbore doubled over in a coughing fit. Blood spilled from his mouth onto the rain-soaked stone.

"Let's get out of here," Aindriu said and pushed Jenny and Kensei down the sidewalk.

Jenny and the others ran north, toward the Department of Transportation. They found a hiding spot behind a cluster of shrubs and watched for Blunderbore. To Jenny's surprise, tourists still walked the streets as if nothing had happened. She looked up and thought, *I guess they believe the gunshots were just fireworks.* The fireworks, which had reached a pitch, suddenly ceased, casting a strange silence over the plaza.

A man's voice spoke from Jack's belt. "Jack, you discharged your firearm. What is going on down there?"

"Shut it off," everyone said in unison.

Jack fumbled with the controls and switched his communicator off.

Jenny looked toward the Waypoint and saw Blunderbore leading a new group of four giants north. She and the others crouched down behind a bush.

"What are Risi doing in Acacia City?" Aindriu asked.

"I don't know," Lin said. "And we're not going to stay and find out. It's my job to get our new recruits safely to HQ." She turned to Jack. "Is your plane nearby?"

"Yup," Jack said. "It's at the airfield."

"Can you take us there?"

"Yes, I have a car parked that way." Jack pointed southwest.

"What about Sadi?" Aindriu asked.

Lin shook her head. "She's on her own."

Suddenly, gunfire sounded from the Department of Transportation. Several security guards were firing at the two Risi who had escaped the Waypoint. Behind them, the Waypoint flashed again, signaling the arrival of more Risi. Blunderbore led his giants to the entrance of the DOT building. A press of aliens and humans jammed the exits as they struggled to flee through the revolving door. The dark giant yanked people out, like he was unclogging a drain, and tossed them down the steps.

Jenny winced as a man flew through the air and rolled down the steps to the street. She made eye contact with the mother of a family of blue aliens trapped inside the building. Jenny grabbed Jack's arm and pointed at the aliens. "You need to help them."

Jack lifted his gun. "You saw what this did to him."

"Or didn't do," Kensei said.

"You don't have to kill him," Jenny said. "Just try to distract him long enough for those people to get out."

Jack sighed and rolled his head, popping the joints in his neck. Then he took aim above the crowd. Two shots slammed into Blunderbore's back, causing the giant to stumble forward. One more hit him in the head. Blunderbore turned and located his attacker. He gritted his black teeth and roared before charging at them.

Grinning, Jack looked back and saw that the rest of the group was already running away. "Shit," he said. He clutched the bags of Penwales coffee to his chest and chased after them.

Jenny and the others splashed through rain-soaked streets. Frightened tourists fled and screamed at the sight of Blunderbore at their backs. Dozens of tourists clogged the row of yellow barriers that separated the pedestrian plaza from car traffic.

Jack slowed to a stop with the others, who all pointed behind him. He turned just as Blunderbore swung his colossal sword. Jack jumped backward and raised his coffee like a shield. The wavy blade sliced through the canvas bag, sending a spray of coffee beans out in an arc.

"Now you did it." Jack snarled as he aimed his gun at Blunderbore's belly and pulled the trigger. Thunderclaps sounded, and the giant jerked back with each shot. The gun clicked empty on the seventh round, and Blunderbore fell to the cobblestone road with a thud. His skin was unbroken.

"Damn." Jack knelt down to gather his spilled beans. "My coffee."

"It's not worth it, Jack." Lin grabbed his arm.

Jack sighed allowed Lin to pull him away from the spilled beans. "The car is this way." He led them to a small yellow and white electric cart with "Acacia City Airfield" printed on the side. It had room for six passengers and a trunk with ample room for luggage. It was parked illegally between two cars.

"Where did you get this car?" Lin asked.

"I borrowed it from the airport." Jack pulled a parking ticket off the windshield and threw what remained of his bag into the back seat.

Everyone found a seat in the small car, except for Aindriu.

"Aindriu, get inside. What are you doing?" Lin asked.

"I'm going back for Sadi." Aindriu turned and ran toward the plaza before anyone could say a word.

"Will he be alright?" Jenny asked.

"Don't worry," Lin said. "He can take care of himself."

"Tough kid," Jack said.

Behind them, the crowd grew excited. Jenny turned in time to see Blunderbore stand up and look around. "*Go, go, go!*" She shouted as Blunderbore charged toward them.

Jack hit the accelerator, and the car's wheels spun on the wet road. He aimed for the sidewalk, forcing people out of his way.

The giant was close behind them.

Jack cut over to the street and sped downhill. The sounds of screams faded as they drove farther away from the terrifying creature. The overcast sky hid the moonlight, creating profound darkness that the little car's headlights fought to pierce. After a few minutes, the giant was out of sight, and they were safe.

"What were those things that attacked us?" Jack asked.

"Risi," Lin said. "Creatures from a parallel world."

"What were they doing here?"

"I don't know," Lin replied. "The Risi haven't attacked humans for over a hundred years, and they've never crossed over to our world before."

17

FLIGHT OF THE PEPPER

The charm of Acacia City faded as they drove away from the plaza. People and buildings looked dull. Advertisements flashed across billboards. Tagged Dumpsters stood out like mile markers. Jenny's body shook from residual fear and adrenaline withdrawal as the Risi attack replayed unbidden in her mind. She still remembered how it had felt when her halberd had pierced the giant's head, how the hot blood had coated her hands. She did her best to wipe it off, but some still remained, dried under her fingernails.

After a few minutes of driving, they reached the Acacia City Airfield. Jack turned the electric car into the main entrance. They passed enormous mushroom-shaped structures that illuminated rows of aircraft, some as small as delivery trucks and others the size of luxury yachts. Stubby concrete lights illuminated the boundaries of the parking zones. They stopped in front of 17D.

Jack carefully lifted the eviscerated coffee shop bag and fingered the cut like a surgeon inspecting a wound. He retrieved the one remaining bag of coffee beans.

"I'm sorry for your loss." Lin touched Jack's shoulder. "But we survived, and you can always get more coffee."

Jack sniffed and nodded. "C'mon. My plane's this way."

Jenny followed Jack to a silver plane with blue and orange highlights. A gaudy painting of a pinup girl with blue skin and red hair adorned the side. The name "Pepper" was written underneath.

Jack unlocked the anterior ramp, and hydraulics lowered it to ground level. One by one, they climbed the slope to the plane's gray interior. It smelled of industrial grease. Blue and orange paint marked various controls and compartments. Eight pressure suits lined the antechamber walls.

Jenny found a seat in the passenger cabin and slid her burstepi underneath. After securing the seat harness, she struggled to find a comfortable position for her aching body. Kensei sat down across from her. After settling into place, he pulled out his sketchbook and set it on his lap. Leon scurried out and perched on his shoulder. Lin sat next to Jack in the copilot's seat.

After some discussion over the radio, they taxied to the runway. The plane's engines roared, pressing Jenny into the molded seat as they picked up speed and lifted off. Once in the air, they made a wide turn and headed east over the Pacific Ocean.

As they were turning, Jenny looked out the plane's window and found Acacia City's historic district and the Waypoint plaza. Vehicles with flashing blue and red lights barricaded streets. A Vertical Takeoff And Landing airplane landed in front of the Department of Transportation and parked in the street. The plane was too far away for Jenny to see anything but its lights. As the plane finished its turn, they rose above a bank of clouds as they headed out to sea.

Jenny looked through her reflection and studied the topography of the distant clouds lit by moonlight. It was her first view of the moon and stars since she'd left home. This was also the first time she had ever been on a plane. Her mom had always planned to take her on a trip after high school. She still remembered the look of joy in Ruby's eyes as they talked about possible destinations. They never did decide on one.

"It'll be about two and a half hours before we touch down," Lin said over the intercom. "Try to get some rest if you can."

I am feeling a bit tired, Jenny thought. *I'll just rest my eyes for a bit.*

~

Jenny dreamed that she was Astrea. She was back in the fort defending herself from monstrous Risi. This time, Blunderbore was there. She faced the monster with the Riftkey and cut him in half.

When she awoke, she found that Lin had left the cockpit and was fast asleep in the seat in front of Kensei.

"You awake?" Kensei whispered. His sketchbook still rested on his lap.

"Yeah." Jenny wiped the wetness from the corner of her mouth with her sleeve. She shifted in her seat and found that someone had put a thin gray blanket over her.

"Can you believe what happened back at the Waypoint?" Kensei scratched the sleeping Leon behind the ears with a pencil.

"No, it feels like a dream."

"Those were actual giants."

"Yeah, I know." Jenny folded the blanket and laid it on her lap.

"And we saw aliens."

"I know." She leaned over and pinched Kensei.

"Ow." He rubbed his arm. "What was that?"

"I wanted to make sure this wasn't a dream."

"You're supposed to pinch yourself."

"I know." Jenny smiled. "Who do you think the cloaked person with the giants was?"

Kensei shrugged. "It had to be someone with a key."

"Yeah, and someone who can control the giants."

"And a reason to send them to the Department of Transportation."

"Remember all the stuff in the basement, and all the Risi artifacts? Maybe the giants knew about it."

"Maybe."

Jenny gasped. "You don't think it was Sadi, do you?"

"What? Why would she do it?"

"Who else could it be? With her power to bring up memories of pain, she could have forced the Risi to do whatever she wanted."

"Are you sure you're not just upset because she attacked you?"

Jenny rubbed her cheek. "No! Don't you think it's strange that she went through the Waypoint right before the attack?"

"It could be a coincidence, and according to you, her boyfriend just got killed by them."

"A tragic accident, but one that didn't ruin her plans."

"What plans?"

"To steal valuable artifacts from the basement and sell them on the black market."

"I don't know, it's a bit of a stretch, don't you think?"

"No," Jenny said.

"Just promise you won't tell anyone else until you have proof."

"Okay, but when I do, I'm telling Lin."

"Fine." Kensei pulled a dark-gray tablet from his backpack. "While you were sleeping, I was researching the Waypoints and I learned that they were all located at antipodes."

"Antipodes?"

"Two locations on opposite sides of the planet from each other. Where are you from?"

"Wellington. It's the capital of New Zealand," Jenny said in a rehearsed manner.

Kensei tapped and slid his finger across the tablet's dark surface. "Okay...your antipode is in Spain." He showed Jenny the tablet. It displayed two square maps side by side, Spain and New Zealand.

That's where the wedding was, Jenny thought. Jenny considered telling Kensei about it, but decided that she didn't want to bring up a memory she still found painful. "Wait, there's a Waypoint in Acacia City and Lin said that it's where Sydney, Australia, would be. Why would there be two waypoints so close together?"

"There aren't. A hundred years after the New Zealand waypoint was discovered, they moved it to Australia, or New Spain as they call it here."

Jenny studied Kensei's face from the side. His eyes looked Asian, probably Japanese, based on his name. But his skin was dark, like an Australian Aboriginal's or an African's. Jenny found his features interesting, but as a skinny, nerdy kid with bad eyesight, he'd likely been teased growing up. She knew what it was like to be teased for being different. "I didn't know you could move them."

"Remember what Lin said? Cabin wants to use them off world, and there was one in that laboratory under the Department of Transportation."

"Oh, yeah."

"But wherever they are, we, as Æons, seem to be attracted to them and their antipodal locations."

"What do you mean?"

Kensei tilted the tablet for Jenny to see. "Look, I'm from Los Angeles, which has an antipode in the Indian Ocean. However, I've been in China for the school year, which has an antipode in Argentina." Kensei dragged the maps until its crosshairs aligned over China and displayed its antipode in Argentina. I believe there are Waypoints on our Earth, and they're all at their original locations."

"Huh, that's weird. I was looking into an exchange program in Argentina. What were you doing in China?"

"Trying to get into a space program."

"You want to become an astronaut?"

"It's my dream."

"Why not NASA?"

"Because China seemed more interesting, and they seem to have a surplus of money to throw at it." Kensei took off his glasses and rubbed his eyes.

"Can I see that?" Jenny pointed at the sketchbook on Kensei's lap.

"Um, sure, but it's not very good." Kensei handed her the pad. "Just some doodles."

Jenny set the sketchbook on her lap and opened it from the middle. Inside were cute cartoon sketches of Leon in a unique drawing style she found charming. The next page displayed a shark in a Hula-Hoop. She turned the page and saw a cat wearing a wide blue tie over a short-sleeved, button-up shirt. It waved one clawed paw as if it were on the way to work. The cat's misshapen head sat atop a too-long neck. Its eyes were an infinity symbol with pupils that pointed in odd directions. Its long whiskers sprouted from full cheeks, and snaggly teeth poked out of a crooked mouth. She snickered at the absurdity of it.

"What?" Kensei asked.

"It's a cat dressed like an...insurance salesman."

"Oh, that's Business Cat."

Jenny giggled. "It's hilarious." Something inside her released, and she couldn't stop laughing. "That ridiculous smile, piggy nose, and cleft chin."

Soon Kensei was laughing along with her. "You really like it?"

"Absolutely." Jenny wiped a tear from her eye. "It's wonderful."

"I'd like to turn it into a webcomic someday." Kensei shrugged and looked down at his hands. "Or something."

"You should," Jenny said.

Lin, who had been sleeping in the seat in front of Kensei, now stirred and sat up. "What are you two laughing at?"

"Nothing." Kensei stuffed the sketchbook back into his bag.

Lin shook her head. "Since you're both awake, we should talk about the mission."

"Okay," Kensei and Jenny said.

"In outer space, Between Mars and Jupiter, there is an artifact called a Terminal. It connects the solar system to other stellar systems in the galaxy."

Jenny noticed Jack turned his head ever so slightly to listen.

"Sort of like Waypoints in space?" Kensei asked.

"Yes, sort of, but currently, our Terminal is locked."

Jenny squinted. "Then how are there aliens on the planet?"

"The Terminal can still receive visitors, but we can't send any out. It's only locked on our end."

"So, once an alien arrives, there's no way they can go back." Jenny thought about her own trip through the VRGo puzzle. "Why would anyone come here, then?"

"The same reason anyone leaves their home. Some want to escape corruption and prejudice; some want a better life for their families."

"With so many aliens coming here, won't Earth become overpopulated?" Kensei asked.

"Earth is a big place," Lin said. "Our environment, energy, and biotechnology are far beyond that of the Earth in the Astrea Realm. We don't have the same resource issues you have."

"So why are we here? If this Earth is so great, it sounds like Selkans are better off here."

"For a time, yes. But eventually, their captors will send someone here to find them, and kill them to preserve their secret."

"What secret?" Jenny asked.

"That Tyr uses Selkans for a strategic advantage on the battlefield."

"What advantage?" Kensei asked.

"It allows them to teleport through space, at a terrible price to the Selkans. The process destroys their minds, and drains their life."

"That's terrible," Jenny said.

"Yes, and that is why we must reveal their secret to the galaxy."

"Okay," Kensei said. "Then why don't you just send a message?"

"Any message we send would take thousands of years to reach the nearest system. The only way to inform the other systems is to unlock the Terminal and send a ship to another system."

"And hopefully," Kensei said, "once the citizens of the galaxy know the truth, they will rise in support of Selkans."

"That's the idea," Lin said.

"So, how do we unlock the Terminal?" Jenny asked.

"With a Riftkey."

Jenny gasped and touched the burstepi with her foot, just to make sure it was still there.

"What's a Riftkey?" Kensei asked.

"It is a tool that only an Æon can use. With it, they can unlock a Terminal by aligning the energy fields inside. These Æons are called Terminal masters and have great prestige and power in the Galaxy."

"So, who gets to unlock the Terminal?" Kensei asked as he looked at Jenny.

"We have invited both of you here to take part in a contest to decide just that. But time is of the essence. If the Selkans' captors knew of our plan, they would send an Æon to take the Riftkey for themselves. Then they would unlock the Terminal and gain control of our solar system. Above all, we cannot let that happen."

"Buckle up back there!" Jack called out.

"We'll discuss this in more detail later." Lin stood and resumed her spot in the copilot's seat.

As they descended, the plane bounced through a bit of turbulence. Electric lights came into view as they dropped out of the clouds, forming the distinctive shape of an island against the dark ocean. They flew toward the western shore, where dozens of tiny islands surrounded a four-lobed cement platform.

Jenny's knuckles turned white as she gripped the arms of the seat. As the plane touched down with a jolt she let out a long breath. The back ramp opened with a hiss, and the scent of the sea drifted into the cabin. Though the air was warm, fear and doubt crept into Jenny's heart like a fog and froze her in place.

Lin put a hand on her shoulder. "Are you ready?"

"Yeah, I think so." Jenny took a deep breath to calm herself, then unfastened her belt and walked out of the plane.

Overhead, the Milky Way stretched across the sky over the cement platform. A white windsock flapped, indicating the direction of the wind. To her left, a group of seagulls called to one another. The plane's engines clicked and popped as they cooled. Jenny walked up to the edge of the landing platform and watched the waves crash rhythmically against its concrete side, lifting it up and down with the undulating ocean.

"What are you looking at?" Jack walked up behind her. He had to shout to be heard over the cooling fans. He looked down and jumped backward. "Whoa!"

"You okay?" Lin asked.

"Yeah, I'm fine." He took a few calming breaths to relax. "You got fuel here?"

"Uh, yeah." Lin led Jack over to a steel plate in the deck. She lifted it up to reveal a panel with various hoses for fuel, water, and air.

Jack took the fuel hose and plugged it into his plane.

Lin joined Jenny at the edge of the platform. She pointed at a group of tiny islands. "That's where the Selkans live."

"They look like green stepping-stones," Jenny said.

"They built all those islands from mud dredged from the seafloor."

"That's amazing," Kensei said. "How do they get them to float?"

"From what I understand, it has a little to do with the soil and a lot to do with the grass."

After Jack refueled the plane, Lin led them to the concrete structure at the center of the platform. It emerged from the blue ocean, and they had to cross a bridge to get to it. There was a stairwell inside that descended below sea level. Inside, it was cool and dark, and the steel teeth of the steps gnawed at Jenny's boots like playful puppies.

At the base of the stairs, they passed through a heavy door. Lin slammed it shut behind them and locked it with the twist of a dial. After passing through a second door, they entered a long, curved room with a white interior. A row of twenty-four doors lined the outer wall.

"Escape pods," Jack said. "Are we on a spaceship?"

"Why, yes." Lin looked impressed. "This is the ship the Selkans escaped in. By hiding it underwater, we hope to avoid any unwanted surface scans."

From the escape pod room, they entered a large, circular room. "This is the ship's bridge and operations." Above them, a dome of glass offered a glimpse of the night sky through several meters of water. They stood at one end of a catwalk that crossed above a cylindrical room filled with workstations. A photo-realistic map of Earth lined its walls.

"Good evening, Lin," a man in a blue uniform called up from below. "New recruits?"

"That's right, Doug. I'm giving them the tour."

"Mazu was looking for you," said a second officer in a blue uniform.

A woman with short, silky black hair appeared through a door at the opposite end of the catwalk. She crossed over to them with the grace and hidden power of a panther.

"Ah," Doug said. "There she is now."

"Mazu," Lin said.

"Mother, I'm pleased to see that you're still alive." Mazu looked like a younger version of Lin, with dark, almond eyes and flawless pale skin. "I heard about the attack on Acacia City and feared the worst."

"We're okay, but I haven't heard from Lance."

"He's on his way here."

"He contacted you?"

"Yes." Mazu grinned. "Perhaps you are losing favor with him."

Lin looked away from her daughter. "Mazu, meet our new recruits. Jenny Tripper and Kensei Drake."

"It's nice to meet you," Jenny and Kensei said.

Mazu bowed to them. When she rose, she was eye to eye with Jack. "And who's this?"

"This is Jack Spriggan, our new pilot."

"We have no need for another pilot."

"He saved us," Lin said, "and he brought his own plane. He could work here as a trainer; that way you can entertain more scientific pursuits."

"Really?" Mazu's eyes narrowed in suspicion. "Is he qualified?"

"You bet I am, sweetie." Jack stepped forward. "I'm retired Navy, and I specialized in hand-to-hand combat."

"Is that so. What was your job?" Mazu asked.

"Dolphin polisher." Jack smirked.

Mazu returned Jack's half-smile before grabbing the collar of his leather jacket. With a twist of her body, Jack was lifted off the ground. She pulled down and rolled her shoulders, flipping him upside down.

As he flew headfirst toward the steel catwalk, Jack did something incredible. He twisted in the air, like a cat, and somehow landed on his feet. He assumed a wide, low stance and waited for Mazu to make another move.

"Not bad." Mazu lifted one eyebrow and gifted him with a slight smile. "He'll do."

Kensei leaned in and whispered to Jenny, "Wow, that was cool."

"Yeah, it was." Jenny looked down at the bridge crew. They had stopped working to watch the interaction.

Lin looked down as well. "Back to work." The crew jumped and turned back to their jobs. "Jenny, Kensei, c'mon," Lin said. "I'll show you to your rooms."

"I need a few things from my ship first," Jack said.

"That's fine," Lin said. "Doug?"

"Yeah," answered the bridge worker who had greeted them when they entered.

"Can you show Jack to his room?"

"Sure." Doug looked at Jack and nodded.

Jack turned around and left the bridge.

Lin led Jenny and Kensei across the catwalk and down a switchback of stairs. "The living quarters are rather generous for a spaceship, but we can't give everyone their own room. I hope you don't mind having roommates."

"No, not at all," Jenny said. In fact, she felt relieved. The thought of being alone right now was terrifying.

"Good, we'll go to Kensei's room first—it's closer."

Their footfalls echoed ahead of them as they walked down a long hallway that circled the ship. Everything was bright and new, from the white walls to the shiny gray floors. As they descended to the next level, they heard voices, and the sound of casual banter warmed Jenny's heart. How she wanted to see them, to join in their laughter, to talk about nothing.

They walked around the long hallway and stopped in front of a door. "You don't have showers or toilets in your own rooms. This is the men's head." She pointed down the hall. "Women are on the opposite side. Don't get them mixed up." Lin smiled.

They stopped at a door farther down the hall. "And here's your room, Kensei."

Kensei took his backpack off and let Leon out. His pet perched on his shoulder.

"Oh no." Jenny patted her back.

"What is it?" Lin asked.

"I forgot my bag on the plane."

"Well, hurry up," Lin said. "You can probably still catch Jack."

Jenny turned and ran back the way she had come. *Stupid, Jenny, stupid.* Her ears burned as she imagined someone, like Jack, finding the Riftkey inside her bag.

Jenny made excellent time as she flew up the stairwell and ran onto the platform. Her lungs were burning, and she had to stop and catch her breath. To her relief, she saw that the ramp to Jack's plane was down. She climbed inside and saw Jack in the cockpit. His back was to her. He was wearing a headset and was talking to someone. Jenny tiptoed through the spacesuit–filled antechamber, careful not to interrupt Jack's conversation.

"I've located the *Endeavor*," Jack spoke into his headset.

Jenny heard a voice leak through Jack's headset, but she couldn't make out any of the muffled words. Still, it sounded familiar. *Who is this man that Jack is talking to?* Jenny thought to herself while she looked under the seat for the burstepi.

"Even though Trey wasn't there to meet me it all worked out." Jack paused and Jenny could almost hear the other man's voice. "You'll like this. You couldn't detect the Endeavor because it's underwater and covered by a concrete shield."

Jenny retrieved the burstepi and stood up. She looked at Jack, then back toward the exit ramp. *I should leave,* Jenny thought, *but then I'll always wonder what Jack is up to.* Jenny made up her mind and tiptoed closer to the cockpit. She put her weight on a seat back as she leaned closer and listened with all her senses. Suddenly, Jenny recognized the other man's voice. It was the same person who had asked, over Jack's communicator, why he had discharged his firearm in Acacia City.

"Selkans are here," Jack said. "I'm streaming the scans to the *Strider's* computer now." He pressed a button on the console.

Selkans? Jenny's heart pounded.

"Yes, you were right. The Selkans are planning to unlock the Terminal with a Riftkey." There was a long pause, then Jack said, "I'll see you in forty-eight hours, until—"

Just then, Jenny's hand slipped off the seatback, and the seat restraints jingled. Her breath caught in her throat. *Did he hear me?*

"Wait, someone's on the plane with me."

As Jack reached into his jacket Jenny quickly back away. The black silhouette of Jack's gun stood out against the windshield. He turned and immediately saw Jenny crouching in the aisle with the burstepi in her hands.

"Oh, it's just you." Jack walked past Jenny to the back of the plane and stashed his gun under a floor panel. "What are you doing out here, sweetie?"

Who is he calling "sweetie"? Jenny tried not to sound scared when she replied. "I came back for my bag." She lifted the burstepi up to show him.

"Good thing I was here." Jack picked up a large duffel. "C'mon. I'll join you."

18

ENDEAVOR

Jenny was afraid that Jack could hear her pounding heart over the crashing waves. *Is he a spy for some foreign government, or a corporate competitor? No, Lin and Aindriu said he checked out. Or maybe Jack is about to kill me to protect his secret.* She pictured him pushing her off the edge of the platform and into the ocean, and shivered.

Jack walked down the ramp and stood on the landing pad.

Well, Jenny thought, *if he's going to pretend as if nothing happened, then I'm going to do the same.* Jenny took a deep breath to calm her nerves and followed him. As soon as she stepped off the ramp, it closed behind her. Jack leaned in close to Jenny as if to say something, but a loud roar interrupted him.

Jenny covered her ears and looked up. An aircraft's lights swirled against the backdrop of stars. A minute later, it touched down on the opposite end of the platform. Jenny saw two men climb down a ladder, followed by a tall man in a suit the color of vanilla ice cream.

The man caught sight of them and approached. Jenny saw that he was handsome, with high, sharp cheekbones and dark hair. He must have been over two meters tall. *Like Rygelus, from the treehouse,* Jenny thought. It was impossible to place his age. He may have been thirty or three thousand, for all Jenny could tell.

He looked familiar. "Are you Lance LaGrange?" Jenny asked.

"Yes, and who are you?" he asked in a rich baritone voice. An aura of gravitas stormed around him, making Jenny feel small and insignificant.

"I'm Jenny Tripper, though I hardly know who I am, I've changed so many times since I woke up this morning." *To think*, Jenny thought, *I attended my mom's funeral, entered two parallel universes, inhabited Astrea's body, escaped from giants—twice—and flew here.*

Jenny held out her hand, which he shook. His hands were like steel wrapped in velvet, and the nails on each of his six fingers were carefully manicured. *He's the second person I met today with six digits*, Jenny thought. *I wonder if it's less rare in this universe. Maybe it's as common as being left-handed.*

Lance smiled. "Miss Tripper, it is good to finally meet you in person."

"It's my pleased—I mean, I'm pleasure to meet you." Jenny felt her face flush with heat.

Lance smirked, then turned to Jack. "You must be Mister Spriggan."

"That's right." Jack took his hand.

"Firm grip," Lance said. "I like that. It will be good to have another pilot on board, especially one with his own plane. We'll have need of it for supply runs."

Jenny saw movement from the door of Lance's plane, then Sadi stepped out into the night air. Jenny's blood turned cold. She could still feel the burning pain in her mouth from Moonlighter's attack. She backed toward the stairwell as Aindriu followed Sadi out of the plane. "I, uh, need to go."

"Oh." Lance looked from Jenny to Sadi and back. "Do you have some better place to be?"

"Um, no, sir. Not better. It's just that Lin is waiting to show me to my room." Jenny continued to back away. "It was nice meeting you. Goodnight."

Jenny held her cheek as she hurried across the undulating bridge to the concrete structure. She ran down the stairwell and found Lin waiting for her in the control room. She slowed her pace and caught her breath. While she waited for her heart to slow down, she ran through the night's events in her mind. *Should I tell her about the conversation on Jack's plane? Now that I think about it, it wasn't that odd, and Jack didn't act surprised to see me. I bet he was talking to his old boss or someone in Cabin. It makes more sense than other things that happened today.* Jenny yawned and stretched her back. *I'll sleep on it before making a decision. All I want to do right now is get these boots off and lie down.*

"I see you got your bag," Lin said. "C'mon, I'll show you where you'll be sleeping." She led Jenny down the stairs and through the halls. They stopped in front of one of many identical doors. "This is your room." She pressed a nearly invisible button on the wall. After a moment, the door slid open with a whoosh.

The door was at the narrow end of the pie-shaped room. A school of yellow fish swam behind a large oval window in the back wall. In each of the side walls were two cocoon-like openings which contained beds, one slept in, and the other with crisp white sheets and a beige blanket. Storage areas surrounded both beds like halos.

A young woman with blue hair and skin the color of honey brushed her teeth over the sink of a kitchenette. Silver tips in her hair glinted in the room's lighting. She finished and joined them. Silver jewelry jangled as she walked. Thin chains looped through her ears, piercing the lobe, auricle, conch, and tragus in turn.

"This is your new roommate, Billo Misra. Billo, this is Jenny Tripper."

"Hey, Jenny," Billo spoke in a subtle Indian accent.

"It's nice to meet you..." Jenny cocked her head. "Wait, I know you. You're a virtual tour guide. I watched you infiltrate Area 51."

"That was a long time ago." Billo smiled.

Jenny looked at Lin. "She's famous back on our world." She looked back at Billo. "My mom watched all your videos." A lump formed in her throat. "You brought her so much happiness."

"Thank you." Billo touched Jenny's shoulder. "It's always a pleasure to discover lives that I've touched. Your mom would love my next series, where I plan to infiltrate the most secure places in the world. I'm going to start with Fort Knox and end with the Sree Padmanabhaswamy Temple. Did she see my latest recording where I base jumped into the swallow cave in San Luis Potosí, Mexico?"

"I don't think so; she passed away a few days ago."

"I'm sorry." Billo squeezed Jenny's shoulder.

Jenny nodded, and they were silent for a moment.

Billo stared at Jenny. "Oh wow, I love your eyes, brown and green."

"Thanks." Jenny returned Billo's gaze and noticed that her eyes were violet. "Your eyes are amazing too."

"They're just contacts." Billo shrugged. "And yours?"

"All mine."

"Wow, that's rare."

"I see you girls are hitting it off already." Lin handed Jenny a yellow envelope with her name printed in big letters. "That's your welcome packet. You should have already received it, but your initiation got interrupted."

"That's one word for it." Jenny took the big envelope.

"Billo, can you show her how to use her Topo?"

"Sure thing."

Lin looked at Jenny. "I'll return in the morning for the remainder of your admission and testing."

"Okay, I'll be here."

Lin turned to Billo. "Make sure she gets plenty of sleep."

"I promise." Billo gave her a knowing smile.

"Have a goodnight, you two."

"Goodnight," Jenny and Billo said in unison.

After Lin left the room, Jenny turned to Billo and asked, "What's a Topo?"

Billo opened Jenny's paper envelope and removed a black cardboard box. Embossed onto its surface was the logo of a rock surrounded by water. "This is your Topo—it's kind of like the tablets we have at home."

Jenny hefted the dense box and turned it over. Printed on the back were a few logos, including Cabin's. She lifted the cover off the package. A dark-gray slab, like polished stone, lay inside. Jenny pulled the Topo free of its packing. At her touch, the stylized logo of rock and water appeared on the screen. Instead of being flat, the logo stood out from the surface. "Oh, Kensei had one of these."

"Who's Kensei?"

"We arrived here together."

"Are you two close?"

Jenny shrugged. "Um, sort of, I guess."

Billo lifted an eyebrow.

"Not like that," Jenny said. "We're friends."

"Oh, okay." Billo smiled and lifted the Topo for Jenny to see. "The surface changes to simulate any texture, even skin."

Jenny traced her fingers across the Topo. Amazingly, the rock felt rough, and the water rippled at her touch. A thin loading bar appeared below the logo. When it was completed, the background of the Milky Way replaced the bar. Then, several colorful icons overlaid the galaxy, each one standing out from the surface. Jenny wanted to run her hand across the screen to feel the different textures at play.

A huge grin spread across Billo's face. "Crazy, isn't it?"

"It's not the craziest thing I've seen today."

"I heard about the attack. I can't believe how calm you seem. I'd be freaking out."

"Would you believe it was actually the second time today I was attacked by giants?"

"Giants?" Billo sat down next to Jenny. "Tell me everything."

Jenny couldn't tell Billo about the Riftkey, so she gave her new roommate a version of her day that didn't involve Cobol. As she finished relaying the facts of the attack on Acacia City, her throat began itching like crazy, and she started coughing.

"It's the siphonophores." Billo stood up. "Everyone gets sick after their inoculation."

"It probably"—Jenny coughed—"doesn't help that I was stuck in a storm drain."

"No." Billo pulled open a drawer. "Probably not." She handed Jenny a hard candy. "Try this. I picked them up in Acacia City. The flavor changes the longer you suck on it."

Jenny unrolled the candy from its wrapper and popped it in her mouth. "Mmm, strawberry."

Billo brought Jenny a glass of water and sat next to her.

"Thanks." Jenny took a sip and sighed. The water cooled her raw throat and ceased her coughing fit.

Billo leaned in, pressing her shoulder against Jenny's, and peered at the Topo. "Click on this one." She pointed at an icon labeled "*Endeavor*." "That's the name of our underwater home."

Jenny depressed the button. The surface of the Topo transformed into a topographic map of a ship with five wings like the petals of a flower. Their room was already labeled as "Billo Misra's and Jenny Tripper's Living Quarters." Common areas like the galley, mess, sickbay, bridge, operations, and engineering stood out. As did offices, lavatories, research spaces, and the gymnasium.

"This is the ship's manifest." Billo tapped a button in the top left corner. A list of names appeared in a new window. "Let's see what they know about you." She scrolled through the list of names, then Billo tapped on Jenny's name. A list of her physical attributes appeared next to a recent picture. It also showed her birth date, place of birth, and current location. There were even links to her relatives, hobbies, interests, and education.

"Happy belated birthday." Billo smiled at Jenny.

"Thanks." Jenny gave her a sheepish grin. "My birthday's been an emotional roller coaster. But even after all that's happened, I miss my mom the most." She looked at Billo. "She really did love you."

"I'm sorry." Billo put her arm around Jenny.

"I feel hollow." Jenny's shoulders slumped.

"I know it may not seem like it right now, but the pain gets less each day."

"How do you know?"

"I lost my mom to cancer four years ago." Billo gave Jenny a smile, but her eyes looked vacant. "Almost everyone here has lost somebody. It has something to do with our abilities. Some gift, huh?"

"Yeah." Jenny wiped at her eyes with the sleeve of her uniform. She turned her attention back to the Topo and closed her biography. Then she opened the ship's manifest and scrolled through the list of names. Jenny gasped as she recognized a name on the list. She shook her head. *No, it can't be the same girl from my high school.*

"What is it?"

"I think I know her." Jenny pointed at the name.

"Adriana Thatcher? She's one of our best recruits."

Jenny tapped on Adriana's name. The portrait of a beautiful blond girl appeared. "It is her."

"How do you know her?"

"I go to school with her." Jenny clicked on "Education" and read "Wellington High School." "What are the chances?"

"Astronomical." Billo retrieved her own Topo and sat down on her bed. "But after coming here, nothing seems that weird. Know what I mean?"

"I know exactly what you mean." Yawning, Jenny set her Topo down and stretched. "I'm exhausted. Mind if I get ready for bed?"

"Not at all." Billo pointed to the storage areas around her bed. "You can put your stuff into any of those cubbies."

Jenny pushed on a cabinet door, and a tall drawer slid out of the wall. It was a closet, complete with rod and hangers. She unpacked her burstepi, making sure to keep the Riftkey hidden as she pulled her clothes out. Then Jenny traded her Cabin uniform for a worn black T-shirt and gray cotton shorts. She noticed Billo watching her and looking at her arms. Self-conscious of her cutting scars, Jenny tucked her arms closer to her side. She dropped the emptied burstepi onto her bed along with her antipsychotic meds. Jenny lay down and slid a picture of her mom into the seam where the canopy of her bed met the upper cabinet. Finally, Jenny took her toiletries to the kitchenette and asked, "Can I use your toothpaste?"

"Sure." Billo waved from the bed. "It's for both of us. Mind if I play some music?"

"Not at all."

Ambient electronic music played from Billo's Topo. "This is music from another universe; isn't that saucy?

"Mm-hmm." Jenny tried to sound enthusiastic while she brushed her teeth. *Everything, including this toothpaste, is from another universe. What effect does that have on my biology?* Jenny brought a glass of water back to her bed and removed the caps from her meds.

Billo sat up. "You don't need those anymore."

"What?" Jenny tapped the proper dosage into her palm and cupped her hand protectively. "My meds? I've been taking these for years."

"But the siphonophores cured you."

"Well...I don't know. I've never missed a dosage." Jenny popped the pills into her mouth and chased them with water.

Billo sighed. "Trust me. Those pills will do nothing but block your abilities."

A list of effects and side effects played across Jenny's vision like ticker tape. "I keep hearing about abilities, but so far I've just had a bit of buzzing in my head."

"Watch."

In the blink of an eye, there was no trace of Jenny's blue-haired roommate. Billo had changed into a man with light, freckled skin and a full red beard.

Jenny crossed her arms self-consciously. "How did you do that?"

"It's a mind trick." Billo's voice was deep. "Like a form of suggestion." In a blink, she changed back to normal. "I can make you believe that I look like anyone." She turned into an identical twin of Jenny.

"That's disturbing. It's like my doppelgänger back home."

Billo changed back to herself. "That's how I was able to get into so many secure locations."

"You had this power back home?"

Billo nodded. "I haven't always had this much control, though." She glanced at Jenny's meds.

Jenny pushed her pill bottles into a drawer and climbed into her bunk.

"I used to think I was crazy. I had hallucinations, voices in my head, and some truly terrible headaches." Billo leaned forward and showed Jenny the underside of her forearms. Tattoos covered a good deal of scarring. "They diagnosed me as a paranoid schizophrenic with Capgras syndrome."

"What's Capgras syndrome?"

Billo pushed her feet up to the ceiling of her bed.

"I just woke up one day, and I thought people were in my bedroom. I saw people with me wherever I went, talking to me. They told me that my parents were imposters. That they had somehow been replaced, like pod people or something." Billo walked her feet along the ceiling of her bunk. "It got worse from there. It spread to several of my close friends too."

"What did you do?"

"I got desperate. I turned to drugs, both legal and illegal. I went on a drug-fueled journey of self-discovery, and by the end, I understood my inner power." Billo shook her head. "I know it's bad, but I got tired of feeling guilty all the time."

"For what?"

"For putting unnecessary stress on my friends and family. They stuck by me, even when I didn't trust them anymore."

Jenny understood how Billo felt. She, too, carried the heavy weight of guilt. After all, she had believed it was her fault that the wedding couple disappeared. She didn't let herself have friends, and she pushed her family away. They couldn't see Astrea. They couldn't know what she did at the wedding. But now she knew that it was the Riftkey that had activated the Waypoint and that the wedding couple was safely back home.

Billo dropped her feet to the floor and pulled up her shirtsleeve. Five tally marks had been tattooed onto her forearm over a row of scars. "This is how many years I've been clean from legal and illegal drugs." She looked deep into Jenny's eyes.

Jenny looked away.

"We've all been diagnosed with some type of mental illness."

Jenny recalled the visits to the psychiatrist and the feeling of helplessness. Was it possible that everyone here had experienced similar bizarre events? "So, we're all among mad people?"

"That's right." Billo gave Jenny her best Cheshire Cat grin. "We're all mad here. But not crazy. Figuring out what makes you different is hard, but that's why Cabin is so incredible. They'll help you understand who you really are without judgment, and without the drug-fueled journey I took myself on."

"That would be preferable."

Billo pointed at Jenny's arm. "So, what does your brand mean?"

"My what?" Jenny looked down at her arm. *I forgot that the Riftkey marked me with its symbol.* "Um, it's a family thing." Jenny pulled her family heirloom free of her concert shirt and showed it to Billo. The circle and triangle of her amulet matched the brand on her arm.

"That's hard-core."

Jenny shrugged and stuffed the amulet back under her T-shirt.

"You really should stop taking your meds." Billo put her feet back onto the ceiling of her bed. "You're not crazy, so try meditation instead.

That's how I learned to control my ability. Once I accepted who I was, my headaches and delusions stopped." She looked over at Jenny. "So, what did the quacks diagnose you with?"

Jenny rubbed her sweaty palms together and stared at the ceiling of her bed for several long seconds. "Bipolar disorder."

"Pfft. Boring." Billo waited for Jenny to continue.

"Then schizophrenia."

Billo rolled her eyes.

When the silence became more uncomfortable than the truth, Jenny sighed. "And Cotard delusion."

Billo lifted an eyebrow. "That's a new one."

"I never felt quiet in my body," Jenny said. "It felt like something was trapped under my skin, constantly buzzing, like some electrical current."

"That's how I felt when I stopped taking my meds."

"So, you know a lot about psychology?"

"I was a psych major in college." Billo rested her head on her hands. "So, what is Cotard delusion?"

Jenny felt a lump form in her throat, and she hugged her legs to her chest. After her mom had been diagnosed with leukemia, Jenny started spending more and more time by herself. She talked about wanting to die and made friends with people at school who cut themselves with razors. She tried it herself. She found that cutting brought a sense of physicality to the pain she was feeling inside.

Still, it wasn't until she ignored her personal hygiene for a week that she was taken to a psychiatrist. She told the doctor about her hallucinations, and Sally. She told the doctor that she was dead. That was why she felt numb; that was why she saw a ghost. The psychiatrist diagnosed her with Cotard delusion and prescribed a regimen of drugs.

Instead of being upset with the diagnosis, Jenny felt relieved that her distress stemmed from an illness. It was like being told that it wasn't her fault that the wedding couple had disappeared. So what if she saw Sally, and felt a strange buzzing in her head. She was just crazy. For the first time in a long time, she had felt joyful, and the drugs reaffirmed her lack of control. Each time the doctor raised the dose, it marked how much it wasn't her fault.

"I saw things," Jenny said. "Things that the doctor didn't believe."

"Like what?" Billo leaned in closer.

"Like ghosts. Well, one ghost. Sometimes I saw strange colors, and felt a buzzing in my head that would give me migraines. And, I don't know if it's related, but people would tell me that they saw me in places I couldn't have been, like at the store when I was actually at home. One time, when I was really depressed, I told the doctor that I was a ghost. Like I was in some sort of half existence, and maybe that's why I saw the world the way I did."

"Wow, that is different." Billo fluffed up her pillow and leaned back. "Listen, the doctors back home don't know what they're talking about. They can only diagnose us based on their limited understanding of the human brain."

"And whatever fits their description of crazy," Jenny said.

"Our disorders are side-effects of abilities they can't comprehend, and the meds keep us from figuring out who we are, and what we're capable of. I used to believe that my parents were imposters, and now my ability is to trick people into seeing what I want them to."

"So," Jenny's eyebrows knit together in thought. "What kind of ability do you think I have?"

Billo shrugged. "I don't know, but I'm sure Cabin will help you find out."

Jenny lay down in her bed and felt the tension in her muscles melt away. "I hope you're right."

Billo yawned. "You ready for bed?"

"Yeah, I'm exhausted."

Billo shut off the music and said, "Lights off." The room's white ambient light turned off, and a dim red safety light turned on.

Jenny pressed the back of her head into the pillow and closed her eyes. The Waypoint key and her mom's amulet weighed against her chest. She was tired, but her mind buzzed with activity. *What is my ability?* Jenny thought. *All I can do is see Sally, and she turned out to be Astrea, my ancient ancestor who unknowingly created my universe hundreds of years ago. And what does that make me, her descendent, her heir?*

Jenny pulled Astrea's key from around her neck and examined it in the dim red light. She thought about Lin's short Waypoint lesson before the Risi attacked, and an idea occurred to her. If the Topo had a connection to the Web, then maybe she could find out what had happened after the raid on Acacia City. She leaned over and picked up her Topo.

"I wouldn't do that." Billo rolled over.

"Why not?"

"Because you'll never get any sleep. Just imagine, hundreds of years of entertainment that parallels ours. All that history. I didn't sleep at all the first night I was here, and I promised Lin that we'd get some sleep."

"I just want to look up one thing."

"Fine, but if you show up to breakfast exhausted, tell Lin that I warned you."

"Deal." Jenny opened the Web browser on her Topo and typed "Acacia City" into the search engine. She clicked on a news headline about the raid at the top of the search results. The article listed the number of wounded and the estimated damage to businesses. As Jenny read, Billo's breathing became deep and regular. Jenny found what she was looking for. The primary target seemed to be the basement of the Department of Transportation. But it didn't say what they were after.

Jenny took Billo's advice and turned the Topo off. As she looked up at the picture of her mom, her mind wandered to the last time Jenny had snuck out. It was four months ago. Her mom had been waiting up for her when she got back later that night. All she said was that she was disappointed, and she let Jenny go to bed. At the time, Jenny thought she'd gotten off easy. Yet, her mind kept replaying the hurt on her mom's face. After a fitful sleep, Jenny woke and discovered that something had changed between them. She realized later that her mom no longer trusted her. Jenny had resolved to earn back her trust, but before she had a chance, her mom had been diagnosed with leukemia. The news had rocked Jenny's world and sent her spiraling into a deep depression. Everything became darkness and shadow. She gave up on living, stopped grooming herself, and cut her arms. Jenny rolled over and opened the burstepi. She pulled the handle of the Riftkey free.

Cobol, are you there? Jenny asked in her mind.

I'm here, Jenny, Cobol responded.

Why have you been silent for so long?

When you put me in that bag, I went somewhere else, and I couldn't reach your mind.

I'm sorry, but Lin said I'm supposed to keep you hidden.

It is better than the storm drain, but I would much rather have my body.

I know—Jenny sighed—*but I haven't had time to look. What does a sword need with a body anyway?*

You can't imagine what it's like to be paralyzed for thousands of years.

No, the few minutes when I couldn't move after falling through the storm drain were long enough.

Billo stirred and snorted. Afraid of revealing the Riftkey, Jenny thrust it back inside her bag and rolled over and looked at her roommate. As she lay there, listening to her beating heart, she thought about how normal it was to be sleeping in the same room with someone famous compared to being in an underwater spaceship in another universe. Then, she thought about how Billo had transformed into other people. *Could Cabin help me discover an ability like that?*

19

ANCHORS AWEIGH

Victus leaned back in the cockpit of the *Celestial Strider* and reviewed the scans Jack had sent. Images of a concrete platform and dozens of small green islands flashed across the display. *These look like Selkan homes, but it's not enough*, he thought. After all, his fate was tied to the success of this mission. He focused on a brown smudge standing on a small green island and silhouetted against the blue water. As Victus increased magnification, a Selkan filled the frame. A sliver of hope slipped into his mind. *This is it.* He smiled. *The infallible proof I need to bring the* Tamarack. *Time to go home.*

Possessing a body was like flexing a muscle. Most Æons could only maintain a connection for a few minutes. Keeping this connection for three days was a feat unique to Victus. As he prepared to leave Hocco's body, an idea came to him: a way to experience something that usually ended in death. He knew it was an addiction. One that he had developed during his time as an assassin. And like most addicts, he was unable to stop himself.

Victus floated down to the belly of the *Strider* and removed his spacesuit. In nothing but a thin bodysuit, he entered the airlock and locked the inner door. A computer's voice warned him that a spacesuit was required in the airlock. A rush of endorphins caused him to shiver with excitement. Victus overrode the safety, and with shaky hands, he opened the outer hatch.

At once, the vacuum of space sucked him out of the airlock. His lungs squeezed shut, and his skin burned from the unfiltered power of the sun. Within seconds, the mucous membranes in his nose and mouth cracked and split. He looked upon the Earth with red eyes covered in frozen tears. Victus opened his mouth in a silent scream as his skin stretched out like a balloon. Through the strength of will alone, he held on to this experience, savoring the tearing of flesh and the burning in his lungs. This was the rush that Victus was addicted to. *You feel the most alive when you're this close to death.* With reluctance, Victus released his bond to Hocco's dying body.

The agony evaporated in a rush as Victus woke alone in a small, dim room. His skin felt dry, and his mouth tasted like cardboard. He lay on a plastic bed in gray scrubs. Nearby, monitors beeped and displayed his vital signs. Victus pulled a plastic tube out of his throat and let it drop to the floor with a wet smack. He pushed himself upright with atrophied muscles.

The door to his hospital room swung open, and two nurses in white scrubs rushed inside.

"Sir." The male nurse grabbed a wheelchair and rolled it to the edge of the bed.

"Food," Victus croaked as he pulled an intravenous infusion out of his arm.

"Yes, sir." The female nurse took Victus's hand and helped him into the chair, and pushed him to the mess hall.

Both the sickbay and the mess hall were located in the central core of the *Tamarack*. The core also included the bridge, living quarters, and gym. These areas had the luxury of artificial gravity, which was maintained by an Æon who could manipulate gravitons. Its hangars, weapons, and engineering sections made up the rest of the ship and were subject to zero gravity and the stress of rapid momentum change.

Victus passed several crew members, but nobody saluted or even acknowledged him. *But why would they?* Victus thought. *I'm not myself right now.* His body was in a state of distress. Though he could possess another body longer than any other Æon, it took a massive amount of calories, causing his body to cannibalize itself to maintain the connection. Even with rapid healing granted by nano-organisms, it would be a few days before his lost muscle tissue could be restored.

Once he reached the mess hall, Victus spent the next two hours, eating until he was full, resting, and evacuating. As his strength slowly returned, Victus rose from his wheelchair and left the mess hall under his own power.

Victus stood in his quarters and faced the mirror in his lavatory. "Complete physical," He said. Victus groaned as the results of his physical appeared around his image in the mirror. The energy demands of maintaining a connection across thousands of light-years were staggering. He had lost ten kilograms in the three days he had possessed Hocco. He probed the stubble on his sunken cheeks and stared into his one blue eye. He avoided looking at the other one. The black-on-black eye that stained his pale, handsome face was like an inkblot on a white sheet.

Victus shook his head and caught himself on the counter after losing his balance. Gathering his strength, he showered and shaved. He wished he could put on his powered spacesuit. It would support him and provide power in his weakened state. *No, I can't show weakness in front of my officers. I need to appear on the bridge in full uniform.* He pulled a duty uniform out of the closet.

Before leaving, Victus ran a comb through his white-blond hair and straightened his black uniform, which now hung loosely around his chest and hips. On the way to the lift, several crew members acknowledged him, and a few even saluted.

The elevator doors opened, revealing two young men in beige cadet uniforms. They silenced their conversation and saluted. Victus returned the gesture and entered, holding on to the railing for support. "Carry on," he croaked. His throat still itched from the feeding tube.

One of the men turned to his companion and continued their

conversation in a hushed tone. He spoke of a romantic encounter with a lady on Lan Station and expressed, with great exuberance, the success of the advice from the famous radio personality, Big Newton. Victus knew Big Newton by another name, Brigham Newton. In addition to being a famous media personality, Newton was a powerful Æon and Terminal master. During the First Galactic War, Newton's forces were undefeated until the introduction of the Terminal Defenders. Postwar, he hosted a popular radio program. People called him for advice, and because no one's troubles were unique to themselves, Brigham's voice affected billions. In this way, Newton held more influence over the galaxy than he ever did during the war.

Newton was strongly suspected of being the master who'd sent the Selkans to Sol. It had been pointless to accuse him because Terminal masters operated independently of the government. An investigation would invite retaliation from other masters and possibly reveal their secret use of Selkans. Victus knew all too well that it wasn't wise to upset the Terminal masters. He reached involuntarily up to his black eye, caught himself, and forced his hand back to his side.

By the time the car stopped on the gym floor, his atrophied muscles were shaking. The men exited, and the doors closed. Victus leaned against the wall. Finally, the car slowed to a stop on the bridge level. Victus straightened his uniform and took a deep breath.

The elevator doors opened to stars twinkling on curved black walls, like pinpricks in an enormous globe. The bridge of the *Tamarack* was a hollowed-out sphere in the heart of the battlecruiser. The *Tamarack's* surroundings were projected on the walls, giving it the appearance of being in outer space.

A junior officer at the tactical station noticed Victus and saluted. "Officer on deck."

Victus searched the young man's face and read his aura. There was some anxiety, but that could be from seeing the admiral walking after being in a coma for three days. He returned the man's salute as more heads turned to watch his approach. Victus feigned strength as he took the ladder up to the officer's deck, a circular platform that rose above the operations center. From this heightened position, it truly felt like they were floating through outer space on the back of the *Tamarack*.

"Welcome back, sir." Marcus Hoff, the captain, took Victus's hand and pulled him onto the deck, making it look like a handshake. The captain of the *Tamarack* was bald, except for a halo of short-cropped salt-and-pepper hair. His nose was hooked like the beak of a raptor. He was Victus's senior by thirty years.

Victus squeezed his hand in silent thanks for the assistance onto the deck, then faced Carmen Jacquay, the wing commander. She had long, dark hair that lay flat against her head in an intricate braid. Victus was always impressed by her knowledge of the ship. Somehow, she could recall every detail of the *Tamarack*'s twelve hangars, including a squadron of corvettes and over a hundred assault fighters and transports.

"How are you feeling, sir?" Carmen met his gaze with fiercely intelligent blue eyes.

"I'm recovering."

Captain Hoff squeezed his thin lips together and grasped his hands behind his back. With his gray eyes and a square jaw, he looked carved from stone. "Doctor Abrams has asked for another assistant."

"Another one?"

"The job is hard."

"The job is essential to maintain this ship's superiority. It takes someone with a certain demeanor—"

"You mean a sadist?" Carmen interrupted.

Victus gave her a level gaze. "If that's what it takes."

"Are the Selkans in the Sol System?" the captain asked.

"They are." Victus nodded and watched as the captain's aura flared orange and yellow with frantic waveform patterns.

Victus turned his back to them. "Recall the crew. We leave for Sol in eight hours. I hate to end station leave prematurely, but time is of the essence. We cannot allow the Selkans to unlock the Sol Terminal."

20

THE WHITE UNIFORMS

Sunlight filtered through blue seawater and created a shifting pattern of light on the floor of Jenny's room. Billo's Topo beeped an alarm. She shut it off and looked over at Jenny.

"Good morning, sunshine."

Jenny groaned because she wasn't ready to be awake.

"How are you feeling today?"

Jenny took a deep breath and was surprised that her throat didn't itch, and her chest wasn't stuffy. In fact, it was like she had been sick her entire life and this was the first day she felt well. Her muscles hummed with energy, and the whole world seemed brighter. "I feel great."

Billo got out of bed and opened her closet. "That's how it goes, one day feeling like shit, and the next you feel like you could take on the world."

Jenny swung her legs off the bed and stood up. Her legs felt like coiled springs. Just for fun, she jumped a whole meter off the ground, and landed with the grace of a cat.

"Wow." Billo smiled. "You must be feeling better."

Jenny's side cramped. "Yeah, but I'm starving."

"I still remember how hungry I felt the day after my treatment. I'll take you to the cafeteria after we get ready." Billo grabbed a bathrobe from her closet.

"Sounds wonderful." Jenny found her own bathrobe and followed Billo to the communal bathroom.

After her shower, Jenny examined herself in the mirror. To her surprise, the scratches from her fall had reduced to fresh pink skin.

"What are you looking at?" Billo asked.

"My back. It was all scraped up after falling in the drain."

Billo touched the sensitive new skin on Jenny's back. "Looks good to me."

"Yeah, it does now." Jenny looked at her forearms and sighed inwardly. The scars from cutting still remained.

They finished up in the bathroom and returned to their room. Jenny opened her closet and rummaged through her bag. She took out some sculpting clay and pulled her short black hair into spikes. Then she donned her white Cabin uniform and pulled her boots on. She had just finished her eye makeup when the door trilled.

"I've got it," Billo said as she attached an earring. "Open door."

The door slid open to reveal Lin and Kensei standing out in the hallway. A night of sleep had revived Lin. The circles were gone from under her eyes, and her hair was in a tight bun. Kensei wore his white uniform without his purple hat. The sides of his dark hair faded up to a pile of dense curls.

"Good morning," Lin said. "Billo Misra, I'd like you to meet Kensei Drake."

"Nice to meet you." The jewelry in Billo's ears jangled musically as she crossed the room. "You arrived with Jenny."

"Yeah. Oh wow." Kensei's mouth hung open. "You're Billo."

"I know."

"I love your channel."

"Thanks."

"My favorite is the time you walked up to the president right in the Oval Office."

Billo smirked. "That was a fun one."

"Billo." Jenny pulled her boots on and stood up. "You know a lot about websites, don't you?"

"Yeah." Billo furrowed her brows.

"Kensei wants to make a webcomic...He's got some hilarious drawings."

"Really?" Billo put a hand on her hip. "Let's see what you have."

Kensei narrowed his eyes at Jenny, then took off his backpack and pulled out his sketchbook. "It's not really that good."

Billo took the book and flipped through the pages. "What do you mean? These are great."

"Really?" Kensei and Billo continued talking.

Lin turned to Jenny and asked, "How are you feeling?"

"Amazing! I've never felt—"

Again, their doorbell trilled.

"Wow, we're popular this morning," Billo said. "Open door."

Jenny's breath caught as the door slid open. Adriana Thatcher stood next to Mazu in the hallway. Only the sun could brighten a room more than Adriana. People gathered around her to soak up her radiance and recharge their spirits. She had the kind of beauty that would make Disney princesses jealous. Jenny waited for the talking birds to land on her shoulders and break into a musical number.

"Everyone, this is Adriana Thatcher," Lin said. "Adriana, this is Kensei Drake and—"

"Jenny Tripper." Adriana shook her head, causing two blond ringlet curls to swing back and forth. She wore a blue scarf over her white uniform that accentuated her eyes. "Hey, Billo."

"Hi, Adriana." Billo leaned forward and stared into her eyes.

"I saw your name on the crew manifest," Jenny said to Adriana, "but I didn't believe it until now."

"It's good to see a familiar face." Adriana looked Jenny up and down. "I like the new look."

Jenny narrowed her eyes. Back at school, Adriana had never said a word to her. *What's she playing at? Stop it*, Jenny scolded herself. *This isn't high school.* "Thanks."

"Hi," Kensei stuck out his hand.

"Nice to meet you, Kenny."

"It's Kensei."

Adriana shook Kensei's hand. "Oh, your hand's all clammy."

"Sorry." Kensei rubbed his hands on his white slacks. "I'm nervous." He looked at Jenny and Adriana. "Wow, you two could be sisters."

"What?" Adriana crossed her arms and chewed her lip. "No way."

Jenny searched for what Kensei had seen. *There's no way we're sisters,* she thought. *Yet, according to my mom, we're both Roma. Hmm, our eyes are the same shape, and we're about the same above-average height and slim build.*

"Let's get going," Adriana said. "I'm getting hungry."

"Get going with what?" Jenny asked.

"Yeah." Billo crossed her arms. "What's everyone doing in our room?"

"I brought you all here for a demonstration," Mazu said.

"What kind of demonstration?" Kensei asked.

Lin ushered everyone to the back of the room, where there was more space for them to stand together.

"It's a side project Adriana and I are working on." Mazu pulled her Topo from the asymmetric pocket in her blue uniform. "I have another location for you to scout."

"Okay." Adriana pulled out her Waypoint key. It had a brilliant-yellow heliodor gem set into the handle.

"What are you looking for?" Jenny asked.

"An artifact called a virosuit," Mazu said. "It should be in an underwater cave system near here. Adriana is helping us locate the entrance before we launch an expedition."

"What is a virosuit?" Kensei asked.

"It's the body of a Riftkey."

"Like a robot or something. Does that mean the Riftkey is intelligent?" Kensei asked.

"Yes, it is capable of thought," Mazu said. "And when it is combined with the virosuit, it will be able to move on its own."

"You two"—Lin pointed at Jenny and Kensei—"pay attention."

Jenny pulled her tuning-fork-shaped key free and held it out in front of her, the way Adriana did. Energy buzzed in her mind as she stared at the key until her eyes crossed.

Adriana looked over at Jenny and shook her head. "You're doing it all wrong."

Jenny frowned. "Then show us."

"Hold it like this." Adriana moved Jenny's key until the tines were free. She moved over to Kensei. "Good, but keep a loose grip." She smiled. "No one's going to steal it." Adriana stepped back and studied both of them. "Much better. Now watch." Adriana held up her heliodor key in her left hand. Her eyes rolled back in her head until only the whites showed.

Jenny felt the energy emanating from Adriana. She focused her mind and grasped on to it. As she did so, the air in front of Adriana shimmered like a mirage, then shattered into thousands of glittering diamonds. The diamond air coalesced into two round portals, like windows. Looking through one didn't reveal what was behind it. Instead, it showed what was behind its mate. *Each one acts like a camera for the other,* Jenny thought.

"What are they?" Kensei peered into the portal nearest to him.

"They are my eyes." Adriana flipped her hair behind her shoulder. "Mazu, can you show me the location again?"

Mazu held her Topo up to one of the portals. Adriana nodded. In an instant, one of the portals passed through the wall and the water, and into the air. They had a bird's-eye view of the *Endeavor's* landing platform, the Selkans' homes, and the main island.

Adriana plunged the portal back into the water. It blurred past countless marine animals until it reached the rocky wall of the coastline. Adriana quickly scanned the rock until she located a dark cave. Her portal moved forward. Light from inside Jenny's room illuminated the cave's inky interior, but it wasn't enough. Mazu pulled a flashlight from her bag and shined it into the other portal. The gray rock lit up.

"We know there's a special kind of Waypoint somewhere under this island." Mazu swung the light back and forth. "One that's linked to an identical Waypoint in the Nimue Realm and connects the two universes. There should be a drastic change in the color and texture of the rock—"

"At the point where the two universes connect," Adriana said.

"Why connect them at all?" Kensei asked.

"We only have theories," Lin said. "It might be to preserve the conservation of matter or maybe to provide energy to the Waypoints and Term—"

"I think I found something," Adriana said.

Clear as day, two distinct types of rock joined together in a perfect circle. "That's it." Mazu reached out toward the anomaly. Her hand passed through the portal, and she squeezed Adriana's shoulder. "You found it. Good work."

Adriana sighed in relief. Quick as a blink, the portals disappeared in a cloud of glittering light.

Jenny shook her head in wonder. "That's the coolest thing I've ever seen."

Adriana grinned. Slowly, and with considerable effort, her eyes rolled forward again.

"What's it like"—Kensei focused on the emerald set into his key —"using an ability?"

Adriana looked up at the ceiling. "It's like re-creating the essence of a strong emotion. While controlling things like your heart rate and body temperature. Does that make sense?"

"Sort of," Kensei said. "It sounds like acting, emoting while staying in control."

Adriana nodded. "Yeah, I guess it is."

Jenny stared at her key. After her mom became sick, Jenny shed enough tears for a lifetime. Ever since her mom died, she'd felt hollow inside. Jenny wasn't sure she had any emotion left to give.

"I think that's enough for now." Lin looked from Jenny to Kensei. "I hope you two learned something."

"We did," Jenny and Kensei answered.

"Good, let's get some breakfast," Mazu said.

"That sounds great." Jenny stuffed her key back into her shirt and got into line behind Kensei as everyone filed out of the room. She caught Kensei staring at Adriana. Jenny leaned over and whispered into Kensei's ear, "You like her, don't you?"

"What?" Kensei jumped. "No."

"Don't worry." Jenny shrugged. "Everyone likes her, but she's oblivious to it."

"Hmm," Kensei muttered.

The sounds of utensils clanking on plates echoed in the hallway outside the mess hall. Jenny's mouth watered at the scent of bacon. Inside, banks of lights ran along narrow slots in the ceiling. People of every ethnicity sat at long white rectangular tables. They all wore Cabin uniforms in gray, blue, and black. Their voices blended into a din of conversation.

"Here are your meal cards." Lin handed Jenny and Kensei each a plastic card. "We have limited supplies aboard the ship, which means we have to ration our food. One point per meal, and one for dessert. You get twenty-eight points a week, so keep track of these."

Jenny looked over at Kensei and noticed something for the first time this morning. "You're not wearing your glasses."

"Nope. I put them on this morning and found that I didn't need them." He shrugged. "I'll have to get regular sunglasses now."

"Or you can let people see your eyes."

Kensei shrugged.

Lance LaGrange approached them. He wore a dashing linen suit with blue detailing at the pockets and buttons. His dark hair had a perfect part down the side, and his smooth face seemed to glow. "Miss Tripper, Mister Drake, you two look splendid."

"Thanks." Jenny looked down at her new black boots.

"It's surprisingly comfortable." Kensei tugged at the bottom of his uniform's shirt.

Lin looked up at Lance. "What happened to you last night?"

"I was supervising the delivery of a new pump when I received a distress call from Mister Ward."

Lin smiled at Jenny and Kensei. "You two go on ahead."

"Thanks," Jenny said. Her stomach was eating her from the inside out. A tall, handsome, dark-haired young man in a blue uniform scanned her meal card. She grabbed a tray and got into the canteen line.

Heat lamps shone down on stainless-steel food bins. Each had a handwritten label listing the dish's name and ingredients. The first item was talo, which looked like a corn tortilla. The next tray held a white fish called wahoo. Jenny took two tortillas and a generous amount of the fish. Next was ota, a cold fish dish. Jenny scooped some onto her plate and added some cooked bananas and mashed taro from the next station. At the end of the line, she took a stainless steel cup and filled it with coconut water.

"Where should we sit?" Kensei asked.

Jenny looked around the room. Sadi and Aindriu sat in a group with several other gray-uniformed recruits. A gaggle of blue uniforms sat in the middle of the room. At the far end of the room, a group of five people wore black. Jenny looked down at her white outfit. *Why couldn't I get one of those?* Jenny thought. "What's with the different uniform colors anyway?" she asked.

"It seems like most of the older people are wearing blue and black," Kensei said.

"I think it has to do with seniority," Jenny mused. "We're in white because we're the newest recruits."

Kensei nudged Jenny and pointed to a corner. Two walrus-like aliens spooned heaps of food between their tusks. "Those must be Selkans."

"Stop pointing," Jenny said, "it's rude." Yet she couldn't take her eyes off of them. They had stout bodies with long arms that tapered down to delicate, long fingers. White tusks jutted a few centimeters from the sides of their mouths. Each had a broom-like mustache sprouting under their broad, flat nose.

"Jenny," Billo called out as she waved from a table in the far corner of the room.

Adriana was sitting next to her and joined in the call. "Over here."

Jenny and Kensei walked over to join them.

"Hey," Adriana said. Her turquoise-blue eyes met Jenny's.

"Hi," Jenny said as she set her tray down next to Billo. "This feels a lot like high school." Her Topo pressed against her ribs as she sat down on the bench. She pulled it out and set it on the table. The others had already done the same.

"Yeah, a bit." Adriana chuckled.

"So, you're both Kiwis?" Kensei looked at Jenny and Adriana.

"We are," Adriana said.

"It's a beautiful country." Billo pushed a strand of silver-tipped hair behind her ear and fixed her dark eyes on Adriana. "What part do you live in?"

"We both live in Wellington." Adriana looked at Jenny. "On the upper island."

Jenny tried some of the salty fish first and found that it tasted excellent when combined with the taro. It was unbelievably delicious. Maybe her newly healed tongue had more taste buds now.

Adriana looked at Jenny. "How'd you end up with Cabin, Jenny? Did Michael give you a VRGo puzzle too?"

"Michael?" Jenny choked and forced a bite of fish down her throat. "The barista at the Black Rabbit?"

"No, he's a waiter at the Imperial Dodo." Adriana furrowed her brow, then she shrugged and laughed. "I guess he has two jobs."

"Yeah, he gave me the puzzle. I thought it was a birthday present at first."

"Oh, happy birthday." Adriana smiled.

"Thanks." Jenny returned her smile and grew uncomfortable with the attention. She stared down at her food.

Adriana didn't seem to notice and turned to Kensei. "And how about you, Ken?"

"Hmm?" Kensei looked up from his Topo.

"How'd you end up here?" Jenny repeated Adriana's question.

"Oh." Kensei swallowed. "Well, that message from Lin said there were boundless opportunities to learn." He held his Topo up. "I mean, look at this thing, it's so cool. Plus, this may be the only chance I ever get to travel to outer space."

Billo stared across the room at Sadi, who was collecting empty trays from tables. Billo leaned across the table and whispered to Adriana. "I heard Sadi had to take extra kitchen duty."

"Yeah," Adriana said. "I wonder what she did."

Jenny looked down at her plate.

"I bet it's because she attacked Jenny," Kensei said.

"What, really?" Billo looked at Jenny. "You didn't mention that last night."

Jenny squirmed in her chair. "I didn't want to make a big deal out of it. Sadi was distraught, and she acted out."

"Tell us," Billo said.

Jenny recounted the events surrounding yesterday's lunch, including how she had stumbled over a dead body in the woods.

"And you think it was Trey?"

Jenny shrugged. "I have no idea, but Sadi was pretty upset."

"That's awful," Adriana said.

"So, she can create pain?" Billo asked. "I always wondered what her ability was."

"Not exactly create," Jenny said. "She can enhance or decrease pain, even the memory of it."

"Well," Billo said, "if Trey really is dead, I can see why she'd be upset."

Adriana narrowed her eyes at Billo. "But Sadi shouldn't have taken it out on Jenny."

"Still"—Billo looked at Jenny—"I think you should avoid her. She's not the type to let go of a grudge."

"I'll try, as long as she leaves me alone." Jenny shrugged. "That reminds me. I meant to look for articles about the attack in Acacia City." She pulled out her Topo and searched for the Acacia City raid. From the results, she found a news article that looked promising. "Look at this." Jenny leaned closer to Kensei. "It's an article about the raid last night." They read together in silence for a minute. "It looks like the only thing the Risi stole was that Waypoint in the basement."

Kensei furrowed his brow. "What would giants want with a Waypoint?"

"Not the giants, the person in the black hood. You know..." She tilted her head toward Sadi.

"Yeah, I know who you mean, but what's she going to do with one?"

Jenny shrugged. "Maybe she's working for someone else?"

"It's still not proof of anything."

"I know." Jenny twisted her fork through her last morsel of food.

"We're not here to find out why the giants raided Acacia City, we're here to unlock the Terminal." Kensei fed Leon a spoonful of cooked banana.

"I know," Jenny huffed and looked from Sadi to the Selkans. The older one waved his arms as he spoke and gestured with his long fingers. "Do you think we'll actually be able to save them?" she asked the table.

"I don't know," Billo answered. "Lin's positivity is infectious."

"But the Selkans are nervous," Adriana added.

"It feels like we're on borrowed time." Billo sipped her drink.

"What's the big hurry?" Kensei asked.

Adriana looked at Kensei. "Their captors could come after them at any moment."

Billo set her fork down and pushed her empty tray to the end of the table. "I just hope one of us wins." She looked over at the grays' table.

"It's not a contest," Adriana said. "It's about saving the Selkans."

"Of course it's a contest." Billo set her chin in her hands and locked her dark eyes on Adriana. "And you have the best chance of any of us to win."

"Yeah right," Sadi said. She stood at the end of their table with a handful of trays. "None of you deserves the Riftkey."

"What do you mean by 'you'?" Jenny asked.

"Astreans. All of you from that other universe. It belongs to us."

Jenny rolled her eyes.

"We are all on the same side," Adriana said.

"Yeah," Kensei said, "we're all trying to save the Selkans."

"I don't care about the aliens. I just want the power and authority that comes from being a Terminal master."

"What authority, where'd you hear that?" Billo asked.

"From Trey."

"And who'd he hear it from?"

"I don't know"—Sadi adjusted her thick-rimmed black glasses—"and I guess I never will."

The table was silent. Nobody wanted to respond to Sadi.

"I'm going to win the Riftkey." Sadi glared at each of them as she gathered the empty trays. "It's a fact." She left the table, carrying the trays to the cleaning station

"She gives me the willies," Kensei said once Sadi was out of earshot.

"Can you imagine her with the Riftkey?" Billo asked.

"I'd rather not," Adriana said.

"I'd try to win the competition just to keep her from getting it," Billo said.

They all nodded.

Jenny looked around the room and saw the same look Sadi had given them reflected on a dozen other faces. "It seems like we're not entirely welcome here."

"It's true," Billo said. "Some people believe the Riftkey belongs to this Earth, but everyone knows about Astrea. She's the original Æon and she came to our Earth."

Lin and Lance walked up to their table. "Jenny, Kensei, come with us, please."

"Are we in trouble?" Jenny wiped her mouth with a paper napkin.

"No." Lin cocked her head. "May I introduce you to the Selkans."

Jenny and Kensei nodded, and Lin led them across the room to the aliens.

The Selkans rose from their bench. They wiggled great mustaches that seemed to grow right out of their noses. Short brown fur covered their bodies.

"This is Jenny Tripper and Kensei Drake," Lin said. "The newest recruits to our program."

"I am Thork'l, chief of our clan," the older Selkan said. He wore a green coat over a white shirt and brown trousers. Blue facial tattoos marked Thork'l's eyebrows and chin. "And this is my son, Kett'l."

Jenny's eyebrows rose. Kett'l's eyes were dichromatic, like hers, but light and dark brown. They shook hands. The Selkans had long, dexterous fingers webbed up to the first knuckle. Their fingernails were the shape of almonds, and their skin felt like warm leather.

"We had a breakthrough in locating the virosuit this morning," Lin said.

"That's great news," Thork'l said.

"What is your progress on the Locator?" Lance asked.

"I'll have it finished by this afternoon," Kett'l said, wiping his large hands on his mechanic's coveralls.

"Excellent," Lance said. "We are on a path to success."

"It would seem so," Thork'l said.

"Are you ready?" Lance asked.

Thork'l nodded.

Lance turned and addressed the room. "May I have your attention, please?" He spoke clearly and with authority. He waited until the room had gone quiet. "I am sure that most of you have heard rumors of the raid on Acacia City." A murmur spread across the room, and he waited for silence to return. "For those of you who have not, last night, a group of Risi entered through the Waypoint and attacked the Department of Transportation. Cabin has offered aid to the city for reparation and to assist those harmed during the raid."

"How many casualties were there?" a woman in a black uniform asked.

"Twenty-four wounded and one confirmed fatality."

The crowd murmured. "Just one? That doesn't seem right. These giants are brutal."

"Who was it?" someone in a blue uniform called out. "Who died?"

Lance took a long breath and lowered his head. "I regret to inform you that it was one of our own. We recovered the body of Randolph Torres the Third from Esperanza Woods. For those who wish to honor his memory, we are holding a memorial service tonight."

People gasped and looked to Sadi.

Jenny sent feelings of compassion toward the gray-uniformed girl. *We don't need to be rivals*, she thought. *After all, I don't feel animosity toward you. Can't you see, I was just in the wrong place at the wrong time?*

Lin stepped forward with her hands clasped and her head lowered.

"While this news is tragic," Lance continued, "it's important that we remain focused on the bigger picture. Yes, we lost one life, but hundreds more still depend on the success of this mission. For the first time in Earth's history, Æons have gathered together for a common cause."

Lance looked around at the room. "Some of you come from our own organization." He gestured toward the table of gray-uniformed recruits. Aindriu cheered and pumped a fist. The other grays applauded.

"Others have come from the armed forces," Lance continued, and indicated the table of black uniforms. Two saluted, but the other three just nodded their heads. "Many of you completed the VRGo puzzle." He nodded to the table in the middle of the room filled with blue uniforms. This was the largest and most eclectic group by far. It was composed of people of many ages and races. They clapped and cheered at their announcement. "And there are those who traveled a great distance to be here." He nodded toward Jenny and the other white-uniformed recruits.

Billo whooped, and Adriana clapped. Jenny waved and felt her cheeks grow warm.

"We are all here to save the Selkans." Lance opened his arms. "But there is more. By unlocking the Terminal, you will usher the entire solar system into a new age and shape the future of galactic relations."

"No pressure," Billo whispered.

"But only one of you can wield the Riftkey." Lance looked slowly around the room. "May the best Æon win."

The room clapped and cheered.

Now I know why Lin wanted me to keep the Riftkey a secret. Jenny touched her burstepi. *It's like showing up to the race with the gold medal. It's not fair to the other competitors.*

Thork'l stepped forward. His deep voice boomed across the room, and everyone went silent. "My people and I thank you all for your dedication and hard work. You have taken us in, shielded us, and given us hope." He placed his hand on Kett'l's shoulder. "Without the Riftkey my son constructed, none of us would be here. We would still be slaves without hope for freedom." He looked across the room, meeting people's eyes one by one. "And you wouldn't have the opportunity to unlock the Terminal."

"Good luck," Kett'l said.

"Thank you." Lin stepped forward. "Now, let me introduce you to our newest recruits, Kensei Drake and Jenny Tripper." She looked toward them. "Kensei is our first recruit to bond with the emerald key." The crowd murmured with excitement. "And Jenny has bonded with Astrea's original key."

The room let out a collective gasp. Jenny felt dozens of eyes scrutinizing her, judging her. She touched the burstepi again. *I'm going to win this contest,* Jenny thought, *and prove that I deserve this Riftkey.*

21

EXPEDITION

Jack sat on the edge of his bed. He yawned and thumbed a sore muscle in his back. Last night, instead of sleeping, his brain had replayed all the poor decisions that had led him to this undersea prison. He looked over at the oval window that provided a view of the ocean and shuddered. He had discovered that he had a paralyzing fear of drowning. Living aboard a sunken spaceship kept him in a constant state of dread. *Well, at least I've got these coffee beans to take back home with me,* Jack thought as he examined the slice in the shopping bag for the hundredth time. *That coffee from Penwales yesterday really was incredible. I wonder if all Earth's coffee is that good. They might have some in the mess hall.* Jack stood up. *Alright, maybe a mug of coffee will settle my stomach.*

Jack left his cabin and took the stairs down to the mess hall. As he walked, he studied the ship's interior. *There's no evidence of construction anywhere,* he thought. *Not even a stray cable. And look at that: Even though the hallway curves, every wall panel lines up precisely with the ceiling and floor. This ship has remarkable engineering.*

Inside the mess hall, people sat clustered by the color of their uniforms. Six people in gray uniforms sat on one side. Jack recognized Aindriu among them, the muscular boy with a shaved head. Five people in black sat in the back. They were all young, no more than twenty-four,

Jack estimated. Then there were about twenty people in blue uniforms, who sat in the middle of the room. Half were young, like the other recruits. The others likely worked for Cabin. He noticed grease stains on a few of their outfits, and four others armed with holstered pistols. *Some sort of security.*

Jack's stomach grumbled as he smelled food. He rushed past the food bins and found the beverage station. *What would Cabin need protection from?* He filled a white ceramic mug with coffee and looked over at the Selkans. *Probably not the aliens or the recruits. No, it's more likely that they're armed in case of someone like me. Which means they must be aware of a security breach.* He inhaled the heavenly aroma of the coffee. *They might already know that Mister Torres was a mole. That would mean that I'm under suspicion.*

Jack sat down at an empty table in the far corner of the room. If he were going to be around people, then he'd make sure that no one could sneak up behind him. *They gave me a blue uniform, so they consider me an employee, but it's still just a disguise.*

Victus's contact, Trey, had supposedly updated every relevant database with records of Jack's service. However, it was doubtful that his quick hack would survive a careful examination. *Good thing I left my gun back on the plane,* Jack thought. *That girl, Jenny, caught me talking to Victus. Did she hear anything incriminating? Did she tell anyone?* Jack shook his head. *No, they would have already questioned me if she had. Not that it matters. My role in this mission is complete, and Victus is on his way. All I have to do is lie low until he gets here.*

Jack took a sip from his mug and sighed in delight. It was creamy, slightly nutty, and much higher quality than anything back on the station. He took another sip. *A better brewing process could reduce the bitterness.* For a moment, Jack allowed himself to daydream. He pictured himself back in the loft above his shop. Through the skylight, he could see ships gathering inside the Terminal.

A group of people entered the room and broke Jack's reverie. It was Mazu and Lin with a group of four kids in white uniforms. He recognized Jenny and Kensei, but not the other two. Lance walked up to greet them, then Lin broke off while the others got their food. After Mazu filled her tray, she split from the group. Jack watched the athletic, dark-haired woman cross the room and recalled his first meeting with her. He smiled. No other woman had literally sent him head over heels the way she had.

Mazu turned away from the food bins and walked toward him. "Mind if I sit here?"

Jack's eyes went wide and he sat up straight. "Uh, yeah, I mean, no." He forced a smile. "I don't mind. It's a free galaxy, after all." Jack's smile faded as he realized how unusual the phrase would be to someone here, on Earth.

Mazu didn't seem to notice. She set down her tray and sat across from him. Jack looked at her mug and made a mental note that she liked cream with her coffee.

"You know," Mazu said as she leaned toward Jack. Her lips were mere centimeters away from his ear. "For someone who wanted a job with us," she whispered, "you're sure acting like you don't want to be here."

The scent of her skin was raw honey, and her hair smelled of lemongrass. Her lips were pink, and her skin was like porcelain. "What do you mean?"

"Hiding in the corner like this. Why don't you sit with the others?" She motioned toward the tables filled with blue uniforms.

Jack shrugged. "I'm used to being alone, plus I'm a bit on edge."

Mazu cocked her head. "Why's that?"

"I don't like being underwater."

"You're from the Navy," Mazu said. "Don't you like the water?"

"Sure, but I prefer to stay above it," Jack said. "That's why I'm a pilot." Jack looked up and asked. "Is it really safe?"

"Oh yeah." Mazu twirled her hair. "Sure, there are a few leaks every now and then. The saline eats away at the seals, but as long as the pumps are working, we'll be alright."

Jack gulped, and his face paled.

"Are you okay?"

"Yeah, just a bit homesick." Jack thought of his dry loft back on Lan Station.

Mazu nodded. "Where are you from?"

"A-America," Jack stammered. "New Madrid."

"Oh, I've always wanted to go." Mazu took a sip of her coffee. "What did you do there?"

"Lots of odd jobs." His knee bounced with nervous energy. "But I mostly repaired boats."

"Oh?"

"Yeah." Jack became more animated as he weaved truth into his lie. "I had my own shop."

Mazu smiled and leaned forward. "What made you come out here?"

"I received an offer I couldn't refuse." Jack clenched his jaw. Sometimes the truth was more painful than a lie.

After finishing her breakfast, Mazu pushed her tray aside and spoke candidly. She talked in detail about the scientific aspects of the mission, like the ecosystem and biology of Selkans and their islands. She was a practicing exobiologist, and being able to study a new alien species up close was a dream come true. As she probed into his background, Jack stuck to the truth as often as possible, altering it just enough to fit into the Earth-based role he had assumed. Jack sighed in disappointment as Lance called for attention. He wasn't sure what to think about their leader. Lance had a much older presence than his appearance would suggest. Jack's eyes went wide. *Could Lance be a Tyran?*

The Tyran's were composed of two distinct races. One that looked identical to humans. The other had pointed ears and a single large bump on their forehead. Both races shared that same ageless face and six fingers on each hand. Jack stared at Lance's hands as he recalled their handshake from last night. *I think he had six-fingers.*

Jack had only encountered one other Tyran in person, his former hegemon, his home planet's leader. Jack had received a medal from the hegemon for his service to Balk during the war. He still remembered the ageless appearance of her face and the six fingers on each hand.

As the announcements wrapped up, Lance approached Jack's table with one of the black-uniformed crew members, a dark-skinned man built like a cargo freighter. Jack glanced at the firearm on the man's hip.

So, I am to be guarded. Jack's heart picked up a beat, and his armpits began to sweat.

"Mister Spriggan," Lance said. "How was your first night aboard the *Endeavor*?"

Jack wiped his hands on his pants and stood up. The last thing he wanted was for this tall, six-fingered Tyran to tower over him. Still, Jack only came up to Lance's chin. "Honestly, not great."

Lance chuckled. "It can take some getting used to." His blue eyes scanned Jack's face. "Mister Ward told me that you were in Acacia City to meet Mister Randolph. What business did you have with him?"

"He said he had a job for me."

"Oh, and how did you know him?"

"He served with me in the Navy."

"I didn't know that he served."

Jack forced himself to maintain eye contact. "Yes, sir. After retiring, we kept in touch through social media. After my divorce..." Jack shifted his feet uncomfortably and glanced at Mazu. Lance noticed the look and lifted an eyebrow. "Well, I was on hard times, so he offered me a job."

"Did he tell you what this job was?"

Jack looked around the room. His gaze settled on the Selkans for a second. Jack jerked his head back to Lance. "He told me the position was for a pilot but that he would only give me the details in person. I had no idea it would lead me here." Jack had spent a good part of his life reading cues and tells. It was an essential skill as a fighter. Something about LaGrange had his guard up.

"I suppose no one could have predicted the attack in Acacia City," Lance said. "It's a good thing you were there." He reached into his coat and pulled out a Topo. "Can you explain why your picture is on Trey's Topo?" Lance asked.

Jack looked at his picture on the screen and shrugged. He hadn't prepared for this, and Jack searched his mind for a suitable answer. "You tell me."

"The picture itself isn't suspicious." Lance returned the Topo to his coat. "But the data attached to it is quantum encrypted. Do you know why Mister Randolph would have encrypted this message?"

"No, sir." Jack shrugged. "But that's a recent picture from my social profile."

Lance rubbed his chin as he studied Jack's face. "If you are going to stay on my ship, I will need you to do some errands for us."

"Yes, sir," Jack said. "I'm here for a job, after all."

"I need you to take the company plane on a supply run after break-fast. Mister Nichols will accompany you." Lance motioned toward the gun-toting man in the black uniform.

"Hey, I'm Marcel." The dark-skinned man held out his hand. Jack shook it.

"And," Lance continued, "you will accompany Miss Song on her mission."

Jack looked down at Mazu. She sipped her coffee and smiled back at him. "What kind of mission?" Jack asked.

Mazu spoke up. "It's an expedition through an underwater cave system about six kilometers from here."

Jack froze. "We're going underwater?" He gulped.

"Is something wrong?" Lance asked. "I assumed a Navy man like you had hours of dive training."

Jack rubbed his face. "No, actually, I was just a pilot. I haven't been diving in a long time." *Actually*, Jack thought, *I've never been diving.*

"No worries." Marcel smiled. "A child could operate a Tumlare suit."

22

FIRST TEST

Jenny nudged Kensei, "Look." She pointed to the far corner of the room. Lance and a man in a black uniform stood next to Jack and Mazu. Even from here, Jenny could tell that Jack looked nervous. *Maybe it has something to do with what I overheard him saying last night,* Jenny thought.

"What do you think they're talking about?" Kensei asked.

"No idea," Jenny said. "But judging by Jack's expression, it can't be good."

A minute later, Lance and the man in the black uniform left Jack's table. Mazu stood up and squeezed Jack's shoulder. She said something to him before leaving the mess hall. Jack remained at the table, looking pale.

Lin, who had been talking to the Selkans, walked over to Jenny and Kensei and asked. "Are you two ready to take your first test?"

Jenny and Kensei looked at each other and said, "Yeah, sure."

Lin led them out of the room and to a large circular room directly below the mess hall. The air smelled of antiseptic, and clusters of hexagonal ceiling lights illuminated a variety of medical appliances. They walked between four mobile examination tables to a corner office in the back. On the door, a handwritten sign read, "Mazu Song, Ph.D."

Inside the office, posters of anatomical drawings lined the walls. Two tall hardwood bookshelves held tomes on natural studies. A couple of jars containing deep-ocean fish stood next to a taxidermied squirrel, platypus, and owl.

Mazu sat behind a simple wooden desk. When they entered, she stood up and cleared a pile of books from one of two aluminum chairs and said. "Have a seat."

Jenny and Kensei sat down.

"I just made some tea; would you like some?"

"Yes, please," they all answered.

Lin took four small, floral-printed cups off a shelf and set them on the desk. Mazu lifted a white teapot and poured a green-tinted mint-and-floral fusion into the cups.

"Thank you," they said.

Mazu moved a little wooden dummy aside to look at Jenny. "You've probably noticed some changes, wounds healed"—she looked at Kensei —"vision improved."

They nodded.

"Right now, your brain is as malleable as a young child's."

"We have a device called an ADD "—Mazu leaned on her elbows —"that can condense months of training into a single session."

"ADD?" Jenny asked.

"An autodidactic device," Mazu said.

"Automatic learning." Kensei's eyes widened. "You're going to make us smarter."

"The concept of accelerated learning is nothing new, but the ADD is on another level."

Jenny lifted her cup and inhaled. The floral scent was like a mild perfume, and the mint tickled her nose. She took a sip. It was divine.

"So, it's like learning without doing anything?" Jenny asked.

"It's not quite that easy," Mazu said. "It's more like boot camp for your brain."

Kensei set down his cup after taking a sip. "When do we start?"

"The sooner, the better," Mazu said. "The ADD has a strong magnet, so you'll have to leave your metal belongings here." She picked up a wooden bowl and set it on the desk.

Jenny pulled her mother's amulet and Astrea's key from around her neck and dropped them in the bowl. Hesitantly, she unstrapped her burstepi, which Mazu set behind her desk. Finally, Jenny removed her earrings and dropped them into the bowl. "Do you have any other piercings?" Mazu looked Jenny up and down.

"No." Jenny looked at her sideways. "That's all." She smiled at the thought of Billo having to remove all her jewelry.

Kensei placed his key in the bowl and set his backpack on the desk, and Leon's pink nose peeked through the flap. "I'll be right back," he whispered. "You'll be safe here."

Mazu nodded and stashed the bowl behind her desk. "Follow me."

Mazu led them a few doors down the hall and entered a room on the opposite side of the sickbay. Yellow signs warned of a powerful magnet, and three large screens displayed controls and readouts. A wall divided the room in half, and an enormous light-gray machine was visible through a window.

"It looks like a PET scan." Jenny had seen a positron-emission tomography scanner while her mom was in the hospital.

"Yes, but unlike your PET scan, this can read and write." Mazu tapped one of the large screens, and Jenny felt the machine hum through the wall.

"What do you mean by 'write'?" Kensei asked. "Are you going to brainwash us?"

"Nothing as droll as that," Lin said.

"First," Mazu said as she tapped at the displays, "we'll identify the domains of the brain associated with learnable tasks. Once we have a map of your brain, we'll create new connections based on logical progressions of your existing model."

"You make it sound like we're computers," Kensei said.

"That's not too far off," Lin said. "After all, our brains are organic computers."

"Now"—Mazu tapped the screen and the ADD machine hummed —"who wants to go first?"

Jenny gulped and held up her hand. If she was going to win this contest, beat Sadi, and prove she was worthy of the Riftkey, she had to be brave. "I will."

"Wonderful," Lin said and opened the door to the machine. It was a big gray tunnel with a plastic halo on one end. The halo looked like one of those old-fashioned hair dryers from beauty salons.

Lin smiled and said. "Have a seat."

As Jenny sat down, Lin lowered the plastic halo around her head. It tightened around her skull, and her scalp prickled with energy. Jenny wiped a bead of sweat from her forehead and looked up at Lin. "Have you done this?"

"No. Unfortunately, my brain's too old." Lin tapped her head. "I'm stuck with what I've got."

Jenny watched Kensei's pale face through the control-room window. "You look more worried than I feel."

He let out a forced laugh. "I don't like small spaces."

"If you're claustrophobic," Mazu said, "we can medicate you."

"No, that's okay, I think I'll be alright."

"I'm ready when you are," Mazu said through a microphone in the control room.

"How are you doing?" Lin asked Jenny.

"I'm okay."

"Just so you know, it will get really loud, but that's normal."

"Okay." Jenny took a deep, shaky breath to calm her pounding heart. She gave Lin a thumbs-up. "I'm ready."

Lin reclined the seat until it became a table. The autodidactic device lit up, and the table slid into the circular opening. The halo clicked and shifted her head into position. Jenny felt her head lock into place.

Lin squeezed Jenny's hand, then joined Mazu and Kensei behind the screens.

"We're synchronized," Mazu said. The machine purred with energy, and Jenny's head buzzed.

A low tone sounded in her mind that slowly grew in pitch. Then, the sound became louder and drowned out all her other senses. Her mind went wild, and her body seemed to vibrate. A bright flash exploded behind her eyelids, and her mind shattered into a thousand dreams. Her eyes fluttered as she learned directional harmonic theory, the emission frequency of atoms, modal vibrational phenomena, quantum mechanics, and so much more. A peculiar tingling moved from her feet up to her head. There was an odd sensation, like a shirt turning inside out.

Suddenly, Jenny felt weightless, and she was standing in the room looking down at her own body, still in the autodidactic device. *I'm having an out-of-body experience*, Jenny thought. She looked down at her hands. They were made of blue light, and a shifting corona surrounded her.

Jenny heard the sound of the machine transition into a low hum and come to a stop. There was a sensation, like a rubber band stretched to its breaking point, and she returned to her own body. A moment later, the table slid out of the device. Jenny blinked at the sudden brightness of the overhead lights.

Lin tilted Jenny's chair upright and lifted the halo from her head. "Well, how did it go?"

"I feel like I just got off the world's longest roller coaster."

"Sounds like fun." Kensei chuckled weakly from the doorway.

Jenny looked at Kensei. An aura of nervous yellow light surrounded him. "You're glowing."

"Yeah?"

"Yeah," Jenny replied. "It's like your whole body is wearing a crown of golden light."

Lin nodded. "Previous subjects have described seeing auras. It's nothing to worry about. It'll wear off eventually."

"Okay," Jenny said as she stood up.

Kensei took her place and Lin lowered the halo onto his head. The chair reclined and slid into the machine.

Jenny and Lin joined Mazu in the control room. A three-dimensional model of Kensei's brain—in shades of blue on black—appeared on one of the two large screens. The second screen displayed schematic views from the top, sides, front, and back. Rows of statistics bordered the drawings.

Jenny turned to Lin. "When I was in there..." She tried to recall the experience, but it was like trying to remember a dream.

"What was it like?" Lin asked.

Jenny kicked her foot. *Did I really see myself?* She remembered what Billo had said. Cabin was here to help. Billo and Adriana had powers, and if Jenny was going to find hers, then she needed to be honest. "It's like I was outside my own body."

"Interesting," Mazu said. "That's the first time I've heard of autoscopy in any of our subjects."

"Do you think it might be related to my ability?" Jenny asked.

"It could be," Lin said. "Keep it in mind as you go through your tests, okay?"

"Okay."

A few minutes later, the ADD powered down, and the table slid out of the circular opening. Lin entered the room and helped Kensei out of the chair.

Kensei returned to the control room. "Wow, what a trip. Hey, Jenny, now you're glowing."

Jenny smiled. "Yeah? What color?"

"White," Kensei replied. "Soft white. Like a rose."

Jenny and Kensei retrieved their belongings from Mazu's office and left the sickbay.

Jenny fiddled with the straps of her burstepi and asked, "When will we feel the effects of the ADD?"

"It's not instantaneous," Mazu said. "And some connections won't be fully established until you seek them."

"How do we do that?" Kensei asked as he checked on Leon.

"The best way is by experience. You'll find that you'll be better at familiar tasks and that you know some things you didn't before. Like languages."

"So, we'll be able to understand people?"

"And aliens," Lin said. "Though you may have some trouble speaking."

"Why's that?"

"Some sounds will be unfamiliar, and you'll have to train your muscles to form them before you can properly speak them."

"That makes sense," Kensei said.

"Where are we going now?" Jenny asked.

"To the testing room."

"Um, Mazu?" Jenny asked.

"Yeah?"

"Could you teach me that flip move you used on Jack?"

Mazu smiled. "Sure, everyone should learn how to protect themselves. Especially from guys like Jack." She winked.

They climbed two sets of stairs to the top level of the *Endeavor*. As they rounded the hallway Jenny heard a familiar sound echo against the white walls of the ship. It was the squeak of shoes on a gym floor. They entered a large room directly above the mess hall that looked like a school gymnasium, and there she saw the source of the sound. Eight people were playing volleyball at the center of the gym, four in blue uniforms versus four in black.

"Here we have our gymnasium," Lin said. "As you can see, it's been set up for volleyball, but we also play basketball, handball, and football in this space." She pointed left at a room filled with free weights and resistance machines. "That room is set up for weight training." She pointed right at a room filled with tumbling mats, heavy bags, and dummies. "That room is for structured activities. You're free to use these rooms any time of day."

"Team sports are drop-in only," Mazu said, "and work on a first-come-first-serve basis."

Jenny pointed toward the back of the gym where a group of people had gathered in front of a row of windows. "What's in that room?"

"That's where we're going." Lin led them around the volleyball game.

A red-haired, freckled young woman caught the volleyball, halting the game. Soon, every eye was on Kensei and Jenny. As they approached the back of the gym, Jenny saw four black boxes the size of refrigerators through a row of windows. A recruit in a white uniform stood in front of one of the cubes with her back to the gym.

"It's Adriana." Jenny stood on her tiptoes and tried to see what she was doing at the large box.

There was a leaderboard next to the room's entrance. The top row read, "Player," "Maze 1," "Maze 2," "Maze 3," "Maze 4," and "Total." Underneath was a list of names sorted by score. The highest score of 423 belonged to Randolph Torres the Third (Trey). Cassadi Stevens followed with 415, and Adriana Thatcher stood in third place with 409.

"I see that Trey's score is still there." Mazu withdrew her Topo. "I should probably remove it."

"Do you know how he died?" Kensei asked.

"Blunt force trauma." Mazu tapped at her Topo. "Likely a blow from a Risi's club."

"Do you know why the Risi attacked Acacia City?" Kensei asked.

Mazu shook her head. "No idea." When she put her Topo away, Trey's name was gone from the leaderboard, leaving Sadi in the number one position.

As Jenny studied the board, one thing stood out. "Why does every player have a score of zero in at least one maze?"

"Each of the mazes tests a different range of frequencies," Lin said. "And no one can sense the full range."

The door opened, and Adriana stepped out. Those gathered around clapped and whooped. On the leaderboard, her name slid to the number one position.

Billo clapped and ran up to Adriana. "I knew you could do it!" she cheered.

Kensei gave Adriana a high five. "Does that mean you'll be the one to go to the Terminal?"

"I wish," Adriana said.

"I'm sure she will." Billo gazed at Adriana with undisguised admiration. Jenny realized it was the same look Kensei wore for Adriana.

Just like at home, Jenny thought. *Adriana has no idea that everyone is in love with her.*

"The day isn't even over yet," Adriana replied. "I'm sure Sadi will just pass me again."

"Jenny, are you ready?" Lin held the door open.

"Um, sure." Jenny felt far from ready for whatever was about to happen, and now she felt self-conscious with Adriana there.

"Good luck," Kensei said.

Jenny felt everyone's eyes on her as she entered the room. Lin followed her inside, and the noises of the ship evaporated as the door swung shut. Inside the room, the windows acted as one-way mirrors, further isolating her from the gym just outside.

Lin approached the first black box. "The goal is to guide a ball through a maze as quickly as possible."

"And the fastest time gets the Riftkey?"

"That's right. Of course, you already have one."

"Is there any point in me taking these tests?"

"Yes. These are actually simulators, designed to teach you how to unlock the Terminal. That way, when you're up there"—Lin pointed up—"in space, you'll know how to use the Riftkey to unlock the Terminal."

"I get it." Jenny tried to infuse her voice with confidence that she didn't feel. "I'll just have to make sure I win."

"That's right." Lin smiled. "After you insert your Waypoint key into the brass plate, the walls will become clear, and the timer will start." She walked toward the exit and opened the door. Sounds from the gymnasium flooded the room.

Jenny stepped up to the first black box and peered inside. She couldn't see anything—no maze, no ball. There was a brass plate set low on the box with a ruby gemstone above a keyhole. The hole looked like a perfect fit for her Waypoint key. She pulled it free of her uniform.

"Try to be receptive and calm," said Lin from the doorway. "And, Jenny..."

"Yeah."

"Good luck." The door swished shut, and the room was silent once more.

Jenny stared at the box and took a deep breath. *If the gems act the same here as they do in the Waypoint keys, then this maze will test...ugh, what did the ruby symbolize? Perception! This should test my ability to control perception.*

Jenny inserted her key, and a steady tone sounded from the box. A panel slid open on the brass plate, revealing a timer set to five minutes. The walls of the box transitioned from black to transparent glass, and the clock started.

Inside was a maze that stretched from edge to edge. A red ball, like a large marble, sat within the labyrinthine walls. In the center, a bronze-lined hole marked the finish. Jenny traced the path from beginning to end and quickly discovered a problem. She had no idea how to move the ball. There were no visible controls.

This must be part of the test.

The walls were like glass. Jenny slid her hands along the sides, feeling for any bumps or depressions her eyes missed in the sides of the box. As she did, the maze floor tilted.

The red ball rolled down a corridor and came to rest against a wall. Tentatively, she brushed her hand along the opposite side of the box. The floor tilted in the other direction. Jenny smiled and placed her hands on the sides of the box. The floor of the maze quivered under her trembling hands. She moved her right hand down, and the floor tilted in response.

The ball rolled, but it was too fast. She overcorrected, and the ball moved in the wrong direction. She sighed, growing frustrated, then remembered Lin's advice. This was just a learning exercise, designed to teach her how to use the Riftkey. She forced herself back to calmness.

Rather than focusing on the path, Jenny decided to get a feel for the controls. After a minute of trial and error, she could guide the ball in any direction she wanted. Yet she lacked a certain finesse when going around corners and bounced the red marble down its course until it dropped into the bronze-lined finish. She stepped back, thankful to have completed the first maze. Jenny glanced at the timer. She had just under three minutes left. Not bad.

The walls of the maze melted into the floor and reformed into a second labyrinth. Its corridors were narrower and contained more traps than before. Jenny sighed. *I guess it was too good to last.* There was a new finish, this one lined with silver, in the back corner.

Jenny placed her hands on the sides while she scouted the path. She tried harder to avoid traps and slow the ball down before each turn. The new strategy paid off, and when the red ball dropped into the silver hole, she had one and a half minutes left on the clock.

This time, she didn't dare to take her hands off the box. A good thing too, as the maze walls melted away and a third labyrinth appeared. This one was full of dead ends, and instead of the hole, a golden cage marked the finish. She found her path through the maze and slid her sweat-slick hands across the smooth wall of the box. As the ball slipped inside the golden cage, the clock stopped with only eight seconds left.

This small victory filled her with a sense of exhilaration. As Jenny pulled her key from the hole, the box grew dark, and the panel closed over the timer. Curious if she could improve her score, she inserted her key, but nothing happened. Shrugging, she approached the second test.

A sapphire gemstone sat above the keyhole. *This one represents the ability to control radiation.* Eager to apply her new knowledge, Jenny inserted her key. The panel slid open, and Jenny noticed some immediate differences. Two waveform patterns appeared on either side of the timer. The left one was on a red background, the right one on blue. A meter, measuring watt-hours from zero to one thousand, sat above the clock.

The walls of the box transitioned from black to transparent.

Jenny gasped. This maze was completely different from the first one. The labyrinth did not rise from the floor. Instead, it was set into the sides of the box. Water filled most of the cube except for a short gap at the top.

This ball was blue and sat at the bottom of a water-filled column. Jenny walked around the maze and found the golden cage on the opposite wall from the ball. Carefully, she traced a path from the ball to the cage.

Jenny placed her hands on the sides of the box, but nothing happened. She searched the cube for controls, and like before, there were none. The timer ticked down. She imagined people outside the room laughing at her, and her ears grew hot.

Well, maybe I could try this one later. Jenny reached down to pull her key out of the socket. A buzz traveled through her arm and she jerked her hand away.

Something about that feeling was familiar. It reminded her of the VRGo test. Jenny pinched the key with her fingertips. Her body buzzed with energy, and patterns of light swam in her vision. A white waveform with peaks and valleys appeared in her mind.

Jenny looked down at the waveforms next to the timer. The red one had dramatic peaks and troughs, and the blue one was more of a spiky pattern. Just as she had done with the VRGo test, she hummed inside her mind. The chaotic humming changed to a steady tone, and the peaks and valleys of her key's white waveform changed. She experimented with different pitches, and the waveform varied in frequency and intensity.

Jenny worked the white waveform until it matched the red pattern.

As she did, the blue ball flashed, and the meter buzzed. Nothing else seemed to happen, so she tried the blue waveform. The ball flashed again, and to her surprise, the water around the ball froze. The ice formed a column that pushed the blue sphere upward until it tipped into the next column of the maze. It fell with a plunk and quickly sank to the bottom.

Jenny clapped with joy. She could move the ball to the other side of the maze on columns of ice. She put her hand back on her key and tried the blue pattern again. The meter buzzed and nothing happened. *What did I do wrong?* She looked down and noticed that the needle on the meter had maxed out. Since the blue one didn't work, she decided to try the red pattern again. As she did, the ice melted away, and the meter returned to zero. She smiled.

By her third sequence, Jenny could melt the ice in one column while freezing the water in the next. After her sixth round, she could control the direction of the freeze. This opened up new routes. Instead of rising to the top of each column, Jenny could push the ball into openings in the wall. Once she reached the last column, she lifted the blue ball on a column of ice until it rested inside the golden cage. Jenny pumped her arm in celebration and looked down. The clock had stopped at 00:01.

A pit formed in her stomach. *That was too close.* Jenny approached the third box on shaky legs. A heliodor capped the keyhole on this brass plate. *This one is electromagnetism.* She inserted her key. The brass panel slid open to reveal two different waveforms on red and blue backgrounds. Above the timer sat a voltage meter. Its needle—which was all the way to the right—read 100 percent.

Inside the box was the most bizarre maze of all. Forty strange mechanical devices—connected by ramps—filled the interior. Half of the devices were red, and the other half were blue. In the top corner, a trapdoor held a yellow ball up from the golden cage below it.

Jenny chose the red waveform and hummed inside her mind until the white waveform synced. Jenny jerked back in surprise as an electrical arc jumped from the yellow ball to a red device, which powered on and rotated ninety degrees. Next, Jenny tried the blue waveform. This time, a green laser shot out from the nearest blue device, bounced off a reflective surface on a red mechanism, and terminated at the floor of the box. The voltage meter, she noticed, had dropped by 10 percent, but with the red device, it didn't drop at all.

Jenny shook her head. *What am I supposed to do?* She tried blue again. A green laser shot out from the next blue device. It bounced off a reflective surface on a red device and hit the floor.

The blue devices shoot lasers, and the red ones reflect them. Jenny shook her head. *I still don't see a pattern.* She chose more waveforms at random. At one point, she activated a blue device and nothing happened. Looking down, Jenny noticed that the voltage meter had reached zero. The timer read 03:23. *What do I do now? I've only activated half the devices.*

Okay, Jenny thought, *each blue device decreases the meter by ten percent, but I've activated twelve. The meter should have reached zero two devices ago. Jenny traced the path back and noticed that two of the red devices had reflected the lasers at two blue devices. That must be the trick, Jenny thought. Looks like I have to adjust each of the red devices so that they feed energy back into the system.*

Jenny worked her way backward. She found that if she focused on the last device she'd powered on that she could deactivate it and get more energy in the bank. Then, she discovered that she could access any of the devices by focusing on them. She targeted the first red device and rotated it until the laser pointed at a blue device. Then, she did the same for each of the red devices until the laser opened the trapdoor, and the crystal ball dropped into the golden cage. The transparent walls of the box turned black, and the timer stopped at 00:18. It was her best score so far.

Jenny wiped her brow as she approached the last box. *These puzzles are exhausting.* Yet, they also filled her with a great sense of accomplishment.

An emerald sat above the keyhole on the fourth test. *This one is for gravity,* Jenny thought as she inserted her key. The panel slid open, revealing a timer and four new waveforms: two on either side of the clock, and two on the top and bottom. The walls grew transparent, and the clock ticked down. The green ball sat in the middle of the floor, but the finish was nowhere in sight. The structure of the maze seemed identical to the first one; however, these labyrinth walls were much shorter, and small geometric objects littered the course.

Jenny touched her key and chose the rightmost waveform. The ball rolled to the right. *Huh, it's like a controller.* The left pattern made the ball go left, and up and down made the ball move forward and backward.

Neat, but what's the point if there's no finish?

Jenny rolled the ball down a corridor of the maze. A small cube was in the way, but instead of bouncing off of it, the ball stuck to the block. Jenny smiled. *It's sticky.* She rolled the lopsided ball to a small cone and picked it up too. But, when she turned toward a big cylinder, the green ball rebounded.

So, there's a size limit.

As Jenny rolled her ball around, she was careful to avoid large objects while she picked up small ones. She rolled up ramps, across bridges, and inside walled areas. Over time, the ball grew unwieldy and lumpy. When she thought it couldn't hold any more, it absorbed all the pieces it had collected so far. The ball grew slightly larger and became a darker shade of green.

The ball felt more massive as well, and best of all, it could now pick up larger objects. She grabbed the large cylinder, then the ramps and bridges she had rolled over earlier. Once she had gathered enough objects, the ball absorbed the pieces stuck to it. It grew a little larger and darkened to an evergreen color.

Now, as Jenny rolled the larger ball around, it picked up entire sections of the maze floor. Underneath, Jenny glimpsed a flash of gold. She doubled her efforts. As more layers came loose, a golden cage soon became visible.

The green ball flashed again, absorbing the objects and growing larger, and darker. The ball moved sluggishly across the floor. The finish was only millimeters away, but it took several agonizing seconds for the ball to crawl inside the cage.

The walls went black, and the timer stopped with nine seconds remaining. As Jenny removed her key, she almost collapsed from exhaustion. At the same time, her heart thudded in her chest, and a sense of euphoria made her body tingle. Behind her, the door to the gym opened, and Lin walked in. Jenny gave a nervous laugh.

"Jenny, you were amazing," Lin said. "Nobody has ever completed every test."

"Really? I'm the first?" Jenny knew the leaderboard results, but she still found it hard to believe that no one else had completed all four challenges.

"What you just accomplished was comparable to a deaf person sitting at a piano for the first time and playing a concerto." Lin took Jenny's arm and led her out. "Sure, you played a lot of wrong notes, but all you have to do is work on your technique."

Smiling, Jenny scanned the leaderboard for her name. Her spirits dropped as she looked lower and lower on the list. Finally, she found her name in last place with a score of 36. The next lowest was Aindriu's, at 124, and he had only completed the first test. Billo had the next-lowest score.

"Your turn, Kensei," Lin said as she held the door open.

"Good luck." Jenny tried to sound cheerful.

"Thanks." Kensei looked a bit pale as he entered the room.

While Kensei was in the testing room, Jenny studied the leaderboard until some patterns emerged from the scores. Everyone except for Jenny had a score of at least 60 on the first maze. A few, like Aindriu, had scored significantly higher.

It seemed that everyone had a much higher score on just one of the mazes. *It must correspond with their chosen key.*

Lin stepped out of the maze room.

"How do people get those really high scores on one test?" Jenny asked her.

"They found shortcuts," Lin said. "Often from a unique ability in their range of affinity."

Just like Adriana, Jenny thought. *I bet she made the laser shoot directly at the trapdoor with her portals.*

"You'll need to find a shortcut to have any chance at winning," Lin continued. "I wouldn't expect you to find one on your first try. It's amazing that you finished the tests at all, let alone all of them."

"Next time I'll have the mazes memorized."

"That won't help," Mazu said. "They change each time."

Jenny exhaled noisily. "Why doesn't the first test have waveforms?"

"It's the perception test," Mazu said. "In my opinion, it's the keystone of all the tests."

"Why? I'm just rolling a ball around a maze. In the others, I'm freezing water, or controlling electricity or gravity."

Mazu paused to gather her thoughts. "True, the other tests are all external, so their effects are more obvious. The perception test requires you to improve yourself, and because of that, it influences all the others."

"How?"

Lin said, "My father liked to tell me, 'A blind man takes a stumbling path through a room, but a sighted man finds the path before taking their first step.'"

Jenny narrowed her eyes. She still couldn't see how rolling a ball around a maze could compete with the ability to heat or chill objects at will. She turned around and watched Kensei work through the tests. So far, he wasn't any faster than her at the first two tests. He failed to complete the electromagnetic test in time, but he was about to start the last maze.

This is his key.

After he'd worked through the gravity test, the box turned black, and Kensei stumbled out of the door as if he were drunk. He slid down the wall with Leon jumping up and down on his shoulder the whole time.

Jenny knelt down next to him. "You alright?"

"Yeah." Kensei's head rolled around on his shoulders. "But my hands feel huge, and the room feels like it's tilting."

"Take your time." She checked the leaderboard. Kensei's name had appeared a few slots above hers with a score of 212. "You did great in there. Way better than me." *Even though you scored zero in the electromagnetic maze and I scored on every test.* "You must have found a shortcut."

"Yeah, maybe." Kensei's head rolled as he tried to focus on Jenny.

There was a jingling sound from Billo's earrings as she jogged up to them. Billo pulled Jenny toward the leaderboard. "Hey! Congratulations on your first test."

"Thanks."

Billo studied the board and pouted at Jenny. "Don't let it worry you; that's a better score than I got my first time."

Jenny sighed and dropped her head. "I'll do better next time."

There was a clamor near the entrance to the gym as a group of gray uniforms walked through the volleyball court. The players stopped their game and yelled for them to go around. The grays ignored them and continued to walk across the court.

Billo screwed up her face. "What a bunch of bullies."

"Yeah." Jenny's eyes focused on Sadi, and she felt her body grow hot.

"I mean, they think they own the place. Just because they're from this Earth, and they work for Lance..."

"Yeah." Jenny tried to listen to her roommate, but there was a pounding in her ears. The grays gathered at the windows to the test room, and for a moment there was silence.

"Jenny, are you listening to me?"

"Oh yeah." She turned to focus on her roommate. Billo had a very dejected look on her face. She obviously was not used to being ignored. "I'm sorry."

"It's okay." Billo lowered her voice so that the grays would not hear her. "So, how are you going to beat them?"

Jenny shrugged. "What, me?"

"You're the first person to complete all the tests."

"Yeah, but my test scores are horrible."

"You just need a little practice."

Jenny's heart gave a little skip. Billo was looking at her with the same admiration she had shown Adriana. *I completed all the tests; that must mean I have more potential than all the other recruits.* "I guess you're right. After all, I did finish all the tests on my first try." Jenny lifted her head, raised her voice, and said loud and proud, "I bet I'll have the high score by tomorrow."

"Is that so, Tripper?" Sadi said from behind them.

Jenny jumped.

"I'll take that bet."

Jenny's body flushed with heat as she turned to look at Sadi. "We weren't talking to you."

"Do you think you can beat me?" Sadi asked. "Or were you just trying to impress your Astrean friend?"

Jenny stood up straight. *I can't back down now.* "You heard right. I'm going to beat you."

Sadi smirked. "Let's make it interesting, then. If you win, I'll take your duties for a week."

"Duties?"

"You know, chores, errands, jobs. And if I win, then you'll take mine."

"It's a deal."

They shook, each giving their confirmation of the bet.

Sadi studied the board. "Last place, Tripper? Good luck." She turned and entered the testing room.

"That could have gone better," Billo said.

23

KATA

Jenny stood in the gym and thought about her exchange with Sadi. *Did I really just bet that I could beat the person with the highest score? There's no way I can win. Maybe it won't be so bad to clear the trays from the mess hall.*

"Jenny," Lin said, "you and Kensei should have invitations on your Topos."

Jenny removed her Topo from her pocket and found the invitation; it was for 13:30. She accepted it. "What's it for?"

"I have daily check-ins with all my recruits. It's your opportunity to tell me how you're doing and how I can help you. Though I don't know what I can do about you and Sadi, but I blame myself for that."

"And while you have your Topo out," Mazu said, "you should sign up for your next test."

"Okay. How?"

Mazu pointed out which application to open and how to schedule a time. Jenny saw that Kensei had already reserved a slot at 20:30. The only remaining time today was at 21:00. Jenny took it.

"Billo," Lin said, "I believe you and I have our appointment in a few minutes."

"That's right. See you back in our room, Jenny."

"Bye." Jenny watched Lin and Billo leave the gym.

Mazu stepped in front of Jenny. "You should not aggravate Sadi."

Jenny took a deep breath. "I'm tired of everyone being afraid of her."

"I understand your frustration. To be honest, I would like to see her taken down a peg or two. Just be careful—this is more than just a game to her. It's more like life or death."

Jenny gulped and nodded. She noticed two young men in blue uniforms studying the scoreboard. One had curly brown hair and hazel eyes; the other was taller, with unkempt black hair and light blue eyes.

Hazel Eyes nudged the tall guy. "Go ahead, ask her."

"No." Tall Guy twisted away. "Stop."

Jenny looked at the young men. "What did you want to ask me?"

Tall Guy went stiff and his face turned red.

Hazel Eyes answered. "Are you really from another universe?"

"Yeah." Jenny looked at Kensei. "We both are."

"That's so cool." Tall Guy leaned against the window to the test room. Inside, Sadi had already moved on to the second maze.

"Did you two just pass the gravity test?" Hazel Eyes asked.

Jenny stood up straighter. "We did."

"That's amazing. Most of us thought it was broken."

The taller one looked into Jenny's eyes. "By the way, I'm Moeshe, and this is Ezra."

"Nice to meet you. I'm Jenny, and that's Kensei."

Kensei's head still rolled around his shoulders.

"I'm pleased to meet you," Moeshe said. Ezra elbowed him in the ribs. "Oh, yeah. Ezra and I wanted to know the trick?"

"Trick?"

"Of how you two passed the gravity test," Ezra said.

"Oh," Jenny and Kensei both started to say. "It's like." Jenny smiled. She pointed at Kensei and said, "You tell them."

"Okay." Kensei pushed himself upright and leaned against the wall. "You know how black absorbs light and white reflects it?"

"Yeah." Both boys leaned forward.

"Well, it's like that, but with gravity. I make the ball more absorbent than the pieces, and they jump right to it."

"So, that's how you did it," Jenny said. "I must be gravity color-blind because all I can do is make one side of the ball heavier so it rolls in that direction."

"I think it's pretty amazing." Moeshe looked at Jenny and fiddled with his hands. "I was wondering...if you have some time...maybe we could discuss the differences between our universes over lunch, if you're free." He glanced at Kensei.

"Uh, sure." Jenny smiled. "I'd love to."

Kensei put himself between Jenny and Moeshe. "But right now, we have more training to do, right, Mazu?"

Mazu grinned at Kensei. "Yes." She faced Jenny. "Did you still want me to show you that move?"

Jenny's face lit up. "Yes, I do."

"Kensei"—Mazu winked and hooked him by the elbow—"let's go."

Jenny waved at the boys. "Goodbye."

Mazu led them to a room on one side of the gym. It smelled of stale sweat. Blue tumbling mats covered the floor, and heavy bags hung from the ceiling. In the corner was one of those wooden men used for practicing martial arts.

"Let's start with the basics." Mazu slipped off her shoes and stepped onto the mats. Jenny and Kensei did the same. "Show me your best stances." Mazu demonstrated by setting her feet shoulder-width apart and bending her knees. She placed one hand forward, palm straight out.

Jenny only knew fencing stances. She turned her body at an angle, to make herself a small target, and slid one foot forward. Kensei stood like he was guarding a basketball player.

"That's good." Mazu stood and walked around them. She pushed and pulled at their arms and legs, and corrected their footing. "If your stance isn't strong, then your technique will be weak." She kicked Kensei's foot into position. "I'm showing you the basics of fighting, but I want you to know that all fights should be avoided if possible." She twisted Jenny's hips. "Real fights aren't choreographed. They're messy, and can mean life or death." She straightened Kensei's shoulders. "Attack as a last resort, and act as if your life depends on it. Aim for tender areas, like eyes—" Her hand flashed forward, and a blast of wind hit Jenny's face. Mazu's finger stopped a centimeter from her eye. "Groin—" Her foot launched up and stopped just below Kensei's groin. He whimpered and covered himself. "And pressure points." Mazu pressed her thumbs into Jenny's and Kensei's throats at the point where neck and collarbone met.

Jenny's body turned to jelly, and she collapsed to the mat. There was a weird tingling where Mazu had poked her. After a few seconds, she regained control and returned to her fighting stance. She watched Mazu warily.

"Your treatment has granted increased strength and endurance, but not technique or reflexes. You'll still have to train your muscles to match your wits."

"What do you mean?" Kensei asked.

"Do you remember how we got to this room?"

"Yeah, we walked."

"But did you have to tell each foot to take a step and when?"

"No, I just thought of where to go—"

"And your legs did the rest."

"Your brain knows how to walk, but you don't have to think about it. The same goes for writing, speech, and even breathing. You may have more knowledge now, but your muscles still need to learn some basic routines."

"Like our stances," Jenny said.

"Exactly. A firm stance is useful, but adaptation is more important." She walked behind them, grabbed the blue mat, and yanked.

Jenny's feet slid backward, and she crashed shoulder-first onto the mat. She rubbed her sore arm and scowled at Mazu. Reluctantly, she returned to her stance and narrowed her eyes at her instructor. Getting thrown around wasn't really what she had in mind for their lesson.

"Use whatever tools you have available, even if all you have are your teeth and nails."

After the rough introduction, Mazu spent the next twenty minutes running through variations of stances. Jenny quickly grew frustrated with her own body. While the ADD had granted her book knowledge of all these techniques, her muscles refused to respond the way she'd expected. She felt sluggish and lacked the flexibility or finesse to hold proper positions. Jenny mentioned this to Mazu.

"You lack muscle memory," Mazu said. "The only way to achieve this is by training. I'll teach you a tai chi kata. I want you to practice it whenever you can. Over time, your muscles will be at the same level as your brain."

Mazu demonstrated the kata once, then twice. On the second round, Jenny copied the movements. On the third round, Mazu stopped her demonstration and made corrections to their techniques. After twenty minutes of slow, practiced movements, Jenny's legs shook with exhaustion.

Satisfied with their level of effort, Mazu led them to the heavy bags. Jenny stepped up to her sand-filled opponent, formed a proper fist, and punched as hard as she could. She hadn't expected much, but her mouth dropped open in surprise. The heavy bag jerked back as if struck by a sledgehammer and swung on its mount.

"Not bad." Mazu smiled. She brought her arm back halfway, then knocked her heavy bag off the hook with one punch. She easily returned the bag to the hook and watched Jenny and Kensei.

After several minutes, Mazu brought them back to the mat. For the next fifteen minutes, she showed them some basic throws and holds, including the one she had used on Jack. After each lesson, Mazu made subtle corrections of position, then had Jenny and Kensei practice on each other. Jenny found that sparring one-on-one was the best teacher of all.

Kensei twisted out of an arm hold, only to have Jenny counter and lock his head between her legs.

"Wow, Jenny, you're good."

"Have you trained in martial arts before?" Mazu asked.

"Just fencing." Jenny blocked an attempted grab. "I guess it helped."

"Yes." Mazu nodded. "The ADD is better at enhancing existing experience than just adding knowledge."

What Mazu said seemed right. Jenny felt fast. Not limb-swirling, bullet-dodging fast, but steady and consistent and with an economy of movement. She'd never had better control over her body in her life.

Mazu looked up at the clock and sighed. "That's enough fighting for today. I have a prior appointment, but before I go, I'd like to see you practice with your keys."

Jenny bowed to Kensei, then wiped the sweat from her forehead. As she reached down for her key, Jenny brushed her mother's amulet. *Would my mom be proud of what I'm doing? If nothing else, I'm having an adventure, and my mom always loved adventures.*

Kensei held his key out. "What do we do with them?"

"Try a pattern you learned from the tests."

Jenny looked at Mazu quizzically. "Like, freezing water or something?"

Mazu shrugged. "Whatever you feel like."

Something in the corner of the room rustled. Leon woke up from his nap and wriggled free of Kensei's bag. Kensei picked him up and placed him on his shoulder, but the sugar glider immediately jumped and drifted back to the bag.

"That gives me an idea." Kensei gripped his key and concentrated. He jumped, and his back hit the ceiling, three meters up. He floated gently back to the floor, stumbled, and fell onto the blue mat.

"Well." Mazu grinned and put her hands on her hips. "I've never seen anyone do that before."

"You might want to work on your landing." Jenny chuckled.

"Whoa, I'm dizzy." Kensei held his head. "Will I always get so dizzy after using my power?"

"There are side effects to your powers." Mazu knelt down and rubbed Kensei's back. "Some Æons have figured out how to prevent them, or at least have learned to live with them."

Jenny thought about her own elusive power. Was it that she could see Astrea, or was there more to it? "Where do these powers come from?"

"That's a good question. It's my belief that humans have always had them. Throughout history, there have been people with rare abilities, like the Irish druids, Mapuche sorcerers, Greek prophets, Siberian shamans, and European witches. But as civilization grew, so did fear of pagan beliefs. These early Æons were labeled as heretics, or mentally insane."

Jenny nodded in understanding. The pressure of fitting into the modern world was overwhelming. So much so that, at one time, being called crazy had seemed the easy way out. At some other time and place, Jenny would surely have been labeled a witch. Instead, she had been diagnosed with a mental disorder. To Cabin, however, she was gifted.

The door opened, and Adriana strolled inside. "Here you are." She approached Jenny. "What do you think you're doing?"

"What do you mean?"

"I heard about your bet with Sadi."

"It's harmless." Jenny shrugged.

Mazu raised her eyebrows.

"Nothing is harmless to her." Adriana looked Jenny hard in the eyes. "The whole ship believes she's going to kill you, and she just might if you give her a chance."

"You made a bet with Sadi?" Kensei asked as he rolled his head.

Adriana looked down at Kensei. "What's wrong with him?"

"Side effect of his power." Mazu stopped rubbing Kensei's back and stood up. "But he'll be alright."

"Ah." Adriana nodded knowingly.

"Adriana, I need to run to a meeting. Can you give Jenny and Kensei a lesson with their keys?"

"Sure."

Mazu left the room, and Kensei rolled over onto his back. "I just need a moment."

"Take your time." Adriana looked into Jenny's dichromatic eyes. "Hold up your key and show me what you can do."

Jenny stared into Adriana's turquoise-blue eyes and thought, *The only reason you're giving me a lesson is that you got here before me. If my mom hadn't died, then I'd have been here before you.* Then Jenny took out her key. She tried to form a waveform from the second maze, but it fell flat. Jenny frowned.

Adriana crossed her arms. "Is that all you have?"

Jenny gritted her teeth. *That's okay, I'll just try another waveform.* She went through another pattern, then another. But like the first one, each waveform went flat.

"Anything?"

Jenny grew frustrated, and as she looked over at Adriana, her mind turned to anger. She thought about high school, where the pretty blond girl was on the honor roll and was the team captain of the girl's football team. Even Ruby wanted Jenny to be more like Adriana. *We're in another universe, and I'm still in her shadow,* Jenny thought. "You think you're better than me." It was a declaration, not a question.

Adriana scrunched her face. "What are you talking about?"

"Perfect Adriana Thatcher, everything comes easily to you. It wasn't enough that you were popular at school, you have to be popular here too."

"This isn't school." Adriana shook her head. "But you're acting like it."

Jenny clenched her fists. "You're just a show-off."

"Why don't you go back to your room, put on some black makeup, and listen to some goth music?" Adriana took a moment to tie her wavy blond hair into a tight bun and used the fork of her Waypoint key to hold it in place.

"At least I have my own identity."

"Is that the one where you use your mom's death to hide who you are?"

Tears welled up in Jenny's eyes, and she charged forward. Grabbing Adriana's legs, she slammed the other girl onto the mat. Jenny reached out to lock Adriana's arm, but the blond girl twisted away and swept Jenny's legs out from under her. Jenny's vision flashed as she hit the mat, and the air left her lungs.

Adriana wrapped Jenny's arm between her legs. "Submit."

The pain in her shoulder was excruciating. "Never." Jenny kicked out with her legs to get leverage. *No, I can't lose. I have to win and prove that I belong here.*

"You know nothing about my life or my struggles. Submit."

"What does a rich, pretty girl like you know about struggling?" Jenny yanked her arm free, almost dislocating it in the process. Jumping to her feet, she stood in the low stance Mazu had just taught her. The two girls circled each other. Rage pounded through Jenny's veins as she feigned a punch and then kicked at Adriana's knee.

From her time spent telling fortunes, Jenny had learned to read every tell of a person's emotions. As they circled each other, she watched Adriana's face. They tested each other's defenses with short jabs and kicks. Jenny knew she had to draw Adriana into a more committed attack. She allowed an opening in her defenses and watched.

Adriana pulled her foot back as if she would kick. But if she were going to kick, she wouldn't put so much weight on it. It was a feint. Jenny raised her arms to block a kick to her head, but actually she prepared for the real attack.

Just as she expected, Adriana kicked with her other foot. The blow was aimed at Jenny's gut. If it had connected, it would have stunned Jenny long enough for Adriana to put her in another hold. Since Jenny was ready, she caught the kick in the crook of her arm. Lifting Adriana's captured leg, Jenny knocked Adriana to the ground.

Jenny wasted no time. She took Adriana's arm between her legs and rolled backward. At the same time, she placed one foot on Adriana's neck and wedged the other under her back. With this leverage, Jenny extended Adriana's elbow almost to the point of breaking.

Adriana tapped the mat and Jenny released her.

Jenny panted and pushed herself up to her feet. "You're a good fighter."

"Thanks." Adriana sat up and breathed heavily. "So are you. Where did you learn?"

"I've been studying fencing since I was eleven." She held out her hand to Adriana and pulled her up.

"My dad started teaching me how to box when I was ten."

"You're lucky. I never even knew my dad."

Adriana looked into Jenny's eyes for several seconds. "Not as lucky as you think."

Jenny bowed her head. "I'm sorry I attacked you."

Adriana massaged her elbow. "I'm sorry for what I said about your mom."

"It's true." Jenny bowed her head. "Everything you said was true."

"Hey." Adriana squeezed Jenny's shoulder. "Forget about it. You wanna get some lunch?"

"Yeah." Jenny smiled. "Sounds good."

Kensei shook his head as he followed Jenny and Adriana out of the training room. "I guess I'll just get my key lesson some other time," he mumbled under his breath.

"Jenny?" Adriana asked.

"Yeah?"

Adriana stopped and turned to Jenny. She pulled on a stray strand of blond hair and chewed her lip. She seemed to want to say something.

"What is it?"

"Do you know anything about your dad?"

"No," Jenny said, looking sideways at Adriana. "Why do you ask?"

"Aren't you curious?"

"Um, yeah. I asked my mom about him all the time," Jenny said solemnly, "but she never said a word."

Adriana looked into Jenny's eyes. "Do you know why?"

Jenny scowled, and a lump formed in her throat. "She said it was to protect him and his family."

Adriana nodded. "I see."

As Jenny thought of her dad, she felt doors opening in her mind. Clues fell together, like pieces of a puzzle spread across many years of memories. *The man from the wedding. The one who gave me a toy. What was his name?* "Thatch—Thatcher." Jenny inhaled sharply.

"My dad has this old house truck full of gadgets." Adriana looked pointedly at Jenny.

"A converted 1962 Mack truck."

"He'd take it around to festivals—"

"And weddings." Jenny stopped and looked at Adriana.

"Yeah."

"I met him when I was eleven." Jenny remembered the magical creations inside. "He said he had a daughter, and he gave me a present."

"The first time I saw you, I knew..."

"You knew?" Jenny's heart thudded in her chest. "Knew what?"

"That you were my sister."

Adriana transformed before Jenny's eyes. She was her sister. She could see it now, and Jenny wanted to know everything about her.

"You're sisters?" Kensei jumped. "I knew it."

"Is that why you never talked to me at school?" Jenny asked.

"Yeah, sort of."

"But why?"

"Because every time I saw you, it reminded me that my dad was unfaithful to my mom."

"Oh." Jenny looked down.

"It's not your fault, it's his. I've never forgiven him. But that doesn't mean we can't be friends, or maybe sisters." Adriana raised her eyebrows.

Jenny nodded. "I'd like that."

Adriana reached out and hugged Jenny.

"You know"—Jenny laughed—"deep down, I think I always knew." They parted and continued down to the mess hall. "So, what's he like?"

Adriana shrugged. "I haven't seen him in a while, not since my parents split up."

"I'm sorry."

"It's okay. It's better actually. Though I never hear from him, except for a birthday card once a year."

Jenny thought about her own birthday. She had never received a card from him, but she didn't bring it up. "What about your mom?"

"She's my mom." Adriana scowled. "She's tough on me, but my older brother can do no wrong."

"Wait, I have a brother too?"

"Yeah, you do." Adriana smiled.

"Do you have siblings, Kensei?" Adriana asked.

Kensei nodded. "Two sisters."

"Older or younger?" Jenny asked.

"Both younger." Kensei described how his single mom wasn't around much because of work. So, he'd helped raise his two younger sisters as much as any father. He cooked meals, braided their hair, and did everything else expected of a parent.

In the mess hall, fried chicken, corn on the cob, mashed potatoes, and bread pudding filled the stainless steel serving bins. Jenny had worked up an enormous hunger from training and was already salivating when she took her tray. After filling her plate, she brought it to the table with the other white uniforms.

Although Billo had finished her lunch, she offered to stay for the company. She pushed her empty tray to the end of the table and leaned forward. "It's Kensei, right?"

"Um, yeah," Kensei mumbled around a bite of chicken.

"I'm a bit of an amateur psychologist."

"Here we go—" Adriana rolled her eyes.

Billo glared at her before turning back to Kensei. "I know about Jenny and Adriana. Now I want to know what your mental illness was."

"I, uh…" Kensei looked around the table for support.

"Don't worry." Adriana put her hand on his. "We were all misdiagnosed with some form of psychosis."

"What was yours?" Jenny asked Adriana.

"Nothing interesting, just migraines and early-onset blindness."

"Oh?" Jenny said. "That sounds pretty serious."

"Yeah, at around six, my migraines got so bad that they'd sometimes leave me blind for hours."

"I had Todd's syndrome," Kensei blurted out.

"Hmm." Billo stroked her chin. "That's a new one."

"My perception would get messed up. Like I'd have trouble telling how big or small something was." He stared at his hands. "My family called it the 'Big Littles.'"

"It must have something to do with your ability. Most of our diagnoses do. Imagine, if we'd have stayed at home, we'd probably be in some mental hospital. But here, we're gifted." Billo transformed herself into Lin and back to herself.

"I want to bring this cure home," Adriana said. "No one should believe that they're crazy or lose their family members to some disease."

Jenny had always believed that Adriana's altruistic personality was an act. Could it really have been genuine? "We totally should. You know, it's weird how we hardly know each other even though we went to the same school."

"I guess we just had to come to another universe."

Jenny laughed. "You know, my mom hoped that we would be friends."

"Because we're sisters?"

"Yeah." Jenny nodded and scooped up some potatoes.

"You're sisters!" Billo said and looked at Kensei. "Did you know?"

"I just found out," Kensei said. "It makes sense, though. Our powers must be genetic. I wonder if my sisters have abilities."

"Then why aren't there more people here?" Billo asked. "There must be more to it than genetics."

Jenny remembered how her mother had been able to see Sally, right before her seizure. "Some people might be carriers, or it might be recessive. Who knows?"

Kensei nodded. "Did you hear that they're calling us Astreans?" He opened his backpack and fed Leon bits of bread pudding.

"Yeah," Billo said. "I like it. It makes us sound exotic."

"Me too," Adriana said.

"Adriana, can you give us some advice on the mazes?" Kensei asked.

Billo leaned forward.

"Well, you can't memorize them," Adriana said. "They're different every time. The only way to win is by finding a shortcut."

"That's what I've been told too," Jenny said. "So how do we do it?"

"You need to find your special ability," Billo said.

"Is that all?" Jenny said.

"Practice," Billo said. "Use your key."

"Not all of us knew our ability before we got here." Adriana looked at Billo.

"How did you find yours?" Jenny asked Adriana.

"As Billo said, it had something to do with my condition, my sudden blindness. Over time, I found that I could restore my eyesight through meditation. When I first touched my key"—Adriana traced its shape under her uniform—"the same sense of peace washed over me."

"That's how it worked for me too," Kensei said. Leon scrambled onto Kensei's shoulder and looked furtively around the room. "You should see my skills."

"You mean hitting your head on the ceiling?" Jenny laughed.

Kensei slumped in his chair. Leon hopped onto his head.

"Speaking of skills," Adriana said. "You are one hell of a fighter, Jenny."

"Really?" Billo looked at Jenny curiously.

Jenny sat up straighter in her chair and squared her shoulders.

"Yeah." Kensei rubbed his neck. "I couldn't beat her."

"Neither could I." Adriana narrowed her eyes at Jenny. "She's got quite a furious streak."

After clearing his plate, Kensei checked his Topo and excused himself from the table. "I've got to go meet with Lin. I'll see you guys later."

They waved goodbye to Kensei, and Billo turned to Jenny. "Everyone's talking about your bet with Sadi."

Jenny sunk lower into her seat as Adriana glared at her.

"Do you really think you have a chance?" Billo asked.

"Well, no one's ever passed every test before."

"Well, I can't wait to see your next round. What time did you get?"

"21:00."

"Ooh, that's rough," Adriana said.

"I know," Jenny said, "but that was the only time available."

"People are scared of Sadi," Billo said.

"For good reason," Adriana added.

"But we'd all love to see her lose," Billo said.

"She won't make it easy for you," Adriana said to Jenny. "I wouldn't be surprised if she tried to take you out of the competition."

Maybe she's right, Jenny thought. She hadn't considered what Sadi would do to win.

The girls spent the rest of their meal talking about things back on their Earth. When they were finished, they dropped their trays off at the cleaning station.

"So, what do you want to do now?" Billo asked Adriana and Jenny.

"I don't know," Adriana said. "We could go swimming."

"I was thinking of something more indoors," Billo said, "maybe volleyball."

Jenny jumped as her Topo buzzed against her side.

"What is it?" Adriana asked.

Jenny pulled her tablet free and checked the screen. "Oh, it's time for my appointment with Lin."

"Better not be late," Billo warned.

"Hey Jenny," Adriana said.

"Wanna hang out after your meeting?"

"Yeah, sure," Jenny grinned. "I'd like that."

As Jenny raced out of the mess hall, someone kicked her ankle. She lost her balance and fell, skidding to a stop on the white floor of the hallway. The sound of laughter was like a punch to her ears. Waves of heat washed over her like hot flashes. She looked back and saw a group of four gray-uniformed recruits. Sadi and Aindriu were among them.

A hand reached down to her. It was Moeshe, the tall young man in the blue uniform. Jenny took his hand and let him pull her up.

Sadi sauntered over with a big grin on her freckled face. "Guess who just got the highest score?"

Jenny's face went sour. All she wanted at that moment was to hurt this girl. "You wouldn't be in first place if Trey were still alive." Jenny covered her mouth and wished she could take back her words.

Sadi clenched her jaw, and she trembled. "Just wait. I'll teach you what pain really is."

"Not if I teach you first."

Sadi's pale face turned red.

Jenny's cheek started to itch, and she turned and ran down the hall.

24

LOCATOR

Jenny's body was hot from embarrassment after Sadi had tripped her. She could still hear the laughter as she made her way from the mess hall. Still, she could have handled the situation better than bringing up Trey. It was never Jenny's intent to hurt Sadi, let alone be on her bad side. But, it was now hurt or be hurt, and Jenny didn't plan to be Sadi's target again. This also meant that she had to win the bet.

Before she knew it, Jenny had reached the top floor. The door to Lin Song's office slid open and Kensei stepped out.

"Hey, Jenny," Kensei said.

"Hi, how'd your meeting go?"

"Not bad." He pulled his backpack onto his shoulders. "But I got stuck with cleaning the men's bathrooms."

"I figured we'd get something like that." An idea crept into Jenny's mind. *If I win the bet, then Sadi may have to clean bathrooms for me.* A grin spread across her lips.

"What are you smiling about?"

"Nothing, I just thought of something funny."

"I was wondering..." Kensei shuffled his feet. "If you're free, maybe we can hang out?"

"Sure, but I have to meet with Lin right now. How about after?"

"Yeah, sounds good." He shrugged his backpack off his shoulders.

Inside Lin's office, a large brass floor lamp illuminated a simple desk in the middle of the small space. A silk-covered box, a bamboo whisk, and a cast-iron tea kettle rested on the wooden surface. In the corner was a cabinet of curiosities. The top shelf held a collection of black-and-white cow figurines. The other shelves held a panoply of kitsch. There were primitive talismans, religious symbols, and bizarre figures.

"Come in, Jenny, have a seat."

Jenny moved from the doorway and sat on a simple wooden chair. Her eyes landed on a half-eaten plate of treacle tarts. Though she had just eaten, her mouth watered at the sight of the delicacies.

"Take as many as you want." Lin pushed the plate toward Jenny. "I love them, but my eyes are bigger than my stomach."

"Thanks." Jenny picked a crispy tart from the plate. "I'm just so hungry all the time."

"Your mind and body are growing and strengthening—that requires a lot of fuel." Lin twisted an owl-shaped ring on her finger. "How's your first day?"

"Good. I'm learning so much. It's all a bit overwhelming." Jenny bit into a tart and immediately wished she had some water to wash it down.

"I know, it's a lot of responsibility to put on you all at once. And I'm sorry, but I'm about to give you one more."

Jenny chuckled. "That's okay." Cabin had provided her with a priceless amount of benefits. It seemed a small price to pay for room and board.

"To protect the Selkans all duties must be performed by those with proper clearance, which means that we all have to pitch in to keep things clean and functional. I have a shift in the mess hall myself. Mazu is responsible for health care and research. As a tradition, our newest members are tasked with keeping the community head clean."

Jenny shrugged. "Yeah, that's what I expected."

"Good. I knew you would understand." Lin's chair creaked as she leaned back. "So, I heard about the fight between you and your sister."

"Kensei told you?"

Lin nodded. "We encourage healthy competition, but not to the point where anyone gets seriously hurt."

"Did you know we were sisters?"

"Of course," Lin said. "We performed a thorough genealogy check on all our potentials."

Jenny chewed her tart in silent contemplation.

"Do you have any questions about the program so far?" Lin asked.

Should I tell her about my bet with Sadi, and how terrible I did on the mazes? And what about the Riftkey, and finding Cobol's body? She decided on her most immediate concern. "I did terrible at the tests. How do I get better?"

"This first round was about learning. You passed all the tests. That's nothing to be upset about. All you need is practice."

That's exactly what my mom would have said, Jenny thought. *I miss her so much.* At that moment Jenny wondered what her mom would think of her now. Would she agree with Jenny's choice to run away and join Cabin to save the Selkans, or would she be upset that she abandoned her aunt? Maybe Lin could provide some insight.

"Do you think my mom would be proud of me?"

Lin took a long, slow breath and leaned forward in her chair. "You were selected by another universe, out of billions of people, to help save an alien race. Yes, I think your mom would be proud of you, and I'm proud of you too." Lin jerked her head back and coughed loud and hard. She snatched a handkerchief off the desk and held it to her mouth. Red spots bled through the white fabric.

"What's wrong?" Jenny jumped up. "Are you sick?"

"Yes." Lin slumped back in her chair.

Jenny's sympathy turned to confusion and betrayal. She was starting to trust Lin. "Are you dying?" Jenny heard the bitterness in her own voice.

"No, Jenny, I'm not dying, I'm just sick."

Jenny wasn't happy with the answer, but she didn't want to continue to talk about this subject either.

"When's your next test?" Lin asked.

"Not until nine." Jenny looked up at Lin. "What should I do until then?"

"Anything you want. Play on your Topo, work out in the gym, or go for a swim in the ocean."

"I didn't cross over to another universe just to work out and swim. I came here to save the Selkans. There must be something more useful I can do."

"Well, there is something that would help me a great deal."

"Yes, anything."

"Can you go down to the workshop and retrieve something from Kett'l and deliver it to Mazu?"

"Sure, what is it?"

"It's a Locator. Mazu needs it to explore that cave Adriana found this morning."

"Where's the workshop?"

"I'll show you on your Topo."

Jenny retrieved her Topo from the front pocket of her uniform. She opened the ship's map. The *Endeavor* had four floors. Lin's office was on the uppermost level of the first floor, and the levels increased in number as they went down. So, the second floor contained the mess hall, and the sickbay was on the third. Lin selected the lowest level, the fourth floor, and the Topo's screen reconfigured into a maze of maintenance corridors.

"This is the engineering level." Lin held a finger on a room, and a blue pin elevated from the surface of the screen. "And this is the workshop. Get the Locator from Kett'l and take it here." Lin selected the third floor and put a pin on one of the rooms. "This is the moon pool, an opening to the ocean. Mazu is getting ready to dive, and may already be waiting for the Locator, so please hurry."

"Don't worry, I will," Jenny said as she rushed out of Lin's office. In her haste, she stumbled over something in the hallway. "Oh, Kensei, sorry. I didn't see you."

"It's okay. It's my fault. It's these long legs." Kensei had been leaning over his sketchbook and drawing with his legs stretched halfway across the floor. He pulled them in and sat cross-legged.

"Were you waiting for me?"

"Yeah," Kensei said as he pulled out his bag and stashed his sketchbook. "Do you still want to hang out?"

"Sure, except now I've got to run an errand for Lin."

"Okay, I'll come with you. Just let me put Leon away." He lifted the sugar glider from his shoulder and lowered him into a rigid box with air holes inside his backpack.

"Yeah, sure," Jenny replied. *After all,* Jenny thought. *Lin didn't say I had to go alone.*

Jenny and Kensei followed the map on her Topo as they descended the stairs. They rounded a corner and almost bumped into Adriana.

"Oh, hey, Jenny, I was looking for you."

"Looks like you found me." Jenny smiled.

"Are you free?" Adriana looked from Jenny to Kensei and back. "I thought we could take a swim or something."

"I'd love to, but I have to run an errand for Lin first."

"Want to come?" Kensei asked.

"Um, sure," Adriana said. "If it's okay."

"Yeah." Jenny rolled her eyes. "It's fine."

"What are we doing?" Adriana asked as she followed Jenny.

"Yeah, what are we doing?" Kensei repeated.

"We're picking something up from Kett'l and taking it to Mazu."

"Where's Mazu?"

"She's in the moon pool getting ready to explore that cave you looked at with your portals."

"Right now?" Adriana sped up to walk beside Jenny. "They weren't supposed to leave until tomorrow."

Jenny shrugged.

"Okay," Adriana said. "Where's Kett'l?"

"He's in the workshop on the engineering level." Jenny showed the Topo to Adriana.

Together, they followed the map down the curved hallway. As they passed the sickbay the entrance to the engineering level came into view. A printed map hung from the wall opposite the broad stairway. The current level filled most of the plan. A miniature of the other floors appeared in the sidebar. Jenny's guts turned to ice as she heard two voices echoing up the stairs to the engineering level.

"That sounds like Aindriu and Sadi," Jenny said.

"What are they doing down here?" Adriana asked.

"I don't know." Jenny ducked behind the wall. "Let's try to listen in."

Adriana caught her hand. "Why?"

"She thinks Sadi led the attack on Acacia," Kensei said.

"Really?" Adriana asked.

Aindriu and Sadi's voices grew louder, and Jenny could hear their feet on the steps.

"I can hide us behind a portal," Adriana said.

Jenny looked at Adriana as if seeing her for the first time. "Yes, please."

Under Adriana's guidance, Jenny and Kensei flattened their backs against the wall. Adriana had her key in hand. "We'll have to be quiet."

Jenny and Kensei nodded. Aindriu and Sadi drew closer.

Adriana's eyes rolled back in her head. The air shimmered and two circular portals crystallized in the hallway. One moved between them and Aindriu and Sadi, and the other was on the other side of them.

"If the portals work," Adriana whispered, "then they'll only be able to see a blank wall when they look this way."

Jenny's hands grew cold, and a trickle of sweat traced a path down her back as Sadi and Aindriu came into view. She pressed herself against the wall with all her might.

"So, Moonlighter, where do you think Lance went?" Aindriu asked.

"I don't know, but I'm sick and tired of not knowing what's going on here."

"Lance trusts us," Aindriu said.

"That doesn't mean he tells us everything."

"Like what?"

Sadi stopped just in front of Adriana's portal. She stared directly into Jenny's face but only saw the hallway. "Like what really happened to Trey."

Jenny put her hand over her mouth and held her breath.

"What is it?" Aindriu looked at Sadi.

"I feel something." Sadi licked her lips. "Something familiar."

"Look, I'm sorry about Trey." Aindriu put his hand on her shoulder. "He was my friend too."

Sadi looked at the hand as if it were an evil creature. Aindriu removed his hand, and they continued walking. Jenny didn't breathe until Sadi and Aindriu were out of sight. Adriana allowed her portals to shatter into millions of crystal facets, but her eyes remained rolled back in her head.

Jenny and Kensei started down the stairs.

"Hey, guys?" Adriana asked.

"Yeah," Jenny and Kensei answered.

"I've gotten pretty good at getting around blind, but I wouldn't mind some help."

"I've got you," Jenny said. She climbed back up the stairs and took Adriana's hand.

The steel floor plates of the engineering level clanged underfoot. Pipes ran uncovered along bare metal walls. The air smelled of grease, and the consistent throb of unseen machinery pulsed in Jenny's chest. They turned a corner and entered a dimly lit corridor. Jenny took out her Topo with her free hand and turned it on. Using the map, they navigated the narrow, serpentine hallways to the workshop.

"Why were Sadi and Aindriu looking for Lance?" Kensei asked.

"I don't know," Adriana said.

"Maybe Lin would know," Jenny offered.

"Yeah, let's ask her when we're done with her errand."

"Sounds good."

Adriana stopped and blinked. "My sight is back." She let go of Jenny's hand.

The farther they traveled, the more pungent with oil and brine the air became. After passing a giant machine that rumbled like a freight train, Jenny checked the map. "The workshop's right over there," she shouted, pointing at a door at the end of a long hallway.

A gravelly voice spoke from behind them. "What're you doing down here?"

Jenny jumped in surprise and turned to see an old man in blue coveralls. His proud belly shadowed stout legs. The man held a blue trucker cap full of bacon in one hand while the other hand stroked an unkempt yellow beard that may have once been white.

"Oh, oh, nothing..." Jenny stammered. "We were just..."

"Looking for someone?" The man pulled a piece of bacon from his hat and took a large, crunchy bite. He noticed Kensei staring and thrust his hat forward. "Just got back from the mess hall. Want a piece?"

"No, uh, thanks." Kensei stepped back. "I just ate."

The old man wiped at his lips with the back of a hairy hand and held it out. "The name's Winchell. I maintain systems and such—keep things from breaking down, and if they do, I fix 'em." When Winchell smiled, his big rosy cheeks pushed his eyes shut.

"Kensei." He shook Winchell's hand. "This is Jenny and Adriana."

"Yer the second set of visitors we had down here. You want to see the Riftkey too?"

"No," Jenny said. "We've come to pick up something for Mazu."

"But," Kensei said, "I wouldn't mind seeing the Riftkey."

"Great," Winchell said. "I'll come with you." He led them to the door at the end of the corridor. A porthole window provided a teaser of the workshop interior. He turned the metal wheel on the door and pushed it open with an elbow.

Objects with impossible geometries rested on shelves in the workshop. A Klein bottle, Möbius strip, and other objects twisted back on themselves unnaturally. A VRGo puzzle and a waypoint key also rested on a large work table.

Kett'l sat on a stool in front of a large black box the size and shape of a refrigerator. At first, Jenny thought it was another maze test, but she saw that it was hollow inside. Kett'l's back was to them, and he hummed an unfamiliar tune. With a hiss, a tendril of smoke curled around his massive head.

"I'll be right with you," Kett'l shouted without turning. "Just adding some finishing touches."

"Wait here and stay quiet." Winchell went to a cabinet and retrieved shaded goggles for each of them. "I gotta get going, I got a pump to work on." He took a bite of bacon from his trucker's hat of plenty, then he picked up a red metal toolbox. "See you all later."

"See you," Jenny and the others said. They donned their goggles and crept toward Kett'l.

Kett'l hummed as he held his hands up to the box. Past his broad shoulders, Jenny could see that the interior was more vast than its outer dimensions, and eight Waypoint keys hung inside the enlarged space. Swirling energy patterns coalesced from the walls of the box and formed a thin silver wire that fused into all eight keys.

The beauty of it was astounding, like seeing four natural rainbows at once. Jenny focused on the point where the wire manifested from thin air and followed the myriad waveforms to the walls of the box.

All the maze waveforms are here in this device, Jenny thought, *but there are so many more.* She felt like a kindergartner staring at a chalkboard covered with formulas of advanced physics. *Somehow, he's manipulating energy into matter. That means Kett'l is an Æon, and so far beyond my ability that I can barely follow.*

The silver wire vanished.

"There." Kett'l stood up and flipped the visor over his eyes. Reaching up into the ceiling of the device, he pulled a hidden lever. There was a bright flash of light, and all eight of the Waypoint keys merged into one. He put on a pair of leather gloves and reached into the box. When he withdrew his gloved hand, he held a Waypoint key. He turned and flipped up his visor to reveal his dichromatic eyes, light and dark brown. "Thanks for waiting, I just had to get through that last part."

Kensei took out his own Waypoint key. "It has the same gem as mine."

"Yes, this is to replace yours," Kett'l's deep voice boomed.

"That was amazing," Jenny said.

Kett'l smiled, revealing the entirety of his tusks. "I've always been good with machines."

"I never thought that creating a Waypoint key was so complex," Adriana said.

Kett'l held up the newly formed key. "The key is impressive." He pointed at the VRGo puzzle on the shelf. "Those puzzles were even harder, but I'm most proud of that." Kett'l pointed at a shelf on the wall.

Outside the workshop, the pumps seemed to chug at the same rate as Jenny's heart. Inside a glass case was an object very familiar to Jenny. The flat of the blade was unbelievably shiny, and the blunt edge was impossibly black. Jenny hugged her burstepi, wanting to speak to Cobol, just to know that he was still there.

"Is that...?" Kensei asked, his mouth agape.

Kett'l nodded. "It is the Riftkey."

"I didn't know it would be so shiny," Adriana said.

"That would be the single layer of nuclei lattice. It gives it a hundred percent reflection rate and is practically unbreakable."

"Why are the edges black?" Kensei asked.

"Actually, the whole Riftkey is black. The shiny part is only a protective casing. According to Mister LaGrange, when activated, the edges break electromagnetic bonds."

"For what purpose?" Adriana asked.

"To unlock the Terminal, one must reshape the flow of its interior. Only the Riftkey can do this."

Kensei moved closer to the Riftkey. "If I win the contest, then I can go to outer space."

"And if I win"—Adriana stood next to Kensei—"then I could save all the Selkans."

Kett'l stood in front of the display case and put out an arm to hold them back. His voice took on a menacing tone. "Do not touch it."

"Why not?" Kensei asked.

"When an Æon touches the Riftkey, they become bound to it for life."

"For life?" Kensei gulped.

"Until the winner of the contest is announced, the Riftkey will not leave my protection." Kett'l spotted the burstepi on Jenny's back. "Oh. You're wearing one of my bags." He ran the material between his long fingers. "Yes, this is one of my first successful builds. A nice bit of weaving, if I do say so myself."

Kett'l stood close enough for Jenny to smell the musk on his fur. "Yes," Jenny said. "It's Lin's. She loaned it to me after my bag was ruined." Kett'l continued to inspect her bag. *I have to do something*, Jenny thought, *before he looks inside and finds the Riftkey*. Then she remembered the impossible patterns Kett'l had been weaving inside the device. "You're an Æon, aren't you?"

"No." Kett'l stepped away from the large box.

"Then what were you doing inside that thing?" Adriana asked.

"It's called a forge," Kett'l said.

"I saw the patterns inside your forge," Kensei said. "You are an Æon."

"I should not have shown you my work." Kett'l growled. "Please do not tell anyone."

"No one else knows?" Jenny asked.

"No."

"Then how do they think the forge works?" Kensei asked.

"They think I know a secret to it, and I would like to keep it that way."

"We won't tell." Adriana stared at Jenny and Kensei until they nodded in agreement. "But, why do you deny it?"

"Yeah, you could use the Riftkey to unlock the Terminal," Jenny said.

"I know it is selfish." Kett'l sighed. "But one day, I wish to return to my home system."

"What do you mean?" Adriana asked.

"Do you not know?" Kett'l searched their confused faces. "Being a Terminal master brings much power, but it is also a great responsibility. Once you are bound to the Riftkey, you are duty-bound to the operation of the Terminal until death."

"Death?" Kensei whispered.

They looked at one another, and Jenny knew they were all thinking the same thing. *Am I willing to be stuck here, in this universe? Do I want to be bound to the Terminal?* Jenny thought, *I may be bound to the Riftkey, but now there's another one, right there. I don't have to be the one to unlock the Terminal.*

"Maybe we should just let Sadi have it," Kensei said.

"No," Jenny said, surprising herself with her ferocity.

"Jenny's right. It's worth the sacrifice if we can save the Selkans," Adriana said. "And I'm sure we can still visit home anytime we want."

"Yeah, I'm sure they'll figure something out," Kensei added. "They would have told us we would be stuck here, wouldn't they?"

"Well, one thing is for sure," Jenny said. "There's no way I'm letting Sadi have that kind of power."

Adriana and Kensei nodded in agreement.

"Oh. I almost forgot." Kett'l pressed a button on the forge, and the opening disappeared. Instead of a deep interior, there was only a black wall. Kett'l walked to a shelf and picked up a long, forklike brass device. "This is the device Mazu needs for her expedition."

"What does it do?" Jenny asked.

"It detects nexum, the material that makes up the Terminal, Waypoints, and their keys. It should be able to find the virosuit."

"Thank you, Kett'l." Jenny took the Locator and turned to Adriana and Kensei. "Let's hurry and get this to Mazu."

25

POSSESSION

The air quality improved as they traveled farther from the workshop. It felt like returning to daylight after a long night. Soon, Jenny, Adriana, and Kensei reached the base of the stairwell, and in a burst of energy, they raced to the top, eager to be the first to escape the dungeon-like engineering level. As they reached the top, they rounded the corner and stopped short.

Sadi stood in the hallway with her arms crossed over her chest. Aindriu and a gray-uniformed recruit Jenny didn't know stood next to her. Sadi's eyes focused on the device in Jenny's hands.

"Is that the Locator?" Sadi looked up at Jenny's face, and her eyes widened. "You're taking it to Mazu, aren't you?" She reached for the Locator. "Hand it over. I'll take it to her."

"No." Jenny jerked the device away. "Lin asked me to deliver it."

Sadi's eyes narrowed. "Why you?"

As Jenny read Sadi's face, she grew terrified. "Because I asked to help."

"You seem to be in the middle of everything," Sadi snarled at Jenny. "I'll give you one last warning, Tripper. Hand it over, or else."

"No." Jenny clutched the brass device to her chest.

Sadi glared at her, and a faint pressure built up in Jenny's skull. Dread chilled her body when she recognized a familiar itching on her tongue. Jenny scraped her tongue against her teeth to relieve the itch, but it only made it worse.

"You were here earlier, weren't you?" Sadi smirked. "No need to answer. I recognized your pain. How did you hide?" Sadi looked at Adriana. "It was you, wasn't it?"

"I-I—" Adriana stammered.

"Leave her alone," Jenny said. "It was me."

"Run!" Kensei yelled.

Jenny hugged the Locator to her chest and ran away from Sadi. She needed to get away and reach Mazu. She would tell Lin about Sadi's behavior. With any luck, her rival would be disqualified from the contest.

They made it halfway around the curve when Sadi's voice rang out behind them. "Pain, pain, come to stay, Little Sadi wants to play."

Jenny whimpered as her tongue exploded with pain. A searing heat cooked it like meat on a grill. Her heart slammed in her chest like a jackhammer, every pulse a flare of pain. Her tongue felt like pulp in her mouth, and she collapsed to the floor from the mind-numbing pain. She hardly noticed the Locator ramming into her breast, or her chin hitting the hard laminate.

"Pain is in the mind," Sadi said, "and your mind is under my control."

"Please, please, no," Adriana begged. Tears poured down her cheeks and dripped onto the white, polished floor.

"I heard that you're both sisters, and Gypsies." Sadi stood over Jenny's prone form. "You know, it used to be legal to kill your kind. Why don't we reenact some history?"

"Don't do this, Sadi," Kensei pleaded. "It's not worth it. You'll be kicked out."

"Only if somebody finds out." A rictus grin split Sadi's face. "I promise I won't leave a mark."

Pain spread over Jenny's body, wrapping her arms and legs in sticky, scalding tar. It reminded her of her worst sunburn, times a hundred. She pictured her flesh crisping and burning.

Sadi looked down at Jenny with passionless eyes. "You don't belong here. Death and pain have followed you. First, you stumble over Trey's body, then you're at the heart of the Acacia City raid. With you three out of the way, the Selkans will have a better chance at survival." Slowly, she reached down and pulled the Locator from Jenny's shivering hands. "And I'll be sure to win the Riftkey."

Jenny screamed as the waves of pain slammed into her body like a sledgehammer. She felt the flesh on her cheek sizzle, then bubble, before falling from bone like hot wax. Jenny was on her side, and the floor was cool against her skin. Her muscles curled her body into a fetal position. Shadows pressed into her vision. Her hands and legs spasmed out of control.

A corner of Sadi's mouth curled up into a smile. Her lips quivered a little, like she was trying to hold back a laugh.

Adriana shook her head violently. "Stop it, Sadi. Please. Stop."

Aindriu looked down at Adriana, then at Sadi, with horror. "What should we do with them?"

"We'll take them downstairs and lock them in a maintenance closet. By the time anyone finds them, the contest will be over. But first, I'm going to take a look inside this backpack." She rolled Jenny facedown and pulled at the burstepi.

No! Jenny shouted in her mind. Her hate for Sadi and her need to survive warred with the feeling of pain. Her consciousness stretched and pressed against her skull. Something yielded inside her mind, and the pain was gone. Jenny was outside her body. Her new form glowed with light, and a single bright thread connected them.

New colors transitioned into view, as if her eyes were adjusting to a dark room. The auras she had seen after the ADD treatment had returned. The other people in the hallway glowed in different hues of color. Formless blotches moved at the edge of her vision. They were only there, *really* there, when glimpsed from the corners of her eyes. Sounds were felt as much as heard.

Sadi pulled the burstepi off Jenny's shoulders, stood and worked at the straps. Jenny roared and charged at Sadi. Instead of colliding with the freckled girl, Jenny felt the world disappear.

～

Jenny was a little girl, but not herself. She sat on a couch in a living room she didn't recognize, watching a TV show she'd never seen before. She could hear two men talking at the front door.

"Cassadi is special, Mister Stevens, and Cabin can help her understand her gift."

"Go away," Mister Stevens said. "I don't need your help."

"We just want what's best."

"Are you implying that I don't know what's best for my family?"

"Not at all."

"I don't like your tone. I have half a mind to come out there and whoop your ass right now."

"That's not necessary, Mister Stevens. I'll be on my way."

The scene changed, and Jenny was sitting outside on the grass watching a large gray squirrel stuff hazelnuts into its cheeks. She laughed at the funny feeling of her cheeks stretching. A dark shape swooped up from behind the squirrel. There was a great rush of air and a flurry of wings. She felt a searing pain in her chest as the owl clutched the squirrel in its talons. She screamed from the pain of it and collapsed to the ground. A moment later, someone lifted her and wrapped her in their arms. They wiped hot tears from her face and whispered comforting words into her ear.

"There's something wrong with that girl," Mister Stevens said.

"She's just sensitive," a woman answered.

Are these Sadi's parents? Jenny thought.

The scene shifted again. Jenny was having dinner with Sadi's parents in a small, dirty kitchen. She smiled at them. She always liked having family dinner.

Daddy took a bite of a chicken breast and turned to Mommy in disgust. "It's undercooked."

Jenny felt a pit in her stomach. Her skin grew cold and clammy. She breathed in quick gasps.

"No, it can't be," Mommy said.

"Are you calling me a liar?"

Jenny hugged her legs tightly to her chest.

"I can heat it up for you."

"Why bother? You'd probably mess that up too."

Mommy stood up and took the plate. "It's no trouble."

"I wasn't done with that." Daddy grabbed Mommy's wrist and twisted. The plate fell to the floor with a crash. "Now you've done it!" He slapped her across the face with the back of his hand.

Jenny massaged her sore wrist and jerked back with the impact of the slap. "Stop it!" she screamed, but Daddy kept hitting Mommy over and over. Jenny felt each impact as if he were attacking her. She cried.

Time slowed as Daddy shoved Mommy into the table. Glasses spilled, along with Daddy's beer. Uneaten plates fell off the table and shattered, scattering food across the floor.

Jenny focused on Sadi's father at that moment. His eyes were wide, showing the whites above and below the iris. A fleck of white spittle formed in the corner of his mouth. Tendons and blood vessels stood out on his neck.

Mommy curled herself into a ball and shouted, "Not in front of Sadi."

Jenny closed her eyes. The pain stopped, but her mom was still screaming. She wanted more than anything for Daddy to stop. Something broke inside her mind. With tears flowing down her cheeks, she forced her eyes open and shouted, "Leave Mommy alone!"

The first thing she noticed was that her parents were glowing. Mommy was red, and Daddy was blue. Maybe if Daddy were red, then he would stop. She concentrated, and a moment later, Daddy clutched his head and screamed. He yelled at her to stop, but it felt good to make Daddy go red. He begged her to stop, but he didn't stop when Mommy begged, so she kept making Daddy red.

Daddy fell to the floor and twisted around like a snake. Spittle flew from his mouth and he clawed at his ears, but she wouldn't stop. Daddy turned black. This felt wrong, so she stopped. She knelt down next to Mommy and tried to wake her up, "Mommy, it's okay, Daddy's asleep." She kept shaking Mommy's shoulder long after she turned black.

The scene shifted. She was older now and had just joined Cabin. It was the happiest day of her life. She met a boy there who understood her like nobody else before. She finally felt like she belonged somewhere, and she allowed herself to be happy for the first time since she was a child.

Now she was standing in a forest, looking down at the dead body that had once been the man that she loved.

~

A feeling of revulsion flooded Jenny's mind. The memory of Trey's dead body brought Jenny back to the present, but Jenny was no longer in her own body or the glowing angelic form. She was in Sadi's body. It was eerie to be standing over her own unconscious body.

"Well, c'mon," Aindriu said.

"Yeah, let's see what's inside," the other gray said.

Jenny looked from the burstepi in her hands to Aindriu and the other gray. Their auras were still visible as ghostly blue light. Sadi's ability tingled at the edge of her mind. After experiencing Sadi's memories, Jenny knew how to use this power. To find memories of pain and enhance them.

Using the Waypoint key hanging around her neck. Jenny visualized a red waveform and focused her energy on it. Instantly, the blue auras around the two grays turned red.

"Sadi, what are you—" Aindriu said as he dropped to the floor.

At the same time, a wave of pleasure exploded inside Jenny's mind. It felt like getting a body massage while soaking in a hot tub. They screamed for her to stop, but she couldn't, it felt too good. All too soon, they fell unconscious. Their auras had turned black, and her ecstasy ceased. She sighed and shook her head as she came to her senses.

Adriana looked up at her with a mix of curiosity and hatred.

"Hey." Jenny knelt down and looked at her sister. "It's me, Jenny. Somehow, I'm inside Sadi's body."

"What?" Adriana looked over at Jenny's real body. "How?"

Kensei sat up and looked from Sadi to the unconscious grays. "What's going on?"

"I'll explain on the way." Adriana picked up the Locator. "Right now, we have to get this to Mazu. Jenny, can you move your body?"

"No. I'm trapped in here. I'm not sure what I did." Then a pressure, like the sudden urge to vomit, pushed against Jenny's mind. She moved in jerky motions as Sadi struggled to regain control.

I have to get away. The thought wasn't Jenny's.

Without saying a word to her friends, Jenny rushed down the stairs and sped through the maze of corridors. As her mind started to tear, Jenny threw herself against the grated steel floor. Like a rubber band drawn to its breaking point, Jenny's consciousness snapped back to her own body. Exhaustion overwhelmed her, and she passed out.

26

MOON POOL

Jack sat at a corner table in the mess hall with a view of the entire room. He was drinking his third mug of coffee when Mazu entered. She held a package under one arm and scanned the room. Jack had to admit the woman interested him, and his mind had wandered to her more than once.

Mazu approached Jack's table and dropped the package next to his empty platter. "I hope it's the right size."

"What is it?" The contents of the package were flexible and weighed more than they looked like they would.

"A wetsuit." Mazu tapped her foot. "We've gotta go."

"Wetsuit, as in water?" Jack's blood froze in his veins. "Right now?" *Damn.* Jack thought. *Victus, where are you? You strand me here, then leave as soon as I send proof of the Selkans. What am I supposed to do, just wait here until you come back for them?*

"Didn't you review the mission briefing?"

"No, I thought I had until tomorrow." Jack's leg bounced with excess caffeine and nerves.

"Well, c'mon, I'll fill you in on the way. But hurry, we don't have much time."

"How long will we be gone?"

"Not long. The cave is only ten kilometers away, and we'll need to do some spelunking. I'd say six hours round trip, tops."

What if Victus arrives while I'm gone? Jack thought. *Would Victus just leave me behind? I wish I knew when he was coming. If they discover I can't swim, my cover will be blown. I'll just have to say no to the mission.*

"Are you coming or not?"

Jack looked at Mazu, and his mind went blank. "Count me in." *Damn it,* Jack thought. He drained his mug, picked up the package, and followed Mazu out of the mess hall.

Together, they descended to the next floor and entered a converted cargo room that smelled of saltwater. Four large mechanical diving suits lined the walls like gleaming silver trophies. A giant robotic arm waited nearby. At the end of the room, a large circular hole opened to the ocean.

Jack gulped as he stared at the rippling pool. Until yesterday, a bathtub was the most water he'd seen in one place for several years. Being this close to the open sea made him break out in a sweat.

"Tell me about your time in the Navy," Mazu said.

"There's not much to tell, really." *I spent most of my time in a spacesuit,* Jack thought, *not a diving suit. Not that I can tell her that.* "I flew marines from one place to another."

"Did you see any action?"

"Only from a distance." *From thousands of kilometers,* Jack thought. Most space combat was fought out of sight from your enemy, using sensors and lidar to 'see'.

Mazu unbuttoned her uniform and pulled her jacket off. Underneath she wore a skintight black bodysuit. Blue lines embedded into the material connected to hard discs at the joints. She left the headpiece off, letting it hang against her back like a hood.

"You need something?" she asked as Jack continued to stare at her.

"Some things are coming to mind."

"Get dressed." Mazu grinned and pointed at the gray package in his hands.

Jack sat on the floor and tugged his boots off. He took off his leather jacket and piled the whole lot in the corner of the room. Next, he unfastened his belt and worked at his uniform pants.

"While I'd love to see how far you'll go, there's a changing room over there." Mazu pointed at a stall in the corner of the room.

"Oh." Jack entered the stall and pulled the door closed. There was barely enough room to turn around. He would have preferred to change out in the open. Sighing, he tore the package open. Inside was a black suit like the one Mazu was wearing. The elastic fabric was a lightweight, carbon fiber weave. Blue lines traveled up each leg, crossing the torso, and continued down each arm.

Jack stripped out of his Cabin uniform. He thrust his bare foot into the first suit leg. *The damn thing is sticky.* His foot refused to go any farther than the knee. He yanked hard, and his other foot slipped on the wet floor. He fell backward into the room's flimsy siding and landed hard on his backside. "Ouch." A cold draft blew over his exposed skin from the gap under the door.

"You alright in there?" Mazu snickered.

"Yeah." Jack's face grew hot. "Just dandy." He was about to get up but found that it was easier to pull the wetsuit on from the floor. Once he had his feet in place, he stood up. He checked that the thin knife strapped to his thigh was secure before pulling the suit over his legs.

"Do you have someone special back home, Jack?"

Jack thought about his ex-wife and touched the finger where his wedding ring used to be. Pepper had been stubborn and feisty. Not dissimilar to Mazu. "Not anymore."

"Oh? What happened?"

Jack worked an arm inside the suit. "Well, my moral judgments clashed with Pepper's smuggling practices. So, we fought. Then divorced." He thrust another arm inside, and like Mazu, he left the suit's hood off. With the suit on, Jack stepped out of the changing stall and presented himself to Mazu.

"Looking sharp."

Jack could feel her eyes rolling over his body. "It's a good fit." Though he wasn't as chiseled as he'd been in his youth, he still sported some of the ripcord muscles he'd earned as a pro fighter. He balled up his clothes and stashed them in the corner of the room farthest away from the water.

The door to the room slid open, and a massive dark-skinned man entered.

"Marcel!" Jack approached the man, and the two performed the handshake the big man had taught him on their supply run. It involved several finger holds, hand slaps, and fist bumps.

"Marcel, you're late," Mazu said, rolling her eyes at the masculine display.

"It's good to see you too." Marcel unstrapped his holstered handgun and checked the safety and the chamber. "I had to make sure I wasn't being followed."

"Always the cautious one."

"It keeps me alive." Marcel stripped out of his black uniform, folded it, and set the whole pile next to Jack's clothes. Underneath, he wore the same black wetsuit Jack and Mazu had on.

"Would you help Jack with his Tumlare suit?" Mazu asked.

"Sure," Marcel said.

"We need to leave as soon as the Locator arrives."

"It's not here yet?" Marcel asked. "Looks good." He patted Jack on the shoulder with a huge hand.

"No. I'm worried," Mazu said. "Lin should have delivered it by now."

"What's the big rush?" Jack asked.

Marcel picked up a hefty controller from the wall. A thick cable connected it to the robotic arm.

"He doesn't know?" Marcel asked.

Mazu shook her head and looked at Jack. "A large ship just arrived through the Terminal. We think it's Tyr."

Victus. Jack almost sighed in relief but stifled his emotions. It was absurd that the man who'd betrayed him, who'd killed Hocco, could stir such a feeling of comfort.

"Tyr?" Jack asked, feigning ignorance. "Who are they?"

"They're the agency that keeps the Selkans as slaves."

If Victus gets here while I'm out with Mazu, Jack thought. *Then there's a chance I'll miss him and be stuck here on Earth.* "Ah yes," Jack said. "Shouldn't we stay and help?"

Mazu studied Jack. "We are helping, by leaving now instead of tomorrow."

"I just thought—"

"The only way we can help them now is to recover the virosuit."

"Virosuit?" Jack cocked his head. *Victus didn't mention that.*

Mazu sighed. "That's enough questions. Time to get in your diving suits."

"I thought I was in my diving suit," Jack said, indicating the skintight black carbon fiber that covered his body.

Marcel laughed. "We're not skin diving."

Using the robotic arm, he plucked a mechanical diving suit off the wall and set it down near the open pool. With its flipper-like tail folded up—to give it a solid base—it resembled a Selkan in shape.

"C'mon," Marcel said. "I'll show you how to suit up."

Jack approached the newly deposited Tumlare suit. Marcel slid a switch at the belt, and the suit flipped open at the waist. "Climb in."

"Yes, sir," Jack answered automatically. He gripped the sides of the suit and stepped onto the flipper-like appendage. *Now, this feels familiar.* During his service, Jack had donned powered suits for heavy work on spaceships.

He heaved both legs inside at once. The hard discs of his wetsuit tugged at his leg joints as they made secure connections inside the suit. He gave Marcel a lopsided grin. "Snug."

Marcel used the mech arm to set two more suits by the pool. After setting the last suit down, he handed Jack a rucksack. "Basic supplies. Food, water, and a survival knife."

Jack opened the pack and found six food rations, a head-mounted light, a water canteen with a purifier, a multi-tool, a paracord, and a thin heat barrier. Marcel showed him where he could store the bag inside his Tumlare suit.

Mazu stared at the door and tapped her foot. "Where is that Locator?"

Marcel retrieved his handgun and stashed it inside his Tumlare suit.

"Expecting trouble?" Jack asked.

"Always."

"If it's dangerous, shouldn't we all have one?"

"If it were up to me, you would." Marcel approached Jack. "But I'm one of a select few who are permitted to carry a firearm."

Jack thought about his own weapon. After arriving at the *Endeavor*, he had returned it to the secret compartment in his spaceplane.

"Damn." Mazu rubbed her face. "I'll have to get the Locator myself."

Jack twisted in his Tumlare suit to watch Mazu cross the room. Before she reached the door, it slid open on its own. A blond girl rushed inside, followed by Kensei Drake with an unconscious Jenny Tripper in his arms.

"What happened to Jenny?" Jack asked. *And how is a skinny kid like Kensei able to carry her so effortlessly?*

"Uh." Kensei looked down at Jenny, then up at him with a blank face. "I, uh..."

"She's fine," the blond girl said. "It seems to be a side effect of her power."

"Oh," Mazu said, "she finally triggered it. What is it?"

Adriana scrunched her face. "I'm not sure."

"Well, we can ask her when she wakes up. I see you brought the Locator."

"Oh yeah." Adriana stepped forward and handed it to Mazu.

"Thank you." Mazu studied the brass-looking device for a moment before setting it next to her Tumlare suit. "If that's all, you can go and report back to Lin."

Adriana and Kensei turned and made for the door.

"Oh, and tell Jenny congratulations when she wakes up."

"We will," they answered and left the room.

After the door closed, Mazu and Marcel quickly climbed into their suits.

Jack just stared at the blue-green water in the pool and imagined hidden terrors lying beneath the surface. His heart thundered painfully in his chest. *At least in space you can see for millions of light-years in any direction.* "So, how do I close this thing?"

"It's easier than it looks." Marcel winked at Jack. "Just do what I do."

Reaching back, Marcel flipped his helmet forward and thrust his hands into the suit's armholes. The chest responded by folding around him like a butterfly closing its wings, locking him into a water-tight cocoon.

Jack steeled himself and followed Marcel move for move. He slipped his head inside the helmet as it hinged forward and his breathing sounded loud. The familiar sound of breathing inside a suit worked to calm him. Next, Jack thrust his hands into the armholes, and the chest hinged closed, clicked, and sealed shut. He could almost convince himself that he was going out for a spacewalk. That was, until Mazu dove into the moon pool, sending a fountain of water into the air. Then, her voice sounded in his helmet. "You'll need to activate your fins once you're in the water."

"Okay," Jack replied.

Marcel tipped over and fell into the pool, causing a flood of water to wash over Jack's feet. Jack's heartbeat quickened. *I can do this*, Jack thought. *It's just water. I drink it all the time.* He took several deep breaths to calm himself. *What did she mean by activating my fins?* Jack twisted around to see the fins, still folded up against the back of the suit, lost his balance, and toppled to the side. He fell into the pool with a plunk. Instantly, the murky water surrounded him and greedily pulled him into its dark depths.

27
———

SECOND TEST

Jenny trod water in the middle of the ocean. Huge waves lifted her up and down in a rhythmic motion. The dark abyss tickled her feet and pulled at her legs. She screamed for help, and her eyes shot open to find that Kensei was carrying her on his shoulders. *That explains the rhythmic movement*, Jenny thought.

"Welcome back," Kensei said.

"Thanks, now can you put me down?"

"Sure." Kensei set her down and leaned against the wall. He fought the dizziness that came from using his ability.

Jenny felt the burstepi on her back and sighed internally. She glanced between Kensei and Adriana and saw their empty hands. "Where's the Locator?"

"We delivered it to Mazu," Adriana said. "While you were asleep."

"Thank goodness." Jenny sighed in relief. "What happened?"

"You saved us," Kensei said between deep breaths. "You were Sadi, or you controlled her body or something."

Jenny remembered the encounter with Sadi, and all the pain and raw emotions from it flooded into her mind. Sadi's life flashed before her eyes. *I possessed her.* Jenny shook her head and rocked on her heels.

"How did you do it?" Adriana asked.

"I don't know." Jenny looked away and saw a map that indicated that they were on the gym floor. "Where are we going?"

"To Lin's office," Adriana said. "To let her know that we delivered the Locator."

"And to tell her what Sadi did," Kensei added.

Jenny thought of the little girl and her abusive father. "No, just let it go."

"Why?" Adriana demanded.

"Because I know she won't try anything like that again," Jenny replied.

Lin sat behind her desk, a game consisting of cards and a collection of colored stones arranged in different numerical groupings pushed to one end. "Hi, friends, did you deliver the Locator to Mazu?"

They all talked over each other in reply.

"One at a time, please." Lin waited until they quieted down. "Okay, I believe you were first, Adriana."

"Yes, we delivered the Locator to Mazu."

"And Aindriu and Sadi were on the engineering level," Jenny said.

"But we snuck by them," Kensei said. "Thanks to Adriana's ability, and Jenny—"

Jenny kicked him.

Lin looked at Jenny and Kensei curiously, then Adriana spoke up. "I think they were looking for Mister LaGrange."

"Interesting." Lin looked distracted. "You know, I can't find him either."

"Did he leave?" Jenny asked.

"I don't know."

"Is his plane still here?" Kensei looked up at the ceiling as if he could see the cement platform floating above the spaceship.

"Yes," Lin said. "All the planes are still up there." She looked back at her young pupils. "But I don't want you three to get distracted," she warned. "The final test is tomorrow morning."

"*Tomorrow?*" Adriana said. "I thought we had a week."

"We did"—Lin sighed—"but recent events have accelerated our timeline."

"Recent events?" Kensei asked.

"A large ship arrived through the Terminal. We believe it's a Tyr warship, come for the Selkans."

The trio gasped. "How long until they arrive?" Adriana asked.

"We have a day, maybe two."

"What about Mazu?" Adriana continued.

"And the artifact she's seeking with the Locator?" Kensei asked.

"We don't have time to wait, and we only need the Riftkey to unlock the Terminal."

They sat in silence for some time.

"Lin?" Jenny asked.

"Yes?"

"I was wondering about Sadi." Jenny paused. "What made her the way she is?"

"Her ability gave her a difficult life, and while Cabin taught her to control it, there were some things we could not heal. There was a traumatic event in Sadi's childhood that caused her to flip her empathic sense."

"What do you mean by 'flip her empathic sense'?" Adriana asked.

Lin weaved her fingers together. "Instead of feeling good when she sees positive emotions, she feels bad. The more powerful the emotion, the worse she feels."

"Which means that she would feel good seeing others in misery," Adriana said. "It's all starting to make sense now."

"What about her parents?" Jenny asked.

"Her father is out of the picture. Her mother brought Sadi to us, and she quickly became one of Lance's pet projects. Now"—Lin ushered them out of her office—"I suggest you focus less on Sadi and more on your tests. Go."

Once they were outside Lin's office, Adriana turned to Jenny and asked, "What was all that stuff about Sadi?"

"Was it because of what happened down there?" Kensei asked. "When you possessed her?"

Jenny turned away. "I'm not ready to talk about it."

"I understand." Adriana held the back of her hand to her mouth and yawned.

"Where do you think Lance is?" Kensei asked.

"No idea," Jenny said.

"Do you still think Sadi is involved?"

Jenny shook her head. "She doesn't know any more than we do."

"Well"—Adriana stretched and yawned again—"I think I've had enough excitement for one day. I'm going to get my chores done before dinner so I can go straight to bed."

"Good idea," Jenny said. "A mindless task like cleaning the bathroom sounds dreamy after this hectic day," Jenny said goodbye to Kensei and Adriana before returning to her room.

Billo was on her bed with her Topo in hand. A drum and bass song played from its hidden speakers. "Hey." Billo turned the music down and waved her Topo at Jenny. "Did you hear that tomorrow is the last day for testing?"

"Yeah." Jenny walked to her closet. "Just a minute ago, from Lin."

"We were supposed to have a week left. I can't believe it's really happening."

"Yeah, it's surreal."

"I hope Adriana can stay on top," Billo said.

"Yeah, me too," Jenny agreed, but she didn't really mean it. She wanted to win, and not just because of her bet with Sadi. After being in the other girl's body...Jenny didn't hold the same sense of anger or fear toward her. It was more about proving to herself that she could do it. That she'd earned the right to wield the Riftkey.

Billo smirked. "The grays are worried about you."

"What? Why?" Jenny opened the drawer to get her meds.

"I don't know." Billo walked behind Jenny. "But I heard them talking about you."

Jenny rotated the amber pill bottles in her hand. "For the past four months I haven't missed a single dose, and now I've missed three." *I've also never traveled to another universe before*, Jenny thought.

Billo watched Jenny in silent anticipation.

Jenny's right foot began tapping the floor. "If I want to win," she said, "then I'll need every advantage." One by one, she opened each bottle and dumped the contents into the trash can. An enormous weight lifted from her shoulders, and she collapsed onto her bed.

Billo applauded. "You've begun your journey to recovery."

After finding the cleaning supplies in a small hall closet, Jenny dragged them over to the women's bathroom. Pulling on a pair of yellow rubber gloves, she set to work scrubbing and rinsing every surface.

Jenny liked cleaning. She even found it meditative. When Jenny had moved into her aunt's house, the place was a mess. She'd spent hours scrubbing and sweeping. When she was finished, the place had looked brand-new.

The repetitive tasks felt good and actually refreshed her energy. After she had finished, Jenny stood and admired her hard work with pride. It was dinner time now, and Jenny was starving.

In the mess hall, Jenny overheard people spreading rumors of a fight in engineering. She could feel their eyes on her as she loaded up her tray. She could hear them whispering as she walked to the table and sat down. To her relief, her friends chose to eat in companionable silence. It wasn't until the end of her meal that someone spoke up.

"It's almost time for Trey's memorial service," Adriana said. "I think we should all go."

I forgot, Jenny thought as the image of Trey's purple, smashed head flashed unbidden into her mind. She pushed her tray away as her stomach churned.

"Yeah," Billo said to Jenny. "And it's a good way to prove that you're a better person than Sadi."

~

Jenny and the other white uniforms joined about twenty other people on the landing platform. The sun had set, and millions of stars lit the night sky. Lin Yuan stood with her back against the ocean and led the tribunal. She spoke eloquently about Trey and his influence on everyone he met. She spoke of his creativity and drive.

"He will be missed," Lin said as she finished. Then she invited anyone else to come up and say something about Trey.

Only Sadi spoke up.

After observing Sadi's memories, Jenny felt an unexplainable bond with her. She felt compelled to honor Trey as well, but Jenny also knew how inappropriate it would be for Sadi. Jenny could feel the other girl staring at her. Hatred emanated from Sadi in waves, and something else: fear. Jenny wasn't sure which was worse.

After the memorial, Lin reminded everyone that tomorrow was the final day of testing. Jenny and the other white uniforms lined up at the stairwell. Behind them, she heard Sadi arguing with Lin.

"You don't even care," Sadi said.

"I do, Sadi. I do."

"What was he doing in the forest alone?"

"I don't know."

Kensei turned to Jenny. "It's time for my second testing. I hope I'm not late."

"You won't be," Jenny replied, turning her attention away from Sadi and Lin. She shuffled behind Kensei as they left the platform. "Mine is right after yours."

"Cool, maybe I'll see you down there."

Adriana looked at Jenny. "How about a rematch while Kensei is testing?"

"You're on."

Adriana proceeded to trounce Jenny on the mats. She won three bouts out of four. Jenny didn't have as much fire as she'd had in their first bout. After all, the last time they'd fought, she didn't know they were sisters. Also, she was nervous about her next test and kept glancing at the testing room. Neither of them commented on Jenny's poor fighting performance. *Perhaps Adriana understands how nervous I am*, Jenny thought.

"Is it time?" Adriana asked and rubbed at her neck.

"Yeah," Jenny said. Adriana gave her a hand up and they walked over to the testing room. Sweat cooled under Jenny's uniform as she watched Kensei work through the last maze. He pulled his key from the box, and the leaderboard updated. His name surged up to the seventh place. Kensei had finished the last maze in record time, and when he stepped out of the room, he didn't appear nearly as disoriented as last time.

Maybe he's getting more comfortable using his ability, Jenny thought.

"Wow, way to go." Adriana clapped him on the back. "That shortcut on the gravity level is really paying off."

"Are some of the shortcuts better than others?" Jenny asked.

"Yes and no." Adriana shrugged. "Look at how high Aindriu's score is on the first test, yet he has one of the lowest scores."

"Besides mine," Jenny said under her breath.

"You absolutely need to find a shortcut," Adriana continued, "but you also have to be skilled in the other tests."

"I wish we had started earlier." Kensei looked at Jenny. "Now we have a lot of catching up to do, and no time to do it."

"I know what you mean." Jenny looked down and kicked her foot. "I'm probably going to stay in the last place."

"Don't say that." Adriana put a hand on Jenny's shoulder. "I know you'll do better this time."

Kensei looked up at the leaderboard and checked the time. "Well, I'm going to bed."

"Same here." Adriana yawned.

"Aren't you going to stay and watch me?"

"I would"—Adriana shifted her feet—"but with the final test coming up tomorrow..."

"And I am really exhausted after training with Mazu," Kensei said.

"Okay." Jenny opened the door to the test room. "Well, goodnight." She let the door close before they could respond. *I don't need them anyway*, Jenny thought. *After all, I'm the only person to complete every test. Now that I know the waveforms, I'm sure I'll move into the top five, if not first place.*

Jenny took a breath to calm herself, then inserted her key into the first test. She worked the ball efficiently through each maze level until it rolled into the golden cage. When she finished, she saw that she was ahead of her previous time, but not as fast as she'd expected.

Don't worry, Jenny. There are still three more tests.

By the time she'd finished the second test, she knew she wasn't going to beat Sadi's score. After the third, she was sure she wouldn't be in the top five. Jenny activated the fourth test. Last time, the placement of the geometric objects seemed utterly random. This time, she noticed an order to them. She charted a path, the way she had on the other mazes, and quickly picked up enough small objects to level up to the next size. Then, she found another route for the medium-size objects. After picking up the large objects, the ball rolled into the golden cage, and she removed her key and left.

The sound of the door clicking shut echoed through the empty gym. She slowly turned around and checked the leaderboard. Her name had risen to fifteenth place, placing her solidly in the middle of the pack. *I only scored 236 points?* Jenny sat down on the floor and held her head in her hands. She felt a little sad and relieved that no one was here to witness her failure. Even though she was alone, she expected to hear Sadi's laughter behind her at any second.

Jenny was too upset to go back to her room. Instead, she decided to work through the tai chi kata Mazu had shown her earlier that day. Jenny entered the training room and assumed the starting stance. She moved as slowly as she could manage. In the case of katas, slower was harder and better for training her muscles.

Being able to finish each test means nothing if I can't find a shortcut, Jenny thought as she worked through the forms. *After all, the ball could only roll so fast. What did Mazu say about the scores? 'The perception test requires you to improve yourself, and because of that, it influences all the others.' They all depend on the perception test. Which means I need to improve myself.*

After twenty minutes, sweat coated her skin and her arms were like lead. She stopped and took a deep breath to slow her racing heart. Sitting cross-legged, she straightened her back and focused on relaxing her body. She opened her awareness to everything around her.

The air vents in the room hummed softly as they circulated clean air. Her heart thumped in a steady rhythm. Her mind drifted away.

Suddenly, a steady buh-da bum, buh-da bum reverberated through her body and echoed in her chest. *What was that?* She stood up and followed the sound. It took her out of the training room to the middle of the gym. It seemed to originate from the skylight. She looked up, peering through the dark water.

The sound was like the heartbeat of the ocean.

28

THE PULSE

Red lights lit the path ahead of her as Jenny left the gym. Though it preserved her night vision, it gave the appearance that she was walking through a lava-filled cave. Her breathing sounded loud in the empty corridor. Jenny didn't know the rules about being up late, and she worried about getting caught.

Soon Jenny reached the *Endeavor*'s control room, where she'd first met Mazu. As usual, workers in blue uniforms peered into their displays. She tiptoed across the catwalk, worried that one loud footfall would give her away. At any moment, they could look up and see her. They'd likely send her to bed, or worse, she'd be kept from the tests or expelled.

Jenny made it across the catwalk without drawing the workers' attention. She entered the escape pod room and sighed in relief. Jenny ran to the stairwell and ascended the steel steps. As she climbed higher, the ever-present beat pounding in her chest grew louder.

The air on the platform was a mixture of brine from the ocean and fuel and oil from the planes. The beat that had drawn her out of the *Endeavor* echoed across the sea from one of the Selkans' islands. The waves caught the orange light from a bonfire and held it like topaz jewels. Organic shapes danced in front of the flames, sending wild shadows across the water's rippling surface.

They were drums! Of course! That's where the sound is coming from. The deep bass boomed in her chest as she slipped off her boots. She sat on the edge of the platform, wishing her legs were long enough to reach the water. Suddenly, a big wave hit the concrete wall, and a spray of saltwater touched her lips. She licked it away just as a deep voice boomed from behind her.

"Hello."

Jenny jerked in surprise and almost tipped forward into the churning sea. She turned to find Kett'l standing behind her in his blue coveralls.

"Sorry to startle you." Kett'l smiled around his tusks. "I was on my way to the celebration." He pointed at the bonfire across the waves.

"Ah." Jenny nodded. "What are you celebrating?"

"Why, the success of the mission. A victor will be chosen tomorrow to unlock the Terminal." He cocked his head at Jenny. "What brought you up here? Did you feel the drums?"

"Yeah." Jenny thumped her chest. "They're like an extra heartbeat."

Kett'l nodded knowingly. "You hear with more than your ears. We call it the music of life. If you know how to listen, you find it everywhere, and in everything." He looked up at the stars and held out thick arms terminating in long, webbed fingers. "You can hear the universe singing."

Last week, Jenny would have thought anyone talking about the music of life was crazy. She couldn't be sure that Kett'l wasn't mad, but that was true of anyone on the *Endeavor*. After seeing the alien Æon weave matter from thin air in the forge, she was far more receptive to what he had to say.

"Join me," Kett'l said. "You can be my guest."

"Out there?" Jenny waved her hand at the island. *With aliens?*

Kett'l nodded and unclasped his coveralls. He pulled the blue clothing down over his generous belly. He stepped out of the bundle, revealing a giant, furry, walrus-like body.

Jenny's eyes widened and heat flushed into her face. She looked away and thought about his offer. *The test is tomorrow, and it's late. Yet, how can I pass up this once-in-a-lifetime event?* She turned toward him, careful to keep her eyes on his face. "Okay, yeah. I'll do it. I'll join you."

Kett'l grinned, displaying large, flat teeth beneath his white tusks.

Jenny stood up. The siphonophores, inhabiting every cell of her body, had increased her endurance, and made her a more perfect machine. She was in the best shape of her life. Jenny removed her uniform and felt unashamed as she stood in front of the alien in her underclothes.

The next moment, Kett'l ran and jumped into the ocean. Crystal-blue water fountained into the air.

Jenny found a hidden alcove on the platform where she could stash the burstepi and her clothes. Satisfied that no one would find her bag, she stepped up to the edge and peered down into the dark water. It churned and foamed as it crashed into the side of the platform two meters down. Before she lost courage, Jenny took a deep breath and leaped.

The cool ocean pulled her down and drew the heat from her body. Salty seawater found its way into her mouth. She clamped her lips shut and clawed upward. She gained the surface and struggled to keep her head above the waves as she looked around for Kett'l. A brown head bobbed up and down several meters away. The Selkan, who had seemed so large and awkward on land, glided confidently through the sea. Jenny swam after him using a freestyle stroke as powerful as an Olympic athlete's. After a minute, she reached the island just behind Kett'l. Fresh green grass tickled her toes.

Kett'l smiled warmly. "You swim well, for a human."

Jenny straightened and puffed out her chest. "Thanks."

The island, which was about 18 meters in diameter, contained a single mud hut. Rows of fish hung from a line to dry. A group of young Selkans danced around a roaring bonfire. Six more banged on huge drums with mallets. The elderly hummed a communal song. Several children played a game of tag. It was entirely domestic and wholesome and filled Jenny with a sense of warmth and security.

Three older Selkans, two men and a woman, approached Kett'l and greeted him by touching palms. The men had longer tusks than Kett'l did. They also had intricate facial tattoos with complex organic patterns in blue ink. After greeting Kett'l, they approached Jenny with their palms facing up. She placed her hands on theirs. They smiled and bowed before rejoining the festivities.

Jenny turned to Kett'l. "It must be difficult to be so far from home."

"It is." He pulled on a thong hanging around his neck and held it out to her. On it hung a glass vial filled with golden sand. "But we bring a small piece of home wherever we go."

Thork'l, Kett'l's father, walked over and greeted Jenny with a big, toothy smile and a warm embrace.

"Welcome to the celebration," Thork'l said.

"Thank you." She looked up at Kett'l. "And thank you for inviting me and making me feel so welcome."

Kett'l touched his forehead and bowed.

Thork'l led them closer to the fire. A group of elderly Selkans sat nearby and greeted her with open palms.

The trio sat on the green grass to watch the young Selkans dance. Their random, organic movements mimicked the fire that danced across the burning logs. Collars of shell and bone around their necks and arms clicked rhythmically. The sights and sounds held Jenny's attention in a hypnotic trance.

Kett'l joined the dancers.

Jenny's muscles pulsed in rhythm with the drum. Her head swayed, and her feet shifted in time with the beat. Then she let herself go. The drums and the humming Selkans guided her. She joined the Selkans, and danced like she was eleven years old again.

Deep down in her heart, she knew this song. It was the music of the universe, and it ignited a light inside of her. The frail flame flickered at first, fragile as a newborn, but it soon blazed as hot as the sun. Tears sprang from her eyes. *Why do I keep my happiness locked away?* She stared up at the sky, and for the first time in a long time, she saw beauty.

Kett'l collapsed onto the soft grass. He was breathing hard. "Phew, it's been a long time since I've danced like that."

Jenny sat down next to Kett'l and heard giggling voices behind them. She turned and saw a Selkan boy chasing a group of five kids.

Kett'l turned to look. "The little one, with the shells, is my sister, Lys'a."

"She's adorable."

The boy jumped over a bench and ran after Lys'a, but as he was about to tag her, she vanished. Jenny's eyes went wide, and she jerked backward.

Where did she go?

Lys'a appeared a few meters away from where she was last seen. The girl giggled and ran from the boy.

"She teleported," Jenny said in wonder.

"Of course."

"Can every Selkan teleport?"

"It's an innate flight response, though it's easier to invoke when we're young and easily frightened."

"That's amazing," Jenny said.

"It's how Tyr uses us in their ships. Though none of us here have been slaves, we were all prisoners to our system."

"What do you mean?"

"Before our escape, the only Selkans to leave our system were in the belly of a warship. Tyr keeps us trapped on our planet. They control our system's Terminal and all the information going in and out."

Jenny leaned forward. "How did you escape?"

"That is a long story." Kett'l reached up and pulled a dried fish off the line. He rolled the fish in his hands and examined the silvery scales. "My people believe that there is one pattern that controls all the energy in the universe and that our ability to teleport comes from that pattern. But a group of human scientists, assigned to study my clan, sought a more scientific explanation." He broke the fish open, peeled off a chunk of white flesh, and popped it into his mouth before offering some to Jenny. She took a piece and chewed the delicious, flaky fish. "Shortly after my sixteenth year, I began to see energy, like the waves of the sea."

"Like the waveforms in the mazes?" she asked.

He nodded. "I named it 'the Pulse' because it feels like a heartbeat to me."

"Pulse. I like that." *It's as good a term as any to describe what's going on inside my head.*

"None of my people understood the Pulse." Kett'l tore off another chunk of fish. "But the human scientists did. They took me aboard their laboratory, the *Endeavor*."

Jenny looked back at the concrete platform. Two planes were visible as black silhouettes against the starry sky. Below them, her friends slept beneath the waves.

"Yes." Kett'l nodded. "The same spaceship that rests underwater. I feared that the scientists were going to study me, but I soon learned that they wanted to teach me. They sheltered me from Tyr and kept me from becoming a slave.

"Over the next seven years, they became a second clan to me. They taught me about science and the galaxy. Even the Terminal master offered her generous knowledge, and trained me as an Æon. As my abilities grew, I worked with them to construct the forge, and finally the Riftkey.

"I was content, for a time. But like any young man, I grew restless, eager to prove myself. In that last year, I dreamed of becoming the Terminal master of my system. You see, the current master was old, and when she passed on, she wanted me to take over. How naive I was."

"Why?"

"Tyr became suspicious of the scientists' reports, and escape became the wiser option. Through great risk, the scientists contacted a group called Unity."

"Who is Unity?"

"They're a group dedicated to establishing equal rights to all people of the galaxy. They suggested a new plan. One that would make our presence known to everyone."

"And when your presence is known, Unity will gain more support," Jenny said.

"That is true, and not something I had considered." Kett'l stroked his furry chin.

"How is it that no one else knows about you?"

"A man named Vae Victus has assassinated anyone with proof of our existence. And because Tyr controls our system, any attempt to broadcast would be rebuffed. When we do get a chance to reveal ourselves, it needs to be bold and irrefutable."

"So, how do you send an irrefutable message to the Galaxy?"

"Unity's plan was for me to unlock a Terminal. As a Selkan Terminal master, no one would deny my existence. And with the backing of the other masters, I could reveal to the entire galaxy that my people were being used as slaves."

"But that's not what happened."

"No." He shook his great, tusked head, and folds of loose skin rippled under his chin. "I never wanted to be master of Sol, not when there's a possibility that I could be master of my own system."

Jenny nodded, she understood his reservation about permanently giving up his home, not when there were other Æons here on Earth. Jenny still wasn't sure if she wanted to accept the role of Terminal master in this foreign realm.

Jenny leaned back against the log and thought about Kett'l's story. In a way, her story was similar. She, too, struggled to understand her ability, and she'd been forced to run away to save herself. Though, instead of the threat of slavery aboard a ship, she had been cursed to live as a fortune-teller before dying of cancer.

"I wanted to refuse," Kett'l continued, "but I couldn't, not when it meant saving the lives of my people. Still, I had one condition. I would not leave without my clan. Unity agreed. When the day came, we all boarded the *Endeavor* and flew toward the Terminal, entering it just as it activated. The timing had to be perfect, or we would miss or be cut in half. For a moment, there was nothing. Then we saw the new stars and I knew we had done it—we had escaped from Tyr."

Jenny watched as one of the Selkan children, a boy, disappeared and reappeared a few meters away.

"After that, Unity directed us to a sympathetic Terminal master, Brigham Newton. He agreed to send us to Sol. After arriving here, Cabin took us in. I showed them the Riftkey and relayed Unity's plan.

"Except the part where you would unlock the Terminal."

"That is correct. We decided to hold a competition to find an Æon to become master. I used the forge to create the VRGo puzzle and multiple Waypoint keys. Meanwhile, Cabin located potential recruits to send the puzzle."

Now we're all competing against each other for the right to unlock the Terminal. "Can you give me some advice on the tests?"

"I'm not sure." Kett'l shook his head.

"What about the Pulse, can you teach that to me?"

"Yes." He stood and picked up two shell cups and filled them with fresh water. Jenny took a cup and washed down the salted fish. "The key to the Pulse is understanding that all things exist as vibrations. If you can see them, then you can control them. Watch." Kett'l turned his attention toward one of the drums.

To Jenny's eye, a black mist formed on one of the drumheads and its deep reverberations went silent. The drummer looked at his mallet in confusion. He experimentally tapped the side of the drum. It made a sound of wood hitting wood. He tried pounding on the mist-covered top again, but it yielded nothing.

"How did you do that?"

Kett'l grinned, and the black mist on the drumhead dissipated. The drummer slammed both sticks against the drumhead, and the resulting boom overpowered every other sound. His fellow drummers glared. Jenny giggled along with a few other Selkans who had been watching.

"Listen," Kett'l said.

Jenny leaned closer to the Selkan.

"Start by syncing your Pulse to that of the drum."

Jenny turned that new sense within her mind toward the drums. She could see the sound waves flowing out into the air. She reached for her key, but Kett'l stopped her.

"Try without your key."

Jenny nodded and visualized the white waveform of her Pulse. She squeezed her hands into fists and narrowed her eyes as she struggled to match it to the drum waves. She shook with the effort.

"You're trying too hard."

Jenny sighed and released her breath. "What am I supposed to do?"

"Don't force yourself into alignment; let it guide you instead."

Jenny did as Kett'l said, but the sound waves from the drum kept changing, and she couldn't keep up with them. "I can't, they're too fast."

"You are focusing on the sound waves. Try looking deeper than the surface of things. That is where you find the heart."

"Deeper?" The sound waves were big and bold, but she pushed past them and dug into the heart of the drum. She felt something twinge at a corner of her brain. It was subtle, like the buzz of a mosquito next to a chainsaw. She had to shut off all her other senses. A single beautiful wave function surfaced. It was at the root of every emanation and separate from the air around it. It was the drumhead. "I see it."

"Good. Now silence it by making an opposite waveform."

Jenny worked and shaped her Pulse until it was a reverse copy of the drum's vibrations. A black mist spread across the drumhead, and, like a pair of noise-canceling headphones, the drum went silent.

The drummer stared at the drum in disgust. He put his ear close to the drum and tapped it with his finger.

Jenny didn't stop there. She did the same to the next drum, then another, until half the drums were silenced. She giggled as each drummer stopped and inspected their drum.

The drummers looked at one another, then one of them turned and pointed at Kett'l. Jenny thrust her hands in her lap and tried to look as innocent as possible.

"Well done." Kett'l squeezed her shoulder. "Now for the next lesson. Watch close: We can also amplify waves." He did something, and the black mist disappeared.

The drummers turned back to their drums. As their mallets hit the drumheads, the resulting boom knocked Jenny onto her side. Worried about the elderly Selkans, she turned and found them laughing and pointing at the confused young drummers. She smiled. They must have seen Kett'l play this game before.

"That's enough for now." Kett'l turned to watch the dancers. "If we keep it up, they'll throw us off the island."

Jenny could tell he was speaking from experience. Even though their lesson was cut short, Jenny had learned a good deal. *Maybe it will help me find a shortcut in the tests.* Jenny watched the children play teleport tag around the island. Lys'a chased after a little boy. Using the Pulse, Jenny waited for the boy to teleport. This time, instead of disappearing and reappearing, she saw the child split into two separate children, one physical, one ethereal. Each ran off in a different direction. As Lys'a grew nearer to the physical boy, it vanished and appeared in place of the ethereal boy.

Is that how their teleportation works? She continued using the Pulse. The next time the boy split, she observed a subtle waveform, like the ones she saw on the drumhead, or the tests. This gave her an idea. Still focusing on the boy, Jenny tuned her Pulse to match his. As his ethereal form ran away from his physical, Jenny inverted her Pulse. Something pulled in her mind like unraveling a thread, and a black mist clung to the boy's body. His ethereal form collapsed back to his physical. Lys'a tapped him on the shoulder. The boy looked confused for a moment, then he giggled and chased after her.

Kett'l gripped her shoulder painfully. He turned his eyes on her, they had become dark and menacing. "What did you do?" There was no cheer in his voice. He blew out his thick mustache in deep breaths as he waited for her answer.

Jenny's mouth hung limp, and her insides turned to ice. "The same thing you showed me."

"We never use the Pulse on living things."

"I'm sorry." A pit grew in Jenny's stomach. She had been so proud of herself, and now she was being scolded. "I didn't know."

"What if you had hurt him, or killed him?" He sighed and forced a more gentle tone into his voice. "You are not wise enough yet, Jenny Tripper."

Jenny's face heated, and her limbs felt numb. The drums pounded through her chest as they watched the dancers in uncomfortable silence. *Why did I do it?* Jenny asked herself. *Kett'l's right, I'm not wise enough.*

At that moment, all she wanted to do was go back to her room and crawl under the bed covers.

The children stopped playing tag, and Lys'a walked up to Jenny.

"Hello." Jenny forced a smile that didn't reach her watery eyes.

Kett'l's young sister returned her smile. "My name's Lys'a."

"I'm Jenny."

"Wanna dance?" The little Selkan held her hands out to Jenny.

After what I just did? Jenny thought. It took all of Jenny's willpower to reach up and grip the girl's hands. Lys'a pulled with all her might and Jenny got to her feet. Lys'a led Jenny toward the fire and started dancing. At first, Jenny's movements felt forced, but the little girl's enthusiasm was infectious. Soon, Lys'a had Jenny dancing along with her. As Jenny held Lys'a's hands and twirled around the fire, her concerns melted away.

After the festivities, Kett'l and Jenny swam back to the platform together. They sat on the edge, watching the embers of the fire die in the distance as the moon crept across the night sky.

"You did well out there." Kett'l took Jenny's hand in his. "I'm sorry I scolded you."

"No, you were right. I was stupid and careless."

"True." He nodded slowly. "But experimentation and mistakes are the best teachers. A little caution is good, but do not let fear hinder your potential."

"I won't." Jenny smiled.

"You and I are special." Kett'l took Jenny's hand in the palm-to-palm greeting of the Selkans. "We share a bond that distance cannot separate."

"What do you mean?"

"Know me, not by this physical body but by the energy contained within it." Kett'l closed his eyes, and Jenny felt something press against her mind, like wind blowing over a curtain.

Following his lead, she closed her eyes. Thousands of waveforms rippled outside her mind, as vast as an ocean. She focused on the pressure at the edge of her awareness and found the shape of Kett'l. She looked past his body and searched for the pattern that infused every part of him, the essence of Kett'l, his signature, his true name. She smiled and opened her eyes.

He nodded. "You found me. And I found you."

～

Later that night, as Jenny lay in bed, her mind replayed the more dramatic events of the day in painful detail. *Why can't I just remember the good experiences?* She took out her mother's amulet, kissed it, and stared at the photograph in the red light.

Hi, Mom. Today was exciting—spectacular, really. I got to dance with Selkans; they're a group of aliens who escaped slavery from a galactic government named Tyr. I discovered that I have abilities. I can see and manipulate energy with my mind, and there are other people like me here. One of them is Adriana. She's pretty cool. I'm guessing you already knew she was my sister, and I understand why you couldn't tell me. There's this other girl, Sadi, who's sort of my enemy, but I don't think she'll be bothering me anymore.

We're all competing for the chance to fly into outer space and unlock something called a Terminal. But I'm not doing very well on the tests. And, even if I do win, I'll be bound to the Terminal for life.

While Billo snored softly in her bed, Jenny pulled the burstepi into her lap. Carefully, she unfastened the strap and opened the flap. She reached inside and grasped the Riftkey.

Cobol? No answer. She pulled the handle free of the bag. *Cobol, are you there?*

Yes, Jenny, I'm here, Cobol said.

I have a question.

I'm ready to answer.

If I unlock the Terminal, will I be bound to it?

Not if you find the virosuit.

Really? It sounded too good to be true, but, of course, it depended on Mazu finding and returning the artifact.

That is my purpose. Once you unlock the Terminal, I can maintain it myself. You and I will be bound to each other, but you will not become tied to the Terminal.

That's a relief. Jenny yawned. *Thank you, Cobol.*

You are welcome.

Goodnight.

Goodnight, Jenny Tripper.

Jenny slid the Riftkey into the burstepi and fastened the clasp.

As she slept, her subconscious mind worked on the mazes. She visualized thousands of patterns that night as she puzzled out different ways to solve each test. Her mind sank deeper in its dream state. She was dancing around the fire with Lys'a. Suddenly, a black mist enveloped the Selkan girl. She screamed, and a pair of glowing yellow eyes appeared out of the dark cloud. It was Blunderbore, the dark giant. He swung an enormous, wavy sword at her head. Jenny now held the shaft of a polearm. Hot blood coated her hands. The giant she had killed stared down at her. His brown eyes were a mix of surprise and sadness.

Jenny jerked awake as the alarm on Billo's Topo beeped monotonously. *Didn't I just fall asleep?* She buried her head in the pillow. *Ugh, I've got to get up. The final test is about to begin.*

29

SPELUNKING

Bubbles sped past Jack's helmet. The depth meter on his heads-up display climbed as the underside of the *Endeavor* shrank. He hit the ocean floor with a sudden jolt. The Tumlare suit absorbed most of the impact, but his teeth still rattled in his head.

I never thought I'd die like this, Jack thought as he tipped forward into a cloud of sand.

"Kick your legs," Mazu said over the suit's comm. She clutched the Locator to her chest and used her fins to hover near Jack.

"My legs?" *They're useless in a spacesuit*, Jack thought.

"You weren't lying, were you?" Mazu asked. "You really don't have any diving experience."

Jack's heart thundered, and his breathing was short and rapid. *Does she know who I am, and that I've been lying to her this whole time?*

"Can't you swim?" Marcel asked.

"No," Jack replied. "I don't know how."

"Maybe there's something wrong with your suit?" Marcel asked.

Jack's head jerked around. There was solid ground below him and turquoise water all around. Mazu kicked a set of flippers that extended from her legs.

These big Tumlare suits are surprisingly graceful in the water, Jack thought.

Marcel swam closer to Jack. "Both feet together, like a dolphin."

"We can't wait here," Mazu said. "Either he figures it out, or he doesn't. We can pick him up on the way back." She turned and swam away. The backwash swirled sand behind her.

Marcel hovered near Jack and shrugged by raising his hands. Then, he turned and joined Mazu.

Okay, I can do this. Jack tipped himself forward and kicked with both legs. Something clicked inside his suit. He felt a vibration in his feet. He kicked again, and this time he lurched upward, but sank back to the seafloor. Jack churned the water with his arms and legs until his legs ached from the effort, and still the distance between his comrades grew.

Jack recalled his first time in a spacesuit. Every movement had been countered by an equal and opposite force. Even subtle shifts had significant effects in space. He had to be aware of every action. *I need to work with the Tumlare suit, not against it.*

Jack studied Mazu and Marcel and copied their movements. First, he flattened his arms against his sides, then he kicked. This time, he paid attention to the feedback from his suit. Soon he found a natural rhythm between machine and sea. Jack stopped fighting against the water and flowed through it.

Overhead, the Selkans' island homes passed overhead like dark clouds. Sunlight lanced from the sky to the ocean floor. Mazu and Marcel were mere dots against the rippling water's surface. Cursing himself for his lost time and energy, Jack increased his intensity and gained on them.

"Welcome back," Marcel said. Mazu grunted.

Jack felt his face grow hot. *This mission isn't off to a good start.* He stayed in their wake and focused on his technique. After a minute, he relaxed and enjoyed himself. The weightlessness reminded him of space, but it was better somehow.

They swam toward a sizeable dark mass. Turquoise water stretched endlessly out to either side. Crabs, turtles, jellyfish, and other marine life accompanied them on the journey. Nearby, a large gray fish broke through a school of yellow-blue fish.

After some time, they came to a stop at a rock wall. A crack marked a cave opening. The twin headlights on the sides of their helmets pierced the veil of darkness. Inside, small animals clung to the walls, extracting minerals and filtering food.

They ventured inside the cave. Large organisms became more scarce the deeper they went. Eventually, even organic specks like dust disappeared. The cave became crystal clear, and cold. It also grew narrower, forcing them to swim in a single file.

After several minutes, Mazu slowed to a stop and pointed at a patch of wall. "This is it. These are the twin Waypoints that connect our universes."

A perfect line separated gray rock from tan. Stranger still, the tunnel was smooth and perfectly round. Jack's heads-up display indicated that the salinity and temperature had changed radically. He also felt a subtle current that moved in and out, like the slow breath of a giant creature.

"Nimue installed these thousands of years ago," Mazu said.

"These are Waypoints?" Jack reached out to touch the smooth rock surface. He traced a gloved finger across the line—not even a crack— that marked where the two Waypoints joined. He moved through the invisible boundary, and his heads-up display went crazy. When it settled down, it showed that the depth had increased and that the water temperature had dropped by ten degrees. "It's like two sets of lips that mark the point where the two universes kiss."

"I couldn't have put it better myself," Mazu said.

"Do you two need to get a room?" Marcel asked.

Jack felt the back of his neck get hot. He pushed away from the Waypoints and swam down the tunnel. Marcel and Mazu followed.

The tunnel widened as they swam upward, and a blue dot slowly grew larger. *Light*, Jack thought. He sped forward, eager to be out of the water. As his head broke the surface, he found himself in a claustrophobic cavern. They stood on an underwater ledge. Two streams fed the pool: a large one that poured out of a substantial tunnel, and a smaller one that trickled out of a small hole in the wall. The source of the blue light came from little worms, like blue threads.

"Bioluminescent worms." Mazu pointed upward.

The Tumlare suits were too heavy and awkward to climb out of the pool, so they left them in the water. In his rucksack, Jack put on his head-lamp and turned it on. Mazu examined the brass Locator then led them down the larger of the two tunnels.

They climbed over and around rock formations and rough gravel. Jack's boots provided a good grip against the slippery stones but no protection against the pointy rocks. His feet, unused to harsh treatment, quickly bruised.

After some time, their path terminated at a rock outcropping. The stream they had been following flowed out of a small opening to their right. A small tunnel above their heads marked the way forward. Without hesitation, Mazu climbed the rock and slipped through the tunnel. Marcel and Jack struggled up the rock outcropping and followed after Mazu. After that, Jack began to notice Mazu's easy feats of strength. *There's something different about her,* Jack thought. *Something special.*

As they ventured deeper, Mazu checked the Locator with more frequency. Oftentimes she led them down a forked path or into a narrow opening that was hidden from view. Some areas of the cave system were as large as a spacecraft hangar, while others forced them to crawl on hands and knees.

"Thousands of years ago," Mazu said from up ahead, "Nimue walked this same path."

"It feels like we're doing more crawling than walking," Jack said.

Jack's legs ached as they wriggled under a ceiling of jagged stalactites. He ran his tongue over his dry lips and thought, *How much farther are we going? We've been going uphill for over an hour. Yet Mazu still bounds up every boulder and crawls through small spaces with ease. How does she do it?*

A sudden movement caught Jack's eye. Tiny jellyfish-like creatures floated through the air. Bioluminescent patterns flashed across their bodies. Since entering the cave, the only sign of life had been the bioluminescent worms.

"Fascinating," Mazu said. "I wonder if they're a spore or some evolved form of the worms."

A blind white lizard stopped and rotated its head in their direction. Near it, a colorless insect, with more antennas than body, crawled across the gray rock. The lizard's long pink tongue shot from its mouth and seized the bug. The lizard chomped noisily at its food as they walked on.

Mazu was in an ecstatic state as she commented on each of the creatures. Jack found her childlike curiosity about the strange life forms quite endearing. She peered closely at a giant, pale creature that looked like living stone, but which worked a sack of air like a bellows. Farther ahead, an exposed section of the wall displayed the skeletons of enormous creatures.

"These are dinosaurs," Mazu said.

"A what?" Jack asked.

"Colossal creatures that once ruled the planet."

The low sounds of unseen animals vibrated inside the rock. There was a deep rumble and some gravel rained down on their heads.

"Maybe they still rule this planet," Jack said.

"Impossible," Mazu said. "They died off millions of years ago."

The next cavern was filled with enormous white crystals that reached from floor to ceiling. Jack's face scrunched up. The air was hot and smelled like ship exhaust.

"Gypsum crystals." Mazu stood and looked around, seemingly unaware of the stifling heat and smell. "They form above magma chambers."

"That explains why it's so hot." Marcel wiped his brow with the back of his arm.

Mazu checked her Locator and led them out of the gypsum chamber. Free of the stifling heat, they decided to rest. They found a level area on a bare patch of rock. Nearby, the stream trickled down the wall to a bed of small gypsum crystals.

Jack pulled out his canteen and found a smooth rock apart from Mazu and Marcel. A wave of euphoria spread over his body as he sat down. It was hard to believe that a week ago he had been in his workshop. Life had been so simple aboard the space station, and he missed it more than he could have imagined. Yet, if Jack had never left, then he would never have swum in an ocean or seen two universes kissing.

"Come, sit with us." Mazu patted the stone next to her.

Jack shrugged and sat next to Mazu. He found a groove in the stone that fit his butt well enough. "I'm surprised Lance requested me for this mission."

"He didn't," Mazu said.

"Then who?"

"I did."

Jack grew suspicious. "Why me?"

"You seemed like a useful guy to have around—you're ex-military, and you have decent reflexes."

Jack shrugged and said, "Nothing like yours." He took a bite of his brick of compressed protein and carbs. *At least my cover story is holding up.*

"What brings you to our noble cause?" Marcel asked.

"I needed a job"—Jack fiddled with his headlamp—"and Trey provided."

"Sorry to hear what happened to him." Marcel tore open a food ration. "Were you close?"

"No, not really. Trey thinks"—Jack swallowed—"or thought, I saved his life. He believed he owed me a favor." He took another bite and listened to the sound of distant water while he chewed. He looked over at Marcel. "I'm new to all of this. Could you explain something to me?"

"Shoot," Marcel said as he chewed his bar.

"In my experience, no one does anything out of the goodness of their heart. What does Cabin get for saving the Selkans?"

Marcel shrugged. "Can't it just be an act of goodwill?"

"Look, I don't mean to be pessimistic, but..." Jack rolled a rock with his foot. "There's gotta be more to it."

"They get the *Endeavor*," Mazu spoke up. "A stellar laboratory full of more advanced technology than anything seen before on Earth."

"That must be it." Jack nodded, but he felt in his gut that there was more to it. Why else would Lance, a Tyran, be involved?

The trio made small talk as they ate. Jack spoke of the aches and pains in his feet. Mazu talked of flora and fauna. After their break, Jack stashed his gear and followed the relentless Mazu farther into the cave system.

As they hiked along the stream, a trickling sound in the distance grew louder. Their path took them upward, and the stream disappeared through a gap in the rock. Soon, the distant trickling sound grew to a roar, and their path ended at a curtain of water. They followed a narrow ridge around the waterfall and found that they were in a deep hole that was a little over three meters in diameter.

"It must have taken millions of years for this waterfall to carve a pothole this large in the rock," Mazu said.

Marcel pulled a plastic stick from his rucksack. With a twist, it glowed bright green. He dropped it into the pothole. A circle of green light lit the dark stone as it fell. After a couple of seconds, it splashed into a pool, giving the clear water an eerie green glow.

"That's about a twelve-meter drop," Jack estimated.

Mazu checked the Locator. "That's the wrong direction." She looked up. "We need to get up there."

Jack aimed his headlamp upward. As the light played across the waterfall, individual water droplets sparkled like gems. Jack aimed higher and found the source of the waterfall flowing out of a crack in the wall about eight meters above them. On the opposite side of the crack, Jack saw another ledge like the one they stood on.

"Look there." Mazu aimed her headlamp at the far end of the ledge. There was an opening that was large enough for them to crawl through. "That's where we need to go."

Jack shook his head, and his headlamp danced across their black suits. "No way. We can't climb this slick wall."

"Speak for yourself." Mazu tied the Locator to her rucksack and put her hand on the cliff. Her fingertips slipped into a tiny crack in the rock. She bent her legs and tested her weight by pulling herself up with one arm. The muscles in Mazu's calves and buttocks flexed as she scaled the impassable rock.

Jack's mouth fell open as Mazu shifted from foothold to handhold. He turned to Marcel and asked, "Does she expect us to do that?"

"No." Marcel pointed upward. "Look."

Jack watched in awe as Mazu pulled herself onto the upper ledge after just a few minutes of climbing. She tied one end of a paracord to a rock outcropping and flung the other end down to them.

Marcel caught the line and handed it to Jack. "You first."

Jack nodded, took the paracord, and looked up. Cold sweat covered his hands as he tied the line around his waist. Then, Jack inserted his fingertips into the same crack Mazu had used. With a grunt, he pulled himself up.

Mazu pulled the line taut as Jack climbed. The stone was damp but not as slippery as he had expected. His boots provided excellent traction, and his gloves prevented rope burn. Still, he took a more plodding pace than Mazu had, even with the paracord supporting him, and after a couple of minutes, his shoulders ached from carrying his own weight.

Several minutes later, the ledge finally came into view. Endorphins flooded Jack's body as his fingers felt the flat surface. Mazu reached down and pulled him up the rest of the way. Jack leaned against the cold rock wall to catch his breath. He looked up, and his headlamp lit the ceiling of the cave. *That's strange,* he thought. Large holes, about a meter in diameter, punctured its structure.

"You made it," Marcel called out.

"Yeah!" Jack shouted back. "Just a minute, I'll get the rope to you."

Jack worked at the knot tied around his waist, then peered over the edge with the bundle of paracord in his hands. Twenty meters straight down, the glow stick still illuminated the pool in soft green light. Marcel had taken the canteen from his rucksack and was filling it under the waterfall. Before Jack could toss the line down, another line appeared and dangled just a meter away from Marcel. *Did Mazu throw another paracord down?* Jack wondered. He traced the path of the line back to its source, but instead of terminating at Mazu, it ended inside one of the holes in the ceiling. "What the...?"

"No!" Mazu screamed. "Marcel, let it go! That's not our line."

Suddenly, a sound, like two rocks rubbing together, echoed down from up above. There was a rush of air, and a dark form shot out from the hole. Jack caught a glimpse of razor-sharp fangs. He looked down just in time to see rows of vicious teeth sink into Marcel's shoulder.

The big man screamed and drew his gun. The muzzle flashed once. Then Marcel screamed louder. Blood spurted from his shoulder. The massive worm had chomped clean through Marcel's arm. The dismembered limb fell to the ledge, still gripping the pistol. The worm pulled back for a second strike and clamped onto Marcel's head. The man went silent, and his headless body dropped to the ground. Jack pushed away from the gory scene. The smell of death filled the pothole.

"We need to get out." Mazu pointed at the opening in the wall which had been indicated by the Locator. "That way."

Jack glanced upward just as two more worms exploded from the ceiling. "Look out!" He grabbed Mazu's arm and yanked her back. The two worms passed the spot where she had been standing and attacked Marcel's remains. Their undulating bodies formed an impassable barrier of rough gray flesh, blocking their exit.

"Forget that." Jack pressed his back against the wall.

"What then?" Mazu asked.

Below them, a great hissing and grinding erupted as the worms fought over Marcel's remains. The abominable sounds made Jack shiver. Above them, three more filaments lowered from the ceiling. Their rope-like tendrils rippled as the worms waved their blind heads back and forth. Their mouths opened with a hiss, and glistening teeth glittered in the lamplight.

"They must use the tendrils to detect their prey." Mazu moved away from the groping filaments.

"I'll be damned if I'm going out as worm food." Jack unzipped his suit and reached inside for his knife. As he did so, one of the filaments wrapped around his arm, and rows of razor-sharp teeth shot toward him.

With a flick of his knife, Jack sliced the tendril from his arm. He sucked air through his teeth as blood welled up on his bicep. The worm roared with a sound like a power drill. Blood sprayed from the wound and covered both Jack and Mazu, and the injured monster retreated back into its hole.

"Why don't the worms come all the way out of those holes?" Jack asked.

"I'm not sure," Mazu said. "But if I had to guess, I'd say it's a defensive mechanism. They would probably cannibalize each other, so the holes provide them with a protective retreat."

Jack said, "I have an idea."

"I'm all ears."

"Since the worms won't come out of their holes, I bet if we go all the way down, they won't be able to reach us."

"You might be right." Mazu looked over at the opening that the locator had indicated, then at the worms. "And it's worth a shot. After they're done with Marcel, it's only a matter of time before they come for us. But the paracord isn't long enough. How do we get down?"

Jack peered over the edge. The three worms still fought over Marcel's remains below them, but he saw the glint of the pistol in Marcel's dismembered hand. Jack was no zoologist, but he knew about muscles. When a muscle relaxed, it stretched. For the worms to stay in their holes, they would have to constantly keep their muscles contracted. "If I can get that pistol and kill one," Jack said, "it may stretch and thin out enough to reach the bottom."

"And we can use it like a rope," Mazu said.

Just then, two worms turned their cone-shaped heads in their direction. A tendril slithered across the ledge toward them. Jack took his knife and stabbed at the nearest worm. His blade rebounded from its tough hide and tumbled into the hole. He cursed.

"Follow my lead." Jack grabbed the paracord he had just untied from his waist and slid down. The friction burned through his gloves, but he dared not let go. Above him, Mazu grabbed the line just in time to avoid the worms' seeking tendrils. However, the worms did find the paracord and followed it down to their prey.

Jack and Mazu landed on the ledge with the pursuing worms surging after them. They backed up against the wall and the worms slammed into the ledge. The rock trembled under their feet.

Nearby, another tendril swung toward Jack. He dropped and rolled to the side, coating himself in Marcel's blood and gore. Marcel's foot hung from a worm's bloody mouth, and the neighboring creatures consumed his other body parts. Jack found Marcel's dismembered arm and pried the handgun from its hand. The same hand that had taught him a special handshake the day before. Mazu lunged backward as another worm slammed into the rock where she had been standing.

"Stay close," Jack yelled as he pressed the gun against a worm's body. Jack pulled the trigger as fast as his muscles allowed. His ears rang as the firearm kicked and sparked against the worm's rocklike hide. Its skin cracked with the first shot and split after the second. Soon, slippery orange blood coated Jack's arm, and the gun clicked empty. The creature went slack and thinned as it stretched.

"Grab on." Jack dropped the empty gun and wrapped his arms around the worm with all his strength. His sliced bicep burned as he slid down the creature's body and splashed into the ice-cold pool far below. He hit the shallow bottom with an impact that drove the air from his lungs. Jack rolled over and pushed himself up to his hands and knees as he struggled for breath. His headlamp illuminated white pebbles and shiny brass fragments. *Oh no*, Jack thought, *the Locator is busted.*

Above him, the dead worm, unable to contract its muscles any longer, slipped out of its hole. It fell twenty meters up and hit the cavern floor like an egg cracking against concrete. Part of the worm landed on Jack, and the weight of its body pressed him into the shallow pool and buried his face beneath the icy water.

Jack kicked and clawed to free himself from the dead thing, but the small white pebbles provided poor leverage. Jack's lungs screamed for air, then darkness consumed the edges of his vision. His hand scattered white pebbles ahead of him. *No, not pebbles,* he realized. *Polished bone.* His skin grew numb as he struggled to breathe, then his vision turned black.

Sensations teased the edge of Jack's awareness. Strong hands reached under his arms. A muted light shone through his eyelids. Something soft pressed against his lips. His chest expanded with warm air. A repeating pressure on his chest. Jack inhaled sharply, then rolled over and coughed up cold water.

"Jack, are you—?"

Jack gasped. He blinked and stared into Mazu's dark eyes. They seemed darker and deeper than before.

Mazu sighed. "You're alright."

"I'm just dandy." Jack winced and clutched his ribs.

Mazu chuckled. "I'm glad you're as tough as you look."

Jack felt a sudden devotion to this woman who had just saved his life. For a moment, he forgot the pain. "How are you?"

Mazu chuckled. "I'm fine." She held up a mangled piece of brass metal. "But the Locator is busted."

A pit grew in Jack's stomach. "So, the mission is a failure?"

Mazu nodded. "But at least we're alive."

Jack propped himself up on one elbow. Pain spiked through his chest as he breathed. "I've been knocked out in fights before, but I've never felt this bad."

"Are you okay?"

Jack pushed on his side and felt some relief from the pain. "I've been better."

"Let me see." Mazu moved closer and palpated his ribs with her fingers. "Well, they're not broken. They're probably just bruised. It will take time to heal, and it'll hurt, but you don't have to worry about a punctured lung."

"That's some good news."

Mazu pressed her hand against his chest and leaned closer, searching his eyes. "Thanks for saving me."

Jack's body tingled at her touch, and he felt her warm breath on his face. "You saved me too, so we're even." Jack's heart beat faster.

Suddenly, the obsidian tip of a spear appeared between them.

Mazu lurched backward.

Jack reached for his gun by reflex, but nothing was there. "What the...?" He looked around and saw dozens of small humanoids covered in blue phosphorescent fur. The humanoid creatures had enormous ears. Warrior types aimed their spears at Jack and Mazu, while worker types carved the dead worm into chunks using flaked obsidian tools. "What are they?"

"I think they're Alfur," Mazu said. "I've heard Lin talk about one named Heather."

Two of the warriors pried Jack and Mazu apart with their spears. Pain lanced up Jack's leg as he gained his feet.

"Well, what do they want?" Jack felt a pressure on his back. He gasped and twisted away as an obsidian spear pierced his suit and pricked his skin. Jack stumbled forward. "I get the point." Jack limped away from the pool alongside Mazu.

Alfur led them along the stream to a rectangular doorway in a smooth rock wall. They passed through the opening and into a huge cavern that smelled of sulfur. A thin layer of water covered the entire floor, and each step stirred up a cloud of bioluminescence. The ceiling glowed red, and Jack could feel the heat of it. To their right, carved from solid rock, was a pyramid with statues of giant worms guarding a dark door. To their left, hundreds of ladders led from the ground floor to holes in the wall where Alfur, both young and old, gawked at the strangers.

Alfur warriors guided them toward the left wall and pushed them toward a hole at ground level. Jack batted a spear away. "I'm not going in there." He arched his back as a spear tip pricked him. He glared backward. The Alfur pointed at the door and yelled. Jack looked at Mazu, who nodded. *Fine*, he thought. He was in no condition to fight anyway. He slouched his shoulders and walked into the dark cavern.

Once they were inside, a group of workers rolled a massive circular stone into place behind them. Jack looked into Mazu's eyes as the cavern's dim light slivered and disappeared.

Jack slid down the cold stone wall until he sat on the rough rock floor. He closed his eyes and pictured himself back in his pod thousands of light-years away. But there was no chance that Victus would find him here. Jack's only hope was for Cabin to find them.

Reluctantly, Jack opened his eyes and saw a faint blue glow emanating from bioluminescent algae on the ceiling. He stood, wincing at the pain in his leg and ribs, and followed the light to the back of their prison.

Mazu sat in the far corner. Her shiny black hair reflected the blue light of the algae. She was crying into her folded arms. Jack felt helpless as he watched this powerful woman brought low. He racked his brain for the source of her emotions. "I'm sorry about Marcel."

"He did his job," Mazu said into her folded arms.

"Yeah." Jack pictured the worm clamping onto Marcel's head. "Poor bastard."

"I'm sorry." She looked up at him then. "It's my fault we're here. It's my fault you're here."

Guilt spread over Jack like a burning blanket. *If you only knew.* "No," Jack said and knelt in front of her. He placed his rough hands on her shoulders. "No," he whispered. "You're a good person. You're trying to save the Selkans. You didn't know about those things."

Mazu looked up. Her eyes were wet, and blue light reflected off her tear-covered cheeks. "That was some quick thinking up there."

Jack looked away. *It would have been simpler if I had died back there.* But the time for simplicity had passed. *Time to be strong. If not for me, then for her.* Jack forced a smile onto his face and turned to face her. "I was just looking out for myself."

"I don't get you."

"What do you mean?"

"Sometimes you seem so far away. Then, other times, you look at me like I'm the only person in the room."

"Oh." Jack looked down and picked at one of the hard plates on his wetsuit. "I don't know what I'm doing here."

"I know what you mean. Unlocking the Terminal. Retrieving the virosuit. It's all so unreal."

"That's not exactly what I meant, but close enough. What's the viro-suit for anyway?"

"According to Lance, we need it to operate the Terminal after it's unlocked."

Of course, Lance would know, he's a Tyran. Jack's face heated up as he thought of the aliens. "So, you need it to save the Selkans?"

"Yes."

Jack slammed his hand against the wall. "Do you really believe that they're being exploited for some supernatural ability?"

"I know it sounds crazy."

"What if we're on the wrong side?"

Mazu searched his eyes. "I understand your doubt, but I've seen them teleport."

So, the Selkans are the secret weapon, Jack thought. "And if Tyr can somehow use that ability, then they'd be invincible in combat. That's how they ended the First Galactic War."

"By enslaving an entire race of people," Mazu countered. "They've only maintained peace by sacrificing innocent lives."

A foul taste grew in Jack's mouth. A week ago, he had considered himself politically neutral. Now, his galactic pride was eroding. "You're right. No matter what their reasoning is, it's not right to enslave anyone."

"That's why we need to unlock the Terminal and reveal Tyr's secret to the galaxy."

I don't want another war, Jack thought, *but I have no love for Tyr either. Especially not Admiral Vae Victus.* Something inside him delighted at the idea of flying his ship in battle again.

Mazu shivered and nestled against him. Jack pulled her close, and she pushed her head under his chin. Within moments, she was asleep, and Jack followed a moment later.

30

FINAL TEST

The skylight painted the gym floor in shifting hues of blue light. Along the walls were tables adorned with fruits, vegetables, cheese, crackers, and meats. A buzz of excited conversation filled the space. The contestants formed a line that led away from the testing-room door. The gray uniforms were first in line, while Jenny and the other white uniforms stood near the back.

"I carried that in." Kensei pointed to a massive pedestal in the center of the gym. Kett'l and Thork'l stood on either side, and the newly crafted Riftkey rested upon it. Around them were four guards in black uniforms with handguns hanging from their belts.

"Patience, everyone, please." Lin Song stood at the head of the line and held the eager recruits back. She wore a loose white shirt with floral embellishments on its wide sleeves. "We'll begin testing at 07:00."

The clock on the wall read 06:56. Kensei stood on tiptoe and counted the number of people ahead of them. "We might not get our chance until lunchtime."

"If we're lucky," Billo said.

"Don't worry," Adriana said. "There will be plenty of time."

"I hope so." Jenny popped a blueberry in her mouth.

At 07:00, Lin turned and addressed everyone in line. "The time has come to put your skills to the test. May the best Æon win."

Lin opened the door and Sadi stepped inside the maze room. Four large screens displayed a live feed of each maze. Lin walked up to Jenny and the other white uniforms. "I'm sorry that you four got the least amount of time to practice, but I want you to know that I'm proud of you. You've each made such excellent progress."

"Thank you, Lin," Jenny said. "Has there been any word from Lance?"

"No." Lin looked back at the entrance to the gym. "I can't believe he would miss the testing."

"He'll turn up," Adriana said.

"Yeah," Kensei said. "I'm sure he'll want to see who gets the Riftkey."

"Yeah…" Lin pondered. "Well, good luck! Not that you need it. You all will do great"

Lin walked over to the pedestal and talked to Thork'l and Kett'l. Meanwhile, Sadi worked her way through the first maze. Her efficiency impressed Jenny. Sadi soon completed the perception test, then the radiation maze by freezing all the water. But, she struggled on the electromagnetic test and failed to complete the gravity maze in time.

The scoreboard updated as Sadi exited the room. She'd earned 435 points, a new high score. Jenny's heart sank. *How am I supposed to beat that?* It was more than twice her own score of 198.

"Damn," Kensei said. "That's a high bar."

"Don't worry, we can do it," Adriana said.

"You can do it." Billo looked at Adriana. "I'm sure."

After Aindriu's test, he left the maze room and approached them. Jenny's muscles clenched in preparation. Leon screeched at the muscular man. Aindriu pushed between them and assembled a cracker sandwich from the snack table.

"Your pet really doesn't like him," Adriana whispered to Kensei as Aindriu walked away.

"Yeah, I can't guess why," Kensei said sarcastically.

"Maybe Leon knows something we don't," Jenny said.

~

It had been three hours since they'd entered the gym. The butterflies in Jenny's stomach grew more restless after each challenger. She struggled to keep doubt from her mind, but it kept creeping in. It didn't help that Sadi's pale face grew smugger as each recruit tried and failed to surpass her.

"Well, I'm next," Billo said. "Wish me luck."

"Good luck." Jenny turned toward the screen.

Billo inserted her key into the brass plate on the first test box. She clumsily completed that maze, but she made up for it on the second test by freezing all the water on one side of the box and pushing the ball to its finish.

If I'm going to win, Jenny thought, *then I'll need to create a shortcut like that. The first test is a mystery. The people who achieved terrific scores just seemed really good at it. They never missed a turn or lost their momentum.*

Billo did poorly on the electromagnetic maze and skipped the gravity test altogether. As she stepped out of the room, her name climbed to the fourteenth position. That put her three places higher than Jenny.

"Good job," Jenny said.

Billo shrugged and stood next to Adriana.

"I guess I'm up now," Kensei said, then entered the room before anyone could wish him luck.

Jenny found herself tilting her body in time with the red ball as Kensei guided it to the golden cage. Next, Kensei muddled through the radiation test by freezing columns of water. He failed to finish the electromagnetic maze, but he shone on the gravity test. The pieces flew toward the green ball, and he quickly exposed the golden cage.

Kensei's name surged up the leaderboard to fifth place. He stumbled out of the testing room and leaned against the wall. Jenny and Adriana rushed to help him.

"Are you alright?" Adriana asked.

"Yeah, just a little dizzy."

"Good job in there, you made it to fifth place!" Jenny grabbed Kensei's purple hat and tousled his hair.

"Stop it." Kensei grabbed his Lakers hat and pulled it down to his ears.

Adriana squeezed his shoulder. "That's impressive for your third attempt."

Kensei leaned his head backward. "Still not good enough to win."

"Well, I hope I do as good as you," Jenny said, "but I'll probably just humiliate myself."

"I doubt that," Adriana said as she approached the door. "My turn."

People set their food down and watched as Adriana stepped into the testing room.

Jenny turned to look at the screen. Like Sadi, Adriana rolled the ball through the first maze with high efficiency.

"Her control is amazing," Billo said from Jenny's side.

"Yeah," Jenny and Kensei agreed.

Like Billo, she was able to freeze part of the second test. It seemed that only Sadi could freeze the whole maze. Instead of taking the electromagnetic test next, Adriana walked over to the gravity maze.

That's right, Jenny thought. *Adriana has temporary blindness after using her ability. She must be saving the electromagnetic for last.* Jenny watched her half-sister struggle to move the green ball around the gravity maze. She obviously gave it her full effort, but she still failed to complete the maze in time. *What is it about that test that so many people have trouble with?* Jenny wondered.

Finally, Adriana inserted her key into the electromagnetic maze. As she enabled one of the laser devices, she used her power to form two portals inside the cube. The laser passed through one and out the other. It struck the trapdoor and released the crystal ball into the golden cage.

The gym fell silent as Adriana groped her way to the door. The scoreboard updated, showing that she had scored 430 points. It was a fantastic number, but not enough to beat Sadi's score of 435.

Adriana stepped out of the room and heard the silence in the gym. "I didn't get it, did I?"

Jenny took her sister by the arm and guided her out. "No. I'm sorry." *It would take a miracle to beat Sadi now,* Jenny thought as she looked to the middle of the gym where the gray uniforms crowded around the Riftkey.

After a minute, Adriana blinked as her sight returned. Her eyes met Jenny's. "Good luck, sister. Remember to breathe."

"Yeah," Jenny said. "Okay."

"That's all she'll be able to remember," Sadi said and laughed along with the other gray uniforms. "I'd take the Riftkey now, but I want to see the look on your face after you've lost."

"Are you ready, Jenny?" Lin asked.

Jenny nodded. Anxiety was causing her stomach to do backflips, and she could feel everyone's eyes on her. She was so nervous that she felt like vomiting. *Okay, let's get this over with.* She thought as she hurried toward the door and stepped inside.

As the door swung shut, the outside world disappeared. Jenny took some time to gather her wits. *This is for you, Mom. And, Bea, I'll prove to you that I'm more than just a fortune-teller.*

Jenny inserted her key into the first box. As the walls to the perception test became transparent, Jenny quickly scouted a path through the maze. She tilted the table, and the ball rolled. Too fast. It bounced off a wall before she gained control and directed it down the next lane.

I'm clumsy. I know I can do better.

Jenny remembered Lin's words: "A blind man takes a stumbling path through a room, but a sighted man can choose the correct path before taking the first step."

Jenny knew that Lin wasn't talking about vision. Lin meant for Jenny to use her new sense, the one that heard tones and formed patterns in her mind. *Maybe I should try the Pulse as Kett'l taught me.* Jenny focused on the ball and hummed in her mind.

Thump—thump—thump, beat Jenny's heart. She felt the texture of her uniform and heard the soft whoosh of the air ventilation. Thump...

The beat of her heart seemed to stop, and the ball slowed to a crawl. A red line appeared ahead of it and showed a bouncing path down the maze. *What's going on?* She stopped the Pulse, and her heartbeat returned to a normal, thump—thump—thump. The ball returned to normal speed and bounced down the path that the red line indicated.

Jenny smiled. *This must be the perception shortcut. No wonder I couldn't see anyone else doing it.* She started the Pulse again. Thump... The ball slowed to a crawl again, and the red line appeared. *Now I have enough control to make this perfect.* With her perception of time slowed, she guided the red ball down each track with meticulous precision until it reached the golden cage.

Mazu was right, Jenny thought, *the shortcut on the first maze will affect my time on the other mazes.* She went to the next maze and used the Pulse. With her increased precision, Jenny guided the ball through the maze on a thin sheet of ice. She realized now that it had only looked like the other contestants were able to freeze one entire side of the radiation test. *Sadi must have even more control to appear to freeze the entire cube.* Jenny then used the same Pulse strategy on the next two tests. She felt good about her performance, but was it enough to beat Sadi? Jenny took her key and walked out of the testing room. As she opened the door, the sound of applause surprised her.

Kensei led the entire gym in a chant: "Jenny, Jenny, Jenny." Some added, "Astrea, Astrea, Astrea." To represent their universe.

Slowly, Jenny turned to look at the scoreboard, but Adriana and Billo rushed up to her.

"You scored 463." Billo stared at her in awe.

"Good job, sister. I knew you could do it." Adriana gave her a hug.

"You did it, you beat Sadi." Kensei patted her back. "And by a lot."

Jenny looked at the center of the room. Kett'l smiled warmly and beckoned her closer. She walked numbly through the crowd, grasping people's hands and returning high fives in a stupor.

Moeshe, the tall, dark-haired boy who had complimented Jenny on her first test, stepped out of the crowd. He winked and gently pushed her toward the pedestal. She had earned the right to wield the Riftkey, and now everybody wanted to see her bond with it.

Jenny hated to disappoint them.

Lin walked up to her and said, "Well done."

"Thanks." Jenny beamed. "Do you think it's okay to show them my Riftkey now?"

Lin nodded. "I think it's okay."

The guards parted as they walked up to the pedestal and the newly crafted Riftkey. The crowd fell silent. Jenny unlocked the burstepi's clasp at her chest and shrugged the strap off her shoulder. At the sound of clapping from outside the gym, Jenny paused with her hand on the flap. *What is that?* Jenny thought. *Is it Lance?* Everyone turned toward the entrance to see.

A tall stranger in black armor darkened the door to the gym. He was flanked by two huge figures in bloodred armor. Gruesome red skulls decorated their face masks. Three normal-sized soldiers in plain black uniforms and black helmets stood behind them. Pistol carbines hung from their shoulders.

Jenny returned the burstepi to her shoulder and fastened the clasp at her chest.

The tall stranger stepped forward and removed his helmet. He looked to be in his mid-twenties and had platinum-blond hair and pale skin. He was handsome, with a sharp jaw and high cheekbones, yet his most striking feature was an entirely black eye.

"Don't stop because of me," the man said. "What are we celebrating?" His blue eye lit up. "Ah. The Riftkey."

"Who are you?" Lin placed herself between the pedestal and the intruders while the contestants took a step back.

The man held himself in perfect posture. "Admiral Vae Victus of the Tyr Ministry of Defense."

Jenny's blood grew cold. *Tyr? They're here?* The floor seemed to drop out from under her feet. *We've lost.*

"And you are?"

"Lin Yuan Song." She stood up as tall as she could, but only reached Victus's shoulder. "Archaeoastronomer of Cabin, and current leader of this team. What are you doing here?"

"I've come to recover stolen property." Victus stepped forward, the rippling light of the sea reflecting off his black armor. "You have nothing to fear as long as you cooperate."

A black uniformed soldier entered the gym and rushed up to Victus. "Sir, it's not on board."

A muscle in Victus's face twitched. He stared down at Lin, and his blue eye blazed with deadly intent. "Where is the virosuit?"

"I don't know what you're talking about," Lin said.

Victus studied her for a moment, then his lips formed a thin line. "Maybe you don't, but you are hiding something." He looked at one of the huge red soldiers next to him. "Perhaps killing someone will loosen your tongue." Victus looked around the room, then pointed at Moeshe, probably because he was a head taller than anyone else. "That one."

The armored soldier stepped forward and raised his arm. In

response, the Cabin guards drew their handguns and took aim. Several recruits screamed and took cover behind the stone pedestal. Others ran to the side and backrooms bordering the gym. A few were too scared to move, including the tall Moeshe.

Jenny's stomach lurched, and her legs felt like cement. She looked from Moeshe to Lin. *Just tell him*, Jenny thought. There were several loud bangs as the Cabin guards fired at the huge red soldier, but their bullets had no effect on its armor.

The armored soldier aimed his arm at Moeshe. Lin launched forward and knocked the soldier's arm aside. There were three flashes, and three bullets flew outward. No, not bullets exactly, more like needles. Jenny saw a red line indicating the path of each round, like the ball in the perception test. The projectiles slammed into the back wall, forming small craters in the white composite siding.

The armored soldier slammed a fist into Lin's side, but she twisted around the punch and grabbed his wrist. Using her shoulder as a fulcrum, she pulled against the joint. Motors whined and groaned. There came a sound like the snapping of a branch, and the armored soldier's arm fell limp. To his credit, he didn't cry out. Instead, he punched at Lin with his other metal fist. But she was too fast. Lin dodged to the side of his injured arm and kicked hard at the armored soldier's knee. He crumpled to the ground.

Kensei ran forward and grabbed him by one leg and said, "Have a nice trip." He spun, once, twice, and let go. The armored soldier soared across the gym and smashed through the mirrored-glass window to the maze room.

The next armored soldier raised its arm toward Moeshe. There was a flash and a testing room window shattered. Somebody screamed and Moeshe stumbled backward and fell to the floor. Two red blotches bloomed in his chest. Adriana ran to Moeshe and dragged him into a side room. Sadi held out her hand toward this armored soldier and said, "I want your pain." He dropped to the ground and writhed in agony.

Three normal-size soldiers stepped forward and raised their pistol carbines at Sadi, Kensei, and the Cabin guards.

I have to do something, Jenny thought. *Maybe I can use the Pulse to stop their guns*. The needle-like fléchettes of the armored soldier were a mystery, but Jenny had a good understanding of how normal firearms worked. She knew that a firing pin initiated an explosive charge in each round, an action that was similar to how the Selkans created sound by hitting their drums with clubs. Jenny seized her key and focused on one of the pistol carbines. Just as the soldier pulled the trigger, she found the gun's firing mechanism and stopped it from initiating a charge.

The gun refused to fire. Sadi was safe, but another soldier had aimed at Kensei. *I need to stop it,* Jenny thought as she focused on the firing mechanism. *No*—her heart sunk—*I'm not going to make it.* Even with her ability to slow her perception of time, Jenny couldn't nullify the firing pin. Luckily, Kensei was suffering the side-effects of using his ability, and he stumbled to the side before the soldier fired. The monitor displaying the first maze shattered.

Two of the Cabin guards fell to the ground, and something slammed into Jenny's left shoulder, wrenching her arm from its socket. *Did I just get shot?* Jenny asked herself. Her left shoulder burned, and her arm hung limp. *I must have.* The adrenaline flooding her body masked most of the pain, and she felt a sudden urge to run. *No, I have to stay.* There were just two more soldiers to stop. *There, that's one.* Jenny switched her focus. *And there's the other one. I did it!* Jenny shouted in her head. Now that all the pistol carbines are disabled, maybe I can relax.

Suddenly, three new armored soldiers appeared in the doorway in their hulking red suits. This time, some sort of blue shield shimmered like an egg around their bodies. One of them stood out from the others. He had a white skull on its black mask instead of red, and gold accents on his blood-red armor.

Damn it, Jenny thought.

The three armored soldiers charged into the gym. Their suits whirred and thudded against the floor. Sadi brought the gold one down right away. Lin and Kensei focused on the second. Aindriu rushed in to attack the third. He ducked inside the armored soldier's reach and exploded like a coiled spring. Aindriu slammed into the soldier's gut with the force of a freight train. The armored soldier toppled backward. Aindriu hooked his foot behind the soldier's leg and shoved. The armored soldier hit the ground with a crash. Aindriu jumped onto the soldier's chest and delivered a flurry of crushing blows. As he punched,

Aindriu's skin peeled away from his knuckles, revealing a glint of metal underneath. The soldier's armored chest buckled and his helmet flipped open. Inside, a young man stared up into Aindriu's face.

"You look soft without all that armor," Aindriu said as he rolled out of the soldier's reach. He tore the helmet free of the suit and slammed it into the man's bare head. Aindriu didn't stop until the young man fell unconscious.

At the gym entrance, a dozen more normal-sized soldiers rushed into the gym and opened fire with their stubby pistol carbines. Red spots bloomed on the black uniforms of the two remaining guards.

There are too many, Jenny thought as she dove to the ground. *But I have to try.* She focused on each pistol carbine, disabling them as she had done earlier, but it was a painfully slow process, and she was so tired. *I need help. Aren't we all Æons here? Everyone here has powers. Why aren't they using them?* Then it dawned on her. *They're scared. They need motivation.* Jenny called out to the recruits. "Fight back! If we all use our powers, we can win."

As Jenny focused on disabling the carbines, a gray-uniformed recruit walked out of a side room. Suddenly, electricity arced through three soldiers, making them spasm and collapse to the gym floor. Then, a blue-uniformed recruit stepped out from behind the pedestal and knocked two more soldiers over with a gust of wind. Suddenly, more recruits stood up and fought. A soldier burst into flames, while his neighbor froze solid.

Jenny felt their powers buzzing inside her mind, like a symphony playing uplifting music. Within seconds, the fight had turned in Cabin's favor. The power of their attacks had thrown the Tyran soldiers into chaos. *We're actually going to win,* Jenny thought as she disabled another gun. *We're going to save the Selkans.*

Victus worked his way toward the Riftkey while his soldiers fought. Kett'l and Thork'l moved to block his way. While the Selkans were bigger and stronger than a human, neither of them were a match for Victus in his enhanced armor. The admiral shoved the aliens aside, then he noticed what was happening to his soldiers. His look of shock transformed to wonder, then determination. Black mist sprang up around a gray-uniformed recruit, and his lightning fizzled out.

The black mist, Jenny thought. *That's what I did on the Selkan island. He knows the Pulse.*

Victus turned his attention back to the pedestal. "The Riftkey is mine."

"Over my dead body," Lin said.

Victus ducked and Lin's foot passed through thin air. She landed from her jump kick and dropped into a low fighting stance.

"It would be my pleasure," Victus said.

Lin slammed a fist into his gut. Victus's armor cracked and he doubled over in pain. Victus held his arms up in defense. He focused on a freckled red-haired girl and nullified her fire ability.

"You chose the wrong group to attack," Lin said.

"You are mistaken," Victus said. "I'm right where I want to be."

Lin kicked between Victus's legs, but he twisted to avoid the blow. Lin punched at his side and then his neck. Victus blocked the punch with the pauldron of his suit. Lin's fist crumpled on the reinforced armor, and the bones in her hand fractured. Lin cradled her injured hand and kicked at Victus's head. Victus caught her foot and held it.

"Enough of this!" Victus shouted. Using the full power of his suit, he kicked the smaller woman in the chest. Lin flew through the air and smashed into the stone pedestal. She collapsed to the floor while the massive block staggered from the impact.

Jenny gasped and rushed toward Lin, sliding across the floor to the base of the pedestal. "Lin! Lin—" Though her shoulder flared with pain, she straightened Lin up to a sitting position. Lin rasped, and blood oozed from the corner of her mouth. "You have so much potential." Lin smiled up at Jenny. "Don't hide from your true nature."

A loud buzz filled Jenny's mind as the black mist crawled over her and the other recruits. A chasm formed in her head, and the familiar buzz was gone. She could no longer sense the waveforms of the world.

Ever since the wedding, Jenny had been keeping the eleven-year-old version of herself a prisoner. The part of her that was Roma. The part of her named Djangini. It was time to accept who she was and let that part of herself be free. "I won't hide, Lin. I'll be true to myself." Jenny choked out a sob as she stroked Lin's smooth black hair.

"Remember Mazu."

Jenny nodded, and suddenly the wind was knocked from her lungs as Victus kicked her in the gut. She slid across the gym floor and screeched to a stop near Adriana. Jenny struggled to breathe, and tears blurred her vision.

"Take the Selkans," Victus ordered. The soldiers shackled Kett'l and Thork'l and led them out of the gym. "At last," Victus said. He approached the pedestal and pulled off an armored gauntlet. He then lifted the Riftkey with his bare hand and smiled triumphantly. Suddenly, his eyes snapped shut, and his whole body shook.

As Victus bonded with the Riftkey, his nullifying effects slipped away, and the black mist receded from the recruits.

"You have the Riftkey." Lin pushed herself upright and faced Victus. "Let them go."

"You are right. I have what I came for." He looked down at the Riftkey. There was a loud crack, and the black edges glowed blue. Sparks lit the air. "But someone must pay for their freedom." He gestured at those who remained alive in the gym. "Will it be you?" He aimed the Riftkey at Lin's chest.

Lin nodded.

Jenny screamed, "No."

But it was too late. As the Riftkey touched Lin's loose white shirt, gray dust puffed into the air. Victus casually flicked the tip upward, carving the Riftkey into her torso, and Lin's body fell motionless to the gym floor.

"You bastard!" Jenny tried to get up and run toward Lin, but Adriana held her down. She didn't have the strength to resist, so she collapsed to her knees. *The Selkans are doomed.* A pit formed in her chest and threatened to consume her. Her soul ripped apart, and her consciousness exploded from her body.

This out-of-body experience was different than before. When Jenny had possessed Sadi, her entire consciousness had transferred into her spirit. This time only half of her left her body, and Jenny was aware of both her physical and ethereal forms at the same time.

Slowly, Jenny's glowing ethereal form turned to look at her physical self, and when her spirit eyes met her physical ones, the rest of the world became insignificant. Death didn't matter. The Selkans didn't matter. This was Jenny's true self, the energy within her physical body made real. The experience was overwhelming. Tears ran down her face. She was overcome with happiness and awe and felt truly free for the first time. She giggled like a child.

Those around me must be thinking I've gone mad, Jenny thought, *but I've never experienced anything so pure and honest.* Jenny saw herself for the first time, bare and open, with no filter. Her truest innermost self. Not just Jenny Tripper, but Djangini the Roma, daughter of Rubelli Tripper, leading back through a hundred more ancestors to Astrea Baillie, the Æon who discovered the Waypoint keys and traveled across universes.

However, maintaining this ethereal form was physically draining. As Jenny weakened, her ghost vanished with a snap and returned to her physical body. She was filled with an oppressive sense of claustrophobia and loss. More than that, her shoulder throbbed with pain worse than before.

Victus set the Riftky on the pedestal and approached the place where Jenny's spirit had stood. She felt his gaze as though he had touched her with it. His hard stare bored into her as if he were peering at something beyond. One eye may have been black on black, but it was his sapphire-blue eye that gave her chills.

All thoughts of joy and happiness evaporated from Jenny's mind. She shuddered as a pressure pushed against her brain and she vibrated like an off-cycle washing machine. The room grew darker, and her body grew heavy.

Victus leaned in close, and whispered into her ear, "I know what you are."

"Go to hell," Jenny growled, cradling her limp arm with her uninjured hand.

All around the gym, the armored soldiers were getting to their feet. Even the one that Aindriu had knocked out.

"You're the one who disabled the guns." Victus placed his boot on Jenny's gun wound and pushed. Her shoulder exploded in pain, and she fell to the floor. While holding her down, Victus turned to address the room. "Mister Spriggan failed to inform me of your talents."

Mister Spriggan, Jenny thought, *isn't that Jack's last name? He* did *betray us. He told Victus that the Selkans were here.*

"It was not my intention to harm any of you." Victus slipped his armored gauntlet back onto his hand. "I am only here for the Selkans." He spread his arms out wide and spoke sincerely. "It is with their help that we have put an end to a century-long war. Already, they have saved billions of lives."

All around her, voices murmured in response.

There's no way anybody really believes him, Jenny thought as she beat at Victus's armored leg. He didn't seem to notice.

"We need people like you." Victus scanned each face in the crowd. "People with the power to maintain peace throughout the galaxy. Come back with us. We know how to properly train you. Join us and you can reach your true potential."

Sadi stepped forward and glanced back at her comrades in gray. "Lance abandoned us. I owe him no allegiance." She looked down at Lin's body, at Jenny, then at Victus. "I'll join you."

"Excellent." Victus held out a hand to her. "Welcome to Tyr, Miss..."

"Cassadi Stevens." Sadi walked up and took his hand.

"Miss Stevens." Victus looked around. "Is there anyone else?"

Aindriu stepped forward. "Me." He walked over and stood beside Sadi. "I'm Aindriu Ward."

Victus smiled and nodded in recognition, "It is my pleasure, Mister Ward."

After that, all the gray-uniformed recruits had offered their loyalty to Tyr. Jenny felt numb. Her strength gave way. Her skin tingled. *This can't be happening*, Jenny thought as she drifted into unconsciousness under Victus's boot.

31

BANISHED

Jenny woke with a throbbing head in her room on the *Endeavor*. She pressed her palms against her eyes to relieve the pain, and fire lanced through her shoulder. *That's right*, Jenny thought. *Someone shot me*. She lifted her shirt and looked under her uniform. White bandages covered her chest and back. A stain of red revealed the location of the wound. She tested her arm. It felt stiff, but it moved well enough. The bullet must have passed clean through. *Wait, where is my burstepi?* Jenny rolled out of bed and looked around the floor. Her heart pounded and a pit formed in her stomach.

Billo had her closet doors open, and she was folding and packing her clothes into a bag.

"Where is it?" Jenny approached her roommate.

"Where is what?" Billo tilted her head toward the door.

Jenny turned and stumbled backward in surprise. Two Tyran soldiers stood in the doorway. They each wore a black uniform and helmet with a tinted mask. Pistol carbines hung from their shoulders.

"Calm down," Billo said.

"What's going on?"

"They're sending us home." Billo shoved toiletries into her bag and zipped it up. "Hurry up and pack. I'll wait for you."

"Home," Jenny said numbly. While glancing at the soldiers, she opened her closet doors with trembling fingers. Her Topo was on a shelf with a bullet embedded inside of it. *It must have protected me from a potentially lethal round.* Her burstepi lay on top of her duffel bag at the bottom of the closet. She sighed in relief. *But is the Riftkey still inside?* Jenny reached inside the burstepi and felt the hard angles of the Riftkey. She wanted to talk with Cobol but—she glanced at the guards—it wasn't worth the risk to remove even the handle.

Jenny thought of returning home, and her face burned with guilt for not saving the Selkans. She quickly stuffed the contents of her closet inside the burstepi along with the picture of her mom from the ceiling over her bed.

Taking one last look at her room, Jenny slung her packed bag over her uninjured shoulder and followed Billo to the stairwell. As Jenny climbed, the diamond-steel steps seemed to gnash at her boots like snarling dogs. When they reached the top, the guards shoved Jenny onto the platform. She blinked at the sudden brightness of the midday sun.

Victus crossed his arms behind his back as he surveyed the operation. Two Tyran spaceplanes accompanied Jack's and Cabin's on the cement platform. Four armored soldiers in their huge red armor walked around shouting orders. The one with the white face skull and gold accents stood next to Victus. Sadi stood on his other side. She had already exchanged her gray Cabin uniform for a black Tyran one. Her long, curly brown hair was in a single braid, and her glasses were gone.

Cabin recruits were lined up under the guard of twenty soldiers in black uniforms. There were fewer recruits now than at the start of the day, and many wore bandages like hers. Behind Jenny, a gray-armored soldier approached from the stairwell. He pushed Winchell, the custodian, into the mass of people and approached Victus. "Sir, that's the last of them."

"Excellent." Victus turned to address the Cabin recruits and personnel. His blond hair flipped about in the wind, and his black armor reflected the midday sun. "I am Vae Victus, a peacekeeper of the Tyr Ministry of Defense. You are fortunate that Tyr has no interest in you." He looked out at the Selkan islands. "My mission is to retrieve stolen military property, not to punish accomplices. Sergeant Alberta will now oversee your evacuation."

The armored soldier with the white face skull and gold accents stepped forward. "You will be sorted into two groups based on your origination," she barked out to the Cabin staff.

In the distance, the roar of engines drowned out the soldier's shouts. Four massive spacecraft skimmed the ocean's surface and came to rest in a surge of water near the Selkan islands. Victus approached Jenny and cradled her chin in one hand. *I know what you are,* he spoke into her mind. *You are like me.* His black-eyed gaze crawled across her face.

A trickle of sweat raced down Jenny's backbone. "You killed Lin," she said aloud. "And you didn't even let me say goodbye."

Victus's lip curled. "Relationships are a weakness." He pushed her away. "The only thing that matters is power. You have some potential, little one. Return with me and I could make you great."

"You disgust me." Jenny turned and approached the group for the Cabin plane destined for Acacia City. Billo, Adriana, and Kensei all joined her, along with three blue-uniformed recruits. She recognized one of the young men. It was Ezra.

Jenny looked around. "Where's Moeshe?"

Ezra shook his head and looked down.

An icy pit formed in her stomach. Jenny thought of Lin and the others who had lost their lives. She glared at Victus, and her blood turned to fire. *How can I share the same abilities as that man?* Jenny shuddered at the remembrance of his touch.

"I'm sorry," she said to Ezra. "Were you two close?"

"No." He shook his head. "We never even met before all this, even though we were both from Acacia City." He looked at Jenny with red-rimmed eyes. "He was a good guy."

Jenny nodded and looked over at her half-sister. "It's funny how big a city seems. Then you cross a universe, and everything seems so small."

"Yeah," Ezra agreed.

A commotion erupted behind them. Aindriu walked among the other group carrying a canvas rucksack. People were shouting at him.

"What's going on over there?" Kensei asked. Leon stood tall on his shoulder as if to get a better look.

"No idea," Jenny said.

After a few minutes, Aindriu walked over to their group. He had a pained expression on his face, like a dog caught in the act of ransacking the rubbish bin. He didn't seem to enjoy his new role within the Tyran ranks. Without making eye contact, he held out the canvas rucksack. "Remove your keys and put them in the bag."

"You're taking our keys?" Kensei asked.

"Yes," Aindriu hissed.

All around them, the Tyran soldiers slid their fingers over the triggers of their firearms. Jenny lifted the chain around her neck and gazed upon Astrea's key. This was a piece of her history. How could she just hand it over? "No," Jenny said. "We earned these."

Kensei looked incredulous. "Yeah, they can't just take them away from us."

Jenny flinched as she saw the soldiers tense. *Would they kill us?* Jenny thought. *Probably. Either way, it's not worth the risk.* She looked around at the injured people and thought of those who didn't make it. "Here." Her shoulder flared with pain as she lifted the key over her head and handed it to Aindriu.

"What are you doing?" Kensei asked.

"Lin is dead," Jenny said. "I don't want anyone else getting hurt, so I'm playing along."

"Thank you, Jenny." Aindriu pointed at the amulet around Jenny's neck. "What's that?"

"It's just a necklace."

"Hand it over."

"But it's not a key." Jenny clutched her mother's amulet in her hand.

"I have orders to remove all unusual items." Aindriu grimaced and took a step toward her. Glints of metal still showed under his knuckles. "Remove it or I will."

The Tyran soldiers took a step closer and raised their pistol carbines. This time everyone noticed. Jenny's hands shook. She couldn't undo the clasp. Suddenly, Aindriu reached out and yanked the necklace. It came free of her neck and took a piece of her soul along with it.

Billo and the three blue-uniformed recruits followed Jenny's lead and dropped their keys into the sack.

"Now you," Aindriu said to Kensei and Adriana. He squared his shoulders and adjusted his stance. "This doesn't have to get messy." He flexed his pectoral muscles and rolled his neck.

Leon stood on Kensei's shoulder and mimicked Aindriu's flexing routine.

Aindriu clenched his jaw and glared at the little creature.

"Just give it to him," Jenny said. "It's not worth it."

"Why are you doing this?" Adriana cupped her key in her hands. "Why did you join them?"

"This world will be—"

Leon screeched and interrupted Aindriu.

"A lot bigger after the Terminal gets unlocked—"

Leon screeched again.

"And I'm going to be on the right—"

Leon screeched a third time.

In a blur, Aindriu grabbed the sugar glider from Kensei's shoulder. With a quick twist, the tiny body hung limp. Aindriu tossed the dead sugar glider back at Kensei. "This is not a game. Do you want to get us all killed?" He glanced back at the Tyran soldiers and spoke in an urgent whisper. "Put your keys in the bag, now."

"You bastard." Kensei cradled his dead sugar glider in his arms. "I'll kill you."

Aindriu stared into Kensei's eyes, daring for him to make good on his threat. He yanked Kensei's key off of his neck and dropped it into the sack. Adriana glared at Aindriu with tears in her eyes, then she lowered her own key into the bag. He pulled the string tight and walked away. The guards directed them to the Cabin plane.

Jenny dragged her feet up the ramp and slumped into the first empty seat. She watched numbly as Kensei took a spare shirt from his bag, gently wrapped up Leon, then placed his body inside the backpack. Adriana squeezed Kensei's shoulder and gave him a hug before sitting down. Jenny chastised herself for not giving Kensei support, but what was the loss of a pet compared to so many people?

Aindriu walked through the plane and entered the cockpit. Apparently, he was their pilot. One of the Tyran soldiers stood guard at the cockpit door while two more took seats near the front. The entire plane tipped backward as one of the huge armored soldiers boarded the plane. The ramp closed behind them. The engines revved.

Across the aisle, Kensei rocked in his seat and chanted, "I'm going to kill him. I'm going to kill him."

Jenny was lost in her own grief. She thought about her mom, Lin, and Moeshe. Jenny felt her neck, naked without the weight of the amulet and the key. She barely noticed the plane lift off the platform and drift out over the ocean.

Gray waves stretched out endlessly beneath them. Then there was light. Red, orange, and pink clouds could be seen in the distance. The ice-cold numbness that gripped Jenny's heart thawed, and a spark of hope kindled into a fire. *Mazu is still out there somewhere.*

The Cabin plane landed around eight that night. Jenny grabbed her bag and followed the others out of the plane. A chill wind from the bay made Jenny shiver. The clouds against the evening sky were the gray of rats. Spaceport security looked the other way as the Tyran soldiers escorted them across the tarmac to the terminal.

The interior of the Acacia City Spaceport was an incredible feat of architecture. Curved supports resembling an enormous rib cage lifted the glass roof a hundred meters above their heads. Shops and restaurants lined the passageways. Advertisements broadcasted messages on humongous displays and holograms. Thousands of people, both alien and human, rushed through the spaceport's terminal.

Did they know an enormous warship orbited the planet?

They exited the spaceport's terminal and waited in Departures. The Cabin recruits huddled together on the sidewalk. Jenny chuckled at the juxtaposition of the giant armored soldier and the regular commuters waiting to be picked up. The other recruits looked at her like she was crazy. *At least I can still find humor in all this darkness*, Jenny thought.

When a large black van arrived to take them to the Waypoint, Jenny looked longingly back at the spaceport. *I'm leaving the one place I truly belonged*, she thought. *The* Endeavor *was my Shangri-la. Where else can I hone my Æon skills or train my ability?* Tears flowed from her eyes as she said goodbye to the non-Astrean recruits. She gave Ezra a hug before getting into the van.

Two of the normal Tyran soldiers took the back seat, and Aindriu took the front seat. They drove to the historic sector of Acacia City and parked near the plaza. Tourists went about their business, though signs of the raid persisted. Broken windows and burned-out structures lined the cobbled street. One of the umbrellas outside The Buzz stood crooked in its stand, its black-and-yellow fabric torn. *I can't believe it's been only two days since the raid.*

Four Songbirds, armed with polearms, stood guard at the gazebo steps.

"Ho," one of them said. "What's going on here?"

"This is Tyran business," one of the soldiers said as he raised his pistol carbine. "Back off."

The Songbirds retreated.

As Jenny climbed the gazebo steps, she thought about the person in the black cloak. "You know"—she looked at Kensei—"we never did discover if Sadi was involved in the raid."

"And we never will."

"You're idiots," Aindriu said as he climbed up the gazebo. "Sadi had nothing to do with it. Now, get on the Waypoint."

"You don't have to send us away." Jenny looked at Aindriu. "Just let us go."

"You'll be safer back home."

Home, Jenny thought. *Would it be so bad to go home?* Time and distance were having an effect on her motivations. For the first time since she'd left, she began to feel homesick. She missed her room, her music, and even her school. As she stood there thinking, Kensei stepped in front of Aindriu, breathing hard through his nostrils and clenching his fists.

"What are you going to do?" Aindriu stood centimeters away from the taller but thinner Kensei. The muscles in his scarred neck flexed, and metal glinted under the skin of his knuckles. "Take your keys back and fight against an entire army? Don't be stupid. This is the only chance you have of saving your lives. Take it."

Jenny loved Kensei, but even after the treatments, he was as awkward as a deer taking its first steps. She knew how this fight would end. "Don't do it."

"Listen to him," Billo urged.

"Please, no more fighting," Adriana added.

Kensei's shoulders slumped, and he turned away. His eyes were red and wet as he entered the Waypoint.

"That's better." Aindriu slid down after him and pulled out his key. "Best to avoid more bloodshed."

Jenny rubbed at her injured shoulder, then lowered herself into the Waypoint. Adriana and Billo followed her down. They all huddled together as Aindriu inserted his key into the Waypoint. He set the dial for the Esperanza Woods and pushed down. The air shimmered as the buildings of Acacia City disappeared. An uncomfortable sensation of movement twisted Jenny's guts.

Suddenly, the smell of moss and soil filled her nose. A natural gazebo, formed of bent trunks and branches, enclosed them. Farther out, a ring of tall trees lined an extensive grassy clearing. Birds chirped and giant insects buzzed. Back in Acacia City, it had been late evening. Here, the sun was at its zenith.

"Everyone off," Aindriu commanded.

They did as he said. Jenny looked back at the Waypoint and saw Aindriu still inside the bowl. In a moment of clarity, she knew he was about to abandon them in the Nimue Realm. "Wait! How are we supposed to get home?"

"That is not my concern." Aindriu disappeared in a flash of light.

Billo gazed up at the ancient, towering trees. "Does anyone know how we actually get back home?"

"No, I don't," Jenny said. Adriana shook her head.

Kensei knelt down in the wild grass. He opened his rucksack and removed Leon's silent form. The tiny sugar glider looked like it could be sleeping. Kensei pulled out a knife from his bag and dug into the topsoil. After forming a shallow grave, he placed Leon inside and covered him with loose soil. He stared at the dark mound for a minute before he stood and joined the group.

"If I ever see Aindriu again, I'll kill him," he said, though, after his brief confrontation with Aindriu, his words seemed empty.

"Ho there," came Rygelus's voice as he crossed the rings of trees. Nimue, his ghost daughter, accompanied him. Her outline had solidified since Jenny had last seen her, and the similarities between father and daughter were shocking. He stopped in front of Jenny. "What are you doing here? What's wrong?"

"Lin is dead." As Jenny said it, emotions welled up inside of her. She dug her fingernails into her palm to keep her mind in the present.

"I'm sorry." Rygelus put a hand on Jenny's shoulder and studied the faces of the other recruits.

"We were—" Jenny started.

"Wait." Rygelus stopped her. "I want to hear all about it, but not here." He looked around as if expecting something to come through the trees. "Come up to the treehouse." Rygelus turned and led them away from the Waypoint. "Brock will want to hear your story as well."

"Yeah, okay," Jenny nodded and followed.

Kensei walked beside her and whispered, "You know him?"

"Yeah, he's the one who found me in the woods."

"Ah."

Rygelus stopped at the foot of a titanic tree. They entered the shed at its base. One by one they climbed up the rope ladder and entered the treehouse through the trapdoor. Inside, it was all hand-carved wood and craftsman styling. Jenny and the others stood in the living area. In one corner, there was a small sitting area with two simple chairs. In the other corner was a dining table made of a slab of live-edge wood and four stout legs. A furry, glowing creature sat on a dining chair. A plate of small cleaned bones lay in front of him. His head, with its long fox ears, barely cleared the tabletop.

"Whoa." Kensei jumped back and pointed at Heather. "What the heck is that?"

"Heather is Alfur," he answered.

"What's an Alfur?"

"Alfur is Heather."

"That's as clear as he gets," Jenny said.

"Isn't this the creature that got you lost in the forest?" Billo asked.

Jenny noted the notch in the Alfur's ear. "He is."

"Heather." Rygelus cleared his throat. "I believe you remember Jenny Tripper. These are her friends."

"Nice to meet friends."

"I'm Kensei."

"And I'm Adriana."

"Billo."

The Alfur wrung his small hands worriedly. "Heather not know Jenny be here."

Jenny stepped toward the table. "The last time I saw you, you were chasing after a tasty treat. Did you even try to find me?"

"Yes, Heather try." The Alfur nodded his head vigorously, causing his long ears to bounce. "But Heather saw Risi. Heather ran away. Heather sorry, Heather is coward."

Jenny waved the apology away. "It's okay. It all worked out anyway."

Jenny looked around the room. A short-bladed knife sat next to a hunk of wood on a worktable. A picture of a frog lay near them.

There was a rustling in the adjacent room, and then Brock entered. His golden locks flowed behind him as he rushed through the house. "What are they doing here?" He asked.

Rygelus looked at Jenny. "Now would be the time to tell us your story."

Jenny proceeded to tell Rygelus and Brock what had happened since she'd last seen them. While she talked, Rygelus retrieved a canvas bundle from a barrel. He laid it on the dining table and unwrapped the oil-soaked wool blankets. Inside were three hunting rifles, a shotgun, two air bows, and four handguns.

"They took our keys," Kensei added.

"Do you have a Waypoint key?" Billo asked.

"No." Rygelus shook his head. "We do not own a key."

"Then we are trapped here," Billo said.

"You can get home through the cabin." Brock unwrapped a two-handed sword from a thick canvas cloth.

"The cabin." Jenny pictured the bare domicile she'd arrived in. Again, she felt a pang of homesickness. She looked over at the Alfur. "So, why is he here?"

"Tell them." Rygelus looked at Heather.

The little man shifted in his seat. "Alfur have human prisoners."

"You do?"

"No, not Heather, other Alfur."

"Someone who passed through the Waypoint?" Kensei asked.

"Could it be Mazu's expedition?" Jenny said.

"But why would the Alfur hold them prisoner?" Adriana asked.

"Humans kill sacred worm."

"Sacred worm?" Kensei asked.

"What's going to happen to them?" Adriana asked.

"Heather not know. Maybe eat."

"No." Jenny's mouth went wide. "You can't eat them."

"Not Heather. Heather like bugs."

"I remember." Jenny turned to the others. "What should we do?"

"We go home, no question," Billo said.

"No," Adriana said. "We've got to save them, even if it's not Mazu, we can't just let them eat humans."

"Aren't giants out there?" Kensei asked.

"Yeah," Billo said. "And I'm not going to risk my life trying to save someone else's."

Adriana looked at Rygelus. "You're preparing for a rescue mission, aren't you?"

"Yes," Rygelus said as he set out ammunition for the guns.

"Why should any of this matter to us?" Billo asked. "It's not even our Earth."

"It's not my city, it's not my country," Adriana said. "There's always some excuse if you're looking for one. But when I see something wrong, I have to make it right. Who or where doesn't matter. And if it is Mazu, there's a chance she could take us back."

"Back where?" Billo looked at Adriana. "To save the Selkans?" She turned toward Kensei. "To get to outer space?" Her eyes searched Jenny's face. "To unlock the Terminal with a Riftkey we don't have?"

"Someone stole the Riftkey?" Rygelus asked Jenny.

"No," Jenny assured him. She pulled her burstepi around and opened the flap. "Well, yes. But I still have the original." She reached inside and pulled the Riftkey free. The mirror-like blade reflected everything in the room while the narrow sides absorbed the light.

Her friends gazed at it in wonder. Heather scrambled off his chair and dropped to his knees in front of her.

"That's a Riftkey." Adriana looked dumbstruck.

What are we doing back here? Cobol asked in Jenny's mind.

It's a long story, Jenny answered. *Just keep listening.* "I promised Lin to keep it a secret, but now she's gone."

"You had that in there the whole time?" Kensei peered into the burstepi. "But it's just a normal bag."

Jenny took the bag and looked inside. He was right. She couldn't see anything inside. She put her hand in and felt Lin's clothes and books deep inside. "It must be some sort of illusion."

"So you have a Riftkey." Billo shrugged. "It hardly matters." She looked down at the wooden-plank floor. "We couldn't even stand up to Aindriu. How are we going to face someone like Victus?"

"Well, maybe if we get to the Terminal before him..." Jenny's voice sounded weak in her ears.

Billo shook her head. "You're as optimistic as Adriana. We don't know where the Terminal is, and even if we did, we'd need a spaceship to reach it."

"I'm sure Lance could get us there," Adriana said.

"Victus has an army and spaceships. Not to mention a big head start."

Kensei pulled his head out of the burstepi. "What if Tyr is right?"

"What?" Adriana snapped at him.

"What if they are doing what's best for the galaxy?"

Adriana glared at him.

"It's the trolley problem."

"What's that?" Jenny asked.

"It's something we talked about in school," Kensei said. "Imagine that you're on a footbridge overlooking a trolley track. Five people are trapped on the tracks and the trolley is rushing toward them. You can stop it by pushing a fat man off the bridge in front of the train. His bulk will be enough to stop the trolley, but he will die in the process."

"What's that got to do with the Selkans?" Jenny asked.

"Don't you see? They are the fat man, and Victus is the one pushing them off the bridge to prevent war."

"I prefer to believe in a third choice," Adriana replied. "That the trolley driver can pull the brake."

"I'm just saying, we don't know what's going on out there." Kensei waved at the sky.

"No, we don't," Adriana said, "and we will never have the full picture. All we can do is give aid to those who need it. In my opinion"—she glared at Billo—"the Selkans need more help than Victus."

Billo looked out the nearest window in silence. After a long pause, she spoke. "Back home I have fans who care about me. I owe *them* my life, not some aliens in another universe." She looked at Kensei. "You could go home and create a fantastic webcomic. I could help."

"And give up?" Adriana asked flatly. "Go home and leave everyone else to their fates? The Selkans risked everything in coming here. Now, we're their only hope. I, for one, couldn't live with myself knowing that I didn't try everything in my power to save them."

"That's you, but it's not how everyone thinks," Billo said.

"And you think Cabin did all this for you?" Adriana said. "For you to have fun and learn new abilities? You knew when you came here that it was a rescue mission."

"Jenny," Billo said. "Your mom wouldn't want you risking your life."

What would my mom want? Jenny wondered. *Ruby always valued life above all things, but would she be happy if I risked my life?* Jenny looked at her old roommate. She respected Billo, and the thought of going home filled Jenny with more joy than she cared to admit. But the thought of going home *now* didn't feel right. Not when there was still a chance to save the Selkans. "My mom would be disappointed in the real Billo."

A look of surprise crossed Billo's face, then she nodded slowly. "You're right. Your mom would be disappointed, but not for the reason you think." Billo's eyes had a vacant, far-off look. Then, her body sagged, and she seemed to age ten years in an instant. "You know what I discovered back on the *Endeavor*?"

Jenny shook her head.

Billo continued. "That I was average—below average, even. My ability didn't help me on the mazes, and it won't help to save Mazu either. At least at home, I was someone. I was popular. I made a difference in people's lives." She looked at Jenny. "You know what would happen if I went with you?"

"No," Jenny said weakly.

"I'd get in your way, or I'd die, or both. My ability is good for sneaking into movie sets and into the White House, but not for fighting bad guys. You're not going to be rolling balls around a maze anymore. This is life or death." Her eyes watered and she shook her head. "They murdered our friends."

"You're right." Jenny squeezed Billo's shoulder. "This whole thing has me scared out of my mind. I can't blame you for wanting to leave."

"Thank you." Billo gave a weak laugh. A smile stayed on her lips, but her eyes remained untouched.

Jenny took a deep breath. "I'm staying. I have to try and save the Selkans."

Billo nodded and turned toward Kensei. "And you?"

"I would never leave my new friends. Adriana and Jenny are going to need me."

"Good, then it's settled." Brock looked at Rygelus. "I'll take Billo back to the cabin while you finish packing."

Rygelus nodded.

Billo faced her former roommate. "Are you sure you won't come with me?"

"I need to do this." Jenny forced a smile. "Are you sure you want to go?"

Billo nodded.

Jenny pulled her into a tight hug. "Be safe."

"You too."

Well, there goes Billo, Cobol said as Brock lifted the trapdoor and escorted Jenny's former roommate out of the treehouse.

32

RESCUE MISSION

Blades, bows, and guns covered the treehouse's dining table. Boxes of ammunition rested on a couple of chairs.

Kensei looked over the collection. "Will this trip will be dangerous?"

"You think?" Jenny asked.

Rygelus put a shotgun and two hunting rifles into a canvas backpack. "We will likely encounter the Risi." He pulled more bundles from under the floorboards and handed them to Jenny. "Put these in your bag."

The bundles contained bedrolls, tents, and a fire kit. They fit comfortably inside Jenny's burstepi next to the Riftkey. Rygelus added water canteens, cooking supplies, and food to her bag.

"Can I have a gun?" Jenny asked as she strapped the burstepi onto her back.

Rygelus browsed the table and picked up a blocky black model. "You ever shoot one of these?" He offered it to her, butt first.

"No." Jenny gripped the firearm with her uninjured arm. A door opened in her mind. It was like remembering a song that she had memorized a long time ago. Jenny held the gun with the nozzle pointed at the ground. She checked that the safety lever was on, removed the magazine, and cleared the chamber. It was empty. She aimed the gun at the wall, with both arms out straight, and checked the sight. In spite of being kept in storage, the firearm was well maintained, cleaned, and oiled.

"You seem to know what you're doing." Rygelus set a box of ammunition in front of her. He pointed at a collection of holsters. "Take your pick."

While Jenny perused the collection, Kensei and Adriana took guns and ammo for themselves. They seemed to have the same skill with firearms that she did. Jenny chose a belt that wouldn't interfere with her burstepi. She rechecked the safety and inserted the gun into the leather holster. Then, Rygelus gave each of them green vests with chest- and back-plate armor. Jenny added four clips of ammunition into the side pockets, along with a flashlight and a slim medkit.

"Why do you have swords and bows with all the firearms?" Jenny asked.

"I mainly use the bow for hunting," Rygelus said as he slid one knife into his boot and another onto his belt. "Out here, stealth is a greater asset than firepower. In a firefight, there's a good chance we'll run out of bullets before taking a Risi down."

"What is it that you do out here?" Adriana asked as she strapped a holster around her waist.

"We're rangers," Rygelus said. "We maintain the Waypoint and defend travelers."

Kensei checked the safety on his firearm and sighted it. "Have you fought lots of giants?"

"Not as often as you would think. We're not out here to kill or risk being killed. A war with the giants is the last thing we want. As it is, they barely tolerate our presence."

"But if we run into them, at least we're prepared." Kensei practiced his draw.

"At best, these make us evenly matched."

"But we've seen them," Kensei said. "All they have is leather armor and clubs."

"And would you trust a handgun to kill an elephant?"

"I wouldn't kill an elephant at all." Adriana snapped her gun into the holster.

"Regardless." Rygelus looked at Adriana. "We should avoid engaging them at all costs. Our survival depends on proper preparation. So, it would help if I knew what each of your abilities is."

"I can create massless portals," Adriana said. "They let me see things far away without moving, but they also leave me temporarily blind."

"Your ability will be useful for scouting our path." He strapped a recurve bow to his back along with a bundle of arrows. He looked at Kensei and asked, "And you?"

"I can affect gravity," He said, "to make something lighter, or heavier."

"That will be very useful." Rygelus laid out several handguns and knives across the large table. Heather flinched at the sound of each weapon banging on the wood. "Does your ability also have a side effect?"

"Oh yeah, I get dizzy and lose my balance for a while afterward."

"But not until you stop using your ability?"

"Yeah, that's right," Kensei said.

"Excellent, then you will carry this pack once it's full. How about you, Jenny?"

"Just the basics," Jenny said.

Rygelus cocked his head and furrowed his brow. "The basics?"

What would be useful for a journey? Jenny thought. *Slowing my perception of time would just make the journey seem longer to me. And there probably won't be any opportunity to control electricity, or use the Pulse to nullify vibrations.* Jenny shrugged. "I can freeze water, or make it boil."

"That's not all she can do," Kensei said.

"I don't know what I did to Sadi." Jenny stared out the window. "And I don't know if I can do it again."

"That's okay." Rygelus paused in thought. "I'll think of something." Rygelus lifted the large backpack full of weapons and handed it to Kensei.

Kensei took the pack, which fell to the floor with a heavy thud. "Whoa, I can't carry this."

"Use your ability," Rygelus said.

"I can't, not without my key."

Rygelus narrowed his eyes. "The keys are only focusing tools. They are not the source of your abilities."

Kensei screwed up his face as he took hold of the backpack and pulled.

His body shook with the effort, but he soon relaxed and focused. A look of surprise crossed his face as the pack lifted into the air. It must have weighed over fifty kilograms, but he slung it onto his shoulder as if it were empty.

"How was it?" Adriana asked.

"It's harder to concentrate without the key, but it's not too difficult to maintain."

"You all ready?"

Everyone nodded.

"Then follow me." Rygelus lifted the trap door and jumped onto the rope ladder. He climbed down the tree with dizzying speed. The rest of them followed. With her injured shoulder, Jenny struggled the most. By the time they all made it to the ground, Brock had returned from dropping Billo off at the cabin.

"Did everything go smoothly?" Rygelus asked.

"Like a greased pig." Brock studied the group. "Can I carry anything?"

"Just your sword." He handed Brock the two-handed weapon wrapped in a leather case. "The kids are carrying everything else."

Brock raised an eyebrow. "And my cooking supplies?"

"In here with camp gear." Jenny shrugged the burstepi.

"The weapons?"

Kensei lifted the backpack off his shoulders as if it were full of air.

"Amazing. Give me a moment." Brock ran into the hut at the base of the tree. There was the sound of rummaging and cupboard doors closing before Brock emerged with a rucksack and nodded.

"Let us make haste," Rygelus said.

Jenny and the others walked single file as they followed Heather through the dense woods. Jenny remembered that on her last trip through the forest, her legs and lungs burned from running after the Alfur. This time, Jenny's legs felt fresh even after an hour on the trail.

"So, what are we going to do when we find Mazu and Jack?" Adriana asked.

"Let the Alfur eat him, for all I care," Jenny said as she followed her half-sister's steps.

"What do you have against Jack?" Kensei asked as he pulled a spiderweb out of his curly black hair. Columns of yellow light shone through gaps in the trees and formed abstract shapes on the path.

Jenny took a deep breath. "I caught him in a lie," she said. Then, Jenny told them about the conversation she overheard aboard his plane.

"That's why Victus said that Mister Spriggan failed to inform him of our talents," Kensei said.

"Yup."

"It's too bad," Kensei said. "I liked Jack. He seemed like an honorable guy."

"Yeah, honorable to himself," Jenny said.

"Maybe he had a good reason," Adriana said.

"He gave the Selkans to that monster," Jenny said. "There's no excuse in the world good enough to justify that."

Over the next couple of hours of hiking, Jenny grew sweaty and dirty. Hunger stabbed at her belly, and her feet were sore. When she noticed that Heather was panting like a dog she asked, "Can we take a break and eat something?"

"You have snacks in your bag," Rygelus said.

"We need more than snacks," Adriana said. "We haven't eaten since breakfast."

"Which was at least ten hours ago," Kensei said.

"And I need to check the bandage on my shoulder."

"If we stop," Brock added, "I'll make my stew."

Rygelus perked up and looked at the group. "Okay, we can stop." He looked around. "We can make camp at the clearing up ahead, but only long enough to eat. The Risi hunt these woods, so we must remain vigilant."

Jenny and the others made camp next to a babbling stream. Large butterflies and dragonflies flew in unpredictable patterns. Overhead, a bird called loudly, and two fluffy brown squirrels chased each other along a low branch.

Kensei dropped his pack, then lost his balance and fell over. He rolled onto his back, looking like he was going to be sick. Jenny retrieved canteens from her burstepi and handed them out, giving the first one to Kensei.

Brock needed a fire to cook, so Rygelus volunteered to keep watch while Adriana and Jenny gathered kindling.

The air was crisp and aromatic in the shade of the ancient trees as Jenny and Adriana set out in search of firewood. Jenny picked up a branch from the base of a huge oak, and added it to her bundle. "I miss Lin," she said.

"Me too." Adriana stared at the dry moss in her hand. "She had a way of seeing the potential in a person."

They walked in companionable silence for a while, searching for kindling. "Tell me something," Jenny asked.

"About what?"

"Tell me a secret."

"Hmm." Adriana adjusted her armful of sticks as she thought. After a short pause, she answered. "My family's dirt poor."

"What?"

"Yeah, not that you would know. We hide it pretty well."

"How can that be? You're so fashionable!"

"It's exhausting." Adriana sighed. "At first, it was like playing make-believe or dress-up. But now, I have to work a nighttime job just to buy the same clothes as the popular girls. Honestly, I was a nervous wreck most days. Continually checking in mirrors and afraid that someone was going to see me at my job. I was in such a perpetual state of anxiety that I started to get migraines and, shortly after that, blindness."

Jenny walked in silent thought as she picked up sticks. *Adriana's appearance is as much of a disguise as my gothness. Could I actually be friends with a girl like Adriana Thatcher? We have a lot in common. After all, we're half-sisters with supernatural abilities.* Jenny smiled. *I'm starting to like this golden-haired girl.* "What about your mom?"

"She's a bit crazy. Married at seventeen, and perpetually a teenager. Can you imagine getting married at our age?"

"No!" Jenny knew that some Roma clans still maintained old traditions and married their daughters at young ages.

"My mom has never mentioned a betrothal for me, not that I mind."

"That's good." Jenny was glad that her mom never discussed betrothal with her. "I don't think we're missing anything."

"Me neither. My mom was never the same after my dad's..." She looked at Jenny. "*Our* dad's indiscretion. I think it messed her up, and as I got older and more developed, she treated me differently. It wasn't until later that I realized she was jealous. But I think my mom swore off the opposite sex altogether to focus on her art."

"Oh yeah? What does she do?"

"Anything she can get her hands on. Paint, clay, wood, found objects, and she's pretty good too. It doesn't pay the bills, though, so she also works as a baker in a grocery store."

"Really? Sounds a lot like my aunt, in a way. After her husband died, she never even dated another man. She's married to her business and is always talking about bills, and how I have to help out. Ever since my mom and I moved into her house, I've just been working for her by giving tarot readings to her clients."

"Wow, your aunt really is living like a Gypsy."

"Yeah." Jenny laughed. "So, what do you do for fun?"

"I love soccer." Adriana grew animated.

"That's right, and you're team captain?"

Adriana nodded. "I practice three times a week. My mom and brother watch every game."

"That sounds nice." Neither Bea nor Ruby had ever watched any of her fencing matches. She couldn't blame them. After all, it was Thatch who'd originally gotten her interested in the sport. "What's our dad like?"

Adriana shrugged. "I haven't seen him in a really long time, but I remember that he was fun, like a big kid. Mom said he wasn't good with responsibilities. He was more interested in goofing off with his friends than spending time with us."

Jenny nodded solemnly, remembering her only interaction with him. "I can see that."

"Right before I came here, we got a phone call from his sister. She told us that he has cancer." Tears welled up in her eyes. She shook her head and continued. "He couldn't even tell us himself."

"Do you think it's the curse?"

"The curse?"

"That's what my family called what we have." Jenny picked up a stick and then dropped it for being too green. "The reason we either go crazy or die from cancer."

"Yeah, I guess he has a curse." Adriana found a stick and added it to her stack. "Even though I haven't seen him in years, I want to cure him. I want to bring him the siphonophores."

"Yeah." Jenny hugged the bundle of sticks against her chest. "When I get home, I'm going to cure my aunt."

With kindling in hand, the girls returned to the camp. Jenny retrieved the fire kit from her burstepi while Adriana formed a pile of dry moss. Jenny added shavings of magnesium and showered the whole thing in sparks. Within seconds, a flame blazed to life. Adriana added more wood until they had a serviceable fire. They nursed the fire until a bed of glowing coals had formed.

"That's good." Brock shoved six large potatoes directly into the coals. "Not too big, though—we don't want to attract attention."

Brock pulled out small bags filled with spices, onions, and carrots. Kensei—who had recovered from his dizzy spell—offered to help. While he chopped onions, Brock worked on a broth.

"I think I can speed this up." Jenny focused on the stew and willed it to boil. The air around them grew cold and the pot bubbled.

"That's amazing." Brock looked over at Jenny.

Jenny grinned. *At least I could be somewhat helpful on this journey,* she thought.

Soon, a heavenly smell drifted out of the pot and made her mouth water. "It smells delicious."

"This recipe has been passed down from father to son for generations." Brock cut a slab of elk meat into large chunks and added it to the broth.

"Do you have any kids?" she asked.

"No, not yet," Brock said as he added the carrot and onion that Kensei had chopped up. "I haven't done well with relationships."

"Is that why you're out here?" Kensei asked.

Brock nodded. "I needed some time away from people for a while."

While the stew warmed up, Kensei took out his sketchpad and drew the trees and stream in the sun's golden hour.

Jenny pulled her uniform off her shoulder to check on her bandage. Red blood had seeped through in spots, but it looked pretty good.

"Can I help?" Adriana asked.

"Um, sure."

Adriana took one of the slim medkits from her vest. Taking out alcohol pads, she cleaned the wound and changed Jenny's bandage. "It seems to be healing nicely."

"Yeah, it's still sore and stiff, though."

"Well, you did get shot. It could have been a lot worse."

"I know, you're right." Jenny thought about those who hadn't been so lucky. She lied back on the soft moss and listened to the babbling of the brook. Overhead, the breeze rattled leaves, and a couple of songbirds sang in the canopy. At that moment, it was difficult to believe that they were on a rescue mission in another universe.

When the stew was ready, Rygelus returned from his watch. As always, Nimue accompanied him. Yet, as far as Jenny knew, only she could see her. Jenny found the bowls in her burstepi and handed them out. While they ate, Adriana created a portal that gave them a bird's-eye view of their location.

Jenny saw that they were near the edge of a massive, circular depression in the earth. It was a caldera, perhaps from a dormant volcano or an impact crater from a meteorite.

"This stew is fantastic," Jenny said. "I can't believe you made it over a fire."

"He is an artist with food." Rygelus smiled at his companion.

Brock shrugged. "It would be better with some freshly baked bread."

"Oh." Jenny dug into her burstepi and pulled out a blue-and-yellow bag. The label read, "The Buzz."

"What is it?" Kensei asked.

Jenny looked at Kensei. "Lin bought me a loaf of bread from that cafe in Acacia City. I don't know how fresh it is—but here."

"Outstanding." Brock took the bread. The crust cracked as he tore it into six pieces, one for each of them. He studied the black-and-yellow bag. "Were you still in Acacia City during the raid?"

"We were," Kensei said. "You should have seen Jenny. An enormous giant charged at us, and she grabbed one of those polearms the guards use. Then, at just the right moment—" He made a thrusting motion.

Jenny shifted in her seat. She didn't want to relive the first time she killed another sentient creature, even if it was in self-defense. She looked at Brock and asked, "Did you see what happened?"

"A little."

"We were in the treehouse during the raid," Rygelus said.

"So, they came through the Esperanza Waypoint. Did you see a mysterious person in a hood?"

"We did," Brock said. "After Sadi came through the Waypoint, we took her to the body you found. She was distraught, so we invited her back to the treehouse. We were curious about what the Risi were doing —after all, they can't travel without a key. We were all shocked when they actually activated the Waypoint."

Kensei looked at Jenny.

"So, it wasn't Sadi." Jenny didn't think it was anymore, not after seeing the girl's memories.

Brock leaned toward Kensei. "So, what happened after Jenny stabbed the giant?"

Kensei was happy to share more details about the raid, though he did embellish the story a bit too much for Jenny's tastes. While he talked, Rygelus took frequent sips from his copper flask, and Heather trembled with fear. When Kensei got to the part with Blunderbore, Brock and Rygelus nodded. They seemed to be familiar with the leader of the giants.

Adriana jerked backward. "I see something." She set her bowl down and pointed at the portal. "There. Something's moving toward us."

"Pack it all up." Rygelus pulled the stew pot out of the fire.

Brock covered coals. Jenny stuffed everyone's bowls and canteens into her burstepi. Kensei slung the heavy backpack full of weapons onto his shoulders. Adriana deactivated her portal.

"Quickly, we must hide." Rygelus handed Jenny the stew pot to store in her bag.

"Where?" Jenny looked around.

"There." He pointed to a grove of fir trees with low-hanging branches. "Climb those trees."

Heather didn't need their invitations. He was already halfway up the nearest tree.

"I need some help." Adriana stumbled around the clearing. Her eyes remained rolled back in her head.

"I've got you." Jenny took her sister's hand and guided her to a tree. She helped Adriana get to the first branch before finding her own tree to climb.

Brock climbed his own tree, but Rygelus took cover behind a trunk.

"What about Rygelus?" Jenny asked Brock.

"Just climb," Brock commanded. "He knows what he's doing."

Rygelus strung his bow and readied an arrow.

"What is he doing?" Kensei asked.

"He's leading them away," Brock said.

With her sore shoulder, Jenny struggled to climb the tree. When she could go no farther, she stopped and straddled a branch. She was only about nine meters off the ground. It would have to be enough. She leaned against the trunk and remained silent.

The songbirds stopped their singing, and the forest grew silent. Across the clearing, a dozen dark shapes emerged from the dense woods. The giants wore padded armor and leather helmets. They carried clubs, javelins, and bows. Several of them each carried an elk carcass on their broad shoulders.

A wild-looking, tattered Risi walked on all fours into the clearing. He sniffed at the air, then pointed in the direction of their abandoned campsite. The giants spoke to each other in a low, guttural language. The biggest Risi barked a command. Several of the giants charged across the clearing in great, clomping strides. Two of them stopped directly below Jenny's tree and peered up through the dense branches.

Jenny pulled her arms and legs closer to her body. She looked over at the others. Heather was the highest, followed by Kensei and Brock. But Adriana was only about five meters up. Jenny feared that her sister would be spotted.

Sweat formed on Jenny's forehead as she reached for her gun. She remembered what Brock had said earlier: We should avoid engaging them at all costs. *But, he couldn't have known we'd be in this situation.* One of the giants leaned against Jenny's tree and peered up the trunk. *I have to try something.* With her heart thundering in her chest, Jenny pried the clasp of her gun open. As she did so, a drop of sweat fell and landed on the Risi's dirt-covered face.

33

SELKAN PREPARATION

The *Tamarack*'s crew began restocking the city-size warship the moment they entered Earth's orbit. It had been months since they had visited any planet. In addition to the basics, like air and water, they imported luxury goods such as sugar and coffee. Now, a steady train of supply ships flew back and forth from Earth's Pacific orbital launch platform to the massive ship.

Victus's spaceplane merged into the supply chain until they reached the *Tamarack*. They broke off and entered the *Tamarack* at hangar eight. The plane jolted as docking clamps gripped it. Then, its passengers and crew floated out of their seats and entered the airlock.

As Victus waited for the air to cycle, he wondered about Jack Spriggan. Had the man run away? Had he been discovered as a spy and killed? Before leaving, Victus had questioned the *Endeavor*'s personnel. The last time anyone had seen Jack was in the mess hall. *I should have interrogated their leader, Lin Song, before I killed her.* He pinched the bridge of his nose. *I screwed up. Now I may never know of his fate.*

At least I did not leave empty-handed. He looked down at Cassadi Stevens. *She's only a few years younger than me,* Victus thought. *And I sense great potential in her. But not as much as that the girl with the black hair. If only she had joined us. Such a waste that any of them had to die. They would all have been powerful allies in our quest to maintain peace in the galaxy.*

The airlock door opened with a hiss, and Victus led Miss Stevens onto the ship. As they floated down the main corridor of the *Tamarack*, he described each station of the ship. Cassadi displayed great interest in the vessel, and he soon found himself enjoying her company.

As they reached the center of the ship, artificial gravity took over, and they walked to the lift. Victus led Sadi up to the crew deck and down a long hallway. He stopped in front of a door. "I hope these quarters will suit your needs, Miss Stevens," Victus said as he opened her assigned cabin.

Cassadi walked inside and went straight to the porthole window with a view of Earth. She unfastened her braid and shook out her curly brown hair.

Victus watched from the door and smiled. "Take your time, look around."

While Cassadi inspected her room, he studied the Riftkey. It was perfection. Two impossibly reflective plates held a block of pure darkness. When activated, that darkness would glow a bright blue that could disintegrate anything it touched.

I will need to have a scabbard made as soon as possible, Victus thought. He looked up at Cassadi, who was inspecting the closet. "I can come back later..."

Cassadi walked up to him and searched his face with her deep brown eyes.

Victus was impressed that she didn't shudder at his black one. "If you need more time."

Cassadi glanced down at the Riftkey, then jerked her gaze away. "You mentioned a task suitable for my talent."

"You are correct."

"And, please call me Sadi." She smiled.

Victus cleared his throat and turned toward the door. "Follow me, Sadi."

Together, Victus and Sadi left the crew deck and boarded a lift down to the lower levels. They exited onto a level with white walls rather than the standard gray found throughout the ship. It was silent here, and well guarded. After passing through three security checkpoints, a muted conversation could be heard from the end of a long hall.

Victus led Sadi into the room at the end of the hall. It was filled with a terrible stench. Sadi pulled the collar of her black Tyran uniform over her nose. Along the left wall, at least twenty Selkans filled a small pen. They lacked space to sit, let alone lie down, and their fur was matted with excrement and urine. Bright lights lit a stainless steel operating table in the center of the room. It was fitted with a surgical halo device and sturdy straps.

Two men in white lab coats were arguing. One was young, a cadet with close-cut hair. The other was old, with wild, white hair. Doctor Abrams was in charge of integrating Selkans to the ship. Currently, he was berating his young assistant. Neither of them noticed the visitors.

Victus approached the doctor.

Doctor Abrams turned slowly to see Victus and Sadi. He glanced at the Riftkey in Victus's hand. "I see you found it."

"I did." Victus set the Riftkey on the operating table. It was a heavy thing, and he had grown weary of carrying it around. *I really need to get a scabbard for it.* He turned to the doctor and asked, "What is going on here?"

"This latest technician refuses to work." He gave the cadet a look of contempt.

The Selkans' constant crying and wailing were causing the assistant to shake with emotion. Victus was disgusted by his display of weakness. He looked down at Sadi and was surprised to see the look of pleasure on her face. She seemed to be enjoying their suffering. He smiled and thought, *This is why I chose you.*

The doctor grabbed his assistant by the shoulders and shook him. "You are a servant to the galaxy." He gestured at the Selkans. "These are only cattle. Do not let emotions cloud your judgment."

"I have a solution to your dilemma." Victus put a hand on Sadi's back and led her forward. "Our newest cadet will not balk at performing the tasks you require."

"Really?" Doctor Abrams looked at Sadi. "And what is your name?"

"Cassadi Stevens," she said through the collar of the uniform.

"Are you trained?"

"I possess a comprehensive knowledge of medical and technical disciplines."

Victus turned to Sadi. "And what is your ability?"

"I can increase or decrease pain."

One of Doctor Abrams's large white eyebrows lifted. "That is useful, quite useful. If I'm correct, you can read pain as well."

"Yes, pain and pleasure."

"And do you know what we do here?"

"No." Sadi studied the Selkans. Some stared at the wall with dead eyes. Frightened children and teenagers clutched at their parents. But a group of three Selkans near the back wall caught her attention. There was a big one in blue coveralls and an old tattooed male. They held a little girl between them.

Doctor Abrams pointed at the cage. "These new Selkans need their plugs installed. This involves shaving their amygdalae."

Sadi's eyebrows knit together. "What for?"

"It allows us to initiate a fight-or-flight response at will." The doctor picked a circular piece of metal off a nearby cart with his gloved hands. "By presenting them with a fear-based scenario, we activate their ability to teleport."

"They can teleport?" Sadi leaned back against the operating table.

"Yes," Victus said. "You didn't know?"

Sadi shook her head. "But how does one Selkan transporting do you any good?'

"Ah, that is the real trick." The doctor set the part down and motioned for them to follow him. They entered a room where the air was clean and cool. Red lights lit twelve pods that lined the walls. A cluster of cables sprouted from the head of each pod and joined the others at the center of the ceiling. A Selkan lay inside each one like they were sleeping in a bed. "They are each taking part in group hypnosis."

"Like a shared dream?" Sadi asked.

"Yes, exactly," the doctor said as he caressed one of the pods. "That way, when we trigger their ability, they all transport together, and amplify it to affect the entire ship."

"That's incredible," Sadi said. "Can you amplify other abilities?"

"Yes," Victus said. "It's how we maintain gravity on this section of the ship and provide an exterior view inside the bridge."

"Could you enhance my ability?" Sadi asked.

"Perhaps," The doctor rubbed his chin. "If you allow me to study you."

"Okay," Sadi said.

"For now, we should let them sleep." Doctor Abrams led them out of the room and quietly closed the door behind them.

"Sadi, are you willing to assist Doctor Abrams in his operation?"

"I still don't know what this is exactly, but I'm eager to try."

"Excellent." Victus turned to the assistant. "You are dismissed. Report to the psych ward."

"Yes, sir." The assistant rushed from the room without looking back.

The doctor sighed. "That's the second assistant this month. I hope this one works out better."

"I have no doubt that she will." Victus turned to Sadi. "Can you start right away?"

"Yes." Sadi looked at the Selkans. "As long as he can be first." She pointed at the big Selkan in blue mechanics coveralls.

Victus studied the alien and felt a pressure in his mind. He forced himself into stillness and reached out toward the big Selkan. *No.* He took a step back. *This alien is an Æon. Such a thing should not be possible.* He looked around and wondered if anyone else knew. "Yes, perform the procedure immediately. Miss Stevens shall assist."

Doctor Abrams opened a black case and withdrew a gun. He inserted a cartridge into the chamber and aimed it at the large Selkan. The little Selkan girl screamed as a dart sunk into his neck just above his coveralls. After a few seconds, the Selkan fell to the floor, unconscious.

The doctor opened the cage door, and the Selkans cowered against the back wall. Together, he and Victus dragged the large Selkan from the cage. All the while, the little Selkan girl screamed and held on to his limp body. Sadi had to hold the girl back just so they could get him out and close the door. Then they strapped the big Selkan to the operating table.

Victus wanted to stay and observe his new ward in action, but he had work to do elsewhere. "Report to me on her progress."

The doctor nodded. "Yes, Admiral."

"Sadi," Victus said. "I will be on the bridge if you need me."

Sadi nodded.

Victus turned on his heel and left the room. The sounds of wailing faded away as the door swung shut.

Inside the *Tamarack*'s bridge, Earth filled the view from below. Lights from hundreds of cities spotted the dark globe, and its single moon shone down from above them. The bridge staff's faces were lit from below by the soft blue glow of displays. Victus walked to the base of the command deck and climbed the ladder. This simple task was made more difficult because of the Riftkey he clutched tightly in his hand.

"Welcome back, sir," Carmen Jacquay, the wing commander, greeted him. "Your plan worked flawlessly. You must be relieved."

"Not flawlessly. Jack Spriggan is missing." Below them, a swirl of clouds floated above the Pacific. Victus leaned on the rail and looked out over the ocean as if he could see where Jack had gone.

"The pilot who verified that the Selkans' were on Earth?" Carmen asked.

"Yes."

Marcus, the captain of the *Tamarack*, said, "We should we send a team to locate him, and to wrap up any loose ends."

"Not to kill him." The wing commander cast a sideways glance at the captain.

Captain Marcus cleared his throat.

"No, Marcus." Victus looked at the captain. "We cannot keep the Selkans' presence a secret, but hopefully, with the aliens back in our possession, no one will believe Unity's claims of their existence."

"If you think that's enough," Marcus said.

"I do."

Carmen nodded in agreement. "What are your plans for getting us home?"

Victus lifted the Riftkey.

"Is that what I think it is?" Marcus asked.

"It is." Victus smiled.

Marcus grinned and clapped the admiral on the back.

"What is it?" Carmen asked.

"This is the Sol Riftkey." Victus turned it so that it reflected the light of the projected moon. "With it, I can finally become a Terminal master."

34

VIROSUIT

The drop of sweat landed on the Risi's forehead. The giant reached up with a massive hand, touched his head, and examined his fingers. Then, he looked up the tree, and his eyes met Jenny's. With a quick, fluid movement, the Risi nocked an arrow to his bow and pointed it at her.

Jenny pushed her back against the tree trunk and yanked her sidearm free of its holster. She wobbled for a moment on the tree branch but steadied herself with her injured arm. Suddenly, she was overcome by an intense wave of fear. In her mind's eye, she saw Sadi looking down at her with curiosity. She was no longer in the forest. Instead, she was lying on a cold metal table in a strange room that smelled like an animal pen.

Heavy straps bound her hands and feet, and her head couldn't move at all. Jenny heard a whirring sound. There was a sharp pinch in the back of her cranium followed by heavy pressure. Pain lanced through her body. Sadi's eyes twinkled, and a grin spread across her freckled face.

"Keep him still," a man said. "Take away his pain."

Sadi nodded, and the pain vanished.

Jenny slipped sideways on the branch, and her stomach lurched. She scrambled to catch herself and dropped the gun. She hung there with her uninjured arm wrapped around the limb. *What just happened?* Jenny thought. *It's like I was somewhere else for a second, but where? And why did I see Sadi?*

Below her, the Risi nocked an arrow to his bow. As he lined up a shot through the tree's branches, Jenny swung her leg over the limb. She felt a jolt, and a javelin-size arrow sprouted from her branch. Before the Risi let loose a second arrow, a roar erupted from the clearing. It was the wild-looking Risi. He clawed at an arrow in his neck. A moment later, the wild Risi fell to the blood-soaked grass with a wet gurgle.

Jenny caught a flash of metal from behind a tree trunk, and her heart lifted. It was Rygelus. She watched as he readied another arrow and took aim. A second Risi roared in anger as he yanked a feathered shaft from his shoulder. The giant turned and pointed at Rygelus.

Bushes and small trees exploded into splinters as the enraged giants charged the archer. Another arrow hit a Risi in the chest before Rygelus abandoned his position and fled farther into the forest. Once the giants were out of sight, Jenny climbed down from the tree and retrieved her gun.

Nearby, Kensei picked up his heavy bag from the base of his tree. "That was close. I thought we were goners."

Jenny holstered her pistol and turned to Brock. "Will Rygelus be okay?"

He smiled. "Nothing on two legs can catch that man."

"Do we wait for him here?" Adriana asked.

"No, we keep going. Rygelus will find us." Brock shouldered his pack. "Heather, please show us the way."

Heather led them out of the Esperanza forest to a rocky caldera that was nearly five kilometers in diameter. At its center, a mud lake belched sulfuric steam.

"What is that?" Adriana pointed toward the far end of the caldera. The edge of an enormous, shiny object glinted in the sun. It was half-buried under an earthen mound.

"That's my crashed spaceship, the *Tricaster*," Rygelus said.

Everyone but Brock jumped in surprise as Rygelus walked up behind them.

"This is the first time I have returned to the site of my daughter's death."

Jenny looked at the ghost of Nimue, who remained next to her father. "You haven't been back here for hundreds of years?"

"Thousands." Rygelus took a pull from his copper flask and returned it to his camouflage jacket.

"Why not?" Jenny asked.

"Being in this place reminds me of the crash, and my memory is perfect."

"What do you mean by 'perfect'?"

"I can recall every memory," Rygelus said. Then he went on to describe every detail of his and Jenny's first meeting. He remembered the exact position of the sun, the air temperature, and the humidity when he found her. He knew what Jenny was wearing, and which foot she'd tripped over in the stream. "And time has not dulled the pain of Nimue's loss." He reached into his jacket for the flask.

"How did she die?" Adriana asked.

"There was once a mountain here." Rygelus held the copper flask out toward the caldera. "My partner, Ramus, and I were in the spaceship on our way to retrieve Nimue from her mission. We did not know that the mountain was a dormant supervolcano about to erupt." He took another drink from his flask. "When the blast hit, our shields failed, and we crashed."

"How did you survive something like that?" Kensei asked.

"We did not," Rygelus said.

"Uh." Kensei looked Rygelus up and down. "You're standing here."

"My mind entered a dormant state while nano-organisms repaired the damage to my body. When I woke, it seemed like the crash had just happened, but days had passed. I found my daughter's charred remains in her room. I buried her along with the Riftkey. Not knowing how to live without her, I left the spaceship to live in the forest. Many years have passed since that day. I have watched the trees grow old and die." He held the flask in trembling fingers. "But I still remember burying my daughter as if it was yesterday."

"It's okay." Jenny gripped Rygelus's arm, keeping him from lifting the flask to his lips again.

"The worst part is that I know part of her remains alive. Her consciousness was bound to both the Riftkey and the virosuit, so her spirit is forced to remain. She could even be here, right now, with us." Rygelus looked around, his eyes passing over the ghost of Nimue, unable to see her.

"It's okay to keep loving her," Jenny said. "I know what it's like to lose someone. I lost my mother to cancer, and I just saw Lin die." Jenny gritted her teeth. "But you have to learn how to let go and move on." She looked at the ghost of Nimue.

Rygelus followed her gaze. "I cannot forget her."

"It's not about forgetting. It's...it's about allowing yourself to change, to become a stronger person. She would want you to live."

"You are wise for being so young." He screwed the cap onto his flask and looked at Brock. "I will try."

Brock squeezed his shoulder. "That's all I ever wanted."

"Hurry, hurry." Heather scuttled behind a rock. "Friends this way."

Heather led them on a secret route around the caldera. There was a strange beauty in this place on the edge of a forest filled with life, next to the harsh environment of the sulfuric lake. Pools of yellow, red, and blue dotted the landscape below while birds of the same colors flew among the trees' branches. Their path ended at a cave whose opening resembled a wolf's head in a permanent howl to the sky.

Heather stopped in front of the entrance. "This way to Alfur home."

Jenny turned on her flashlight and entered the cave. The tunnel walls were dark and smooth as if hollowed out by a humongous drill. It was even tall enough for Brock to walk without ducking. Springs of water trickled down the surface of the walls and raced down the sloping path. The only trouble they encountered was that their path ended at the intersection of a more massive tunnel.

Heather pointed in the upslope direction of the new tunnel. "That way lead back outside." Then, he pointed downslope. "Alfur home this way."

They followed the stream downward, and the passage grew more complicated. The path meandered, and the walls became jagged. There were stalactites to bump your head on, and stalagmites to stub your toe. At one point, the rescuers had to squeeze and scrape through a narrow cleft in the rock.

Once they were through, the air changed. It grew warmer and carried a smell that reminded Jenny of chemistry class. Ahead of them, a couple of blocky rock formations stood in front of an enormous cavern. As they approached, the rock formations moved. They weren't rocks at all, but Alfur in some type of stony armor. Each stood a foot taller than Heather and carried an obsidian-tipped spear. Their heads were different too. With their small ears and massive skulls, they resembled pit bulls. One of the guards turned and shouted. His deep voice echoed through the chamber.

Heather ran forward and took a passive posture before them. After conversing with the guards for a minute, Heather returned to the rescuers. "Alfur not happy with Heather."

"Big surprise there," Kensei said.

"Strangers not welcome here."

The guards lowered their spears at them. Brock gripped the hilt of the greatsword strapped to his back.

"No fight," Heather pleaded, and his body shook. "Alfur guards use poison weapons. Alfur never have visitors. No trust."

"That's alright." Jenny stroked Heather's back. "Tell them we just want our friends back."

Heather relayed the message to the guards and returned to Jenny. "Alfur let friends go. Must leave weapons here."

There were some words of protest, but Brock finally unstrapped his sword, and Rygelus removed his bow. The rest of them removed their guns and knives. Jenny was allowed to keep her burstepi.

Once they were disarmed, the guards led them inside the cavern. A few centimeters of warm water covered the entire floor, and each step in the shallow lake stirred up a cloud of bioluminescence. Above them, the ceiling glowed like a perpetual lava fireplace. Hundreds of holes pockmarked the wall to their right. Small glowing heads peered through to watch them. To their left, a pyramid—cut out of solid, dark rock—stretched from floor to ceiling.

The sight of the structure nagged at Jenny's memory. It looked familiar, but where had she seen this pyramid before? As Jenny focused, the air grew as dense as water. Circular waves moved languidly out from the face of the pyramid. She had felt this calling before. First with the Riftkey in the ruins of the fort, then with Astrea's Waypoint key in the basement of the Department of Transportation. *That's it*, she realized. She had seen this pyramid at the climax of her vision. Jenny grabbed Heather's hand and pointed at the pyramid. "What is that?"

"Alfur worship there."

"It's a temple?"

Heather nodded. Two smaller, more delicate Alfur stepped in front of the guards. They were children who wanted to see the visitors. More Alfur climbed down from their homes in the wall and crowded around them.

Like Heather, these newcomers had fox-like faces and glowing fur. A rattling sound caught Jenny's attention. Five warriors escorted a bent and ancient Alfur. His thin gray fur glowed dimly beneath an outfit of bleached bones. He leaned on a staff adorned with beads and studied them through the empty eye sockets of a subterranean predator that he wore as a mask.

Heather stepped forward. "This Deedleoh. Alfur leader."

"He looks like a witch doctor," Kensei said.

"How do you know?" Adriana asked.

"I saw it in a documentary. They often wear masks like that and lots of bones."

Deedleoh spoke, and Heather translated. "Friends kill sacred worm." The witch doctor rattled his staff. "Must pay price."

"We can pay." Rygelus held out his flashlight and turned it on and off to the wonder of the crowd.

Brock pulled out a steel compass and displayed it to the guards. They studied the device in awe.

"No." Deedleoh pounded his staff and pointed at the temple. "God judge." The Alfur gazed at the pyramid as if hypnotized.

"So, how do we pay?" Adriana asked.

Heather shook his head and trembled. "Touch god."

"What does that mean?" Kensei asked.

As Jenny studied the dark rectangular door, she felt a familiar siren call. Curiosity won her over. "We'll do it, but you must let us see our friends first."

Deedleoh nodded and pointed at a stone wheel. "Friends watch. If fail, friends die." The guards rolled aside a massive stone with a set of primitive pulleys. Jenny—along with Adriana and Kensei—followed Heather to the back of the cell. Brock and Rygelus chose to stay behind to prevent the Alfur from trapping them inside.

A weak voice spoke to them from the darkness. "Jenny?" Mazu blinked against Heather's bioluminescence. "What are you doing here?"

"We came to save you." Tears filled Jenny's as she crouched down and took Mazu's hands in hers.

"What's wrong?" Mazu asked.

"Your mom." A lump formed in Jenny's throat, and she couldn't speak. *First my mom, then Lin. How much death do I have to endure?*

Kensei shifted his feet.

"What is it?" Mazu asked. "What happened to Lin?"

Adriana crouched down next to Jenny and said, "She's dead."

Mazu's eyes widened in shock. She stood up and dusted off her black bodysuit. When she spoke, her face was placid, and her voice sounded distant and cold. "How?"

"Tyr arrived for the Selkans," Kensei said. "We fought them, and a man named Vae Victus killed her."

"That bastard," Jack said.

Jenny faced Jack with clenched teeth. "It's your fault. You're the reason Lin is dead. You betrayed us."

"No." Jack stood and held up his hands. "I didn't—"

"The night we arrived at the *Endeavor*, I overheard you telling someone about the Selkans. It was Victus, wasn't it?"

Mazu looked at him. "What is she talking about, Jack?"

"He tricked me." Jack reached out to touch Mazu's arm, but she pulled away. "Victus possessed and killed a friend of mine. He forced me to come here, to Sol. I just wanted to get back home..." He looked into Mazu's eyes for a moment before glancing away. "I know what I did was wrong."

"Too late." Jenny clenched her fists. "You can rot in here for all I care."

"No." Pain and conflict reflected in Mazu's eyes. "I believe him, and Jack saved my life. Anyway, he's not the one who killed Lin."

"You weren't there." Jenny shook as anger and sadness wrestled for dominance.

Mazu took Jenny's hands. "No, and I'm sorry about that. But there's been enough death already, wouldn't you agree?"

Jenny breathed heavily through her nose and nodded. "Fine, we'll decide what to do with him later. Now, I have something to show you." She shrugged the burstepi off her shoulders and pulled the Riftkey free.

"You won!" Mazu hugged Jenny. "I knew you could do it."

Ah, it's good to be out, Cobol said in Jenny's mind.

Not now, Cobol, Jenny replied.

"Well, I did win, but..." She put the Riftkey back in the burstepi and slipped it onto her shoulders

"That's not the Riftkey that Kett'l created," Kensei said.

Mazu knitted her brows. "I don't understand."

"This is the Riftkey that Astrea lost," Jenny said. "I found it in the forest ruins. Lin wanted me to keep it hidden."

"Then what happened to the other one?"

"Victus stole it," Kensei said.

"He has the Selkans too," Adriana said.

"And with the Riftkey he'll unlock the Terminal and control this system," Jenny said.

"That's not the only bad news." Mazu looked at Adriana. "I failed to find the virosuit, and the Locator is busted."

"That's okay," Adriana said. "We're just glad that you're safe."

"Do you know why we're locked up?" Jack asked.

"You killed one of their sacred worms," Kensei said.

"Those things are sacred?"

Heather nodded. "Punishment is death."

"Then why are we alive?" Mazu asked.

"Worm meat feed Alfur." Heather looked down. "So not eat humans."

"That's some relief," Jack said.

"Until they run out of worm meat," Jenny said.

"How did you get them to free us?" Mazu asked.

At that moment, two armed Alfur entered the cell and spoke to Heather.

"You're about to find out." Jenny turned and followed the Alfur out of the dank chamber.

"Where are we going?" Mazu asked.

"To the temple," Kensei said, "in order to touch their god."

The pyramid-shape temple sat within a half-circle alcove. In the water's reflection, the half-circle became a full circle. Bas-relief sculptures of huge fanged worms surrounded the black rectangular door. Alfur of all shapes and sizes gathered around the entrance. The young—who glowed brighter than the adults—clung to their parents' fur.

As Jenny ducked under the low ceiling of the entryway, a chill settled into her bones. A long hallway led them deep inside the pyramid, and the red light of the cavern transitioned to soft blue light. The source of the blue light emanated from hundreds of Alfur seated within an amphitheater. Their murmuring voices quieted as they entered. More carvings covered the temple's walls. They depicted a funeral ritual in which Alfur gave their dead to the giant worms to devour. Other panels were like illustrated instructions for building homes and preparing food and drink. Another pictograph showed giant men who roamed the forest and killed Alfur on sight.

At the center of the amphitheater was a sculpture of a massive worm —which stretched from floor to ceiling—and held a human-size silver statue on its coiled body.

"The virosuit." Mazu rushed down the steps, but a wall of poison-tipped obsidian spears blocked her way.

For the first time in Jenny's memory, the ghost of Nimue left her father's side. She walked down the amphitheater steps and stood next to the virosuit. *That's Cobol's body*, Jenny thought, *and apparently the object of Alfur's worship.*

"Whoa," Kensei said. "It looks just like the Silver Surfer."

"The Silver Surfer?" Brock asked Kensei.

"Yeah," Kensei said. "You know, the herald of Galactus. Oh, that's right, you wouldn't know."

"I don't even know about that," Adriana said.

Jenny looked at the others. "We need that suit if we're going to unlock the Terminal."

"So, we're really doing it?" Kensei asked.

"I'm in," Adriana said. "Let's save the Selkans."

"But we have to get back to Earth Prime." Jenny looked at Mazu and asked, "Do you have a Waypoint key?"

"Yes." Mazu looked at them quizzically. "Don't you have yours?"

"No." Jenny's face went sour as she remembered Aindriu yanking her mother's amulet from her neck.

"They were confiscated after Tyr arrived," Kensei said.

"I'm sorry," Mazu whispered.

"It's okay."

"So," Adriana said. "How do we get it out of here?"

"Jenny must touch"—Rygelus looked at Kensei—"the Silver Surfer."

"Yes, but..." Heather wrung his small hands. "All Alfur that touch statue die."

"What?" Adriana looked at Jenny. "You can die from touching it."

"Yes," Heather said weakly.

"Only those who are not Æons die from direct contact with the virosuit," Rygelus said and looked at Jenny. "It's like when Brock touched the Riftkey, but a hundred times worse."

"How do you know that?" Jenny asked.

"My daughter was an Æon. She could touch the virosuit without harm."

There was a loud rattling sound as Deedleoh, the witch doctor, shook his staff. Once he had their attention, he spoke to Heather. "God judge now."

Jenny took a step forward, but Adriana grabbed her shoulder. "Are you sure about this?"

"Don't worry," Jenny said. "It won't kill me." *At least I hope it won't*, she thought. *It's time to find out if I'm worthy.*

The witch doctor led her down the steps toward the giant worm sculpture and stopped an arm's length from the silvery virosuit. Up close, she saw that geometric lines crisscrossed its shiny skin like the branches of a tree. Its face was a polygonal facsimile of a human's. The ghost of Nimue stood next to the virosuit and caressed its face.

As Deedleoh spoke, the Alfur leaned forward as one. It sounded to Jenny like a sermon. His voice was not loud, but it was filled with passion and held the attention of his people. Jenny unclasped her burstepi and gripped the handle of the Riftkey. There was a crack like thunder as she pulled it free, and sparks formed in the air around the blade. The Alfur ducked down and screamed. The witch doctor backed away from Jenny, and the guards held up their spears.

You found my body! Cobol exclaimed in Jenny's mind. *And an entire temple, just for me? I am quite flattered.*

Jenny approached the virosuit, but before she could touch it, the ghost of Nimue grabbed her wrist. It was real, physical contact. Jenny's mind exploded like a thunderstorm and everything went black.

It was dark and silent. Jenny's blood and bones felt like ice. After a few minutes, or maybe hours, her body warmed. Her heart pumped, forcing oxygen, nutrients, and enzymes throughout her body.

"The vitrification has reduced your metabolic and brain functions," said a familiar man's voice. "But the cryoprotectant is being flushed from your system now. You should be able to hear me."

A red glow penetrated Jenny's eyelids, and she gasped for air.

"Careful, I have you, Nimue." Warm hands guided her arms and legs into a sitting position.

I'm Nimue now? As Jenny's eyes opened, a stab of pain shot down her optic nerves. A cloud of steam rose from her skin, further obscuring her vision.

Rygelus held her. He looked exactly the same age as he had back in the temple, with the same angled eyes, pointed ears, and that strange bump on his forehead. "How do you feel?"

"Like I have the galaxy's worst hangover." Nimue croaked the words out of her parched throat. Just like in her vision of Astrea, Jenny was relegated to being a passenger, forced to relive Nimue's memories, and unable to enact her will in this world.

But this isn't like Astrea's vision, Jenny thought. *It's all fuzzy and indistinct as if I'm watching it through a scratched-up, dirty lens. Huh, this time I can't smell or taste anything.*

Rygelus draped a thick, soft blanket around her bare shoulders and rubbed her back. As a passive observer, Jenny felt his touch, but could not respond. Nimue pulled the blanket around her with one hand and massaged a cramp in her side with the other. "Now I know why they call cryosleep 'the icy womb.'"

Rygelus's bushy eyebrows inched toward each other in concern. He brushed Nimue's long black hair over her shoulders. Then, he picked up a white mug printed with the name of the ship, *Tricaster*. "Here, drink this. You will feel better."

"Thanks." As Nimue sipped at the thick beverage, Rygelus ran a hand through his unruly brown hair and smiled at her.

Time skipped forward like this memory was incomplete. Jenny's mind whirled as she struggled to interpret the new setting. The gray blanket was still wrapped around her, but her mug was now empty and sat on a shelf near the corner of a strange bed. A silvery human form stood in the corner of the room. Blue light radiated from a network of veins in its shiny skin. *Is that Cobol?*

Nimue opened the closet and withdrew a pair of loose, dark-gray pants and a gray-blue shirt. She pulled them on over the black bodysuit she already wore.

"I missed you all these years." Rygelus walked to the far end of her room.

"To me"—Nimue picked up a pair of black boots—"it's like I just saw you yesterday. I thought it was the same for you." She sat on a fold-down aluminum bench and buckled them on.

"It has been thousands of years since we left. I haven't been dormant all that time." Rygelus pressed a button, and the entire wall became transparent. A blue sky filled the wall, and sunlight filled the room.

Nimue walked up to the window and put an arm around her father. "Then make the next couple of minutes feel like days."

Rygelus hugged his daughter, and together, they watched turquoise-blue ocean waves crash into the rocky coast of an island. After a few minutes, Nimue looked up at her father and said, "Take me to Ramus so that we can be done with this mission and return to mother."

Time skipped forward, and they were in a new room. Specialized instruments covered every surface of the circular walls. Jenny recognized the four black maze boxes used in Cabin's testing. At the far end of the room, a tall man stood with his back to them. He was studying a holographic display of the Riftkey. Without turning, he said, "Welcome back, Nimue."

That voice is familiar, Jenny thought.

"Thank you, Ramus," Nimue said, "but it doesn't feel like I've been away."

"Ah yes, you have been in cryosleep." He stared at the hologram. "You may be interested to know that I have identified the properties of nexum."

"Is that all you learned in thousands of years?" Nimue asked.

"I have also refined the serum." Ramus waved in the direction of several black fluid-filled cylinders. "I have only been researching nexum in my free time. While I understand its properties, I have no way of reproducing them. I have compared it to every possible material and alloy, including the theoretical, but nothing comes close."

"Eliminate the impossible," Nimue said, "and whatever remains must be the truth."

"Yes." Ramus touched the hologram. "I must discover what remains, even if it takes another thousand years. It could be the key to exploring the galaxy." He looked pointedly at the silvery android, who had followed Nimue and Rygelus into the lab. "Cobol has been less than helpful in this whole process."

"Do you know how you were made?" Cobol asked Ramus.

"I know what I am made of, and how I work."

"As do I," Cobol said, "but I do not know how I was made."

"You have a point." Ramus walked away from the data that streamed across his displays. "Perhaps if I wish to reproduce this technology, then I must first create life."

Ramus turned to face them. Jenny would have jumped back in surprise if she could have because she was looking at Lance LaGrange. Like Rygelus, he looked identical to the last time she had seen him. Even his dark hair was carefully parted the same way.

Rygelus leaned against a table. "Can you tear yourself away from your work long enough to help us with the Waypoints?"

"Absolutely."

Time skipped forward, and they were in a new room. Eleven, vertically stored Waypoints lined the walls. Ramus walked around the perimeter running his hand over each one as he approached the control panel. With a tap, the black screen came to life.

Nimue turned to Cobol. "Are you ready?"

"I am." Cobol's polygonal face shifted to mimic speech.

Nimue gripped a handle behind Cobol's neck. With a tug, she removed something, and his body slumped over. *It's the Riftkey,* Jenny thought. Then, Nimue and Jenny were somehow inside the virosuit, but it wasn't like wearing a suit, it was more like she was the virosuit.

Please hurry, Cobol said through their psychic link. *Being trapped in this hunk of metal makes me claustrophobic.*

The vision skipped forward, and Nimue, as the virosuit, lifted one of the massive Waypoints from its resting place. She carried it off the ship and walked across a rocky coastline. Ocean waves crashed against the shore, sending spray and foam into the air. She jumped into the churning water. Jenny waited for the shock of cold that didn't come. Nimue walked freely along the ocean floor and entered a cave through a cleft in the rock.

An hour passed, or maybe a day for all Jenny could tell through the degraded vision. This time they were in a forest. Nimue carried another Waypoint up a mountain and into a gaping crack in its side. A steady wind blew out of the cave as if the Earth was breathing. After reaching the bottom, she took a path that sloped down to an enormous cavern with a broad, flat floor covered in a shallow layer of water. The ceiling of the cave glowed red with heat.

This is where Alfur live, Jenny thought. *Over there is where the pyramid will be.* Her reflection in the water was that of the silver virosuit.

Nimue exited the cavern and entered a complex cave structure. She took the Waypoint through a passage carved by a burbling stream. Albino cave dwellers skittered at their approach. She sped through a hot, crystal-filled cavern and out into a rocky tunnel. Finally, she came to a stop in front of a deep pool lit by bioluminescent worms. Their soft blue light reflected in the still water.

There was a great splash as she jumped into the pool. She carried the Waypoint deeper and deeper underwater until the Waypoint could go no farther into the tunnel. Using the virosuit's powerful fists, Nimue pounded the stone wall until it formed a smooth circle. She then wedged the Waypoint into it.

Nimue paused, as if in thought, and the Waypoint vanished. The tunnel beyond changed, and there was a surge of water.

"The final Waypoint is active," Nimue said out loud. She turned and made her way back through the cave complex. Her feet fell in a steady rhythm as she splashed across the water-covered floor of the large cavern. Overhead, the ceiling glowed with an ominous red light.

"Are you close to the surface?" Rygelus asked through some link they had to the virosuit.

"I am—"

"Hurry," Rygelus said as if he hadn't heard her, "we are detecting seismic activity in the area."

Nimue was halfway across the cavern when a loud boom caused her to stumble. She skidded to a stop in a spray of water. A loud ringing sounded over her communicator.

"Dad...Dad!"

"A volcanic eruption," Rygelus said. "Engine malfunc—"

The cavern disappeared and Jenny woke up on Nimue's bed in her cabin. Her hand was wrapped around the Riftkey.

Where am I? Jenny thought. A loudspeaker blared somewhere, and flames of purple, yellow, and green licked at the walls. *I am back on the Tricaster.* She couldn't tell if she was hot or cold. She screamed in agony as orange flames consumed the bed. Her vision failed as her eyes exploded and the skin peeled off of her muscles. There was so much pain, and then everything went black. She expected oblivion to follow death, but she was surprised by what came next.

The pain was gone, and Jenny was floating in an ocean. Above her was an endless black sky filled with stars. Suddenly, an enormous, black tidal wave thundered toward her. She raised her arms to cover her face, but the wave was so vast, so impressive, that there was no possible escape. All she could do was admire the immensity and awesome power of it. She put her arms down and accepted oblivion.

35

TRICASTER

"Jenny?" Adriana's voice was small and distant. "Jenny, can you hear me? Please wake up."

Jenny struggled at the surface of an immense ocean. A storm raged overhead. Thunder boomed from every direction, and her body spasmed with each lightning strike. She swam toward the sound of her sister's voice. A bolt of lightning struck the water near her.

Jenny's eyes shot open. Nearby, a giant sculpture of a worm stretched from floor to ceiling. In its coils was the shining form of the virosuit, Cobol's body. Deedleoh, the witch doctor, was shouting at the audience, trying to pull their attention back to him. Heather had collapsed to the ground and appeared to be crying.

"You're awake." Adriana squeezed her hand. "I was so worried."

Jenny's mind buzzed with new knowledge. Lance LaGrange, the CEO of Cabin, was an ancient alien. He had come here with Rygelus and Nimue to install the Waypoints. *And somehow, I used the virosuit as my body.* Jenny got to her feet, still clutching the Riftkey.

The Alfur lurched backward. Heather sat up and looked at Jenny. A smile spread across his face. "Jenny alright." Deedleoh stopped shouting at the auditorium and turned to look at Jenny.

"Your nose," Adriana said.

Jenny touched her nose and found that it was bloody. Not only that, but her ears had bled too. "What happened?"

"You had a seizure," Rygelus said.

"For how long?"

"Almost a minute," Adriana said as she took Jenny's hand and helped her stand up.

"It felt like hours," Jenny said. As she looked at Rygelus, she remembered how he had held her after waking from cryosleep. "I had a vision that I was your daughter, Nimue. I know now what I have to do." She took a step toward the virosuit.

Adriana took Jenny's free hand. "Are you sure about this?"

"Yes, I'm sure." Jenny squeezed her sister's hand and pulled away. She looked at Rygelus. "When I touch this, your daughter will be released from her half existence."

Rygelus's thick eyebrows flew up. "She is here, right now, is she not?" he asked. Jenny nodded. Rygelus looked away as tears gathered in the corners of his eyes. His chin quivered, but he gritted his teeth to hide it. After a moment, he turned his reddened eyes toward Jenny and nodded. "I am ready."

Jenny nodded back, then turned toward the virosuit. She looked at its polygonal facsimile of a human face and remembered it speaking to her. Jenny slammed her hand onto its chest. Every nerve in her body exploded. There was a collective gasp as the ghost of Nimue materialized for everyone to see.

"I can see her." Rygelus's voice quivered as he stepped up to his daughter. "After all these years, I can finally see her."

"Father," Nimue said as she smiled.

"Nimue. I have so much I want to tell you."

Nimue held up a finger to silence her father. "I already know. I've been with you all these years. Now, all I ask is that you finish the mission, then find my mother."

"I will." Rygelus wiped at his eyes. "I promise."

"I love you."

"I love you, always." Rygelus reached out and embraced Nimue.

"Goodbye, Father."

Rygelus's body shook. "Goodbye, my daughter."

As Nimue began to fade away, she turned to face Jenny. "Thank you for freeing me."

Rygelus stumbled forward as Nimue disappeared. For a while, he stared at his empty arms.

Brock pulled Rygelus into his massive chest.

Now, what do I do? Jenny asked Cobol.

You must place the Riftkey on the Virosuit's back.

Jenny remembered that Nimue did something similar in her vision. *But to gain access to the Virosuit's back, I'll have to roll it over. The Alfur aren't going to like this,* Jenny thought as she wedged herself between the virosuit and the statue that held it. The Alfur guards rushed forward with their spears pointed at her, but her friends moved to intercept them.

"What are you doing?" Kensei asked as he dodged a spear thrust.

"I've got to roll the suit over."

"Do what you have to do," Mazu said. "We'll protect you."

Jenny put her back against the virosuit, and her feet on the statue. She bent her knees and shoved hard. Slowly, the heavy virosuit slid and toppled from its perch and hit the ground with a thud. Jenny followed the virosuit down to the ground and swung the Riftkey in a wide arc to keep the guards away. The virosuit lay on its side with its back exposed. She saw a groove there, just the right size for the Riftkey. She lined the key up, and like a magnet, it snapped into position. The hilt of the Riftkey extended up from the virosuit's back, but the seam where the two met was almost invisible. Blue light glowed under the virosuit's silvery skin.

Cobol jumped to his feet. "I feel better!" he said with a spin-jump that shook the amphitheater enough to shower dust from the ceiling. The Alfur shrieked in surprise. Some wept, while others laughed or shouted. Deedleoh struggled to gain their attention. Cobol looked out toward the auditorium. "Hello, everyone." The polygonal facsimile of a human face mimicked speech. "I am Cobol."

The Alfur stopped shouting and crying. Their mouths hung open, and their eyes went wide. A few of them even ran out of the temple.

"Nice to meet you, Cobol. I'm Kensei."

"And I'm Adriana."

"I know," Cobol said. "I met you both at the treehouse when Jenny revealed me to you." The android looked at Mazu. "I have not met you, but you seem familiar."

"I'm Mazu. You may have known my...mother, Lin."

"Yes, I also met Lin at the treehouse."

"I'm Brock."

"And you already know me," Rygelus said.

"Ah yes, Rygelus. I am pleased to see you once again." Cobol turned to face Jack next.

"I'm Jack, and now that introductions are out of the way, I suggest we get out of here before the Alfur trap us, look." Jack pointed toward the exit.

They all turned toward the exit. Deedleoh rattled his staff and five Alfur guards, armed with their obsidian-tipped poison spears, moved to block the way. Another guard held Heather's arms behind his back. The witch doctor spoke excitedly.

"I don't want to hurt them," Jack said, "but I will if I have to."

"What's going on?" Jenny asked. "What's he saying?"

"Humans must leave." Heather struggled against the guard's grip. He looked up at the pictographs carved into the walls of the temple. "God must stay. God teach Alfur."

Cobol nodded at the witch doctor. Without turning, he spoke to Jenny and the others. "Go now. I will join you once you are free of the temple."

Jenny and the others nodded. The Alfur guards allowed them to leave the temple without incident. Each step they took through the water stirred up some bioluminescent algae.

"What do we do about Cobol?" Kensei asked. "Don't we need him to unlock the Terminal?"

"We have to trust that he knows what he's doing," Jenny said.

"And what about Heather?" Adriana asked.

"It's not like we can take him to outer space," Jack said. "Unless he has his own spacesuit."

Once they were about halfway across the cavern, a ruckus sounded from the pyramid. Looking back, Jenny saw Cobol charging out of the temple. A second later, the five spear-wielding guards exploded from the exit and ran after him. The witch doctor emerged a moment later.

"Run!" Cobol yelled.

Water splashed underfoot as Jenny and the others raced across the cavern. They paused at the exit just long enough to retrieve their bags and weapons. The air whistled, and spears cracked against the wall. They ran up the tunnel, ducked under stalactites, dodged stalagmites, and scraped themselves on the coarse rock. After a few minutes, they came to a stop.

"It seems like they gave up," Brock said.

"Good," Jack panted. "I need a rest." He took a seat on a nearby pile of rocks. Above them, water trickled down the wall and joined up with a larger stream of water running down the side of the cave.

"But why?" Adriana looked at Cobol. "We stole their god."

"Don't worry," Kensei said. "I bet they'll be telling the story of his resurrection for generations."

"I do feel bad for Heather though," Jenny said.

"Yeah, poor Heather," Adriana said.

"Why, it's not his fault?" Kensei said. "They may even consider him a saint, or something."

"Yeah," Jenny said. "I guess you're right."

Mazu stepped up to Brock. "Do you have extra weapons? We may encounter Risi on our return to the Waypoint."

"You're in luck." Brock put a huge hand on Mazu's shoulder. "Kensei is our traveling armory."

"Here." Kensei slipped the backpack off his shoulder and handed it to Mazu. He stumbled and leaned against the stone wall for support.

"Thanks." Mazu easily lifted the heavy pack and sorted through the firearms. She pulled out a semiautomatic assault rifle and then handed the bag to Jack.

"Now," Cobol said. "Jenny and I must unlock the Terminal."

"We can't," Jenny said.

"Why not?"

"It's too late."

"Victus has another Riftkey," Kensei added, "and he's already on his way to unlock it."

"Does Victus know about your Riftkey?" Jack asked.

"No, do you think I would still have it if he did?"

"What's your point, Jack?" Mazu asked.

"My point is that a ship like the *Tamarack* needs a lot of supplies."

"So?" Adriana asked.

"So, Victus has the Riftkey and the Selkans."

"Thanks for the reminder," Jenny said.

"He believes that he's won," Jack continued. "He won't be in any hurry to leave the system. He'll take his time and allow the *Tamarack* resupply. He might even allow shore leave. Which means—"

Adriana clapped her hands. "We can get to the Terminal first!"

Jack nodded.

"How long will it take to get there?" Jenny asked.

"Well, it took six hours to walk here from the Waypoint," Kensei said. "And the flight from the *Endeavor* to Acacia City took three, not to mention the drive..."

"You forgot the most important detail," Adriana said. "The Terminal is in outer space."

"We can take my ship," Jack said.

"That's great," Kensei said. "Thanks, Jack."

Jenny the others stopped at the intersection in the cave.

Jack turned to the group and asked, "Now, which way do we go?"

Kensei pointed to the side passage. "That's the way we came in."

"And where does this path go?" Jack pointed further up their tunnel.

Kensei shrugged. "Heather said it was another way out of the cave."

"Watch out," Brock said. Something whistled through the air, and Brock yanked Jenny backward. An arrow the size of a javelin punched through his leg just above the knee. Brock dropped to the ground and rolled against the wall.

More large arrows buzzed out of the darkness and cracked against the rock. Jenny scrambled for cover. She drew her firearm with a trembling hand and took a deep breath as adrenaline coursed through her body.

Together, Rygelus and Adriana dragged Brock away from the side passage. The big man grabbed the arrow and snapped the thumb-thick shaft. Brock was about to pull out the head when Adriana put her hand over the wound.

"Leave it," Adriana said. "It may be preventing blood loss." She tore a strip of cloth from her shirt uniform and tied it around the wound. The makeshift bandage instantly turned red with blood. "You'll need to stay off your leg."

Brock grunted in reply.

A deep roar sounded from the side passage. With shaky hands, Jenny aimed the beam of her flashlight up the tunnel. Light glinted off the weapons and armor of a group of Risi. An arrow exploded against Cobol's chest as the android ran to meet the enemy. The glow from his veins lit the Risi's faces in cold blue light.

Cobol fought like someone who had missed out on a thousand years of brawling. One iron sword shattered against his shoulder. He punched another giant in the chest, knocking him backward. The android was much smaller than the Risi but proved to be equal in power. Yet there was only one of him, and more giants surged forward, pushing him back and running around him.

Jenny's ears rang as she, and everyone else fired at the incoming Risi. Her injured shoulder ached, but she pulled the trigger as fast as she could into the mass of giants. The air was filled with the sounds of gunfire and shouting. Her nose burned from acrid gun smoke. When her weapon clicked empty, Jenny picked up more ammo from a pile between her and Adriana and slammed the clip into place. She grew numb to the sound of gunfire as if she was acclimating to a hot bath. On the other side of the intersection, Jack, Mazu, and Kensei still defended their position. "Aren't you glad you came with us, Kensei?" Jenny called out.

"There's nowhere I'd rather be," he called back.

"Less talking." Rygelus dropped his gun and set an arrow to his bow. "More fighting." There was a twang, and an arrow sprouted from a giant's eye socket, causing it to trip and land face-first on a stalagmite.

Another giant fell and slid to a stop just centimeters away from Jenny's face. Its body twitched from the throes of a death spasm. Her gun clicked empty just as another Risi charged at her. She ejected the clip and clambered at her side for another one. She looked up just as the Risi swung a crude, hooked sword at her head. Jenny pushed backward and held up her arms to block the attack. At that instant, something released inside her mind. Her consciousness erupted from her body and entered the giant.

Images of hunting and fighting flashed like a movie in her mind, and to her surprise, impressions of family and love as well. *No, I can't get distracted by memories, as I did with Sadi; we're in a fight for our lives. It's them or us.*

Through force of will, Jenny conquered the Risi's mind and possessed its body. Her sense of taste and smell were heightened, which was more like a curse, as the giant suffered from severe body odor and halitosis. Jenny turned and charged toward the other giants. She swung her hooked sword downward. The blade sank deep into a giant's shoulder. The injured Risi looked shocked and betrayed. Jenny yanked her sword free and slashed again, driving the confused giant to the ground. She fought a wave of nausea from the gore of it and looked for her next opponent. The sight of two glowing eyes set in a face the color of asphalt froze her in place.

"I recognize you," Blunderbore's voice was like a landslide. "You are the same humans from the city we attacked." He stepped into the light. He wore only a loincloth, exposing a body that seemed sculpted from obsidian. The bright-orange mane of his hair ran from his head to his waist. Two daggers the size of rapiers hung from a leather belt. "Father didn't want you killed that time, but he is not here now."

"Not this guy again," Jack said.

"And you are without your weapon."

The remaining Risi stepped back as Blunderbore flourished his *flamberge*, a gigantic, wavy sword.

Cobol stepped up to Blunderbore. "I will not allow you to kill them."

"My first challenger." Blunderbore flexed and grinned. "You think you can stop *me*?" The cave quaked as he charged toward Cobol.

Jenny's skin quivered as Cobol hit the ground hard.

Blunderbore put a foot on the prone android and looked around the cave. "Who is next to die?"

Still in control of the other Risi, Jenny charged Blunderbore. She barely caught sight of the *flamberge* before she snapped back to her own body. She sat up and rubbed her neck. "That hurts."

Suddenly, Jenny felt light-headed, and her vision narrowed to a tunnel. "Not again." *It seems like the side-effect of my ability is passing out,*

Jenny thought. The last thing she saw before blacking out was Cobol twisting Blunderbore's foot, and the dark giant crashing to the ground.

~

Jenny woke in time to see Blunderbore throw Cobol into the wall. The android hit with a loud crack. Stone and dust rained down on his silver skin.

"Is that the best you have?" Blunderbore spun his flamberge around his dark body. "I hoped for better sport."

Brock pushed himself to his feet and limped forward. "I challenge you."

"Brock, *no*," Adriana said. "You need to stay off your leg."

But Brock ignored her and held his two-handed sword above his head. While he was a large man, at least two meters tall, he was dwarfed by Blunderbore, who was almost four meters in height. It was by skill alone that Brock held off the giant's attacks. Using his sword an extension of his arm, Brock's blade searched for a chink in the dark giant's defenses. Blunderbore swung his flamberge downward, but Brock parried the strike and countered with a pommel blow into the dark giant's groin.

Brock heaved his *Zweihänder* in an overhand attack. Blunderbore took the blow on his forearm. The blade failed to bit, and the giant counterattacked with a punch to Brock's injured leg. He roared in pain. Blunderbore followed up with a kick to Brock's broad chest. The man flew against the wall, hitting his head against the rock, and fell unconscious to the ground.

Adriana ran to Brock's aid, and Blunderbore pursued her. But, before the giant could strike, Adriana's eyes rolled back in her head and a portal opened in front of Blunderbore's face. The giant stopped in confusion. To his eyes, it seemed like Adriana and Brock had disappeared.

Seeing Blunderbore's confusion, Cobol charged and slammed into the giant's chest. The android wrapped his metal arms around the giant's wrists like a pair of handcuffs. Gunfire rang from Jack's side of the cave. Blunderbore's dark flesh rippled with each impact, but the rounds tinkled harmlessly to the ground, doing no harm to the giant.

Blunderbore laughed, even as he struggled against Cobol. "No weapon can harm me."

"No, but a key can," Jenny said as she ran toward the android. "Kensei, throw me at him."

"What?"

"Just do it," Jenny insisted as she gripped the handle behind Cobol's head and pulled the Riftkey free.

"I get it," Kensei said as he took hold of Jenny's uniform and tossed her up toward Blunderbore's head.

Time to end it, Cobol said.

As Jenny flew through the air, she activated the Riftkey. The glowing blue edges ignited with a loud crack as Jenny passed through the veil of Adriana's portal. As soon as she saw Blunderbore's yellow eyes, she slashed with the Riftkey. A gray mist erupted from the blade as it bit through the giant's neck. Jenny landed on the cave floor with a jolt and rolled to a stop.

The other Risi looked from the dead body of their champion to his head, which flashed orange and black as it rolled down the cave. One of the giants backed away. Soon, they had all turned and ran back toward the cave entrance.

"Let's get out of here," Jenny said as she returned the Riftkey to the virosuit, "before they change their minds."

"Good idea," Rygelus said as he tried to lift Brock off the floor.

"Let me carry him," Kensei said. He slipped his long arms under Brock's back and lifted the huge man onto his shoulder in one smooth movement.

As a group, they made their way up the tunnel. Jenny blinked against the brightness of daylight as she exited the cave. Below them, a crescent-shaped patch of trees surrounded the *Tricaster*, Rygelus's crashed spaceship. Beyond that, a field of mud bubbled with hot, sulfuric gases. Brock looked even paler in sunlight.

Mazu pulled out a medkit from Jenny's vest and tied a tourniquet around his leg to arrest the blood flow. "He needs medical attention right away."

"Then, let's go." Jenny started back toward the Waypoint.

"Not that way," Mazu said.

"Why not?" Jenny asked. "We could take him to Acacia City, right Kensei?"

"Yeah, I think I can carry him that far."

"No," Mazu said. "He won't make it unless we operate on him immediately. We need to get in there." Mazu pointed at the crashed ship, which, from this angle, appeared half-submerged in the rocky soil. Trees and undergrowth had long ago grown over the mound of dirt that was pushed up when the ship impacted.

Rygelus narrowed his eyes. "That spacecraft crashed thousands of years ago."

"Trust me."

Rygelus's face was etched with pain. Looking out toward the ship, the place of this daughter's death, he swallowed hard and gritted his teeth. "We will take him to the ship."

Jenny slowly picked her way down the rough surface of the ridge. Loose rock tumbled ahead of her as she struggled to stay upright. It must have been much worse for Kensei, who was single-handedly carrying Brock.

Once they all reached the caldera floor, Mazu led the way to the derelict spaceship.

"How do we get in?" Jenny asked as they reached the ship.

Mazu ran her hands across the smooth silver surface of the spacecraft.

"There should be a door right around here." Rygelus scraped moss away until the outline of a door became visible. He located a panel and pressed a silver button. "It won't open."

Kensei shifted Brock to his other shoulder.

Mazu pounded on the door.

"Adriana," Jenny said, "maybe you can unlock it."

"How?"

"You were the best at the electromagnetic maze; maybe you can see what's going on with the door."

Adriana looked at Brock and nodded. "I'll try."

Her eyes rolled back in her head, and two crystalline windows formed in the air. She pushed one of the portals into the wall, and a display of circuitry appeared on the other. It reminded Jenny of the third maze test, where they had to complete circuits to open the trapdoor. Adriana twisted and moved her portals inside the wall, and with a hiss, the door slid open.

"You know," Adriana said, "I could almost feel the circuits. I bet with more practice, I won't have to use portals to see them."

Without Cobol's glowing veins, it would have been pitch-black. Ceiling and wall panels were scattered on the floor, revealing the guts of the ship. Girders and supports were warped and broken. Walls were blackened by fire. It was cold inside the dormant spaceship, and the sweat on Jenny's uniform caused it to cling to her skin like cellophane.

"This way." Mazu led them down the curved hallway.

"How do you know where to go?" Jack asked.

Mazu looked at Brock and said, "We don't have much time."

They entered a circular room. Unlike the rest of the ship, the lights were on here, and everything appeared intact. It looked familiar. In fact, it was the same laboratory that Jenny had seen in her vision with Nimue. But it had changed since she'd last seen it. There were now two fluid-filled tanks, containing gigantic fetuses with asphalt-colored skin, and a third, smaller tank that contained a human-sized female fetus.

Mazu ran to a cabinet and pulled out medical supplies. She pointed at a stainless steel table. "Set him up there."

Kensei laid Brock down on the table before collapsing onto the floor. Rygelus squeezed Brock's huge hand and spoke reassuring words to his friend.

From the opposite side of the room, a voice spoke from behind a large black box. "Who's there?" Then, Lance peeked around the box. "Mazu. What are you doing here?"

"Saving this man's life," Mazu said as she gathered supplies into the crook of her arm.

"*It's Lance,*" Kensei said.

Adriana turned to Mazu, "Did you know that he was here?"

"Of course I did," Mazu said as she set the supplies onto a tray next to Brock. "And be glad I did."

After seeing Lance in this same room less than an hour ago, Jenny didn't feel surprised at all. So, she instead asked to assist Mazu in opening and arranging the medical tools and supplies. After Adriana and Kensei overcame their shock, they joined in.

Rygelus couldn't tear his gaze away from Brock's face. He didn't know anyone named Lance, nor did he care. "I knew this day would come"— Rygelus wrung his hands—"but I didn't expect it to come so soon."

"Don't start mourning yet." Mazu set additional supplies on Brock's broad chest and pointed at the blood-soaked pant leg. "Cut the clothing away from the wound."

Rygelus picked up a pair of shears and cut Brock's eviscerated clothing off. "Should we not remove this?" Rygelus touched the broken end of the arrow, which looked more like a broom handle sticking out of his leg.

"Not yet," Mazu said as she cleaned the wound. "I believe it may be blocking an artery."

"Rygelus." Lance approached and put his hand on Rygelus's shoulder. "It is good to see you again."

Finally, Rygelus looked away from Brock and at this man named Lance. His eyes widened for a moment before turning his gaze back on Brock. "I wish it were under better circumstances."

"He will live," Lance said. "Mazu is quite skilled."

After the wound had been cleaned, Mazu pushed a thick needle into Brock's arm and set up a drip line of plasma. While holding a bandage to the wound, she pulled the arrow free and mopped up the dark blood that oozed from the hole. She inspected the wound and announced, "The artery is intact. He should be fine, but he'll need to rest." Mazu picked up a curved needle and a spool of black thread and sutured the wound.

Lance looked around the group and his eyes landed on the android. "Cobol?"

"Yes, sir."

Lance studied the android and nodded in understanding. "I see that Lin had her own secrets."

"Sir?"

"What are you doing here, on our spaceship?" Rygelus asked Lance.

"Continuing our original mission," Lance said. "We were meant to produce an Æon, and train them to unlock the Terminal, so that is what I have been doing."

Jenny recalled Nimue's vision as she studied the embryonic tubes. "Were you trying to create life?"

"After being trapped in this realm for thousands of years, with no chance of escape, yes. Without all this," Lance waved at the embryonic tubes. "There would be no Lin, no VRGo program, no Mazu."

"What's he talking about?" Jack asked.

Mazu ignored them and continued suturing Brock's leg.

"Tell him, Mazu," Lance said.

Mazu sighed and faced them. "I'm a clone."

Lance shook his head. "You were born here, but you are not a clone. You are a genetically distinct engineered human."

"Whose genetic material did you use?" Rygelus asked.

"Bits of Nimue and Astrea," Lance said.

"You used my daughter's DNA without asking?"

"You abandoned our mission, so I did what I had to."

"You dug up her grave."

"You buried the Riftkey." Lance looked at Rygelus. "You abandoned the mission. After Astrea left, I believed that the Riftkey was gone forever, so I took her Waypoint key and left for Earth prime. I left to help all future Æons while you stayed here and sulked over your dead daughter."

"Did you create Blunderbore too?" Jenny asked.

"Yes, along with Lin."

"Why?" Adriana asked.

"I couldn't count on discovering another Astrea, not by mere chance," Lance said. "I needed Blunderbore to control the Risi, and I needed Lin to help me find another Æon."

Just then, Jenny recognized what the large black box was that Lance had been working on when they came in. She pointed at the device and asked, "Is that Kett'l's forge?"

Kensei looked where Jenny was pointing. "It is." He looked at Lance. "Did you steal it?"

At that moment, all the dots connected in Jenny's mind. "You used Blunderbore to steal the Waypoint from the Department of Transportation, and you took it to the *Endeavor*. Then, when Tyr attacked, you stole Kett'l's forge and brought it here."

"That means that you have a Waypoint here that leads back to the *Endeavor*," Kensei said.

"Yes." Lance pointed at the backroom through an open door. "A government like Tyr—who could enslave the Selkans—could not be allowed to have the forge. After Mister Torres revealed himself as a mole, I invented a plan to bring the forge here, and when a suspicious ship entered through the Terminal, I knew it was time to take the Waypoint."

"You could have asked Kett'l," Jenny said. "He would have understood."

"I could not allow Kett'l to know the location of the forge, for his own safety."

"Believe him," Jack said. "I know firsthand how Victus can retrieve information."

"You're the one who brought him here," Jenny said.

"Do not blame Mister Spriggan," Lance said. "He is more innocent in all this than you know."

"Did you kill Trey?" Adriana asked.

"I needed to find out exactly when Tyr would arrive, so I invited Trey to meet me in the forest. I planned to interrogate him, but Blunderbore jogged his memory a little too hard..."

"All this time"—Jenny shook her head—"Sadi has been taking her hostility out on me when it should have been you."

"Miss Stevens has suspected me ever since I picked Mister Ward and her up the night of the raid. When she asked about the cargo, I told her that it was a new water pump for the *Endeavor*, but as you know, it was actually the Waypoint. I knew that she did not entirely believe me, but I could not reveal my plan to her."

"You are just as bad as them." Adriana glared at Lance. "You killed Trey, unleashed those monsters in Acacia City, and now you've turned your back on the Selkans. All for what, a big black box?"

"A box that made your keys." Lance placed his hands on top of the forge and stared into its depths. "I do not expect you to understand the significance of such an invention. You could not know what lengths I would have gone to obtain this. That I have been trying and failing to reproduce this technology for thousands of years."

"I know," Jenny said as she recalled her vision with Nimue. "And you should also know that the forge won't work for you," Jenny said. "Kett'l was an Æon. The forge only enhanced his ability to craft nexum, much like the keys enhance our individual abilities."

"Yeah," Kensei said. "He's like a quantum mechanic or something."

Lance dropped onto the stool and ran a six-fingered hand through his hair. "That explains much. The lack of visible controls had me perplexed. After all this time"—he shook his head—"I am back to nothing."

"No, not nothing," Adriana said. "We could still save the Selkans."

"How, Miss Thatcher?" Lance asked. "If you are here, that means Tyr has the Riftkey and the Selkans. Or am I wrong?"

"You're not wrong," Adriana said weakly, "but there must be something you can do."

"Yeah," Kensei spoke up. "If you save Kett'l than he can operate the forge. Plus, he built it, so imagine what else he could create in his lifetime."

"You make a good point." Lance smiled and stood up from the stool. "We must get Jenny to the Terminal. Follow me." Lance walked between two worktables and put his hand on the doorway. "This Waypoint will take us to the *Endeavor*."

"From there," Jack said. "We can fly up to my ship and beat Victus to the Terminal."

"What if the *Tamarack* follows us to the Terminal?" Kensei asked.

"I have a fleet near Mars that can defend you," Lance said.

"You have a fleet?" Jack asked.

Lance shrugged. "You never know what's going to come through the Terminal."

Jenny and the others nodded in approval. It was a plan.

Over on the table, Brock groaned and stirred. "Rye," he called out, half-delirious from the pain medication. "Where are we?"

"I am here," Rygelus said. "We are safe."

"Rygelus, will you be joining us?" Lance asked.

"No." Rygelus looked into Brock's face. "I will not abandon my friend."

Lance nodded. "How about you, Mazu?"

"I have a patient to attend to, and the next few hours are critical to his survival," Mazu said. "Go, save the Selkans."

"I..." Jack crossed the room and grabbed Mazu's hand. "I just wanted to say goodbye, in case I don't make it back."

Mazu wouldn't make eye contact with him, but she didn't try to pull away. "Don't even consider the possibility."

Jack swallowed past a lump in his throat. "Look." He took Mazu by the shoulders, forcing her to look at him. "I never wanted to work for Victus. He tricked me. I know that what I did was wrong. But I'll do everything in my power to make it right."

"I know." Mazu nodded and put her hand on his stubbly face. "Just get Jenny to the Terminal."

"I will." Jack clenched his teeth. "If it's the last thing I do."

Jack turned and joined the others as they entered the Waypoint room. Lance looked back at Rygelus one last time before he followed them inside. The five of them slid into the obsidian bowl of the Waypoint, then Lance inserted his key.

36

GRAVITY WELL

Traveling through a Waypoint, on an ancient starship, with an android was a new memory for Jack to add to a rapidly growing list of new experiences. And, to say that he had experienced more in the last three days, than his previous thirty-three years of life, was significant for a veteran of a galactic war.

Jack, and the others, now stood in a dark room that was just large enough to hold the Waypoint. Color-coded pipes and conduits ran in parallel lines across the walls and ceiling. The chill air carried the scent of industrial lubricants, which reminded Jack of his workshop back home.

"Where are we?" Jenny asked.

"The engineering level of the *Endeavor*," Lance said.

Jack wasn't surprised that Lance, a Tyran, had engineered the attack on Acacia City. After all, they were known across the galaxy for their plotting and scheming. It was how they held the highest positions of power in each system.

There was an audible splash as Jenny stepped out of the Waypoint.

"Was that water, Miss Tripper?" Lance asked.

"Yeah, it's rising up through the floor."

"That means they scuttled my ship," Lance said.

Jack eased himself out of the Waypoint. The water came up to his ankles, but the bodysuit he donned for Mazu's expedition kept it from reaching his skin.

"We've got to get out of here," Kensei said as he rushed for the exit.

"Wait." Jack grabbed his arm. "There might be soldiers out there."

"I can find out." Adriana's eyes rolled back in her head.

Suddenly, two windows crystallized in midair. One moved through the door while the other displayed dark hallways lit with red emergency lights. Murky water covered the floor. Adriana ran through the maze of corridors and up to the next level. The sickbay was empty but showed signs of recent use. Blood-soaked bandages and first-aid supplies littered every surface.

Adriana's portal moved to the next floor and into the mess hall. It showed tables with abandoned trays of food but no signs of life. Jack's stomach growled at the sight of food. The Alfur didn't starve Mazu and him, but a diet of insects didn't fill his needs. Mazu, however, had eaten everything they provided and claimed that the insects were an excellent source of protein.

The water now reached his calves, Jack noted.

Adriana's portal now showed the gym. There was a sign of battle here. Pools of blood had dried on the shiny wooden floor. Adriana entered the control center next. Broken glass and electronics littered the floor, but there were still no signs of life.

The water was now up to Jack's knees.

Adriana's portal climbed up the stairwell and out into the sky. Jack had to shade his eyes from the sudden blast of sunlight. He squinted against the light and saw two large and dark spaceplanes parked on the gray platform. One belonged to Tyr, and the other was Jack's plane, the *Pepper*. There was also the first signs of life. Three Tyran soldiers in black uniforms and a red marine in a hypersuit walked among the planes. In the background, two black ships hovered in midair over the Selkans' islands.

Suddenly, one of the hovering Tyran ships fired a volley of plasmablasts at an island. A geyser of dirt and water flew into the air, and mud swirled on the ocean's surface. The room plunged into darkness. Adriana leaned back and rubbed her eyes.

"The *Endeavor* is all clear," Jenny said. "We should go."

"Agreed, Miss Tripper," Lance said.

The ship groaned and tilted under the weight of the rising seawater. Jack caught himself against the wall as the sea level reached his groin. He pushed off the wall and leaned to one side as he followed Lance. By the time they reached the stairs, the water was up to his waist. He ran up the stairs and leaned against the wall to catch his breath.

"It's dry up here," Kensei said.

"For now," Jenny added.

"I just remembered something," Jack said. "Every ship that travels through the Terminal needs a negative-energy buffer."

"What does that do?" Kensei asked.

"It keeps your ship from disintegrating when the Terminal activates."

"I knew of the buffer," Lance said, "but no ship in my fleet is equipped with one. I will try to contact them from the control room and warn them."

Just then, Jack remembered his Jacket and watch in the moon pool room. "Go on ahead," Jack said as he ran off toward the moon pool. "I'll catch up with you."

Inside, Jack spotted his bundle of clothing floating near the door. He gripped the doorway and leaned into the water. He was able to pull his jacket from the bundle, but his boots were gone. He pulled his watch from his jacket pocket and hurried to join his comrades.

Water burbled out of the lower level and chased Jack all the way to the residential level. The smell of mess hall food lingered in the air. Just a couple of days ago, this space had been so full of life. Now, the corridors were dark and dank.

Jack ran up the next stairwell to the control room. Kensei and Lance searched through a pile of broken electronics. Jenny, Adriana, and the android tried the workstations.

"That's what you went back for?" Jenny pointed at the leather jacket.

"And this." Jack showed her his watch and then strapped it on. "Is anything here functional?" he asked, gesturing to the electronics.

"No," Lance said.

"You can use the subspace radio on the *Pepper* to contact your fleet."

"We will have to." Lance dropped a large black box and stood up.

"Fine, let's get out of here before we all drown." Jenny pointed at a trickle of water that had snaked its way into the room.

The group passed through the escape-pod room, up the stairwell, and paused at the door to the platform.

"Miss Thatcher, will you please peek through the door again?" Lance asked.

"Sure." Adriana's eyes rolled back in her head. Two more portals appeared in front of her, and one flew through the metal door. The stairwell lit up as daylight poured in through the display.

Two Tyran soldiers and the red marine patrolled the area.

"So, how do we get past them to your plane?" Jenny asked.

"We have to kill or distract those Tyran soldiers."

"You have weapons." Lance looked at Jenny, Adriana, and Kensei, who each still had handguns strapped to their belts. "Can you do it?"

"No good." Kensei shook his head. "We used all our ammo fighting the Risi."

"I have a gun hidden under a floor panel on my plane. If I can sneak on board…" Jack said.

"I will be your weapon," Cobol said. "I am indestructible, after all."

"Can you handle the soldiers long enough for Jack to get to his plane?" Lance asked.

Cobol peered through the portal. "Yes."

There was a tremendous groan, and the stairwell jumped. Water roared below them.

Adriana gasped. "We forgot to shut the airlock."

"Hurry." Kensei looked over the rail at the rising water.

Jenny stood closest to the exit as Cobol opened the door.

"Wait," Kensei said. "Weren't there four soldiers earlier?"

But Kensei's warning came too late. As the door swung fully open, Jack saw a Tyran soldier waiting on the other side. The soldier aimed his pistol carbine into the stairwell and fired. The sound was deafening as bullets ricocheted off Cobol's head and shoulders, protecting those in his shadow. Jenny twisted out of the way and took cover behind the open door. Jack dropped onto the steps as rounds pinged against the wall.

Cobol charged the Tyran soldier like a silver missile. The man grunted as he hit the bridge, and his carbine flew from his hands. Cobol headbutted the man, shattering his nose in a spray of blood. Then, the android stood and lifted the man over his head. The soldier managed a short yell before hitting the water with a splash.

"Was anybody hit?" Adriana asked.

"No," Kensei said.

"We are all okay, Miss Thatcher," Lance said.

"Thank goodness," Adriana said. "Jenny?"

"I'm fine." Jenny emerged from behind the door. "Just a little shaken."

Outside, bullets pinged off of Cobol as he charged the next two soldiers. The android sent one flying off the edge of the platform. Without slowing, he picked up the next soldier, spun him once, and sent him tumbling into the sea.

There was an air-splitting boom, and another Selkan home turned to rubble.

"I think I can get to the *Pepper* now." Jack stepped out of the stairwell.

"No," Lance said.

"No?"

"They'll be expecting that."

"What, then?"

"I will take your spaceplane," Lance said, "and draw the enemy away from here. Then, you can steal their plane and sneak past the *Tamarack's* defenses."

A smile spread across Jack's face. "I like the way you think."

"Once I'm clear," Lance continued. "I'll radio to my fleet and have them meet you at the Terminal."

Jenny smiled, "I'm ready, let's do this."

Outside, Cobol charged the marine in the hypersuit. The soldier aimed his arm cannon and fired at Cobol. But, the android barely slowed as he rammed the armored soldier in the gut. The red marine stumbled backward, almost falling over. The android wedged his fingers into the clamshell cockpit of the hypersuit. With a loud crunch, the cockpit shell flew off and landed on the platform with a dull thud. Cobol plucked the squishy meat from its casing and tossed the shocked marine off the platform.

With all of Tyr's soldiers defeated, Jack and the others rushed out of the stairwell. Kensei stopped and picked up the marine's discarded pistol carbine. Lance ran toward the *Pepper*, and Jack jogged up to the Tyran spaceplane.

A man and woman in the dark-gray uniforms of Tyran officers occupied the Tyran spaceplane's cockpit. The pilot, a woman, had short black hair and a wine-stain birthmark that covered half of her face. Jack was awestruck. Where he was from, natural peculiarities like this were a sign of beauty.

The copilot leaned forward and shouted into the communicator: "*Tamarack*. This is Skalla Four-Twenty-Three. Hostiles are attacking." The pilot pressed a series of buttons, and the spaceplane's engines roared to life.

Cobol ran up to the cockpit and dragged the pilot and copilot out of their seats. Kensei aimed his confiscated pistol carbine at them. They looked frightened and kept glancing at Cobol.

These aren't hardened soldiers, Jack thought. *It's likely the first time they've ever had a gun pointed at them.* Jack felt a little sorry for them.

From the cockpit, a female voice spoke over the communicator: "Skalla Four-Twenty-Three, repeat. Did you say 'hostiles'?"

"What do we do with them?" Adriana asked Jenny.

"We should tie them up." Jenny looked around the spaceplane for something to use.

"First"—Jack pointed into the cockpit—"we've got to respond to that call."

"Then go." Jenny found a set of restraints, which were likely for restraining the Selkans, in the cargo hold.

"I'd wager that there's a camera too," Jack said.

"Should we go back to your plane?" Kensei asked.

Outside, the *Pepper* roared to life and lifted off the platform. Within moments, the two Tyran spaceships—which had been blasting the Selkans' islands—turned and gave chase.

"Too late," Adriana said.

How did I end up as the only adult here? Jack thought. "There's got to be something we can do. Wait, Jenny, I saw you possess that giant in the cave." *The same ability Victus used to trick me.* "You can save us."

"What?" Jenny looked down at her boots. "No. I don't..." Jenny threw the restraints to Jack.

Jack caught the plastic straps and secured them around the copilot's wrists. "If we don't answer them"—Jack pointed at the cockpit—"then there's no chance we'll save the Selkans."

The female voice repeated from the cockpit. "Skalla Four-Twenty-Three, answer or we will assume that hostiles have compromised your position."

"You have the power to control people." Jack cinched the copilot's legs to the seat.

Jenny looked away and then back at him. "So what?"

"You need to possess her." He nodded at the pilot. "Then you can tell the *Tamarack* that everything's fine."

"It's a good idea," Kensei offered.

Jenny glared at Kensei and looked to Adriana.

"I don't see any other option." Adriana shrugged.

"Fine." Jenny sat down and concentrated. "Hey, I think I'm getting the hang of this."

The pilot smiled and looked at Adriana. "Hi, Adriana."

"Jenny?"

The pilot nodded. "It's me, your half-sister."

"Yup," Jenny said. "She's me. I know, it's all very complicated."

"You're possessing her, and you're still in control of your body?" Adriana asked.

"Yeah, I know, it's crazy," Jenny said.

"Can you lower that gun, Kensei?" the pilot asked.

Kensei looked back and forth between the pilot and Jenny, then lowered the gun. "I don't think I'll ever get used to that."

As Kensei lowered the gun, the pilot rushed into the cockpit and activated the comm. "This is Lieutenant Sona Jackson. ID Six-Thirty-Three-Seventy-Eight."

Jack's heart drummed in his chest as a video screen activated. He pulled Kensei out of view of the cockpit and sat down next to the copilot.

"You made a big mistake." The copilot said in a deep voice with a distinctive drawl.

"Can you shut him up?" Jack asked.

"Yeah." Kensei grinned. "I have an idea." The lean, dark-skinned boy pinched the man's shoulder near the neck. Within a few seconds, the blood drained from the copilot's face and his head lolled to the side. Kensei leaned back and smiled. "I've always wanted to do that."

"What did you do?"

"The Vulcan neck pinch."

Jack looked at him blankly.

Kensei sighed. "I just increased the gravity he experienced and starved his brain of oxygen." His head lolled. "Whoa, here comes the dizzy spell."

"You induced g-LOC." Jack smiled at Kensei. "Nice one."

From the cockpit, a woman's voice spoke over the comm. "Sona, what's going on down there?"

"An unknown group of hostiles appeared on the platform." Sona looked back into the passenger area. "We attempted to assist, but they overpowered our guards and escaped in the smuggler's spaceplane."

"They overpowered the red marines?" the voice said.

"Just one," Sona said.

"Where's your copilot?"

"He was injured, I treated him, and he's resting in the passenger cabin."

"Well, I'm glad you're safe."

"Same here. I've got supplies to deliver, and I need a flight plan."

There was a long pause, and Jack exchanged nervous glances with Adriana and Kensei.

"Granted. And, Sona?"

"Yes?"

"Will you bake some of your special brownies when you get back?"

"Sure thing, Ruth." Sona laughed, a throaty trill that sounded foreign given the situation.

"Proceed to hangar eleven."

There was a beep from the console. "Thanks, Ruth. Sona out." She sighed and shut off the communicator.

Shortly after the video disappeared, Jack dropped into the copilot's seat. "Nice work, Jenny. That's a useful ability." *When it's not being used against me.* Jack thought as he looked over the flight plan sent from the *Tamarack*.

"Thanks," Jenny said.

Jack checked the instruments and finished the preflight routine. "Special brownies, huh?"

"I'm apparently a good baker no matter whose body I'm in."

Jack finished the check. "It all looks good. I doubt they suspect a thing."

Jenny, still in Sona's body, left the cockpit and sat next to the unconscious copilot. She picked up the plastic restraints and fastened herself to the seat before releasing the pilot.

"Hey," Kensei said, "You didn't pass out this time."

"You're right," Jenny said, "and you didn't get super dizzy."

"I guess we're both getting better."

Jenny's stomach growled. "Oh man, I'm so hungry. I think I still have some dried fruit in here." She rummaged in the burstepi until she found the dried fruit. While eating, she thought back to her vision of Nimue. *Did she really possess the virosuit?* she asked Cobol.

She really did, Cobol answered.

The engines roared. Jack pulled back on the stick, and the spaceplane rose into the air. They hovered over the turquoise waves for a moment. The nose inclined, and they rose up to the thin white clouds.

Kensei watched out the window. "Where are we going?"

"North," Jack said, "to the orbital launch system."

"Why don't we just head straight toward your ship?" Kensei asked.

"This plane doesn't have the power or fuel to escape Earth's gravity well."

"Kensei," Jenny said, "I bet if you made the ship lighter we could go straight to Jack's ship."

"No way, it's not a backpack—this is like a thousand times heavier."

"I'm sure you can do it."

"Fine, I'll try." He unbuckled himself from the seat and knelt down. The air seemed to bend around him like a magnifying lens. He gasped and collapsed to the floor. "I can't, it's too big."

"It's just a matter of perspective." Jenny unbuckled her harness and held his shoulder. "I know you can do it."

Kensei placed his hands on the floor. This time, the bubble grew until it surrounded the spaceplane, and their speed doubled.

"Wow, kid." Jack's ears popped as the cabin pressure equalized. "How long can you keep this up?"

"As long as you need." Kensei smiled.

"Then I'm altering course." Jack pressed a series of buttons. "Next stop, the *Celestial Strider*."

Jenny walked up to the cockpit. "So, what makes this ship of yours so special?"

"It's an elite military vehicle built during a time of peak conflict in the galaxy," Jack said.

"When was that?"

"About nine years ago."

"So, it's old?" Jenny teased.

Jack leaned on his elbow and narrowed his eyes at Jenny. "No military ships have been built for seven years. Plus, I've been maintaining and upgrading her all that time."

"Sounds like you've just been keeping her running."

"No, she's the pinnacle of military design and technology."

"Nine years ago."

"There's been nothing like her before or since."

"Well, I hope you're right." Jenny turned and walked back to the passenger cabin.

Outside, the sky transitioned from blue to black. Jack leveled the ship and entered a lower orbit to intercept the *Strider*. There was a commotion in the passenger cabin. Jack looked back to see the kids laughing as they spun in midair. He smiled. They deserved to have some fun.

37

CELESTIAL STRIDER

Jenny raised her hands to keep from hitting the ceiling as she floated weightless in the stolen Tyran spaceplane. Adriana and Kensei followed her lead and unbuckled their harnesses. Soon the three of them were laughing as they tumbled through the air, bumping into one another. After a few minutes of floating in zero gravity, Jenny grabbed on to a safety bar to rest. She looked out the window. It was black and littered with stars, but one star glowed brighter than all the others.

"Hey Jack, what is that?" Jenny asked.

Jack unbuckled from his harness and flipped backward out of his seat. He redirected himself around Kensei and Adriana to land gracefully next to Jenny. He peered out the window. "Oh, that's the *Tamarack*, Tyr's warship."

Kensei joined them at the window, which was getting crowded. "It must be huge."

"She's got a crew of over ninety-six thousand," Jack said, "and enough firepower to subdue an entire planet."

"Oh, is that all?" Adriana said.

"No," Jack answered honestly. "She's also carrying a squadron of capital ships and hundreds of fighters."

"Is that's why she's so dangerous," Kensei said.

"Not entirely; she can also teleport."

"Is that what they are using the Selkans for?" Cobol asked.

Jack nodded.

"Do you think they know we're here?" Kensei asked.

"I doubt it," Jack said. "At least not until this spaceplane fails to arrive. Still, that gives us some time to prep the *Strider* before we launch for the Terminal."

Suddenly, red lights flashed around the cabin. Something inside the cockpit beeped.

"What is that?" Jenny asked.

"We're approaching the *Strider*. I have to turn the spaceplane around to decelerate." Jack flipped, pushed off the wall, and floated back to the pilot's seat.

"Why do we have to turn around?" Adriana asked.

"There is no friction in space," Cobol said. "So, the only way to decrease velocity is by accelerating in the opposite direction."

"Ah, that makes sense."

"Sit down and buckle up," Jack said. "We're coming in hot."

Jenny fastened her seat restraints just as the spaceplane spun around. As they turned, a strange-looking ship came into view. It was white and black, with two arms running in parallel to its fuselage. *It kind of looks like a sleeping swan*, Jenny thought.

"I thought you said your ship was a fighter." Kensei peered through the window.

"Yeah," Jack said. "What of it?"

"It looks so new."

"Of course." Jack looked at them, confused. "She has a self-healing hull. She'd be a mess of dents and holes otherwise."

"Is that a body?" Jenny pointed at an object floating a hundred meters from the rear of the *Strider*.

Jack initiated the auto docking program and drifted out of the cockpit. He peered out the window and sighed. "That's Hocco, an old friend of mine. Victus possessed him and tricked me into coming here."

"I'm sorry," Jenny said.

"It's okay," Jack said. "We weren't that close."

"Still," Adriana said. "It's a terrible thing to do to anyone."

Jenny sat lower in her seat. It wasn't so long ago that she did something similar to Sadi. *Am I any better than Victus? What if he started out just like me?*

"Victus leaves a trail of death everywhere he goes," Kensei said. "We have to stop him."

"We will," Jenny said, then pointed at the pilot, Sona, and her unconscious copilot. "But first, what do we do with them?"

"We'll leave them in orbit here," Jack said. "And we'll come back for them after we've unlocked the Terminal."

After the spaceplane had docked to the *Strider,* Jenny and the others passed through its airlock into Jack's ship. Overhead, a spinning light changed from red to amber, then green, giving hued glimpses of the *Strider's* industrial interior.

Jack swung the hatch open and inhaled deeply. "Ah, it smells like home."

To Jenny, it smelled of grease and burned metal. Pipes and electrical wires ran along almost every surface. Several crates were locked magnetically to the walls. "Your home looks like a storage container."

"It's the cargo bay," Jack said. "What did you expect?"

"A state-of-the-art military vessel," Jenny said.

"Well, next time we can take your spaceship."

Once everyone was clear of the airlock, Jack closed the hatch and set Tyr's spaceplane loose. He ushered them into the next room, where eight blue lockers lined the walls along with eight black spacesuits.

"If you're going to fly in my ship, you've got to wear a pressure suit." Jack opened three lockers and handed a bundle to everyone but Cobol. "Put these on first."

Inside each bundle was a skintight dark-gray bodysuit. Jenny and Adriana went to the airlock to change while Kensei and Jack stayed in the locker room. The zero gravity made things difficult, but working together, Jenny and Adriana managed to get their bodysuits on. Jenny pulled the hood over her spiky black hair, leaving only a small opening from the top of her eyes to her bottom lip. Something rigid lined the fabric along her jaw. Adriana tied her blond hair into a bun and pulled on her hood. With their bodysuits on, Jenny and Adriana joined Jack and Kensei.

Jack took a black spacesuit off the wall and gave them a brief tutorial on its use. The rigid lining along the jaw was for communication by bone conduction. Jack said it could pick up a whisper underwater. "Jenny, since you're going to be out there walking along the Terminal, let me show you how to control the magnetic strength of your boots."

After Jack taught her the magnetic-boot-strength controls, Jenny and the others each floated into one of the stiff, armored spacesuits. Then, they spent a couple of minutes practicing what they'd learned. Thanks to the ADD, they were all quick learners.

"Now that you have your suits on," Jack said, "I'll need each of you in a gun pod."

"Gun pod?" Adriana asked.

"There are couches in the pods that will cushion your soft, squishy bodies under high acceleration," Jack said.

With the spacesuit tutorial over, Jack led them out of the locker room and into the hub of the ship. "This is where the arms attach to the fuse-lage. From here, you can go that way up to the cockpit"—Jack pointed as he talked—"or back to the engines. Two of you will go into the starboard arm, and the other two into the port-arm." Jack pointed to his left and right, at hatches set into the wall.

Jenny was first into the hub, followed closely by Cobol.

"The ship looked bigger from the outside," Jenny said.

"She's not as cozy as the *Endeavor*." Jack pounded on a wall, which sent him flying off in the opposite direction. "But in a battle, you're gonna appreciate the two meters of armor, shield, and active defense system a lot more."

Jack opened a hatch and backed away. "Jenny and Cobol, you take the starboard arm."

Jenny held on to the hatch and stuck her head inside. Her breath came out in white puffs. "It's cold."

"It won't be after I store the air."

"'Store the air'?" Jenny asked.

"In case we get hit," Jack said. "Don't worry. You'll be safe in your pods."

"Okay." Jenny crawled into the tunnel. "If you say so."

Cobol followed behind her, and Jack closed the hatch behind them.

Jenny struggled with the basic task of pulling herself through the corridor. It was tight, and zero gravity made it difficult to grasp each rung. She quickly reached the end of the arm joint, and the path branched left and right into the arm itself. Jenny went left and floated down a longer corridor until she reached another hatch.

The lights turned on as Jenny entered the gun pod. She closed the hatch door and locked it with the spin of a wheel. The pod was small, about two meters in diameter. Large yellow warning labels depicted stick figures suffering a range of maladies from asphyxiation to explosive decompression. *How comforting*, Jenny thought. "I thought Jack said we'd be safe here," she said out loud.

"Better than floating in space," Jack answered over the comm.

Jenny flinched. *I'll have to be more careful with what I say. There are probably cameras in here too.* She stuck out her tongue just in case.

The crash couch, which looked like a futuristic dentist's chair, occupied most of the pod. Stubby joysticks and controls were built into the arms. Jenny sat down and grabbed one of the joysticks on the arm of the chair. Suddenly, the walls of the pod seemed to disappear. To her left, she could see the fuselage of the *Strider*. In front of her, twin gun barrels pointed out to open space. A green target reticle appeared between the gun barrels. Three blue reticles, numbered "one," "two" and "four," came into view along with a top-down diagram of the *Strider*.

"Whoa," Kensei said through his comm. "I feel like Luke Skywalker in the *Millennium Falcon*."

Jenny was just getting comfortable when she heard a whirring sound, and her pod rose above the fuselage of the *Strider*. *The arm is rotating*, Jenny realized. When it came to a stop, it was perpendicular to the main part of the ship. Jenny could now see the ship's port-side arm. She waved and said, "Hi."

"I see you," Adriana said over her comm.

Jenny smiled at hearing her sister's voice. She experimented with the control until she figured out how to select objects on her display. She chose the blue reticle labeled with a one, and a camera view of Adriana appeared in the bottom right corner.

"I see you too."

A loud crunch followed by the sound of chewing played inside the hood of her bodysuit.

"Which one of you is eating?" Jack asked.

"I am," Kensei said. "I found some chips in here."

"You should know, those are probably a few years old."

"Gross," Adriana said.

"They're good," Kensei said. "Vacuum packed."

"Enough chatter," Jack said. "All doors are locked and sealed. Close your helmets and connect the umbilical under your seat to your chest valve."

Jenny pulled her helmet down and twisted it until it clicked. There was a whooshing sound, and Jenny breathed in the stale air of the suit. She felt around under her seat and found the umbilical. She lifted a hatch on her chest plate and attached the nozzle. Immediately, the couch latched onto her spacesuit from her shoulders to her feet and pulled her into its embrace.

"I see positive connections from each of the human passengers." Jack paused. "Evacuating the air now."

A pump hummed from somewhere in Jenny's pod. It quickly grew quieter inside the pod until it was utterly silent. Not like the quiet of a bedroom at night, but the complete absence of sound.

"You all ready?" Jack asked.

Jenny jumped at the sound of Jack's voice. Her heart raced, and her body vibrated with anticipation. "Ready."

One by one, each of the other passengers said, "Ready."

"Suit pressurization in three, two, one..."

Jenny gasped as fluid flowed through the umbilical and into her suit. The bodysuit created a watertight layer, keeping the liquid from her skin. But the warmth spreading down her legs felt like peeing herself.

"Something's wrong," Kensei said.

"Yeah," Adriana said. "Something's flowing into my suit."

"Calm down," Jack said. "That's your oxygen supply."

"What?" Jenny said. "It's liquid. Aren't we going to drown?"

"No, you won't," Jack assured her. "I know it's strange at first, but I promise you can breathe it."

"I've seen plenty of space movies," Kensei said, "and this isn't in any of them."

"Why do we need to breathe liquid?" Jenny asked.

"To prevent your bodies from being crushed when we accelerate to fifty Gs."

Kensei made a choking sound. "Fifty Gs?"

"Okay, I get it," Adriana said. "Still, a little warning would have been nice."

"Sorry," Jack said. "I just forgot that you guys have never flown in a spaceship before."

Jenny tried to imagine she was in a warm bath. But once the liquid reached her neck, the illusion faltered, and she panicked. She took one last gulp of air as the clear fluid covered her cheeks.

"Let it in," Jack said. "With the CO_2 scrubbers, you can breathe normally, and we can't go anywhere until you're acclimated."

Jenny opened her eyes, and to her surprise, she could see clearly through the watery fluid. It was slightly salty and effervescent. Then she gagged. She needed to breathe, but her mind wouldn't let her breathe from her mouth. The fear of drowning was too ingrained, too primal. Her lungs began to burn. *If my mouth doesn't work, then I'll try my nose.* At first, it felt like rinsing out her nose with a neti pot. The fluid filled her nasal passage, then flowed down the back of her throat. She kept inhaling until the fluid entered her lungs. She fought against her instincts as she coughed, letting the air out in a bubbling rush. She gulped a breath in, expecting to choke, but sucking more liquid into her lungs. Then she was breathing the liquid in and out. Jenny sighed. *It worked.*

Jack always hated breathing in the fluid, but he at least had years of training on his side. As he gulped the liquid into his lungs, his brain only protested briefly before he was breathing in and out as usual. *They're just kids. Younger than I was when I first enlisted,* he thought. The console beeped. It was a message from the *Tamarack*. *Precisely on time*, he thought as he pressed the play button.

"To the pilot of the *Celestial Strider*. Please proceed to the *Tamarack*, hangar five. You have two minutes to comply before we open fire."

Jack zoomed in on the *Tamarack* and noted the hundreds of torpedo holes, cannon blisters, and launch tubes that marked the hull of the Defender. He checked the status of his passengers. Two of them still hadn't acclimated to the fluid. After two minutes, the console beeped three times, and a red light lit up. The *Tamarack* had them on target lock. *Time's up.*

Lasers fired from the *Tamarack* only to be reflected tangentially back out to space by the *Strider's* shield. Muzzle flashes lit along the *Tamarack's* flank as it fired guns and torpedoes. Impacts lit up the *Strider* as the energy dispersed in a blue glow. The cross-section diagram of the *Strider* flashed and displayed damage to the aft section.

"Is someone shooting at us?" Jenny asked.

"The *Tamarack*," Jack said.

"Isn't that bad?" Kensei asked.

"Yes, but we're out of range of her primary weapon."

"What weapon?" Kensei asked.

"The nuclear lance."

"The nuclear what?" Adriana asked from her picture in the bottom right of Jenny's display.

"It's a focused atomic explosion that can punch through any armor with a massive particle beam. Fortunately for us, it's not effective at this distance."

"That's good," Kensei said.

"I hope you're all ready." Jack's voice sounded muffled and distant through the fluid, but the communicators built into their bodysuits were able to transmit and receive sound through bone conduction, even while submerged in breathable fluid. "We're burning, in twelve, eleven..."

A woman's voice picked up the countdown from ten. When it reached three, Jack said. "Engaging thrusters...now." *I'm going to be sore tomorrow.* Jack clenched his body as the thrusters ignited. He grunted as the seat slammed into his back, and every vertebra realigned. *I'm not as young as I used to be.*

~

Flashes of blue lit up outside, and the ship rumbled. Jenny's spacesuit became rigid as the *Strider* jumped into motion like a bullet from a rifle. The remaining air squeezed out of her lungs, and it felt like a million needles stabbed her body. Sudden changes in acceleration, like what the *Strider* had just initiated, were more common in head-on collisions. Incredibly, the liquid-filled spacesuits did their job and none of the *Strider's* passengers turned to jelly.

Jenny sank deeper into the couch. *It feels like a speeding train hit me. No, more like being crushed under a train.* The ship hummed and vibrated through her seat. There was a flash of blue light, and her pod rumbled. Then, there was a bright orange explosion, and the ship shook like an earthquake. All Jenny could do was hold on and focus on her breathing. It was frustrating to be so helpless.

Just then, a swarm of targets appeared as red dots on the edge of Jenny's display. *Finally*, Jenny thought, *there's something I can do to help.* She gripped the joysticks and selected one of the crafts to target. A diagram with details manifested in the bottom right corner, replacing her view of Adriana. They were small, uncrewed spherical ships, equal parts weapon, and thruster.

"What do we do?" Jenny was thrown to the side as Jack spun the ship.

"Nothing," Jack grunted. "Drones are too small for you to hit."

Too small to hit. Jenny puffed up her cheeks and blew out. Which didn't have the same effect in her fluid-filled spacesuit. The drones entered Jenny's target range, and her fingers itched. They strafed the *Strider's* vital systems, and red dots appeared on the ship's diagram. *To hell with it*, Jenny thought. *I'm not going to sit here and let them pick us apart.*

Jenny targeted one of the drones and activated her gun. The pod spun to track the target. Gas blew out the pod's twin gun barrels and ignited into purple plasma. A low vibration ran under Jenny's seat as tungsten slugs fired. The drone disappeared in a tiny orange explosion.

"Nice shot, but save your ammo. The PDCs will take care of them." Jack spun the *Strider* in a tight spiral to prevent the drones from focusing their fire on a single zone. As he did, the point-defense cannons fired and destroyed the remaining drones with ultimate efficiency.

"There are still five targets left," Kensei said.

"Interceptors," Jack said. "They're out of firing range."

"I see them." Jenny selected one. Unlike the drones, these were crewed ships, sleek and black.

"They're gaining on us," Kensei said.

"No," Jenny said, "they're passing us."

"Why aren't they attacking?" Adriana asked.

"They don't have to," Jack said.

"Why not?"

"Because they know our destination. They'll fly ahead and wait for us at the Terminal."

"So, what do we do?" Jenny asked.

"I'm going to cloak the *Strider* until we're clear of the Tamarack."

"You have a cloaking device?" Kensei asked. "Why didn't you use it before?"

"Because I have to shut off the primary drive. Now, let me give you some tips on how to operate your pods."

38

SOL TERMINAL

Between the *Strider*'s intense acceleration, and breathing the oxygen-rich fluid, it felt like an elephant was sitting on Jenny's chest. After a few hours, she was too exhausted to talk. Even moving her eyes felt like work. So, Jenny resigned herself to facing forward and focusing on each breath with her eyes closed. At least her bond to Cobol didn't require her to move any muscles. *Cobol?*

Yes, Jenny.

How do I unlock the Terminal?

I was wondering when you were going to ask.

I just assumed you would tell me when we got there, but now I'm curious.

I understand, Cobol said. *After we arrive at the Terminal, we must walk along its outer surface until we reach a lock. Then you must remove the Riftkey from my back and insert it into the opening. The waveforms of the bolt will appear to you, and you will have to match them to the energy of the Terminal.*

Oh, like the mazes. Jenny yawned. Lin had said that the tests would prepare her for unlocking the Terminal.

Yes. That is their purpose, Cobol answered. *And, after you align all twelve locks, the Terminal may be activated by selecting a destination.*

That's nice. Jenny blinked slowly. *How long will it take?*

Given your limited mobility in magnetic boots, I estimate it will take two and a half hours, not including the time it takes you to align each lock.

Sounds good, Jenny thought. The next moment, she fell asleep and dreamed that she was back on the *Endeavor*. She had finished the last maze and had stepped out of the room to thunderous applause. As Lin walked toward her, Victus picked up the Riftkey from the pedestal. Jenny tried to call out and warn Lin, but no sound came out, and her muscles felt like cement. The crowd was still cheering as Victus thrust the Riftkey into Lin's back.

Jenny jerked awake with the sudden feeling that she was falling. She looked around in confusion. *That's right*, she thought. *I'm in the* Strider's *gun pod, breathing liquid, and I'm weightless. That must mean that we've stopped accelerating and I can talk again.* Indeed, it no longer felt like an elephant was sitting on her chest. "Where are we?" Jenny asked.

"Halfway to the Terminal," Jack said. "How was your nap?"

"Good." Jenny stretched her neck and flexed the muscles in her legs and arms to circulate her blood.

"You all stayed awake longer than I expected," Jack said.

"From here, we turn around and accelerate in the opposite direction," Kensei said. "Like in the spaceplane."

"That's right," Jack said.

"So, what's the plan for when we get there?" Adriana asked.

"Once we're sixty thousand klicks out, I'll cut the primary drive and activate the cloak," Jack said. "Then we'll coast the rest of the way to the Terminal."

"We're going to sneak up on them," Kensei said.

"That's the idea," Jack said. "Space combat is like any combat; it's about hitting them before they can hit you."

The stars outside spun around as the *Strider* flipped to face the opposite direction. When the roller coaster ride ended, Jenny took a deep breath to ready herself. The thrusters ignited, and she was thrown backward.

Over the next few hours, the kilometers quickly ticked down. At around sixty thousand, the seat stopped crushing her, and Jenny was weightless once again. They turned around, and the distance to the Terminal continued to decrease at about 120 klicks per second.

We're finally here, Jenny thought, *we're finally going to see the Terminal.* She zoomed in her display to look at the artifact. But at this distance, the ring looked small, dark, and unimpressive. "Is that what all the fuss is about?"

"Yeah," Kensei said. "It doesn't look like much."

Do not be fooled by its appearance, Cobol sent to Jenny. *Its technology is far beyond anything humans can conceive.*

"Where did it come from?" Adriana asked.

"No one knows," Jack said.

As they drew nearer, the lidar targeting system in Jenny's pod highlighted five sleek, dark ships inside the Terminal.

"I see the interceptors," Kensei said.

"Good," Jack said. "Remember, the guns will give away our position, so choose your own target and fire as soon as you're in weapons range. With luck, you'll destroy them before they even know we're here. Got it?"

"Got it," they answered.

Jenny's heart pounded as she gripped the joysticks on each arm of the chair. She worked with the other three pods to select targets. When Jenny armed her pod, the gun barrels turned to point directly at the enemy ship. A large red circle indicated the weapon's range; when it became green, it would be time to fire. Jenny's nerves tingled as they crept closer and closer to the enemy. As soon as the red circle touched her target, it turned green.

All at once, they fired in synchronized perfection. Purple plasma belched from her gun barrels, then tungsten slugs flew at a generous fraction of light-speed toward their targets. Against all the odds, the shots missed, and the interceptors scattered in different directions. A moment later, the diagram of the *Strider* flashed red.

"What's that flashing?" Jenny asked.

"We just flew through a tracker net," Jack said.

"Is that bad?" Kensei asked.

"Only if them being able to see us is bad."

"It's bad," Kensei said.

On the diagram of the *Strider*, Jenny noticed two dots emanating little radio waves. *Those must be the trackers.* One was in front of the cockpit, and the other had lodged itself on the joint of the starboard arm, the same arm she was in. There were several beeps in quick succession, then ten new dots appeared on the lidar.

"What is that?" Adriana asked.

"Torpedoes," Jack said. "Hold on."

Stars spun in the background, and Jenny was pressed down into her seat. A second later, she was shoved violently backward. Four of the ten dots had disappeared, leaving six torpedoes.

"Stay on target," Jack said.

"For what?" Jenny asked.

"The interceptors."

Jenny had forgotten about the enemy ships. She quickly worked with the others to exchange targets as they twisted and turned through space. The gun pods were like dragon heads as they belched purple plasma. Seconds later, two of the interceptors exploded, but the remaining three evaded their best attempts as they wiggled through space like they were intoxicated. All the while, the six torpedoes closed in on the *Strider*.

For a second, Jenny became weightless before being jerked sideways. A sharp pain lanced down her injured arm, causing her to yelp.

"You alright, Jenny?" Adriana asked.

"Yeah, it's just the gun wound."

They were now flying straight toward the Terminal, and the torpedoes were directly in front of them.

"Are you crazy?" Kensei asked.

Something vibrated through Jenny's seat, and there was a flash of orange outside. One of the torpedoes disappeared from her lidar, leaving five.

Jenny rocked back and forth in her seat as Jack performed an acrobatic maneuver to put them behind one of the interceptors. Jenny and the others focused their fire, and the ship exploded. Just two left. Jack flew through the debris, and two of the five remaining torpedoes disappeared. There was another flash, and the ship shook.

"Brace for impact," Jack called out.

Jenny cried out as her chair smashed into her. The starfield was spinning, and she felt like a load of laundry in the washing machine. The gun pod's displays flickered, then blinked off. Red emergency lights lit the compact space. The *Strider* came into view for a second, then it flew away. Jenny noticed that its starboard arm was missing.

Jenny heard someone shouting as the oxygen-rich fluid drained from her suit, but she couldn't make it out over her own coughing. A pump drained the remaining fluid from her suit, leaving her gasping for air. But soon, she was breathing as usual, a sound that seemed too loud after the silent fluid.

"Jenny!" Adriana shouted over the comm.

"I'm here." Jenny coughed.

"Are you okay?"

"I've been better."

"The torpedo blew the starboard arm off," Kensei said.

"Yeah." Jenny knew she was breathing too fast and hard, but she couldn't help herself. "I figured that out. What do I do?"

"You need to get out of there," Jack said.

"Yeah, but how?"

"Unhook your umbilical," Jack said. "Your suit has about eight hours of oxygen. That should be long enough."

"Long enough for what?"

"For you to unlock the Terminal before we pick you up. But, once you're unhooked, you won't be able to communicate with us."

"Okay." Jenny almost laughed at the absurdity of the situation. Hearing their words did calm her enough that she could gain control of her breathing and study her surroundings. In her heads-up display, she saw that her oxygen was only at 86 percent. *It will have to do.* Jenny found the umbilical and unhooked it from her chest. Because the arm was rotating, she drifted toward the outside wall.

Come to the center of the arm, Cobol said in her mind.

Jenny crawled along the wall and braced herself against the back of the seat. She took hold of the hatch's wheel and twisted, then pulled the door open and jumped out into the tunnel. The spinning was making her dizzy, so she closed her eyes as she crawled down the ladder. Cobol was waiting for her at the center of the arm.

Jenny held on to the last rung of the ladder and looked out at the wreckage. Shards of metal left a spiral trail through space. The Terminal was roughly ten kilometers away, but that distance was growing every second.

What do we do? Jenny asked.

We have to jump. Cobol climbed out through the wreckage and grabbed a jagged section of metal. The stars spun behind him and Jenny fought her growing nausea by closing her eyes. When she was confident that she wouldn't vomit, she opened her eyes and searched for a handhold. She worked her way along a honeycomb-shaped lattice until she stood next to Cobol.

I'll go first. Cobol crouched and waited for the arm to spin around. Then he leaped and floated straight toward the Terminal.

Jenny crouched down and gauged the arm's momentum. *This has to be perfect*, she thought. *In zero gravity, there's no way to alter my course. If I'm off, then I'll be left floating in space until the oxygen runs out.* Once she had a sense of the timing, Jenny took a deep breath, let it out, and then jumped with as much precision as she could summon. *Now all I can do is wait.*

Lights streaked behind the Terminal as the *Celestial Strider* and the last Tyran interceptor fought to the death.

Jenny was about twenty seconds behind Cobol and at least a hundred meters. *Oh god, oh god, oh god. This was stupid*, Jenny thought. An icy fist gripped her heart. She was too high. *Oh shit, I miscalculated my jump. No, no, no. I haven't come this far just to fail now.* Jenny tried to swim toward the Terminal for a few seconds. *I'm going to miss. I'm going to die.* Then, she remembered the valve on her chest. *Maybe if I vent some air...* she thought.

Jenny twisted her body until her chest pointed away from the Terminal. *Not too much*, she thought. *Otherwise, I won't have enough air to walk around the Terminal.* Jenny lifted the flap on her chest and felt for the nozzle. Very gently, she gave it a twist. There was a brief whoosh, then a sucking sound. *That should do it.* Jenny wriggled around to see if it worked.

Up ahead, Jenny saw Cobol touch down on the Terminal's surface.

The distance between them shrank rapidly. Jenny stretched out with both arms and Cobol reached up to catch her. For an instant, Cobol's hand brushed hers, then she was cartwheeling over the Terminal. *That's it.* Jenny gasped. *I'm going to die out here.*

A hand gripped her foot.

I've got you, Cobol said.

Thank you, thank you, thank you, Jenny thought as her boots clicked into place. *I never want to do that again.*

∾

The outside of the Terminal was wide enough for two cars to fit side by side. It was perfectly flat except for a deep groove about four centimeters wide that bisected the surface. The entire ring seemed to be composed of the same obsidian-colored material as the Waypoints.

This way, Cobol said as he walked casually along the surface of the Terminal.

Jenny wasn't as comfortable in her spacesuit. Moving in the magnetic boots was a new experience. But she remembered Jack's training and adjusted the magnetic strength until it felt most natural.

Here's the first lock. Cobol pointed at a rectangular hole that interrupted the groove and turned his back to Jenny. *Take the Riftkey and insert it into the bolt.*

Overhead, the *Strider* streaked by them. Its engines blazed, and its two remaining rail guns fired back at the pursuing interceptor.

Do not hesitate, Cobol warned. *Your friends fight so that you may complete the mission.*

I know, Jenny said, but she couldn't look away. The *Strider* spiraled around the Terminal, using the ring as cover. She could see the damage from where the torpedo had broken the arm off. Her breath caught as one of the *Strider*'s thrusters exploded.

Cobol stood there waiting for her to take the Riftkey, but she couldn't look away. Not now, not when her friends were about to die. Jenny's guts tightened as the interceptor closed in. Suddenly, the enemy ship exploded in a flash. Jenny flinched as debris crashed into the Terminal. *What was that?* Jenny thought.

It must be Lance, Cobol replied.

Six fighters—in silver and red—raced past the wreckage of the interceptor. The *Strider* limped into view for a moment, then it engaged its cloak and vanished into the dark of space. Jenny almost jumped for joy but thought better of it. Sunward, a whole squadron—composed of interceptors, gunships, and assault craft—sped toward the Terminal.

He must have gotten a message out. Jenny sighed in relief. *Okay, I'm ready.* Jenny turned to Cobol. As she pulled the Riftkey off his back, the empty virosuit tugged at something inside of her. She ignored the sensation and activated the Riftkey. Its edges blazed with blue light. *What if I accidentally cut the Terminal?* she asked Cobol.

Do not worry, the Riftkey cannot cut through the same material it is made of.

That makes sense.

On Earth, the Riftkey had moved like it was underwater, but out here, it was as light and whippy as her fencing foil. Jenny positioned the Riftkey above the lock. *Now for the moment of truth.* She thrust the Riftkey down until it clicked into place. In her mind's eye, she saw waveforms of blue, yellow, and green. *It is just like the mazes,* Jenny thought.

Now you must merge the lock's waveforms until they form one continuous pattern with the Terminal, Cobol instructed.

I see it, Jenny thought. The Terminal displayed a single white waveform. By merging the blue, yellow, and green lock waveforms together, she could connect them to the white waveform of the Terminal and make one continuous line.

Jenny focused on the blue waveform, altering its peaks and valleys until it matched part of the Terminal's pattern. She worked on the yellow one next, and once the two waveforms combined, they formed a more complete part of the Terminal's energy profile. But, before she could even start on the green one, the blue waveform reset back to its original form. *There's a time limit. What do I do now?* she asked Cobol.

That is for you to figure out.

Thanks. Like with the tests, Jenny thought, *this must have to do with perception.* Jenny turned her focus inward and controlled her breathing. She felt her heartbeat and the pressure of the suit on her skin. Time seemed to slow down. For one breath and one pulse, she worked on the three waveforms. Jenny's mind split into two parts as she manipulated the patterns like a spider weaving its web. When the lock clicked into place, a feeling of pure joy washed over her, and the groove bisecting the Terminal glowed with a soft blue light.

I did it. Jenny pulled the Riftkey free and snapped it into place on the virosuit's back.

Yes, I see it. Just eleven more to go, Cobol said.

As Jenny made her way around the Terminal she watched Lance's fleet. At some point, she felt a door open in her mind. She saw that the ships were positioned in defensive formations. Jenny counted around 150 ships: Smaller vessels, barely visible in the distance, formed a wall at the front line. Nine medium-size corvettes and six destroyers remained farther apart. Two frigates—about the size of the *Tamarack*—and one enormous spacecraft formed up in the rear.

It had been two hours since Jenny and Cobol had reached the Terminal. Jenny removed the Riftkey from the tenth lock and returned it to Cobol's back. The groove, running down the center of the Terminal, now blazed a brilliant-blue color. The release-and-attach rhythm of her magnetic boots, which was so novel at first, now seemed tedious. Her oxygen level had depleted to 23 percent, but with only two more locks to go, she had plenty of time.

How will they know when I'm done?

After the final lock is aligned, Cobol answered, *the Terminal will activate in a flash of white light.*

That should do the trick.

Suddenly, the hairs on the back of Jenny's neck rose. She looked sunward and saw a bright, moving light. As she watched, it grew to the size of her thumbnail. *Oh no.* With her heart pounding, Jenny watched the rapidly growing shape of the *Tamarack* as she raced toward the eleventh lock.

Jenny plucked the Riftkey from Cobol's back and inserted it into the slot. As she worked on the eleventh lock, she tried not to let the approaching warship distract her. When she was done, the groove glowed a bit brighter.

Before Jenny could remove the Riftkey from the lock, a thump echoed through her mind. Looking around, she saw that the *Tamarack* had transported to the rear of Lance's fleet, near the Terminal. *It can teleport,* Jenny thought.

All at once, hundreds of spaceships swarmed out of the *Tamarack's* many hangars. Then, rays of light lanced out from holes in its side. They looked like enormous flashlights flicking on and off. But these left behind a trail of spiraling plasma embers. The lights struck Lance's largest ship, instantly overloading the shields and carving through its armor.

That must be the nuclear lance, Jenny thought. *The other ships don't stand a chance against that weapon.*

By the time Lance's flagship retaliated with ballistics and missiles, the *Tamarack* had already disappeared. The projectiles passed harmlessly through the spot where the *Tamarack* had been. The *Tamarack* reappeared on the opposite side of the flagship and immediately fired its nuclear lances. Molten metal fountained from the flagship, and the colossal ship went dark.

In the meantime, both of Lance's frigates had turned their weapons on the *Tamarack*. Zippy corvettes and destroyers accelerated into the fray, and in the midst of battle, a voice spoke into Jenny's mind.

STOP US.

Jenny froze in place and focused on the source of the voice. It was coming from the *Tamarack*. But who could it be? She closed her eyes and concentrated. The voice conveyed fear and pain, but, above all, hope. And there was something familiar about it.

STOP US.

Kett'l? Jenny gasped and opened her eyes.

Please help, Kett'l begged.

I'm here. Jenny whimpered from the fear and pain she felt through their connection. *What can I do?*

Kett'l sent a picture into her mind. It was the pattern that Jenny had used on the Selkan boy. The one that kept him from teleporting. She felt the burn of shame from Kett'l's admonishment rise in her body. She also remembered how Victus had nullified all the Cabin recruits in the gym. *What are you asking me to do?*

Don't let them use us to teleport their ship. Kett'l sent her an image of a dark, circular room. Tubes and cables descended from the ceiling and plugged into a dozen fluid-filled pods, each with a Selkan inside.

Jenny shuddered. *I didn't know.*

Please help.

I will, she said to him. *I will.* She looked out at the ships. The *Tamarack* still dominated the battlefield. Several of Lance's ships were derelict wrecks, the occasional spark, and exhalation of gas the only sign that they had once been alive.

Kett'l didn't want me to use that waveform on living things, Jenny thought, *but now it's the only way to save him, and us.* Jenny concentrated on her connection with Kett'l and formed the pattern in her mind. Nothing happened.

It is happening again, Kett'l sent to her as his fear spiked.

Jenny cowered onto the surface of the Terminal. *I don't know what to do.* She looked down at the eleventh lock and the handle of the Riftkey. A thought came to her then. *The Waypoint key helped me focus my ability. What if the Riftkey works the same way?*

It will, Cobol said.

Jenny pulled the Riftkey free of the lock. She focused on her connection with Kett'l and formed the pattern in her mind. The effect was like hooking an amplifier up to a guitar. She felt a surge of power in her mind and she saw black mist explode around Kett'l and quickly spread to the other eleven Selkans. Jenny had just taken away their abilities the way Victus had done to the recruits back in the gym.

Thank you, Kett'l sent to Jenny. *You freed us, and now we can sleep.*

You're welcome. Jenny smiled.

Without the Selkans, the *Tamarack* could no longer teleport away from danger. Its shields flared blue as torpedoes, ballistics, and lasers found their mark. There was an explosion midship. Wreckage and bodies flowed out like a river, and one of the *Tamarack*'s segments went dark. Though injured, the warship was far from disabled. It moved with a speed that belied its size. Weapons fired from every surface of its cylindrical body to hit every ship within range.

At least I gave Lance's fleet a fighting chance, Jenny thought as she returned the Riftkey to the virosuit.

As Cobol came to life, he yelled into Jenny's mind, *Look out!*

Jenny turned in time to see a black troop carrier hovering several meters above the Terminal. Four massive armored soldiers jumped out of the back. Cables shot out from their hips and pulled them down to the surface. Each soldier was as wide as a truck, and two of them spanned the width of the Terminal.

The soldiers' red-painted skulls grinned as they lifted their arms to shoot, and the troop transport tilted downward to aim its massive gun turret at her. Even a small tear in her suit would be a death sentence, as the remaining 16 percent of her oxygen would vent into space. But there was nowhere to hide, and there was no running away. She had been so close to unlocking the Terminal. She thought of her aunt, who was probably worried sick about her. Now, Jenny would never return home to show Bea all that she had achieved.

There was a sudden flash, and the troop transport exploded. Shrapnel blasted in every direction. Though she could see explosions, the only sound could hear was her own breathing. The bulk of the transport smashed into the Terminal, hitting two of the four armored soldiers and dragging them out into space.

Cobol charged forward.

Jenny engaged her perception ability just as the remaining two soldiers opened fire. Everything moved in slow motion, and red lines marked the path of the fléchettes. Jenny's muscles screamed in protest as she twisted away from the deadly projectiles. The soldiers followed her path, forcing her toward the edge of the Terminal and the endless void of space.

There's only one way out of this, Jenny thought as she jumped off the edge of the Terminal. The stars spun around her as she contorted her body and attached her boots to the side of Terminal. She was safely out of sight from the armored soldiers. *I hope my disappearing act was convincing.*

Jenny? Cobol asked. *Are you still there?*

I am. Hold on, I'm coming to help. Jenny circled around the underside of the Terminal and resurfaced behind the armored soldiers. Up close, they towered over her. Fortunately, Mazu had taught Jenny how to handle a larger opponent. *Lin and Aindriu were able to take these guys down, I can too,* Jenny thought. She hooked her arm through one of the soldier's legs and bent her knees. With a surge of strength, she twisted her body, and the enormous soldier came free of the Terminal. Jenny rolled him over her shoulder and hurled him out into space. *I did it!*

Jenny turned her attention to Cobol, who still struggled with his armored soldier.

Suddenly, a cable struck the Terminal near Jenny's foot, and the soldier she had just thrown slammed into her back. An enormous arm wrapped around her neck and tugged at her helmet. Jenny snaked her uninjured arm in front of her face to protect herself, and her back popped as she strained against the powered armor.

It was impossible to break free of the soldier's grip, but there was one hope. *If I could just reach the Riftkey...* With her injured arm, Jenny reached out for the Riftkey on Cobol's back. *Just a little more*, she thought. The armored soldier lifted Jenny away from the Terminal. She didn't have hip cables to save her. If the soldier threw her out into space, she'd drift away until she died of asphyxiation.

Just then, Cobol tore open his soldier's cockpit in a spray of metal parts. Inside, a young man, around twenty-five, wore no protection against the vacuum of space. His exposed body thrashed against his restraints as air exploded from his lungs. His skin swelled to the point of splitting, and the moisture around his face crystallized.

With a grunt, Jenny stretched out for the Riftkey, but her fingers only grazed the handle. Cobol stepped backward, and Jenny wrapped her fingers around the grip. As she pulled it free, she activated the Riftkey and swung backward. The arm around her neck went slack, but she was still in danger of drifting away. Jenny grabbed the soldier's arm and pulled herself back down to the Terminal and attached her boots.

39

DOPPELGÄNGER

Jenny stood frozen as she watched air and blood vent from the armored soldier she had just killed. *There's a man in there, probably not much older than me,* Jenny thought. Knowing that he would have killed her didn't lessen her horror.

Jenny, Cobol spoke into her mind.

Yeah, Jenny replied numbly.

You need to keep going. There is only one lock left...

Jenny looked up at the battle raging overhead. Dozens of fighters chased one another around the Terminal, and half of Lance's fleet had been destroyed by the *Tamarack*. Their derelict shells sparked and expelled gas as they drifted lifelessly against the stars.

Victus is winning, Jenny said. *What's the point?*

Because there is still a chance, and if you stop now, their sacrifice will have been for nothing.

Jenny blinked dry eyes and looked down at the Riftkey. She took a long shuddering breath to calm her nerves. *You're right.* She snapped the Riftkey into place. *Just one more lock to go.* She forced a smile onto her face. *Let's do it.*

As Jenny made her way around the Terminal, she saw another Tyran troop carrier hovering above the final lock. Two figures leapt from the back of the carrier and descended to the surface using their hip cables.

Oh no, Jenny thought, *not again.*

One of the figures was an armored soldier with gold details on her suit. Jenny knew that it also had a white skull on its black face mask instead of red. She had seen this armored soldier before, it was Alberta. Which meant that the other figure, which wore a black armored space-suit and held the stolen Riftkey had to be Victus.

I will handle this, Cobol sent to her.

Thanks. Jenny dropped to the ground as Alberta raised her arm to fire. *All I have to do is stay back and let Cobol handle them.*

Alberta's arm flashed, but it wasn't bullets that struck Cobol, it was something sticky, like glue or foam. Within seconds, the android was covered from head to foot and bound in place.

I cannot move, Cobol said.

Oh no. Jenny ran to him and tried to tear the foam away, but it was no use. The stuff was as strong as steel. Cobol was indeed trapped.

Behind Alberta, Jenny saw that Victus had reached the final lock. He held his Riftkey out, ready to thrust it into the Terminal.

You must stop him, Cobol said in her mind. *If he succeeds in aligning the final lock, then he will become the Terminal master and control the solar system.*

No! Jenny replied. A surge of rage flooded through her. *I haven't come this far to just let him win.* Though Cobol was trapped, his back remained free of the foam. She gripped the handle of the Riftkey and yanked it free. Like before, she felt a pull from the empty virosuit, and she remembered how Nimue had carried the Waypoint through the cave by possessing the suit. She thought briefly about possessing the suit, but she knew it would do her no good as long as it was trapped.

Jenny's heart pounded as she walked around Cobol. Thump—thump—thump. Holding the Riftkey in front of her like a shield. Alberta aimed, and Jenny activated her perception ability. Time slowed to a crawl, and a red line extended from Alberta's arm to Jenny's chest. *I doubt she will be using the foam this time,* Jenny thought to herself.

Thump, beat her heart. In her altered state, Jenny's heartbeat seemed to take a minute to complete. More red lines appeared as the needle-like fléchettes flew toward her at the perceived speed of a baseball pitch. Jenny easily moved the Riftkey into the path of each fléchette, deflecting them out into space.

Jenny's heart went thump as she marched forward. The red lines that marked the path of each fléchette made them easy to block, and Jenny grew cocky. She started to relax. *I have this. I can beat her.* As Jenny walked closer and closer to Alberta, she had less time to block each round.

Then, the worst happened. She failed to block a fléchette aimed directly between her eyes. Jenny's muscles flared in pain as she jerked her head back, but she failed to dodge the round completely. The needle-like fléchette grazed her helmet's face mask, and a hairline crack spread across the glass. The sound of escaping air whistled in her ears.

Thump, beat her heart.

Jenny ignored the crack in her mask. *I have to make myself a smaller target*, she thought. Jenny took another step forward, released the magnetic hold on her boots, and dove at Alberta. She flew forward, hovering just above the Terminal, and held the Riftkey directly in front of her. She easily deflected each shot as she quickly closed the gap between them. As she came within striking distance, Jenny activated her boots and planted her feet. Blue light flared as the Riftkey cut clean through Alberta's gun arm. Metal and flesh turned into gray sludge, and the dismembered limb flew out into space.

Thump, beat Jenny's heart as she slashed again, this time in a wide arc. The Riftkey passed through Alberta's waist, and the pressure inside the armored suit blew it apart.

With Alberta defeated, Jenny disabled her ability, and her perception of time returned to normal, and her heart beat in normal time. Behind her, the virosuit was trapped in foam, and ahead of her, Victus worked at the final lock.

He hasn't unlocked it yet, she thought. *I can still stop him.*

Jenny ran past the stumps of Alberta's legs as fast as her magnetic boots allowed and swung at Victus's head. Victus pulled his Riftkey from the twelfth lock and blocked her attack.

You can't have it, Jenny spoke into Victus's mind.

You are wrong, Victus answered. *After I kill you, I will be the one to unlock this Terminal, girl.*

You'll find that I'm not so easy to kill. Jenny thrust her Riftkey at his chest.

Victus backed away and glanced at Alberta's remains. *What a waste,* Victus said. He took a wide fighting stance. *I will take pleasure in destroying you.*

Jenny widened her own stance and held the Riftkey in front of her. Before joining Cabin, she only had basic training in saber combat, but after the ADD treatment, she felt like a master. Jenny feinted a stab at his head, and Victus parried her attack downward. She adjusted her footing and blocked a swing at her midsection. They spun their Riftkeys at each other, narrowly dodging and parrying each blow. To an outside observer, the Riftkeys would have looked like blurs of light, forming glowing parabolic curves through space.

You are skilled, girl, Victus said.

Thanks. Jenny slashed at his leg, arm, and head. *You're not so bad either.*

Victus blocked her combination attack and held her back with minimal effort. He deflected her next attack and countered with a thrust. As his aggression increased, Victus turned single attacks into combinations of two or three. His onslaught was more than Jenny could manage. As he advanced, she was forced backward, past Alberta's remains, and toward the trapped Virosuit.

You still have much to learn. Victus charged at Jenny with a flurry of blows.

Jenny's muscles burned from protecting herself, and air whistled out of her cracked mask. She didn't have the strength or experience to face a foe of Victus's caliber. He was an experienced Æon in a powered suit. All it would take was one minor slip, and his Riftkey would slice her suit open.

Jenny turned her thoughts to the Riftkey. *I'm sorry, Cobol. He's too powerful.*

No, he's not, Cobol said. *You can beat him if you use the virosuit.*

What? Jenny thought to herself. *But the virosuit is trapped, isn't it?*

Victus pointed his Riftkey at her chest. *You are nothing,* Victus said in

Jenny's mind, *and unless you join me, you will always be nothing.*

You killed Lin. Jenny gazed into his black face mask. *I'd rather die than join you.*

Victus charged, and Jenny barely got her Riftkey up in time to block him. She stumbled backward and bumped into the virosuit. Jenny felt its pull as she ducked under a slash. As Victus's Riftkey struck the virosuit, some of the foam disintegrated in a puff of dust. and the virosuit remained unharmed.

That's right, she thought, *the Riftkey can't hurt the virosuit.* Jenny came up with a plan. She spun around the virosuit, keeping it between her and Victus's Riftkey.

You are only prolonging the inevitable, Victus said as he slashed at her. He missed Jenny and hit the virosuit. More of the foam disintegrated. Jenny slid her own Riftkey along the skin of the virosuit. All the dust from the foam created a cloud around the suit and obscured her vision. After a few more slashes, the virosuit was mostly free of the foam, and it was time to enact her plan.

With her back against the virosuit, Jenny focused on her breathing, her heartbeat, even the blood flowing through her veins. Like when she had possessed Sona, the pilot, Jenny embraced her inner self. In her mind, she saw herself as an eleven-year-old girl back when she still loved Roma life. Electricity sparked in her neurons as she drifted into a state between sleep and waking, between dreams and reality. Her mind split in two, and Jenny was both outside and inside her body. Jenny's other self, her doppelgänger, drifted toward the virosuit. As she accepted its invitation, her doppelgänger was pulled inside like water into a drain.

As the cloud of foam dust cleared, Victus swung his Riftkey at Jenny's unprotected head, but her doppelgänger blocked the attack with the virosuit's arm. Victus stepped backward, surprised by the suit's sudden movement. Jenny's doppelgänger slammed a metal fist into his gut, and his magnetic boots came free of the surface. He flipped toward the edge of the Terminal, but before he drifted out into space, a pair of cables fired from his hips and pulled him back down to the surface.

Meanwhile, Jenny ran toward the final lock and thrust the Riftkey into the bolt.

Victus rushed to stop her, but Jenny's doppelgänger blocked his path.

Knowing that the Riftkey had no advantage, he placed it onto his back and faced the virosuit with a wrestling stance. Her doppelgänger swung her metal fist at him, but Victus ducked the blow. He hooked his arm around the back of her neck, and with a twist, Victus pulled the virosuit free of the Terminal's surface. Jenny's doppelgänger quickly grabbed his arm and did a complete flip to regain her feet, but Victus had gotten away from her.

Meanwhile, Jenny sighed in relief as she shifted the last waveform of the twelfth lock into alignment. The groove dividing the Terminal blazed with beautiful azure light. *I did it*, she thought to herself. *I unlocked the Terminal.* Jenny rocked back on her heels and smiled. *Now, how do I activate the Terminal?* she asked Cobol.

Another Terminal needs to accept your connection request, Cobol replied. *Once a connection is accepted, you may remove the Riftkey.*

Okay, send a request.

As Victus ran toward the final lock he said, *You may have unlocked the Terminal, girl, but I can still take it after you're dead.* He pulled the Riftkey from his back and swung at Jenny's head. Just then, her doppelgänger slammed into his back, and he missed.

Jenny's doppelgänger grabbed Victus's wrist and twisted. The Riftkey came free of his hand and hovered in space. Victus grabbed the Riftkey with his other hand and swung at Jenny, but her doppelgänger dragged him away by the waist.

Three Terminals are accepting requests, Cobol said. *Balt, Ava, and Fen.*

Balt, connect to Balt, Jenny said frantically as Victus and the Virosuit fought just a meter away.

Connection refused.

Try Ava.

Connection refused, Cobol said.

Fen? Jenny held her breath.

The connection was successful. Interesting...

What?

The Fen Terminal is locked.

So Sol wasn't the only lock Terminal, Jenny thought.

That seems to be the case.

Jenny looked down at the final lock. *Now, what do I do?*

Remove the Riftkey, Cobol instructed, *and the Terminal will activate.*

Jenny pulled the Riftkey free of the lock, and the Terminal hummed beneath her feet.

Thirty seconds until activation, Cobol said.

Victus fired the cables from his hip and pulled himself free of the virosuit's grip. He ducked a lunge and kicked backward. Jenny's doppelgänger stumbled.

Jenny glanced up at the spaceship battle and found the *Tamarack*. Lance's fleet was directing all its fire at the warship's engines. A second later, its rear exploded in a bright flash of light, and the mighty warship went dark.

That must have been the reactor, or something, Jenny thought. Hope sparked in her chest, and a smile spread across her face. *Even if Victus does manage to kill me, another Cabin recruit will just take my place. Even Sadi would be better than Victus.*

We captured your ship, Jenny spoke to Victus's mind. *You've lost.*

Victus looked up at the derelict *Tamarack*, and Jenny's doppelgänger took that moment to slam her shoulder into his abdomen. She grabbed both of his legs and pulled. Victus slammed his fists into the virosuit's back to no avail. He grabbed her arms and twisted. But without leverage, he could not break free.

Jack said that anything caught inside the Terminal would be disintegrated, Jenny thought.

Jenny's doppelgänger pulled Victus's boots free of the surface, and she carried him to the edge of the Terminal.

Stop, Victus pleaded. *Don't do this. You will bring war back to the galaxy.*

You can't condemn an entire species to slavery and call that peace, Jenny said.

You may save a few hundred Selkan lives, Victus continued, *but you are dooming billions.*

Goodbye, Vicky. With one hand under his arm, and the other under his chin, Jenny's doppelgänger threw Victus toward the center of the Terminal.

Jenny held the Riftkey up to the virosuit's back and thought, *It's time for us to become one again.* As the key snapped into place, Cobol returned to his body, and Jenny's doppelgänger returned to hers.

Now, I want to see the moment of Victus's disintegration, Jenny thought as she walked up to the edge of the Terminal. As she squinted against the bright blue light, she saw Victus flipping through space. He was already twenty meters away and still moving. Jenny thought about Lin and the other members of Cabin who had died because of him. *You are all about to get justice*, she promised them.

Then it appeared that Victus had stopped spinning. *That can't be*, Jenny thought as she leaned out for a better view. Through the blinding light, two black serpents sped toward her face. She tried to dodge, but it was too late. One of Victus's hip cables flew past her, but the other stuck firmly to her face mask like a gecko's foot. Air whistled through the glass as more cracks spiderwebbed out from the impact; still, it held. Her oxygen, however, dropped from 5 percent to 3 in a matter of seconds. *I really am going to die out here*, Jenny thought.

As Victus retracted the cable, Jenny dropped to her knees with the sudden force. He was drifting toward her and had already gone from fifty meters away to forty.

Ten seconds until activation, Cobol said in her mind.

No! Jenny sent to Victus. *If I'm going to die, then I'm taking you out with me.*

Jenny breathed out as she gripped her helmet and twisted it free. Instantly, her suit sucked tight around her body like shrink-wrap. The part of her face not covered by the bodysuit swelled from exposure. Her tongue felt like a bratwurst, and saliva fizzed and popped in her mouth.

With her helmet in both hands, Jenny took careful aim and threw it with all her might. It sped downward and slammed into Victus's chest. *That will slow you down*, Jenny thought to herself even as the mucous membranes lining her nose cracked. Blood froze into stalactites in her nostrils. The moisture on her eyes crystallized, and she couldn't blink. Through her blurred vision, Jenny saw a black mist form around Victus just before the inside of the Terminal turned utterly black. It flashed a brilliant white, and Victus was gone.

Jenny felt Cobol's strong arms wrap around her waist. He pulled her off the Terminal, and then they were drifting, weightless, through space. Jenny's vision narrowed to a tunnel, and everything went black.

40

THE CABIN

Jenny's head throbbed, and her skin was on fire. She dared to open her swollen eyelids and found herself on a hospital bed in a sterile white room. *This doesn't look like the* Strider, *it's too roomy, and white, and clean,* Jenny thought. To her left, a gray-haired man with a friendly face tended a drip system that carried blood and clear fluid to each of her arms. With an effort, she rolled her head to the right and saw Adriana and Kensei sitting on chairs next to her bed. Jack was leaning against the wall next to Cobol.

"You're awake!" Adriana jumped up from her chair.

Jenny tested the soft tissues in her mouth with her dry tongue and winced as she touched her bruised face.

"That looks like it hurts," Kensei said as he stood.

"Yeah, it does," Jenny said in a rattly voice. It was painful to speak.

"You look pretty good," Adriana said, "for someone who took her helmet off in outer space."

"Well, I feel awful."

"I can't believe you survived exposure," Kensei said. "I'm kind of jealous."

"I'll let you try it next time." Jenny smiled, then winced and touched her aching head.

"I mean," Kensei said, "normally you'd be unconscious within fifteen seconds. Then your blood would boil after a minute. You were out there for ninety seconds, and you didn't even blow up."

"Stop it, Kensei." Adriana touched Jenny's hand. "You know that kind of stuff only happens in movies."

"Where am I?"

"We're aboard the *Tamarack*," Jack said as he pushed off the wall and stood at the foot of her bed.

"*The Tamarack, how?*" Jenny asked.

"After Lance's fleet disabled the *Tamarack*, they boarded her and brought all the injured here."

Jenny propped herself upright with her elbows. Her head protested the movement, and she grew dizzy.

"Easy, master," The gray-haired man said. "You're still recovering from exposure."

Master? Jenny stared blankly at him. Her eyes went wide as her memories slowly returned to her. She remembered her fight with Victus, how her doppelgänger had helped her, and finally unlocking the Terminal. But, she had thrown her helmet at Victus and she had suffocated. "How am I still alive?"

"I picked you up," Cobol said, "and jumped into the Strider's airlock."

"Where I was waiting for you," Kensei said. "We saw the whole thing. You were amazing out there." He went on to explain what had happened after the *Strider's* arm got blown off. When Jenny reached the last lock, Kensei moved down to the airlock to pick her up. "So, how does it feel to be the Sol Terminal master?" He asked.

Jenny tried to feel excited, after all, she was a Terminal master, but she only felt numb. It was all too overwhelming. She was happy that it was all over, and more than anything, she wanted to go home. "I don't know," Jenny shrugged. "Relieved I guess."

"What happens now?" Adriana asked. "Now that you're bound to the Terminal, do you have to stay here, in this realm?"

"*No.*" Jenny's voice cracked and she coughed painfully.

The nurse offered Jenny a pouch of water to drink. "Just small sips for now." His voice was full of warmth and concern.

Jenny put the pouch to her lips and experimented with the nozzle.

The cold water felt wonderful against her swollen gums. But when she swallowed, her throat felt like bloody ribbons.

"Jenny is free to leave," Cobol said. "My purpose is to operate the Terminal."

"What about Sadi and Aindriu?" Jenny asked.

"Sadi's in the brig," Jack said, "but Aindriu was caught in an explosion."

"Is he dead?"

"No," Kensei said, "but he's in a coma."

"Look what we found." Adriana lifted a familiar-looking rucksack.

"Is that...?"

"It is." Kensei lifted a chain around his neck and revealed his Waypoint key.

Adriana pulled two objects free of the rucksack. One was Jenny's Waypoint key, and the other was her mother's amulet. "I believe these are yours."

Jenny slipped them both over her neck. The weight against her chest felt right, as if everything was in its proper place. She wondered about Kett'l, and how they had stopped the *Tamarack* from teleporting. Somehow, they had shared a connection across a great distance. She tried reaching out to him again but got no reply. "What about Kett'l and the other Selkans?" Jenny croaked.

"They're all free." Adriana smiled. "And if you've recovered enough, some of them would like to see you."

"Sure."

Adriana held the door open to reveal a line of Selkans waiting outside the room. Adriana motioned to the first person, an old woman, who then entered the room. Jenny recognized her as one of the elders from the night she'd celebrated with Kett'l. The old woman stopped at the foot of Jenny's bed and held out a hand. Something round and shiny sat upon her leathery, creased palm. She thrust her hand forward, urging Jenny to take it.

Jenny slowly sat up. Her head swam, but she took a deep breath and forced the pain away. She leaned forward and wrapped her hands around the old lady's offering. Tears raced along the Selkan woman's wrinkles and wet her fur. "Did I do something wrong?" Jenny asked.

The old lady said something, but Jenny didn't understand. "What is she saying?"

"She's saying thank you," Cobol said. "That you're her savior, and that everything she has is yours."

Jenny turned the offering over in her hand. It was a large shell button with a beautiful etching on its surface. It was likely the only possession the Selkan woman was able to keep when the Tyran soldiers took them.

The old lady bowed out of the room, and an old Selkan man entered. He approached Jenny's bed and offered her a smooth, dark stone with a stunning swirling pattern carved by the natural effects of water and sand.

A lump grew in Jenny's throat as she took the man's hands into hers. She gazed out at the long line of Selkans. *This is going to be hard, maybe even harder than facing Victus.*

One by one, Jenny attended to all the Selkans waiting outside her room. Not all of them carried gifts, but each wanted to see her, touch her, and give her thanks.

After the last Selkan had come and gone, a mound of artifacts had formed at the foot of Jenny's bed. She didn't feel right taking their possessions, but trying to return the gifts would have been an insult. By accepting these tokens, she was acknowledging their suffering and loss.

"Is that everyone?" Jenny peered out into the hallway and asked, "Where's Kett'l?"

Adriana hung her head.

"Where is he?"

"He's in another hospital room," Kensei said.

"Take me to him."

Jenny pulled the tubes from her arms and threw her legs over the side of the bed. She stumbled as her feet hit the floor, but she made it into the waiting wheelchair. Adriana pushed her down the hall to a larger hospital room.

Inside, a doctor and two nurses tended to twelve bedridden Selkans. The emaciated aliens had shaved heads that revealed the deathlike pallor of their skin. Their brown fur appeared dull and lifeless, and their tusks had been filed down or removed.

"These are the Selkans who were connected to the *Tamarack*," Adriana said.

Jenny rolled her wheelchair over to where Thork'l stood. The old, tattooed Selkan held onto Kett'l's hand. His son's head had been shaved, like the others. His dichromatic eyes stared blankly at the ceiling.

"Kett'l, I'm sorry."

Kett'l's hands trembled at the sound of her voice, and his eyes shook in their sockets.

"What's wrong with him?" Jenny asked.

"They modified his brain to connect to the ship," Kensei added.

"It's like they're in a constant state of fear," Adriana said. "The doctors have to keep them medicated."

Jenny took Kett'l's hand. His once warm, strong fingers felt cold and weak. His body shivered, and he mumbled incoherently.

Thork'l was beside himself with grief. He looked around the room at the other Selkans. "None of them have been able to talk. I knew that this is why they took our people, but I've never seen a ship slave in person."

Jenny turned to the doctor. "Is there anything to be done for them?"

"We're doing everything we can to make them comfortable. It's all we can do for now." He looked into Jenny's eyes. "Believe me, master, I had no idea this atrocity was happening on the ship. We always believed that they were using secret technology, not people, to teleport the ship."

It was a sunny Wednesday morning in Acacia City. It had been four days since Jenny had first entered the city. She adjusted her duffel bag. Inside were her custom-tailored Cabin uniforms, along with the tokens the Selkans had given her. She wore the emerald-green dress that Lin had bought at Mary Ann's Fine Custom Tailoring.

Jack zipped up his leather jacket and pulled the collar over his neck. His breath spiraled up and around his head.

"It's cold," Adriana said as she stepped out of the black car that had picked them up from the Acacia City Airfield. She took a blue scarf out of her bag and tied it around her neck.

Kensei adjusted his purple Lakers hat and looked over at Jenny. "I'm nervous about going back home. I'm not sure if my mom will be relieved or angry."

"I know what you mean." Jenny took his hand and squeezed it. "But either way, it's because she cares about you. I bet my aunt is out of her mind with worry."

Altogether, they climbed the steps of the gazebo and stepped into the obsidian bowl of the Waypoint. The Songbirds watched over them as Jenny inserted Astrea's key into the lock. She selected the Esperanza Waypoint and pushed down on the key.

The buildings of the Acacia City historic district vanished, and the trees of Esperanza Woods emerged into view. Lance and Mazu were waiting for them at the edge of the Waypoint. A large plastic case sat on the ground between them.

Rygelus and Brock were there as well. Brock was using a pair of hand-carved wooden crutches to keep off of his bandaged leg.

"Miss Tripper," Lance said.

"Yes?"

"Another Terminal unlocked after you opened Sol's."

"What?" Jenny asked. "When? Which one?" She didn't know which question needed answering first, but she hoped he would answer them all.

"The Fen Terminal was unlocked two and a half hours after Sol's opened."

The world spun, and the ground seemed to drop out from under Jenny's feet. It was amazing that she was able to stay upright. "That's the system I sent Victus to."

"That's what I thought," Lance said.

"Victus is still alive?" Kensei asked incredulously.

"It would appear so, Mister Drake. Now, I have something to ask of Sol's Terminal master."

"Okay..." Jenny said.

"Will you be the spokesperson of Sol?"

"Me?" *I get nervous if I have to speak in front of the class*, Jenny thought. "What do you need me to do?"

"I need you to negotiate with the other Terminal masters to protect Sol until I rebuild my fleet."

"Okay." Jenny nodded. "I understand, but I need to go home and see my aunt first."

"Thank you," Lance said. "All I ask is that you return."

"I promise."

"Speaking of Jenny's aunt." Adriana turned to Mazu. "You told me that we could bring the siphonophore treatment home to heal our families."

"Ah yes," Mazu said. "We did." She picked up the large plastic case and opened it. Inside were three wooden boxes. She took one out and lifted the lid. A set of vintage-looking ink bottles and pens rested on red velvet lining.

"Is that a calligraphy set?" Kensei asked.

"It's supposed to look like one," Mazu said. "We've heard that it's challenging to fly with foreign liquids in your world, so we disguised the treatment in case you need to travel."

"That's very thoughtful, thank you," Adriana said as she took one of the boxes.

"I have something to give you too," Jenny said to Mazu. "When I first met your mom—I mean, Lin—she gave me this bag to hide the Riftkey in. She made me promise to give it back after saving the Selkans, so..."

Mazu stepped forward and took the burstepi.

"It has a bunch of her things inside, and, well, I thought you should have it."

"Thank you, Jenny. She left behind a legacy for me to live up to."

"No." Jenny smiled. "She would have wanted for you to live your own life." Jenny wondered if her mom would be proud of what she had done. "Be yourself."

"You're right," Mazu said as she took Jack's hand.

"Why have you been avoiding me?" Jack asked.

Mazu shrugged and looked away. "I didn't think you'd want anything to do with an engineered human."

"That doesn't matter to me," Jack said as he searched her eyes. "Half the people I know are genetically engineered. I'm not a hundred percent pure human myself."

Mazu smiled, then she and Jack led the way through the forest to the cabin.

The smell of moss, wood, and decomposed leaves filled her nose, and the ancient trees of the Esperanza Woods swayed and groaned in the breeze. Butterflies the size of her hand and dragonflies the size of birds fluttered through the air.

Jenny stood with Adriana and Kensei at the base of the cabin steps.

"This was quite the summer break," Kensei said.

"It's winter for us," Adriana said.

"I'm actually looking forward to going back to school," Jenny said.

"Me too."

Adriana was the first to leave. She said her goodbyes and hugged everyone before entering the cabin. After a minute, there was a flash of light, and Mazu asked who would be next.

Jenny turned to Kensei. "You go next." She wanted to look around the cabin, and she didn't want to hold him up.

"If you insist," Kensei said his goodbyes, then rushed up the steps.

When it was her turn, Jenny entered the cabin and looked around. The stacked log walls and wooden floors seemed more charming now. She looked in the corner for the pile of rags that had been Heather, but of course, the Alfur was not there. She did find her black hat, however, right where she left it. Jenny picked it up and placed it on her head.

Jenny took a deep breath, shifted the duffel bag to her back, and approached the wooden ladder. The upside-down VRGo puzzle waited for her at the uppermost rung. She started climbing. As her head and shoulders entered the cube, she felt something pull her upward. The walls of the cabin disappeared as she flew through time and space.

Jenny tumbled out of the VRGo puzzle box and banged into the closet door. She reached out to catch herself, but only succeeded in pulling her clothes off their hangers. Outside her room, she heard someone climbing the creaky wooden stairs.

"Jenny!" Bea called out. "Is that you?"

Jenny's heart fluttered at the sound of Bea's voice. "Yeah." She slid the closet door open. "It's me."

Bea flung the bedroom door open and rushed forward with her arms out. Then, she stopped herself after remembering that Jenny didn't like to be touched. She stood just inside the room and smoothed her long floral dress over her legs. Jenny stepped forward and wrapped her arms around her aunt. Bea raised her eyebrows in surprise, and her body went stiff. Then she relaxed and enjoyed the embrace.

When Jenny pulled away, Bea held her at arm's length and looked her over. "Where have you been?"

Not knowing what to say, Jenny just shook her head.

"What are these bruises from?"

"Would you believe they're from vacuum exposure?" Jenny laughed.

"I would."

Jenny cocked her head. "Wait, what?"

Bea smiled. "After finding your note, I panicked at first, but Michael arrived a few minutes later and explained everything..."

"And you believed him?"

"No, not at first. I thought he was crazy." She shook her head. "He said you were in a parallel universe."

"He told you that?"

"Yes, then he said that you had been recruited to save an alien species."

Jenny shook her head and sat down on her bed. "It's all true."

"I know." Bea nodded. "He had a device he called a Topo. He showed me things about his world, things that couldn't be from here, like movies and music that never existed, and spaceships and aliens."

"It all sounds so crazy." Jenny looked at Bea with tears in her eyes. "I was so upset about losing Mom. I'm sorry I left. I should have realized that you were in pain too."

"Shh, it's okay," Bea said, pulling her into her bony arms. "I was your age when my mother died. I should have remembered how I felt then. I lost a part of myself that day. Ruby may be gone, but she'll also always be with us."

Jenny nodded. "I know, and now I believe it too." She touched her mother's amulet under her green dress.

"You're so grown-up now." Bea searched Jenny's eyes. "I'm sorry I pushed you so hard to learn my business. All I wanted was to prepare you for when I'm no longer here, to give you the means to take care of yourself."

"That reminds me." Jenny reached inside her duffel bag and removed the calligraphy set. "I have something for you." Jenny popped the latches open and revealed the siphonophore vials inside.

Bea cocked her head. "Calligraphy?"

"No, this is the cure to the family curse. It will repair the genetic defect in our DNA."

"What do I do?"

Jenny fit a vial into the injector. "Just roll up your sleeve."

Back at the Sol Terminal, a spaceship covered with hundreds of antennas—giving it the appearance of a huge porcupine—arrived to send and receive the galactic news.

ACKNOWLEDGMENTS

I want to start by thanking my wife, Natalie Perrin. She stuck by me through the five years it took to complete this book. She put up with me constantly killing off beloved characters and changing the plot, but did so with love and patience (maybe a touch of frustration). She is the single best person I know.

Next, I'd like to thank Lynsey Griswold, Michelle Hope, and Alida Winternheimer who provided editorial expertise and keen insight in bringing my story to life.

Furthermore, I couldn't have finished this story without research and inspiration. In addition to reading a substantial stack of books, I also read plenty of blogs, listened to dozens of podcasts, and watched hundreds of videos in preparation for this story. Special thanks to: *Writing Excuses*, *Mythcreant*, and *Writership* who helped to refine my craft; and YouTube channels like *Because Science*, and *Isaac Arthur* provided me with topics, research, and inspiration.

ABOUT THE AUTHOR

Nicholas Marson is a Portland, Oregon native, where he raced outrigger canoes and grew to love coffee. He's two meters tall, and once lived in a tiny house. He graduated from Oregon State University with a degree in biology and graphic design. He is an older brother to two siblings, a husband to an incredible wife, and a father to a princess in training. Now he lives in Eugene where he works as a web developer and translates daydreams into words.

Learn more at, https://www.nicholasmarson.com/.

www.ingramcontent.com/pod-product-compliance
Lightning Source LLC
Chambersburg PA
CBHW021121260626
47169CB00005B/1393